A Scot to the Heart

"I've been wondering about one thing for some time . . . What you said to me that night in the oyster cellar."

Another flush of arousal went through her. She was just barely keeping to the safe side of the line she mustn't cross with him as it was. *Friends,* she sternly told herself. "What any woman would say, in the midst of such a crush," she replied lightly. "A polite thanks for your assistance."

The captain came a little closer. "Then I seriously misheard. I thought you said . . ." His gaze dropped to her mouth.

For a moment she felt again his arms around her . . . She tasted his mouth on hers, hot and seductive. She felt the wild spike of longing that it could mean something . . .

"What?" she said, hating that her voice had gone breathy. "What did you think I said?"

He was an arm's length away; her feet were rooted to the ground. "Whaur hae ye been aw ma life?" he whispered in a deep Scots purr.

Also by Caroline Linden

ABOUT A ROGUE

WHEN THE MARQUESS WAS MINE
AN EARL LIKE YOU
MY ONCE AND FUTURE DUKE

SIX DEGREES OF SCANDAL
LOVE IN THE TIME OF SCANDAL
ALL'S FAIR IN LOVE AND SCANDAL (novella)
IT TAKES A SCANDAL
LOVE AND OTHER SCANDALS

THE WAY TO A DUKE'S HEART
BLAME IT ON BATH
ONE NIGHT IN LONDON
I LOVE THE EARL (novella)

YOU ONLY LOVE ONCE
FOR YOUR ARMS ONLY
A VIEW TO A KISS

A RAKE'S GUIDE TO SEDUCTION
WHAT A ROGUE DESIRES
WHAT A GENTLEMAN WANTS

WHAT A WOMAN NEEDS

Caroline Linden

A Scot to the Heart

Desperately Seeking Duke

AVONBOOKS

An Imprint of HarperCollins*Publishers*

This is a work of fiction. Names, characters, places, and incidents are products of the author's imagination or are used fictitiously and are not to be construed as real. Any resemblance to actual events, locales, organizations, or persons, living or dead, is entirely coincidental.

First Avon Books mass market printing: July 2021

Print Edition ISBN: 978-0-06-291364-7
Digital Edition ISBN: 978-0-06-291365-4

Cover design by Guido Caroti
Cover photograph and illustration by Glenn Mackay
Cover photograph/digital art by Allan Davey
Cover images © Arina_B/Shutterstock; © I love sticky rice/iStock/ Getty Images
Author photograph by Allana Taranto/Ars Magna Studio

FIRST EDITION

21 22 23 24 25 BVGM 10 9 8 7 6 5 4 3 2 1

To Eric

Even more my hero after 2020

A Scot to the Heart

Chapter One

1787
Fort George
Ardersier, Scotland

The broken wheel was the last straw.

The company had been out for a fortnight on the most miserable assignment, repairing roads in an incessant misty drizzle. They were within two miles of Fort George's warm, dry beds and hot food when a wheel of the equipment wagon found an overlooked hole and tilted with a groan and a sickening snap of spokes.

Efforts to raise it were in vain. Resigned, the men and officers unloaded the shovels and pickaxes and other tools onto their own backs and began the weary trudge to Ardersier.

When they reached the long, narrow bridge into the fort, an eternity later, there was an outburst of exclamations—relief, pain, profanity toward the army for the road detail and against God for the fecking rain. Their captain, leading his tool-laden horse through mud that covered his ankles, his sodden sash draped over his head, silently agreed, and vowed he would ask the colonel for three days' leave for the men. On days like this, he hated the army, too.

At very long last, after unloading the tools, dismissing his men, and delivering his horse to the stables, he turned toward his own lodging. As a captain, he had cramped quarters in one of the long buildings facing the Firth of Moray—not that anyone could see the firth today.

"Welcome back, sir," said MacKinnon as he let himself into the two small rooms that were home. "The colonel's wanting you."

Dripping wet, slathered in mud, half-starved and tired almost unto unconsciousness, Andrew St. James just stood in the doorway, his hand still on the latch. "What—*now*?" he asked hopelessly.

His man nodded. "Aye, Captain. Posthaste, he said."

Bloody saints, I hate the army, Drew thought.

"Damn it." He unbuckled his sword belt with stiff fingers. MacKinnon passed him a towel to mop his face as he stripped off his wet clothing.

He longed for a hot bath and shave, to say nothing of putting off his uniform for a comfortable banyan, but he'd learnt the hard way that the colonel's impatience overrode his attention to matters of dress, so he pulled on fresh garments. MacKinnon ran a hasty brush over his jacket, handed him his bonnet, and gave a crisp nod. "I hope it's good news, Captain."

He gave a grim nod. That would run counter to his luck of late. "Aye, let's hope."

He didn't expect it would be. These summonses rarely were.

He strode through the open square, holding his cloak close around him as he went. From one barracks drifted the sounds of a piper and laughter of men at ease. The scent of pipe smoke and roast mutton followed him across the quadrangle, blackening his mood even more. He ought to be sitting down to his own dinner instead of dancing attendance on the querulous colonel. With more force than necessary, he banged on the door of the colonel's house.

Colonel Fitzwilliam enjoyed superior housing and dining. The aroma of roast beef and fresh bread hit like a punch when the servant let him in, setting his temper to simmering. Whatever Fitzwilliam wanted to see him about had better be damned important, he thought as he waited in the office.

The colonel came in several minutes later, a scowl on his florid face and a napkin still tucked across his ample abdomen. "St. James," he said irritably. "What took you so long?"

Drew kept his gaze on the swords hanging above the mantel. The clink of silver on china and the light lilt of Mrs. Fitzwilliam's laugh reached his ears. A dinner party. Probably with syllabub. His stomach growled resentfully. "We've only just returned from detail, sir. The equipment wagon broke a wheel."

Fitzwilliam scoffed. "Ought to have hurried back. There's a letter for you, and I was told to deliver it personally and immediately."

Drew glanced at him, startled. "From whom?" His muscles knotted. It must be bad news from home. Who else would write to him that urgently?

"From London," said Fitzwilliam, unlocking the top drawer of his desk and rummaging inside. "A prissy solicitor for the Duke of Carlyle."

The knot of worry dissolved. He frowned in amazed astonishment. "Carlyle!"

"You're acquainted with him?"

"No, sir," he said slowly. "He's a distant cousin—very distant. I've never met the duke."

The colonel grunted and thrust out the letter. "The solicitor said I was to put it straight into your hands, and only your hands."

He took the letter with a brief bow and slid it inside his coat. On no account was he going to read it in front of Fusty Fitzwilliam. "Thank you, sir. Is that all?"

The colonel pursed his lips, displeased. "What does it say?"

He managed a tight smile. "I shall read it later, after I've had dinner. I can't imagine it's anything significant. My family has had naught to do with Carlyle since my grandfather's day."

"You'll have to tell me what it says," retorted Fitzwilliam, his face growing ruddier. "I received a letter with it from Sir George Yonge himself, with orders to grant you leave from your duties as requested by that missive there." He jerked his head toward the pocket where Drew had stowed it.

"Ah," he said after a startled moment. "I'll be sure to do that, sir."

Fitzwilliam glowered at him. "Do, Captain."

Dismissed, he bowed and left, barely remembering to fling his cloak over his head in time to avoid being drenched a second time.

As he ran back across the square, though, his

mind raced ahead, hundreds of miles away to Carlyle Castle. He'd never been there and never received any communication from the duke, either. What on earth could the Carlyle solicitor want from him?

By the time he reached his lodgings again, he had begun to wonder, even hope, if there mightn't be some legacy, either newly left to him by an obscure relative or recently discovered by the solicitor. There had been no word from the St. Jameses of Carlyle Castle in the dozen years and more since his father and grandfather had died. His mother always said she wasn't surprised, since they hadn't cared when either was alive.

Not that Drew would refuse anything from them now. On the contrary, he would accept even a small inheritance with gratitude—and alacrity.

It was the letter from the secretary at war that unsettled him. Why would Sir George Yonge care that he was granted leave to accept a legacy? Why would Carlyle's solicitor ask the head of the army to intervene?

He tore open the letter as soon as he gained the shelter of his lodging. MacKinnon had laid out a generous dinner which normally would have driven all other thoughts from his mind, especially after a day like this one. But tonight he stood just inside his door, ignoring the water dripping off him, and read the letter from his distant cousin's solicitor.

"Trouble, sir?" ventured MacKinnon after several minutes.

He raised stunned eyes. "Bloody hell," he whispered.

A FORTNIGHT LATER he found himself five hundred miles away cantering up a long winding road to the castle. It was a monumental structure of weathered gray stone, with crenelated towers and a drawbridge through a stone arch that had certainly once held a portcullis—if it didn't still hold one. It was not unlike some of the fortresses to which he'd been posted during his years of army life, and he wouldn't have been surprised to see a regiment come marching crisply around the corner. Never would he have guessed that this was a home.

In the courtyard he flung himself off his horse; he was late. He'd been requested to present himself today, but he'd been delayed by everything from bad weather to a broken saddle girth.

The butler was waiting for him, and he was shown immediately to a room. A servant brought a tray of breakfast, sausages steaming gently in the tureen. Famished, Drew snatched as many bites as he could, trying to set his clothing to rights as a servant silently gave his coat a swift brushing.

"Her Grace requests your presence," said the butler, far too soon.

He crammed a roll into his mouth, washed it down with a gulp of coffee, and strode after the man.

Unaccountably his hands shook as he checked the buttons of his coat. Mr. Edwards, the attorney, had charged him to be prompt and here he was, darting in at the last moment, covered in dust and bleary-eyed from the long trip from Inverness. He dared to hope it was a generous legacy.

The room he was shown into was ornate beyond anything he'd ever seen. Not even the Duke of

Hamilton's house, which he'd viewed once with his family, held a candle to this. The walls were covered in burgundy damask, hung with a dazzling selection of artwork. The carpet beneath his boots was thick and richly patterned. Tall, mullioned windows looked out over an endless stretch of verdant lawn. It was fit for royalty.

The woman sitting on the ornate chair, though, was no queen but a duchess. Drew had managed to learn that much: Sophia Marie St. James, Duchess of Carlyle. She was short and plump, wearing a black silk gown that surely cost more than a captain made in a year, and on her finger glittered a ruby the size of an acorn.

On guard, he took a seat. Another fellow, already seated, cast him an assessing glance. Handsome, lithe, elegantly posed in his chair. But his velvet coat was worn at the elbows and cuffs, and there was something calculating in his eyes. Drew gave a curt nod of greeting, and the fellow returned it with a languid smile.

"Good morning," said the duchess briskly. "I trust your journeys were without incident."

"Yes, Your Grace," he said.

"It was perfectly delightful," said the other fellow, managing to convey the exact opposite meaning. Drew wondered who he was.

"Excellent," said the duchess, eyeing him coolly. "No doubt you wonder why I summoned you to Carlyle. Mr. Edwards will explain."

He had barely noticed the man, clad as he was in black and sitting behind Her Grace. Edwards was the solicitor who'd written to him and got him special leave from the army.

"On the fourteenth of April last," the solicitor said, "Lord Stephen St. James, youngest brother of His Grace the Duke of Carlyle, fell ill and died."

"I offer my deepest sympathies, madam," Drew murmured.

"Thank you, Captain," said the duchess. "That is very kind of you."

"Unfortunately, Lord Stephen was His Grace's nearest living heir," Mr. Edwards went on. "Carlyle himself has no children or wife."

He had spent so much time thinking about legacies and who might leave him something. It was literally the only reason he could find to explain why he had been summoned to Carlyle Castle with all possible speed from Inverness.

His great-grandfather had been the third Duke of Carlyle. His grandfather, a younger son, had fallen out with his brother, the fourth duke, and been banished from the family estates. Drew's father had always said that was more blessing than curse, and no one had ever attempted mending the breach. It was as if their family had come into being with his grandfather—appropriately named Lord Adam—and no previous generations existed.

But they had. And Drew, like his father before him, was an only son. Like a thunderclap from above, he realized why he was here.

He glanced swiftly at the roguish fellow beside him, wondering how closely related they were. That must be another St. James cousin. He knew virtually nothing of the family beyond his grandparents.

"Lord Stephen has also left no wife or children," announced the duchess. The sunlight winked on her ruby ring. "In their absence, it appears the dukedom will pass upon my son's death to one of his cousins." She gave both of them pointed looks. "In short, to one of you."

By God, it was a legacy beyond his dreams. "That is most unexpected news, Your Grace," he said, trying hard to keep calm. "May I inquire how . . . ?"

"Certainly. Mr. St. James"—she flicked a glance at the other fellow—"is the great-great-grandson of the second duke. And you, Captain, are the great-grandson of the third duke."

Drew forced down the urge to shout aloud. *Hold fast,* he told himself. "This is quite shocking news, ma'am. But is there no one—?"

The solicitor drew breath, but before he could speak, the duchess did. "No," she said shortly, glaring at the lawyer. "There is no one nearer."

No one nearer. And the fellow beside him had a lower claim than his own, if his hasty mental logic was true.

Mr. Edwards was speaking again. "As you may not know, His Grace the duke suffered a tragic injury many years ago." Drew had not known that, but if the duke were a hale and hearty fellow he would surely find a bride and commence trying to sire an heir, rather than drag in distant and heretofore unwanted cousins from the outermost reaches of Scotland. "It has rendered him unable to take a wife and father direct heirs, which means there is no chance either of you will be supplanted in the chain of succession." Mr. Edwards laid out a large sheet of paper. "I have taken the liberty of documenting the family here, as you see."

Like a pair of puppets worked by the same

strings, Drew and the man beside him leaned forward to study it.

"This documentation will be invaluable when the time comes to assert a claim," said the solicitor, adding with a hint of warning, "particularly as neither of you is a direct descendant of the current or previous holder of the title."

His eyes raced over the lineage. There was his name, and his father's and grandfather's . . . leading back to the third duke. Precious few other names fell in between.

Great God above, he was heir presumptive to the Duke of Carlyle.

"I see this has been something of a surprise to you," said the duchess as both men sat in stunned silence. "It has been no less alarming to me."

The cousin beside him, who had been fairly quiet, stirred. "I wouldn't precisely call it *alarming*," he drawled in cynical amusement. "A surprise . . . I'll grant."

Drew frowned. What made the man react with insolence to such indisputably good news? Better for himself, he acknowledged, but since he had neither son nor brother, this man must be the next in line. *His* heir.

The duchess gave the impertinent fellow a filthy glare. "The rules of inheritance are firm. The title and entailed lands must descend through the male St. James line, and they *will*. One of you will be the next duke—Captain St. James, most likely"—she glanced at him—"or Mr. St. James, in the event tragedy befalls the captain."

I'm resigning my commission, Drew thought. *On the*

morrow. Only an idiot would stay in the army and risk dying of dysentery now.

"There is a considerable fortune attached to the estate, naturally," the duchess continued. "It is an enormous responsibility, and neither of you has the slightest preparation to assume it. I have had both of you investigated." Her expression was distinctly unimpressed as her gaze swept over them. "The results were hardly reassuring, but we must deal with what we must. Neither of you has taken a wife yet."

He snapped to alertness. "No, ma'am."

"Not one of my own," murmured the roguish cousin with a hint of a wicked smile.

Blessed saints. Drew glared at the man. What was wrong with him? The duchess's expression turned frigid, although the solicitor seemed to be biting back a smirk as he shuffled his papers.

"Nor have you taken any pains toward respectability, sir," Her Grace snapped at him. "That is what troubles me, and that is why I sent for you. The Duke of Carlyle wields great power and must do so with dignity and decorum."

"It is an awesome responsibility," Drew said quickly before his cousin could say something even ruder. "I hope I may become worthy of it."

The duchess inclined her head his way. "I expect it of you, Captain." She paused before adding sourly, "And of *you*, Mr. St. James."

Drew would swear the man grinned.

"I understand this may be a difficult request," the duchess said. "I am prepared to help. Mr. Edwards will disburse to each of you five hundred pounds immediately. I trust you will use it wisely, and return in six months' time more sober, refined gentlemen. If I am satisfied with your progress, I shall grant a further sum of one thousand five hundred pounds per year, to continue as long as you remain respectable."

His heart thumped hard. Five hundred pounds! With fifteen hundred to follow. It was a bloody fortune.

Mr. St. James asked another question, which he barely heard. All he could think of was the money and what it would mean to his family. They were getting by in Edinburgh, but now he could see them comfortably settled. He could give his sisters dowries—two hundred pounds or more, each. Agnes with her intelligence and warm heart, Winnie with her humor and beauty, and Bella with her charm and high spirits . . . all three would surely find good matches. And his mother deserved to have proper servants again, and not have to work in the shop in Shakespeare Square—

He brought himself up short. Edinburgh? He could bring his sisters to *London*, for a real Season. Gowns from Paris, a carriage of their own, entrée to all the most fashionable and intelligent society they wanted. They would be the family of a duke-in-waiting.

Did that make his mother and sisters ladies? How thrilled Winnie would be. He must ask.

The duchess and Mr. St. James had been sparring as he sat woolgathering. Mr. St. James must have offended Her Grace again, from her tone. Drew glanced in pity at his cousin. No discipline, that one. He'd clearly never been in the army, if he thought this was the way to ingratiate himself with those who outranked him.

"This offer is intended to *help* you," Her Grace said witheringly. "Do not delude yourself that Carlyle runs itself, or that a steward can be hired to do it all. You are both young men, neither raised with this expectation. It will be difficult for you to adjust, but you must rise to the occasion. I urge you to accept this proposal and take it seriously."

He cleared his throat. "Yes, of course, Your Grace. It is extremely generous of you."

"It is not generosity," she snapped. "I have no wish to see Carlyle run into the ground! I wish to see it descend to someone who will appreciate its majesty, care for its dependents, and preserve it for future generations. To that purpose, each of you has six months to establish yourself as someone capable of becoming that man. And you needn't fear that the funds would cease if I should die." She glared at Mr. St. James again, as if guessing what he was about to ask. "I will leave instructions in my will to continue the annuity so long as my conditions are met."

Drew had never had the freedom to be disreputable or irresponsible, though he suspected the other man had.

"What shall those conditions be, Your Grace?"

"Respectability," she said, still looking down her nose at Mr. St. James. "No outrageous behavior. Sobriety. The Dukes of Carlyle have long held positions of power in Westminster, and you would do well to take an interest in politics so that you are prepared to acquit yourselves well when you sit in the House of Lords. If you do not, someone else will be happy to take advantage of you, sooner than later." She paused. "And I have always felt a wife settles a man. I do not require that you marry, but the next duke will need an heir. A suitable bride is invaluable."

"We must marry?" That jolted him out of rosy thoughts of selling out of the army and settling his family.

"The Duke of Carlyle will need an heir," she repeated. "If you do not provide one, Captain, Mr. St. James would become the heir presumptive."

Not bloody likely, thought Drew as he and his cousin exchanged swift, measuring glances.

"Mr. Edwards will answer any further questions." The duchess rose to her feet, rousting a large ginger cat from beneath her chair.

He leapt up and rushed after her. "If I may, Your Grace . . ."

She looked up at him. "Yes?"

He smiled and ducked his head. She was a tiny woman, and he had learned that his height intimidated dainty females. "You spoke very deliberately about the importance of marriage."

"Yes, Captain," she said with a trace of impatience. "Not only does a good wife make a man more reliable and stable, she is necessary for a legitimate heir."

"Of course," he said hastily. "I only meant to inquire how you might suggest I proceed. As an army man, I have had few opportunities of meeting any lady who would be worthy of becoming a duchess."

Her demeanor thawed slightly. "Yes, I see. Do you intend to remain in your post?"

Only as long as it takes to clear out of the barracks. "I don't believe I could do justice to this new responsibility and fulfill my duties. In fact, I don't know how I could undertake to learn anything about Carlyle from Fort George, let alone enough to assume the dukedom. I wonder if perhaps I ought to find a situation somewhere nearer?"

It had not escaped his notice, when Mr. Edwards unfurled the family document, that the current duke was nearing sixty. A man of that age, who had suffered a serious injury that rendered him incapable of marrying and siring a son, whose mother had undertaken to locate new heirs . . . This was not some vague, airy expectation. This, Carlyle Castle and the title that went with it, might well be his within a few years, even months. There was no time to lose—nor did he wish to.

The duchess's expression warmed. "Yes, Captain, I believe that would be a fine idea. You would have Mr. Edwards to explain things, and naturally I would be here." She eyed him up and down again. "With the right valet, you'll be a handsome enough fellow. I daresay there are a number of ladies I might introduce to you, who would be deserving of your interest."

Drew smiled. While he still supported his mother and three sisters on a captain's pay, a wife and children were luxuries he couldn't afford.

But as heir to the Duke of Carlyle, with fifteen hundred pounds per annum . . .

"I would like that very much, Your Grace," he said.

Chapter Two

Two months later

Edinburgh was just as he remembered it. From the London road it seemed to rise up out of the earth as a kingdom on a hill, the stone houses clustered like acolytes at the foot of the castle, which surveyed the verdant plain imperiously from its perch.

Drew hadn't been here in over a year, thanks to his posting at Fort George. On his way to Carlyle, there hadn't been time to stop and visit his family. But now . . .

Now he had plenty of time, and vast quantities of news.

His family occupied a small house just off the High Street. It was evening, and his mother and sisters would have closed up the shop by now. But the only one home when he arrived was Annag, who had been his nurse years ago and refused to leave the family even when means grew tight. Now she was all-purpose help to his mother and sisters. "Oh, Master Andrew!" she exclaimed at his entrance. "Here you are, come at last! And about time, too. Your mother's been fair worried."

He laughed, embracing the short, gray-haired

woman who was almost as dear to him as his own mother. "I wrote to her when I would arrive." Though it did not surprise him to hear his mother had been fretting, hoping he would appear three days early.

She pursed up her lips. "And you sounding as English as Butcher Cumberland."

Drew grimaced. "Aye, I've been in England these six weeks," he said, slipping back into the Scots she spoke. He'd got used to speaking clipped English for the duchess.

"May you recover from it soon," she said tartly. "None of that here, laddie!"

"No, ma'am. Where are they now?"

"At the Monroes' for dinner. I'll send round—"

"No, no, just tell them I've arrived. Tomorrow will be soon enough to talk." He winked at her and turned toward the door.

"They'll want all the news!" she protested, hurrying after him.

"And tomorrow they shall have it, along with the gifts I brought." He grinned as her eyes grew wide. "Till the morrow, Annag."

Duty satisfied, he stepped back out into the street and took a deep breath. It was not an unwelcome surprise to find them out. After a hard week of travel, to say nothing of the weeks of study and instruction at Carlyle, the prospect of a night free tasted as sweet as honey.

As eager as he was to see his family again, he had written to an old friend, begging a bed. Felix Duncan had replied as expected that he was welcome to it. Drew swung back into the saddle and took his horse to a stable before walking up the street, saddlebags over his shoulder, to Duncan's lodgings in Burnet's Close.

"Come in," came a muffled bellow at his knock.

He entered to find his friend practicing feints in front of a cheval glass, pausing to adjust his stance after each stroke.

"Are you rehearsing to fight yourself?" he asked with amusement.

"If I'm to face an equal, I must." Duncan eyed himself critically and raised his elbow to create a more elegant line from hip to wrist.

"Very good. And if you're ever looking to face someone *better*, I'm at your service."

Duncan abandoned his posing. "Better! Not better. Only taller and with longer reach. God's eyes, man, you're a mountain."

Drew obligingly flexed one arm. "The result of tedious hard labor. You might try it."

Duncan, who had never done a day's hard labor in his life, propped his épée on his hip and glared at him. "And will it make me taller? Lengthen my arms? I think not."

He snorted with laughter. "Nay, you're a hopeless cause. Doomed to be a reedy little man forever . . ."

Duncan growled and raised his sword, and Drew made a show of yawning in reply. His friend's face eased into a lopsided grin. "For all that you're a rude one, 'tis good to see you again, St. James. Welcome."

"Aye," he agreed as he clasped Duncan's outstretched hand. "Many thanks for the use of your spare room."

Duncan resumed his position in front of the glass. "Anytime you need it." He raised his épée, watching himself in the mirror again. "Although you're worse than an old woman, hinting at wondrous revelations and not telling me what brings you back to Edinburgh when you ought to be marching around Fort George in the rain." He lunged, pausing to flick his queue of ginger hair over his shoulder and slant his eyebrows threateningly.

Drew grinned again. It was true he'd told Duncan some whopping stories when they'd been mischievous lads ducking their tutors in the labyrinth of narrow alleys in and around the Cowgate. "This time, Duncan, I've got a revelation so wondrous even you won't believe it."

He went into the spare room where his trunks had already been delivered. One of them was familiar; it held his belongings, other than the essentials in his saddlebag. The other, larger trunk was new, full of gifts and trinkets for his family, lovely frivolous things suitable for the mother and sisters of a duke.

The sight of it sobered him. It was a Trojan horse, that trunk, a lavish gift that would subtly inject the elegant, rarified world of Carlyle Castle into his family. After the way the previous duke had treated his grandfather, Drew's family had wanted nothing to do with the castle. Now, though, they had no choice, and that trunk was meant to change their minds.

He'd written to his mother only that he appeared to have expectations from the ducal branch of the family; it had felt like hubris to write it down and send the news into the world, unfettered and liable to run amok. Mr. Edwards, the solicitor, was keeping the whole matter quiet. No one outside Carlyle Castle knew of the duchess's plan.

At times Drew had wondered wryly if that was to make it easier to bend him and his cousin to the duchess's will, but the solicitor claimed it was for his own sake, to spare him the intense glare of scrutiny that would fall upon the heir to the dukedom. And that meant very few people in England, and no one at all in Scotland, had any idea that the future Duke of Carlyle trod the plainstanes of Edinburgh this evening.

In truth, he still hardly believed it himself. The Carlyle inheritance seemed like a dream. Even in the midst of Mr. Edwards's strictures or explanations of some finer point of the estate, part of him had thought it wouldn't really be his, that some other heir would miraculously emerge at the last moment and leave Drew and his rakish cousin empty-handed. Only now that he was here, about to uproot his family and begin shouldering the burden of Carlyle, was it sinking in that it was his future. This next month would be the last of his life as Captain St. James, ordinary Scotsman and soldier.

As expected, Duncan followed him within minutes, a towel around his neck and two drams of whisky in his hand, one of which he held out. "All right, then, what is this wondrous and incredible revelation?"

For answer, Drew handed him a sealed packet. Duncan tossed back his drink and set down the glass to unfold the papers. For all his rakish ways, Duncan was a judge's son and an advocate himself, and more intelligent than he acted.

"Jesus, Mary, and Joseph," he exclaimed a few minutes later, still reading. "Is this—is this real?"

Drew nodded, stripping off his coat and tossing it

on the wingback chair near the window. He longed for a bath and wondered if Duncan would agree to a naked plunge in the Firth, as they'd used to do.

"Carlyle?" said his friend incredulously. "Carlyle? *You?*"

Drew gave a mocking bow. "At your service."

After another shocked moment, Duncan put back his head and roared with laughter. "You—a duke! You—the veriest devil of a child, a peer of the realm! You—the wild Scot, a proper Englishman!"

That last made him frown. "I was not wild, and I won't be an Englishman."

"Oh nay, never." Grinning fiendishly, Duncan folded the letters and tossed them back at him. "It might take a while, but you'll become one. No more Scots for you, only King's English. You'll wed a pale Englishwoman and your grandchildren will never venture north of the River Tweed."

Tight-lipped, he replaced the documents in his trunk. "That's lunacy speaking." Even though he'd consciously spoken crisp English at Carlyle, and all but invited the duchess to find an appropriate wife for him. Of course she would choose an English lady . . .

"Is it?" murmured Duncan with a devilish gleam in his eye. "We'll see about that." He left the room, and Drew went back to unpacking his things, irate at his friend for speaking such blunt truth.

Several minutes later Duncan was back, a slim book in his hand. "If you're going to remain a Scot, you'll need help."

The Widower and Bachelor's Directory, read the title. Frowning, Drew opened it, and gave a bark of disbelieving laughter as he realized what it was. "A guide to rich ladies and where to find them, eh? What rubbish is this?"

"Not rubbish," countered Duncan, still smirking. "Invaluable intelligence for the man in search of a wife!"

"Who said I was in search of a wife?"

Duncan arched his brows. "A single man with expectation of a wealthy dukedom will be in want of a bride. And even if he's not in *want* of one, he shall have one thrust upon him, whether he wills it or no. Every unwed woman between the ages of seventeen and seventy will fling herself—or be flung—into his path until one of them trips him up and drags him to church, like a wild boar caught in a snare and trundled off to market."

"You're the only one in Edinburgh who knows," returned Drew, annoyed. "I'd prefer to keep it that way. If women start flinging themselves at me, I'll know whom to blame."

Duncan snorted. "Aye, as if I'd go about telling all the lasses you're about to be rich beyond their dreams. 'Tis of course the only way any sensible woman would take you . . ."

"You're about to get to practice your fencing in earnest."

His friend waved it off as he held out the silly little book. "Keep it! I know all the eligible ladies in town already. And once word gets out that there's a ducal heir on the loose, you'll need to know which ones to fend off."

Drew replied with a suggestion that would have made any soldier blush. Duncan only grinned, beyond pleased with himself. "If you're to depart the realm of ordinary men soon, we must make your last days memorable. Let me change my coat."

That was more amenable to his humor. He'd been at the castle for six weeks, always minding his tongue, constantly alert. A wild, carefree night was just the respite he needed.

To his relief, Duncan's idea of *memorable* turned out to be much the same as it had been in years past. At an oyster cellar beneath a tavern they met up with two other old friends, Adam Monteith and William Ross, and all proceeded to gorge themselves on oysters, well lubricated with strong Scottish porter. There was nothing anywhere to match the taste of oysters from the Firth of Forth.

He had never been to this cellar. There were several in Edinburgh, and some seemed to migrate around town. The gathering was lively, packed to the walls and operating at a dull roar of laughter and conversation.

At another table sat a large group of people including several ladies. They laughed and chattered with a gaiety that caught his eye, and made Drew think of his own sisters.

Well—not exactly in the same way.

Finally Ross caught him looking and nudged him. "D'you fancy her?"

There was no doubt whom Ross meant. The woman at the head of the table was mesmerizing. Not only was she one of the merriest people in the room, inciting roars of laughter at her table, but she positively glowed. Her dark hair was loosely twisted up, and her gown was a brilliant blue. It was her eyes, though, that captured his attention.

Those dark eyes danced with wicked humor and glee and made him want to know what had put that sparkle there.

As if she'd heard Ross's question, she glanced his way. Caught, he gazed boldly back, and her mouth curled in an impish yet mysterious way before she shifted her attention away from him. Drew turned back to his porter, trying to hide the flush of heat that had gone through him and set his heart racing.

Ross nudged his shoulder again, brows raised knowingly. He shrugged, and stole another glance over his shoulder.

At some point a piper set up in the corner and began to play. In an instant the tables were shoved aside and figures formed for a country dance. Duncan leapt over a table to join in, as did Monteith and Ross. Drew threw his coat in the corner with everyone else's and took his place.

The dance was as boisterous as the interlude before it had been. Within minutes he was out of breath, laughing as he swung first one lady, then another on his arm. There was no chance of conversation, over the drone and wail of the pipes, the stomping of so many feet on the wooden floor, the shouts and laughter of the dancers and those cheering them on. It was hot and fast and exuberant, and he loved it. There had been nothing like this at Carlyle, nor at Fort George. Colonel Fitzwilliam, the old prig, disapproved of his officers attending social gatherings.

He was so caught up in the dance that it gave him a genuine start when the next woman turned to take his hand, and he recognized the alluring beauty from the other table. The one who had smiled at him.

Hand in hand they spun around each other, then separated. Each time the dance brought them back together, Drew stared. Up close she was more than mesmerizing. Her dark hair was coming out of its pins, trailing down her back and flying around her as she circled the other dancers. Like the other ladies, she picked up her skirts and tapped her feet with energy. Her color was high and her face fierce with joy. And when she caught him staring at her, she only gave him that infectious flirtatious smile again.

The dance came to an abrupt end when someone tripped and sprawled on the floor. The piper stopped playing just as the fallen man began vomiting. With cries of alarm, the dancers scrambled away from him.

By sheer chance, Drew and the mystery woman were crowded together into a back corner, pushed almost behind the piper by the crush of people hurrying for the stairs. Someone shoved him in the back, and then the woman stumbled against him. Instinctively he put up an arm to shield her, and her eyes flashed toward him in gratitude.

He could only think of one thing.

"Who are you?" he asked, lowering his head to hers and stubbornly blocking the stream of people from this quiet corner. She smelled like the sea and oranges and woman.

She gave him a gleaming glance and said something he couldn't quite make out over the roar of the crowd. He leaned down more. "What? What's your name?"

Her hands came up on both sides of his face. For one breathless heartbeat, she pressed her lips to his in a sudden, searing kiss. He felt it to the soles of his feet and the roots of his hair; every nerve seemed to snap with the shock and beauty of it, as if she'd struck him with lightning. On pure instinct he cupped one hand around her nape and kissed her back.

Before he could manage to put an arm around her, though, she released him and ducked under his elbow into the crowd surging up the stairs. Even with his height advantage, he lost all sight of her in an instant.

His mouth still tingling, he waited out the worst of the exodus behind the stairs, then pushed his way through the room to retrieve his coat. Duncan was lying on a table, tapping his toes and laughing at Ross, who turned out to be the fellow who had lost his dinner all over the floor. Ross leaned weakly against a table leg, his arms thrown around it for support and his face white. Monteith was arguing with the landlord, who had fought his way downstairs and was scowling at the spray of sick all over his floor.

With a lurch Duncan rolled off the table. "Let's go," he said. "Monteith! Bring what's left of Ross." He tossed a pair of guineas toward the landlord, whose aggrieved expression didn't change even as he snatched the coins from the air.

Out in the street, they heaved Ross between them, Drew and Monteith both trying to make sure the man's face was angled away from them. Chairmen in Highland garb trotted past carrying sedan chairs, their boots thumping on the cobblestones. A dog barked somewhere nearby. Lopsided, winded, and more than a little drunk, they staggered through the streets, Duncan singing something bawdy in Scots and Ross moaning at him to be quiet.

"Monteith," Drew said over Ross's head lolling on his shoulder. "Who was the woman in blue?"

"Eh?" Monteith squinted at him. "Which one? Half the females there wore blue, St. James." The last words came out slurred.

He gave up. Monteith was even drunker than Duncan, who was frightening away the stray cats that prowled the streets. Someone flung open a window and yelled at him to be silent, which made him begin another verse, louder than ever.

Tomorrow. Once Duncan sobered up, Drew would find out who she was. He could still taste her mouth on his, and he yearned to taste it again.

Chapter Three

It took forever to get the easel in just the right position. The morning light was excellent, but the windows were narrow and admitted little of it. Opening the sashes helped, but the drapes still obscured the view, until she took them down.

And after all that effort, Ilsa Ramsay noted with chagrin, she was out of green paint.

Well. Perhaps the hills ought to be more violet than green, now that she thought about it.

Aunt Jean came into the room and stopped short. Ilsa preferred to think it was in appreciation of her painting skill, which had improved tremendously in the last few months. She daubed another burst of heather onto her painting of the distant Calton Hill, replicating the vista out the drawing room windows.

"Are the draperies in need of cleaning?" asked her aunt after a moment.

"No," said Ilsa. "They were blocking the view."

Jean picked up one corner of a drapery, lying in a heap on the sofa, and clucked over the loose threads where a ring had torn away. "And did they offend you, as well?"

"I didn't tear them down, that ring was already

loose." Carefully she added tiny highlights of light blue to the heather. Yes; the hillside did look much better with some heather. Pity the real one couldn't be so easily improved.

Jean dropped the drapery. "I suppose I'll have to sew it back on."

"You needn't put yourself out. I didn't mean to create work for you." She tilted her head critically to survey her work. "I like the room brighter. Perhaps I'll never rehang the draperies."

"What? Anyone will be able to see right in!" Jean sounded appalled.

"Only if they climb a ladder propped against the front of the house, which would be notable even in Edinburgh." Ilsa resisted the urge to roll her eyes. The building across the street was a small concert hall, with blank windows on this level.

Jean threw up her hands. "Ach! What goes through your head, child? Of course we need draperies!"

"We don't, actually. They've been down for an hour and the house is still standing."

Her aunt's face puckered in frustration. "That's not what I meant!"

"But isn't it the important question? We don't need draperies. We like them. They demonstrate how stylish we are to anyone who calls. But the panes are well-fitted and there are no draughts, and right now draperies only impede the fresh, clean breeze." She carefully placed another tiny dot of blue on her painting. "I think it may be far more beneficial to our health not to have them."

"There's no arguing with you," muttered her aunt.

Ilsa smiled in relief. "Thank you, Aunt, I am so pleased we are in agreement."

"Hmph." Jean folded her arms. "I never said that."

"As long as we don't argue about it, you are quite entitled to disagree with my every word." She ran the brush around the bottom of the paint pot, then peered inside as if more green paint might spontaneously appear.

"You know, Ilsa, not everyone would be so tolerant of your whims," warned her aunt, reopening a line of contention that had plagued them many times before. "No gentleman would put up with—"

"Yes!" Ilsa got to her feet and began unbuttoning her smock. "No gentlemen. That is a most excellent rule."

Jean puffed up in offense. "Such a broad condemnation! 'Tis unfair of you."

Ilsa laughed. "I've not condemned men! Only *gentlemen*. I adore my papa and Robert."

Jean put one hand to her brow wearily. "Robert is not a man."

"Nor is he a gentleman, which makes him perfect." Ilsa hung her smock on the sconce by the fireplace.

The drawing room door opened. "Oh my, you've got rid of the drapes," exclaimed Agnes St. James.

"No," said Jean firmly, taking down the smock.

"Yes! What do you think?" asked Ilsa.

Her friend surveyed the bare windows, which appeared much larger without the heavy damask draperies surrounding them. There was a fine view, off to the left, of the distant hill over the rooftops. "It's much brighter without them."

"It is. I like it."

Agnes's approval soothed the faint rumble in Ilsa's conscience. Agnes would say something if it were entirely disreputable not to have draperies at her windows. Ilsa didn't see how it could be, but she'd come to distrust Jean's opinion on anything regarding propriety. Agnes was at least a neutral judge.

"Robert is pestering the butler," her friend told her. "He sent me to inform you."

Ilsa grinned. "You mean, he sent you to scold me about neglecting Robert. He must be fretting for his ramble in the park, poor dear."

"*Poor,*" said Jean disapprovingly under her breath.

"I would have taken him myself if Mr. MacLeod had not told me you were up," Agnes went on. "I didn't expect to see you so early. You came in rather late."

She smiled in memory of last evening's fun. "I wish you could have come with me."

Agnes laughed. "My mother would never approve of me going to Mr. Hunter's! I would be marched right home to a blistering scold."

"We can't have that," said Ilsa in sympathy. "I hated to leave you alone, but I'd given my word to Miss White."

Agnes waved it off. "I'm glad you went. Was it wonderful?"

Ilsa thought of the tall, handsome fellow who had embraced her so protectively. "It was marvelous."

"Staying out until all hours isn't dignified," said Jean sternly. "Miss St. James has the right idea. Stay home and stay out of trouble."

Ilsa shared a glance with her friend. Agnes would

have loved to be in that oyster cellar beside Ilsa, dancing and drinking punch and enjoying herself.

But Agnes's mother thought oyster cellars were no place for unmarried girls—even though plenty of ladies went these days. It had been her condition for allowing Agnes to come stay with Ilsa: she must follow all the rules of behavior that she was held to at home. Agnes had been so keen to come, and Ilsa so keen to have her, both had agreed.

"It *is* the right idea to stay out of trouble," said Agnes demurely. "Which is why I must go if you are able to see to Robert. My mother will be expecting me in the shop."

"Indeed, I shall be entirely proper all day, visiting my solicitor and taking tea with Papa," Ilsa told her.

"That is excellent," exclaimed Jean approvingly. "I knew you would be a steadying influence on her, dear Miss St. James."

"Thank you, Miss Fletcher," replied Agnes, choosing not to contradict this provocative statement. Well, Jean was not *her* aunt; Agnes did not need to argue with her over this or anything. Ilsa said nothing.

Jean eyed the crumpled draperies. "Now that these are down, they might as well be cleaned. I'll send the maid in to get them."

"Of course." Ilsa had learned to accept an olive branch when one was offered.

When her aunt had gone, she tossed aside the cap from her head. She only wore it to prevent paint getting in her hair, no matter how Jean scolded her that a widowed lady ought to wear it all the time. "Shall we have a leg of lamb tonight? I consumed so many oysters last night, I can't face anything from the sea for a week."

Agnes made a small grimace. "Alas, I'm dining at home. Mother sent word my brother has returned, and she'll have us all around her table again for the first time in over a year."

"Of course," said Ilsa after a tiny pause. "Welcome home the captain with my best regards."

"Thank you." Agnes rolled her eyes. "He's hinted he brings news from our cousins in England. My mother is hopeful it's a legacy of some sort. She's already begun scouring listings in the New Town, certain we shall be moving to a grand new house."

"You are not as certain, I take it," observed Ilsa.

"Not in the slightest." Agnes pursed her lips. "That family never cared for us. I cannot believe they're about to start now, not in any meaningful way. And even if they did, Mother would insist Drew take all the benefit—aside from her new house, of course."

"Why should he take all the benefit?" asked Ilsa in surprise.

Agnes shook her head. "It would be only fair. He joined the army when he was eighteen and sent his pay to Mother so we would have food and clothes."

"Brothers do such things?" said Ilsa in mock astonishment. "Remarkable!"

Agnes laughed. "He's a good sort. *If* there is a legacy—which I highly doubt!—he may have it with my blessing. After a dozen years in the army, he's earned it."

She smiled. "How generous you are. He must be a good sort." One of her favorite things about the

St. James family was their closeness and honest affection for each other.

"He is! At least, he can be. You'll like him."

An image rose in her mind, a sober, straightlaced fellow in a red coat who spoke in single syllables and avoided anything fun. He'd gone into the army when faced with penury, after all—not for him the usual escape routes of marrying a rich girl, gambling, or piracy. What's more, he chose the *English* army. Not very dashing, joining the English.

Unbidden she thought again of the tall, dark-haired Scot from the oyster cellar. That one had a bit of the devil in him. Too bad she would never see him again.

"A dutiful army man who likes to write letters teasing about possible legacies." Ilsa tapped her chin and pretended to think. "Doesn't seem likely, but one never knows." Agnes just laughed.

She walked with her friend down the stairs. "I do hope you'll meet him." Agnes put on her hat. "I doubt he'll be in town long."

"Perhaps," said Ilsa vaguely. Even his name was prissy and proper. Andrew the Saint. Saint Andrew the Self-Sacrificing. He sounded dreary and dull. She wouldn't refuse to meet him, but neither was she eager.

Agnes left for her mother's shop in Shakespeare Square. Ilsa went into the butler's room, where Robert stood watching Mr. MacLeod polish the silver. At her entrance, he sighed in relief. "Mrs. Ramsay! I didn't like to disturb you, but—"

"I know." She smiled as Robert came up to her, his big brown eyes hopeful. She bent and kissed his forehead. "Yes, my darling, just a moment."

She turned back to Mr. MacLeod. "Two for dinner tonight. Miss St. James will be dining with her family. No fish or shellfish. Lamb, if you can find a prime leg of it."

"Very good, ma'am." He smiled and bowed.

Ilsa left the room, Robert at her heels. Jean had disappeared. Ilsa would wager a handsome sum that by dinner, that loose curtain ring would have been repaired, the drapery sponged and pressed, and the whole thing hung back on the rail. Jean vigorously fended off any hint that they weren't the most eminently proper house on the street.

Ilsa had meant it when she said she didn't want to argue over that, but it seemed inevitable. Jean militantly maintained her status and respectability. At times it seemed like that was *all* Jean did—fuss over the china, the draperies, the exact height of a hemline, or the precise way to hold a fan. A slight slip greeting a new acquaintance would provoke a lengthy scold. A low-cut gown might make her tight-lipped for days.

Not only did Ilsa crave an escape from all that fussing and fretting, she didn't think most of it was important. And she was so tired of toeing the many, many lines laid down by people who told her that all her desires and interests were wrong or unseemly.

She put on her jacket and hat and opened the door, waiting patiently as Robert made his way down the steps. "Well done," she told him, and he nudged her elbow in reply. She smiled. Robert was the perfect companion. He couldn't dance in an oyster cellar, but neither did he scold her, or tell her she was too bold, or say anything disagreeable at all. She patted him on the back and they set off, side by side, for the open fields at the foot of Calton Hill.

This was the part of Edinburgh she loved best. Away from the increasingly dingy and cramped confines of the Old Town, away from the construction dust and noise of the New Town, just a bright, windy day on the hill with no one but Robert. Here she felt at peace, free from society and propriety.

"Should we run away to the Highlands?" she wondered aloud. "I've heard they are beautiful and wild, and not filled with disapproving matrons."

Robert shook his head, plodding along beside her.

"Too cold? Too far?" She sighed, running fingers over his back. "You're probably right. Glasgow? No, too near, and too like Edinburgh." She gave him a little pat. "I have it! We could hide ourselves on a ship to America and go on a grand adventure."

He snorted and wandered off, showing her what he thought of that idea. Ilsa smiled fondly, watching him amble across the grass. "You can dismiss the idea that easily because you don't have to see Mr. MacGill today," she called after him.

She did not enjoy visiting her solicitor. He was reputed to be the best in Edinburgh, or so said her father. Her late husband, Malcolm, had also employed MacGill, keeping things like money and investments entirely out of Ilsa's sight, let alone her control.

But then Malcolm died, and suddenly all that money was hers. Papa had wanted to handle it for her, but Ilsa was done with that, even if it meant she had to deal personally with Mr. MacGill, with his pompous manner and patronizing little smile.

As if she were very fortunate indeed to have even a moment of his attention.

One day I shall withdraw all my money and buy a ship, she thought. *I would like to see India or Spain or perhaps the South Seas.* And wouldn't that give Mr. MacGill the shock of his life.

She knew it would never actually happen, but it gave her great pleasure to *imagine* it happening.

After a long, refreshing ramble she and Robert returned home. He trotted right past her to his room at the back of the hall. It had been Malcolm's private study when he was alive, but now it was Robert's domain. He would settle in for a long snooze, snoring fit to rattle the windows. Ilsa went upstairs and girded herself to face the lawyer with a proper walking dress and coiffure of which even Jean would approve.

Despite arriving before the time of her appointment, she was still kept waiting. Idly annoyed, she entertained herself by counting the carriages that drove past. Mr. MacGill's offices in St. Andrew's Square were large, handsome, and ostentatious, with tall windows facing the square. She wondered why she paid him so much when he irritated her to no end.

She had counted twenty-eight carriages by the time the clerk showed her in. The solicitor came to take her hand and lead her to a chair. He always began with fawning smiles and pleasantries. If only he listened to her with as much solicitude.

"Now, Mrs. Ramsay, what can I do for you?" he asked at last, when she was settled in a chair and had declined his offer of tea.

"I would like to sell my shares in Mr. Cunninghame's trading company."

He was astonished. "Madam! What can you mean? I do not recommend that!"

"I understand," she replied evenly. "But I would like to do it, and they are my shares. Will you see it done?"

"Are you in want of funds?" he said in reproach. "I should have anticipated as much. It is not unusual for a recently widowed female to be unaccustomed to the handling of money. If there are bills to be paid, you must send them to me—"

"Mr. MacGill, I know very well how to live within my means. I am not burning my money on new gowns or slippers." She gave him a determined smile. "Sell the shares, please."

She was slowly reading through the volume of information Malcolm had left behind. Now that he was dead, there was no one to stop her from examining everything in his desk. The Cunninghame trading company was very profitable, but its trade was appalling.

MacGill took a deep breath and seemed to change tack. Adopting an expression of paternal concern, he said, "It would be a very large sum. What would you do with all that money?"

She gazed out the window thoughtfully. The house across the street was under construction, and men were raising a heavy beam into position. "There are so many enterprises here in Scotland in want of investment. I like fabric. Perhaps I'll invest in linen production." She had also seen the reports of increasing trade with America. Scotland had enjoyed a brisk trade there before the war, and now that it was over, there seemed every opportunity for it to resume.

Mr. MacGill clicked his tongue. "I see. Of course a woman would take an interest in fabrics. But, my dear Mrs. Ramsay, investments are not made so impulsively. Let us wait a few months and see how you feel then, shall we? If in six months you still desire to sell, I shall speak to Mr. Fletcher about it."

"It is not my father's money. If my late husband were sitting here, would you say the same to him?" asked Ilsa, still watching out the window. If she looked directly at the solicitor, she would be tempted to throw something at him. "Would you scorn his wishes as idle fancy and impulse, not likely to endure?"

Malcolm had done many things on nothing more than idle fancy and impulse, and men like MacGill had only helped him, often when they should have stopped him. Not one of his friends or associates had tried to keep him from the duel that killed him.

Mr. MacGill went pink in the face. He was a pale man, and it was easy to make him flush. "Mrs. Ramsay. That is immaterial."

Before Ilsa could reply, the clerk slipped in. Silently he brought a letter to Mr. MacGill, who gave the man a look that bordered on gratitude. As if he couldn't wait to be free of her, even after making her wait half an hour for this appointment. With barely a glance at Ilsa, the lawyer unfolded the letter.

"Good heavens," he exclaimed almost immediately. Turning his back to her, he whispered furiously to his clerk, who snapped to attention like a pointer catching a scent. Frowning, Ilsa tilted her head and caught a few words: "waiting," "properties," and "Carlyle."

Almost before she could comprehend what was happening, Mr. MacGill was on his feet, offering her his hand. The clerk scurried out of the office. "My dear Mrs. Ramsay, I do apologize but an emergency has arisen—I must cut this interview short. Shall we speak again in six months?"

She rose to keep him from looking down on her. "Why? What is this? Mr. MacGill, we had an appointment! I only ask a very little of your time now and then."

"Indeed, and you have had it." He reached for her hand.

Ilsa stubbornly refused to move. "Are you throwing me out?"

"No, no," he soothed her, even as he extended his other hand toward the door. "But I must turn my attention—"

"Sell the shares," she said, her voice rising. "Sell them, Mr. MacGill, and deposit the funds into my account. I insist!"

"Madam, I will do no such thing," he snapped, dropping her hand. "What foolishness! You will thank me for it when we speak again in six months."

Frustration boiled inside her. Wordlessly Ilsa turned and stormed from the room without acknowledging his hasty bow. She threw open the door herself, almost striking Mr. Leish, the sanctimonious clerk.

Behind him stood a man, tall and broad, dressed

finely enough to be a lord. An *English* lord. So that's whom Mr. MacGill considered far more important than she, Ilsa seethed as she strode past the lot of them.

Men. MacGill brushing her aside without a moment's hesitation, that arrogant Carlyle fellow demanding his attention with the snap of his fingers, and Leish smirking at her dismissal. Anger carried her blindly to the street, and then all the way to the foot of the Canongate, where her father's house stood.

He was still at the table. Fashionable people dined later, but Papa clung to his preference for an early meal. She suspected he spent the more fashionable dinner hour at a tavern, with cards in his hand. "You're early, my girl!" he said jovially when she came in. "Come in, child! Have some cake."

"How are you, Papa?" She kissed his cheek and waved off the offer of cake in favor of pacing the dining room. "I've just come from Mr. MacGill's office. He has lost my custom."

He blinked at her as he chewed a bite of cake. "Why, now?"

"He refused to do what I asked of him. Would you tolerate that from him?"

MacGill had been Papa's solicitor for years. Ilsa had always thought that was because MacGill was the best, but in the last year she'd come to think that Mr. MacGill only had a *reputation* for being the best. MacGill's fees were exorbitant enough to make one believe he was incomparable, but his service was another matter.

Papa pushed back his plate. "Calm yourself, child.

No doubt he has your best interests at heart. What did you ask him to do, that he refused?"

"I told him to sell my shares in Mr. Cunninghame's trading company."

Her father's face grew stormy. "Ach, Ilsa, why?" he said irritably. "I counseled Malcolm to make that investment, and now you'll sell it?"

She hadn't known that. "You know what Mr. Cunninghame trades in?"

"Sugar and tobacco."

"And you know how that is produced."

"I know he made a ten percent profit on his last two years' voyages!"

"I don't care to profit from slave-grown goods."

"You'll care when your income wanes," he told her.

She rolled her eyes. "As if there's money to be made only in sugar and tobacco! I fancy linen manufacture, perhaps. Something made here. Something Scottish."

His mouth pursed, but then eased. He winked at her. "I know just the thing—cabinetry!"

Her father was Deacon of the Wrights, head of the largest group of carpentry tradesmen in town. Nobody made a finely turned table leg or an intricately carved wardrobe like Papa. His craftsmanship was unequalled, as was his larger-than-life personality. No wright in Edinburgh could have asked for a fiercer champion on the town council, which controlled most of what went on in Edinburgh, and beyond.

And no one had a better talent for disarming her temper. Ilsa laughed. "As if I've not profited enough from cabinetry! But perhaps that's a thought. I'll sponsor some boys to be educated and apprenticed as wrights."

He scoffed. "Where's the profit in that?"

"If you hired them, I would get a share of the income from their work." She beamed at him.

"Eh, when I'm dead you'll have a share of the income from the entire shop's work." He glowered, but she knew he would hire any boys whose education she sponsored. Both of them knew William Fletcher couldn't deny his only child anything.

"I don't want to think about that far-off event." She kissed his cheek. "But I *am* through with Mr. MacGill."

He sighed. "Leave the man to his business. He knows what he's about."

"He dismissed me," she replied. "After making me wait half an hour for our appointment. He was patronizing and short-tempered, and after all that, someone more important than I arrived, and Mr. MacGill all but threw me out the door."

Papa pushed back his chair, frowning. "I'll speak to the fellow. It's not right to treat a woman that way. Who could possibly be more important than you?"

"Some English fellow. He looked rich."

He patted her arm. "The scoundrel! Leave MacGill to me. He'll not be short with you again." He walked with her to the hall and helped her with her cloak, as he'd done since she was a child. Ilsa had given up fighting his little attentions when she was sixteen. He fussed over her because he loved her, and because he had no one else to fuss over. Her mother had died when Ilsa was four, and her father had never remarried. Jean had come to live with them and help raise her, but Papa had always been the center of her world, and she his.

"Mr. Lewis Grant asked me to give you his greetings," Papa remarked as he tied the bow.

"Who?"

"Mr. Grant," he repeated with a twinkle in his eye. "You remember, the handsome—and very successful—wine merchant in the Grassmarket."

"No, I'm afraid I don't recall him," she lied. Her father had begun mentioning possible matches for her in the last few months. By some strange coincidence, they were all prosperous merchants and gentlemen with whom Papa did business. Ilsa was having none of them.

"I'll be sure to introduce you to him," he said, not fooled. "Again. Perhaps next time you'll remember him as fondly as he remembers you, eh?"

"Good-bye, Papa."

She left him and walked toward home, feeling at loose ends. She would prefer to go sit in the coffee shop with Agnes for an hour with a lady's magazine and giggle at the pompous poetry in it, but Agnes was needed at the mercer's shop with her mother, and would be with her family after that. Sorcha White was attending a lecture at the Botanical Gardens with her mother. At home, Jean would scold her about the draperies again or say she should call on Lady Ramsay, Malcolm's acerbic grandmother who had never much liked Ilsa.

She went instead to the bookseller's shop. She passed the selection of novels and poetry, not in the mood for something fictional, no matter how entertaining. She picked up books on fauna, and

Italy, and one beautiful book which turned out to be a history of England. That she shoved right back on the shelf, and blindly pulled out another.

A History of America, Volume One, read the front page. Her fingers slowed. It was a few years old, but finely printed and bound. Her own words of that morning to Robert echoed in her mind: *We could hide ourselves on a ship to America and go on a grand adventure.*

Ilsa knew that she had a very comfortable life, all things considered. She had a father and an aunt who loved her dearly, even if they did not understand her. She had a comfortable home, thanks to Malcolm; he'd been one of the wealthier men in town, before he'd gone and got himself killed. She had Robert, whom she adored without reservation, and she had good friends like Agnes St. James. Many others were never so fortunate as she had been.

But at the same time . . . She'd never been free to do what she wanted. Her aunt had been a strict guardian, her father indulgent but largely absent, and her husband hadn't really wanted a wife, but rather an ornamental doll. When Malcolm died, and she'd realized that for the first time in her life there was no one to tell her what to do, what to wear, whom to speak to, or what she could buy . . . Well, the first thing her heart had craved was a little adventure.

With a snap she closed the book and went to pay for it. It wasn't the same as stowing away on a ship to America, but now she was free to *read* about doing it, at least. She would take what she could.

Chapter Four

Drew slept late the next day, thanks to the quantity of beer and oysters he'd consumed the night before. It had been after three in the morning before they got Ross safely delivered into the hands of his disapproving manservant, accompanied Monteith to his lodgings and shared a bottle of brandy there, stopped at the canal for a quick bathing swim, and finally staggered back to Burnet's Close.

And now Duncan was killing a cat in the other room, from the sounds of things.

He heaved himself out of bed, barely avoiding hitting his head on the slanted ceiling under the eaves—Duncan's spare room was clearly meant to house a dainty lady or a child instead of a grown man—and went into the other room.

"What in God's name is that noise?" he demanded, plugging his fingers in his ears.

Duncan glanced over the violin tucked under his chin. "Music, St. James. A very gentlemanly pursuit."

"Aye, for gentlemen who live alone in the middle of a moor."

"I'm practicing, not performing." Duncan scraped the bow across the strings again, producing a discordant whine that made Drew wince.

"No wonder you're not performing. You're an affront to that instrument." Duncan ignored him, fiddling with the tuning pegs. "And you're violently out of tune."

"All art requires suffering."

"By the artist," he retorted. "Kindly spare the audience."

Duncan put down the violin. "You're the rudest guest I've ever had. You insult my fencing form, and now my musical talent."

"If you had any talent, I would heartily insult it. Besides," he added as he turned back toward his room, "I'm the only guest you're likely ever to have, with the appalling noise you make."

He closed the door of his room and lifted the ewer. Duncan's manservant had filled it, although so long ago the water was stone-cold. In the army, one got used to that. He reminded himself that he was back in Scotland, mere Captain St. James once more, and he ought not to pine for the luxuries that Carlyle Castle had supplied, like warm washing water and a footman to shave him.

Duncan barged in while his face was still half-covered in shaving soap. "What ducal frolics shall you get up to today? I find myself agog to see how an English duke behaves, and if it's any better than a lowly Scot."

Drew flicked soap at him. "I must pay a call on the solicitor today."

At once his friend—who practiced law himself when he wasn't being a menace to music—struck a pose, his nose high in the air and his fist clapped arrogantly on his chest. "Bloody lawyers. Which one?"

"David MacGill, in St. Andrew's Square."

Duncan lifted his brows. "Only the most expensive for the Carlyles, I see."

"Is that so?" He wiped the soapy remnants from his chin and unrolled his sleeves. "What do you know of him?"

His friend lifted one shoulder. "Wealthy—thanks to Carlyle, I presume. Thinks of himself as a modern man, less a Scot than a gentleman of Northern Britain. His offices are in the New Town, which tells you enough."

Drew took out one of his new English suits. The duchess had raised her brows at his plain woolen breeches, and Mr. Edwards had sent him straight back upstairs to change the one time he dared wear a philibeg. The duchess, Edwards had warned him, did not approve of that. A tailor had been sent for posthaste, and Drew soon had a new wardrobe of very English breeches, waistcoats, and coats. Might as well keep to it while on Carlyle's business.

"What business have you got with a solicitor?" Duncan apparently had nothing else to do with himself, although his questions were less irritating than his violin playing.

He buttoned up the waistcoat and tied his neckcloth. "Confidentially, aye? The duke's not in good health, nor has he been for many years. I never even saw the fellow while I was there. But he owns a property here, which no one's visited in twenty years or more. It's all been left in the charge of this MacGill, with no one from Carlyle the wiser as to what he's done with it. I'm to call upon him and find out."

He had agreed to the errand readily, curious to

see what the duke owned in Scotland. Mr. Edwards assured him that it was not much, only one estate, and could be concluded in a matter of days. All he wanted was a review of the records and instruction to Mr. MacGill to have the property put in order, against the likelihood of being offered for sale soon.

Drew wondered at that. He knew who would buy those Scottish lands: aristocrats intent on enclosing them and forcing the cottars and other tenants off them. While posted at Fort George, he had seen displaced families straggle into Inverness, reduced from independent farmers to subsistence crofters. He'd never thought to have a say about any of it, but now . . . He was deeply interested in seeing for himself.

After a quick bite at a nearby coffeehouse, for Duncan kept no food at all in his lodging, Drew walked up Bridge Street over the canal where he and Duncan had stripped down for a frigid swim last night. The New Town, as the rising development across the bridge was called, had grown considerably since he was last here. The streets were level, with proper sewers, and the buildings were of clean, uniform stone, unlike the cluttered hodgepodge of the Old Town.

As he walked, he mentally girded himself for conflict. He had dealt with solicitors before. When his father died, he'd had to step in and sort out his family's affairs, untangling the mortgage and loans Father had taken against the mercer's shop. Later, when he went into the army, he'd gone back and tried to make arrangements for his mother and sisters. He'd got a headache from the dry, stuffy air inside the pompous solicitor's office, to say nothing of the sanctimonious lecture on how his father had mishandled everything. He had come away with no good opinion of the legal profession.

It was an entirely different experience as the Carlyle heir.

He arrived at David MacGill's law offices in spacious, elegant St. Andrew's Square and gave his name. He had made no appointment, not knowing precisely when he would arrive and not averse to catching the solicitor off guard anyway. With a sniff, the clerk took his letter from Mr. Edwards and vanished through a mahogany door. Resigned to waiting, Drew hung up his hat and took a seat, but within moments the clerk was back.

"Please, Captain, this way," said the man breathlessly, now smiling and bowing.

Surprised but pleased, he got to his feet. As they approached the polished door, raised voices sounded angrily behind it, and then it burst open. Drew took a hasty step backward as a lady emerged, her mouth set in a furious line and her eyes flashing. Her skirts swung wide as she strode past him.

He stared, dumbstruck. It was the mystery woman from the oyster cellar, now attired in the finest manner with her hair pinned up in very fashionable curls. Her gaze touched him like a flash of lightning, scalding with contempt, and then she was gone, snatching her cloak and hat from another clerk who'd come running to sweep open the door in front of her.

For a moment he was stunned breathless. In daylight she was even more mesmerizing—and she hadn't shown any sign whatsoever that she remembered him.

"Who was that?" he asked the clerk hovering at his side.

"Madam was on her way out," the man assured him. "Mr. MacGill will attend you now, sir."

His mind lingering on the woman, Drew went into the inner office. He didn't have an appointment, but MacGill had practically thrown her out in order to see him.

"Come in, sir, come in!" MacGill was a sturdy fellow with a headful of fair curls. He bowed and scraped and offered three types of refreshment, all of which Drew declined.

"I hope I've not called at an inconvenient time," he said.

"Not at all, Captain!"

"Yet there was someone in your office," he replied. "She did not look pleased as she left."

A frown flashed across MacGill's face, but he gave a small laugh and waved one hand. "Mrs. Ramsay is the widow of a client of mine. I've served her family for years. She was quite content to make arrangements to discuss her business at a future time."

Content was possibly the last word Drew would have used to describe her expression, but he had a name at last. Mrs. Ramsay.

"In the future," he told the solicitor, "I do not expect you to dismiss anyone in favor of me."

"No," said the lawyer after a startled moment. "As you wish, sir."

He nodded once. It would have to be enough. Now he hoped Mrs. Ramsay had *not* recognized him, so that she wouldn't blame him for her summary dismissal from her own lawyer's office. He opened the leather case of documents he had brought from Carlyle Castle and tried to put the intriguing woman from his mind.

Stormont Palace, the duke's Scottish property, was a fine mansion that had been in Carlyle hands for over a hundred years, with extensive grounds and gardens. It was some fifty miles away, near Perth. Edwards believed it had been decently cared for under MacGill's hand, but he strongly advised Drew never to take that for granted.

Mr. MacGill nodded when informed of Drew's purpose, his thumbs hooked in his waistcoat pockets. "I've no doubt you'll find all in perfect order there, Captain."

"One hopes," said Drew. "I intend to visit it myself, so we shall see."

MacGill's brows rose. "Indeed, sir! I shall send word along at once."

He smiled briefly. "If it is in perfect order, is that necessary?"

The lawyer blinked, then nodded. "True, true! Ah . . . well, what shall I show you, then?"

For hours he pored over the records the solicitor brought out. Stormont Palace did appear to be in fine condition. Though not profitable, it supported itself. Surely with a little effort it could be brought into even better shape, and be a valuable piece of the ducal portfolio instead of a burdensome afterthought.

When he stepped back out into the square, he was mildly surprised by the angle of the sunlight. He'd been there longer than expected, and MacGill had never left his side. He wondered how many other clients had been turned away during his visit. Shaking his head at the difference between a lowly new lieutenant and the heir to a duke, he walked back to the Old Town, to his mother's house, where he had promised to dine.

Unlike yesterday, he found everyone at home this time. Isabella and Winifred ran to fling themselves at him with shrieks of welcome. Laughing, he caught one in each arm, then had to adjust when Agnes joined them. He looked over their heads to see their mother, Louisa, smiling at the sight of them all.

"Save me, Mother," he exclaimed. "I'm overwhelmed!"

This brought a round of protest and even mild abuse. "Such a soft little man you've become, in the army," scoffed Bella.

"I daresay we shouldn't tell his colonel that three girls can overwhelm him," added Winnie.

He huffed. "Like a flock of geese, you are. *Honk, honk, honk*, and so much flapping of wings . . ."

"Andrew," said his mother in gentle reproof. "That is ungentlemanly."

Abashed, he kissed her cheek and then swung her off her feet in an embrace, grinning as his mother squawked indignantly and his sisters burst out laughing.

"Well!" Flustered, Louisa clapped one hand to her head, adjusting her cap. "At least we know it's really you. Come in, come in!"

Dinner was a feast, with his favorite dishes in every course and good Scotch claret throughout. He inhaled happily. He'd missed his mother's kitchen, and when Annag brought in the crowning glory, the roasted beef, he might have moaned in ecstasy. He certainly ignored his sisters' teasing about his appetite, right through the sweets course.

"'Tis more than the rest of us could eat in a week," whispered Winnie, eyeing his plate.

"How fortunate the army has the feeding of him," said Bella. "Our cupboards would be bare."

"I'm being appreciative," Drew retorted, ladling more cream on his plum pudding. "'Tis the finest meal I've had in months, even including at the castle."

"And are you going to tell us why you've been to Carlyle Castle?" asked his mother, raising her eyebrows. Instantly the room fell silent, and all three sisters turned to him with expectant faces.

He swallowed his bite of pudding and laid down his fork. She'd been very restrained—all of them had been. He'd got to enjoy a delicious dinner in peace. "Aye. But I warn you, we'll need more claret."

"Why?" demanded Bella as Agnes jumped up and began pouring.

"Papa always said they were the coldest people there at Carlyle," put in Winnie. "I couldn't possibly hate them more!"

"No," he said, holding up one hand. "You'll not hate them when you hear." Agnes raised a skeptical brow, but the younger girls looked interested. He took a deep breath. "The duke is in poor health. His younger brother died a few months ago."

Someone made a dismissive noise under her breath. "How unfortunate," said Louisa, shooting a sharp glance around the table.

Drew leaned forward. "The brother was the duke's

heir." No one's expression changed. "The duke has no children, nor even a wife. When he dies, the title will have to go to a male St. James, descended from a previous duke."

Bella sucked in her breath. Agnes jerked in her seat.

"You?" said Winnie incredulously. "*No.* Drew, you can't mean . . ."

He nodded, watching his mother's face turn pale. "I appear to be first in line for it."

The girls erupted in shock, babbling questions and exclamations. One hand at her throat, Louisa reached for her claret and drained the glass.

"Well, Mother?" he prompted. "Do you think I'm a liar, too?" Agnes flushed; she was the one who'd voiced blatant disbelief.

"No," Louisa said. "But—but it is too incredible, Andrew!"

"So thought I, but the duchess was quite clear. Her solicitor has a chart of the family, and there's no one between the current duke and me." He spread his arms. "You'd better get used to calling me Your Grace, sisters."

Bella hooted, Winnie threw her napkin at him, and their mother scolded both. Only Agnes gave him a peeved frown. "Of course we won't. Don't be vain."

He grinned at her. "Vain! When I've brought a trunk full of gifts for my dear family?" He held up one hand as Bella fairly leapt out of her seat in excitement. "I left it with Felix Duncan. You'll have them tomorrow."

"Felix Duncan," said Louisa in disapproval. "Andrew, you ought to stay here, with us."

"Agnes has already taken herself off to stay with her friend," piped up Bella. "She's left her room for your use, Drew."

"But if *you* don't want it, may I take it?" asked Winnie eagerly before he could speak. "It's so unfair Agnes has a room to herself, and now she's not even here—"

"She'll come back," said Louisa, "particularly if Andrew is not staying with us."

"I've given my word to Mrs. Ramsay!" protested Agnes in outrage. "Mama, you said I might stay with her for a month—"

"Who is this friend?" interrupted Drew, his attention caught by that name. He glanced at his sister's flushed face. If by some strange chance her friend was the same woman he'd danced with in the oyster cellar—the same woman who had kissed him and then disappeared—he couldn't imagine his mother approved of Agnes spending time with her. He, on the other hand, was keenly interested to know more.

"My dear friend Ilsa Ramsay," said Agnes. "She very kindly offered me a room in her house when you wrote that you were coming to visit. She's so pleased to have me, Mama! And you must admit it is easier in front of the mirror in the morning, if I'm not here—"

"That is true," agreed Bella. "She spends an eternity brushing her hair and uses all the warm water."

"I do not!" Agnes turned back to their mother. "And she has such a small household, she says my company is very welcome and brightens her day immeasurably. Please say I may stay, Mama."

"There's no reason to impose on Mrs. Ramsay if your brother won't be here." Louisa looked to him. "Surely you'll reconsider? Felix Duncan is such a scapegrace."

Under no circumstances did Drew want to live with his mother again. He loved her, but he was a grown man. He'd specifically told Mr. Edwards to find a property with a separate cottage for his mother's use. The solicitor, thinking he meant to avoid any conflict between his mother and a future, yet-to-be-found wife, had nodded; Drew had never told him it would be necessary even if he never married.

"I have no intention of putting you out," he said. "I'm pleased to stay with Duncan, but that doesn't mean Agnes must change her plans." He turned to his sister as if he'd just had the happiest thought. "Perhaps you should invite her to dine with us, Agnes, if her society is so quiet and limited."

Silence descended on the table. Bella and Winnie looked sideways at their mother, while Agnes turned pink. Louisa sighed. "No one would call Mrs. Ramsay's society quiet or limited," she murmured. "Agnes, I have no wish to argue with you. You may stay with her for the month you promised. Andrew, you are most welcome here—"

"I'm already settled with Duncan, so Winnie is welcome to take Agnes's room." He said it in his captain's voice and his mother gave in, to Winnie's squeal of delight.

After dinner he sat and obligingly answered question after question about Carlyle Castle and the duchess. His family still had the mixture of animosity and curiosity that he'd felt before his visit there, and from time to time they would shake their heads over his description of something, like the tall, narrow windows in the formal dining room that dated from the castle's Norman past or the long gallery filled with dour-faced portraits of past St. Jameses.

Finally their mother clapped her hands. "'Tis late! As thrilling as this news is, the shop will not run itself tomorrow. Andrew, walk your sister to Mrs. Ramsay's, if you please."

"Mama, it's two streets away," Agnes muttered.

"Aye, and there have been robberies in this town of late!" Their mother gave a stern look. "Bankers, silversmiths, even a grocer's shop. Who knows but that our own shop may be next!"

Drew opened his mouth to say something about that—his family wouldn't need to labor in a shop much longer, thieves or no—but realized she was right about the time and said nothing. Winnie and Bella fell upon him with more hugs and reminders to bring their gifts the next day. Agnes followed him to the door and put on her cloak. They bid their mother good-night and went out into the street.

"Tell me about this dear friend who invites you to live with her," he said as they walked along the dark High Street. The oil streetlamps cast only the faintest circles of illumination.

Agnes gave him a look, half reproof, half amused. "You'll like her, Drew."

"Will I, now?" Above them, a window creaked open, and he pulled his sister away from the oncoming deluge of waste. "Why is that?"

"Ilsa speaks her mind and enjoys life."

That, he thought, fit the woman he'd seen last night. But what Agnes was saying was more important at the moment. He gave her a considering look. "Something you've not been able to do."

Her mouth turned downward. "Not much, no."

Agnes was twenty-four and still unmarried. William Ross had once said she was a very handsome lass, until Drew gave him a narrow-eyed look and Ross shut his mouth. The fellow was right, of course—Agnes was tall and slender with their mother's blue eyes and their father's dark hair—but Drew knew him too well. Agnes deserved better than Ross.

"I think that will change," he told his sister now. "The duchess has granted me an income. No more captain's pay, aye? There'll be money for new gowns, a carriage . . . perhaps even a Season in London, if you and Winnie and Bella are so inclined."

Her brow puckered. "You're going to make us English."

"No," he said at once. "Just richer Scots."

"With an English castle." She gave him a look. "And an English title. That makes you English."

He clenched his jaw. "I didn't tell Mother yet, but the Carlyle solicitor is searching for a house for us, near the castle."

Agnes gaped at him. "In England? You—you want us to leave Edinburgh?"

He stopped walking. "Don't you want to? Dark narrow streets, people emptying their piss pots on our heads, a shop that demands all your time . . . I thought you'd be pleased to hear of it."

She bit her lip. "I never wanted to go to England. I'm not going to inherit anything."

"But I intend to settle a proper dowry on you."

"The income from the duchess is that generous?"

No, it wasn't, not with all three sisters already of marriageable age. Drew hoped to give each of them five hundred pounds at least. Edwards had hinted that something more might be arranged but had not yet committed to it.

At his hesitation, Agnes threw up her hands. "So you're to be the next duke, and will be treated as such, because that's what the duchess wants—a respectable heir. And we'll be the poor relations, to whom nothing is owed or due, but who are now expected to uphold the dignity of a family who never cared tuppence for us. I knew they would never want anything to do with us. And you're a fool, Andrew St. James, if you think you mean much to them, either."

"Agnes," he tried to say, but she backed away from him.

"Good night, Drew. I'm happy for you, truly I am, but don't presume I'll go along with your plans." She turned and hurried into the house behind her.

His fingers curled into a fist. Damn. Agnes, as usual, wasn't wrong. He would have to do better, looking out for them. How ironic if it should turn out to have been an easier task when he had no expectations at all.

As he turned away, his gaze caught on the windows above him. They glowed with light, unobscured by any drapes, and a woman was silhouetted at one side, a book in her hands.

Drew stopped. He backed up for a better view. Agnes came to join her, and the woman turned away. He wondered if she'd seen him.

The one thing he did not wonder about was her identity. Ilsa Ramsay was unquestionably the woman who had kissed him last night.

Chapter Five

Armed with a name, he had much better luck finding out about his mystery woman.

"Ilsa Ramsay? Aye," said Duncan over pints in a tavern. "An eligible widow. Her father is Deacon of the Wrights, and her husband was a banker—poor bastard."

"Why?"

"Got himself killed. He was a hotheaded sort and got into a quarrel with an Englishman and they ended up dueling over it. Shot Ramsay through the heart." Duncan shrugged. "There was a trial and the man was acquitted."

Drew drank in silence. A banker's widow. "When was that?"

Duncan thought for a moment. "A year ago, more or less." He peered over his beer. "Why?"

There was no reason not to tell Duncan that he'd been struck by her in the oyster cellar, nor that he'd seen her at MacGill's office. Instead Drew said, "She's friendly with my sister and invited her to stay during my visit to Edinburgh. My mother thought I would stay with the family, and there's not an empty bed."

Duncan shuddered. "Live with one's family! Nay, not for all the royal jewels of England." He paused, then asked casually, "Which sister?"

"Agnes. I think my mother doesn't like it, but she's allowed Agnes to go."

A faint smile crossed his friend's face. "Nay, I imagine not."

"Why not?"

"You know why," said his friend. "Probably the same reason you couldn't take your eyes off her that night at the oyster cellar."

Drew choked on his beer. "Oh?" he croaked. "Is that she?"

"Aye." Duncan was smirking. "Thought certain you'd've found that out by now, the way you were staring . . . So this was all brotherly concern?"

"Of course. What else?" He raised one hand at the publican for more beer, to avoid that smirk.

Now his friend laughed at him. "Mrs. Ramsay's above your touch—one of these modern Scottish lasses, she is, independent and rich enough not to need a husband. Although . . ." His blue eyes glinted with mischief. "It must be said, no other lad in Edinburgh has a dukedom to dangle in front of the woman."

Drew replied with a good-natured curse; Duncan replied in kind, and they fell into a mutually amused silence.

A modern lass, Duncan called her. By that he meant a vivacious, spirited woman of wit and intelligence—precisely what Drew had seen the other night. No wonder Agnes liked her.

And it only intrigued him more.

ILSA HEARD THE door but was still startled when Agnes burst into the drawing room. "Would you like to come to tea?" asked her friend breathlessly. "With my family."

Slowly Ilsa closed her book. She had just reached the portion about Christopher Columbus, who found the ports of the Mediterranean "too narrow for his active mind," with which she sympathized. Not that she wouldn't welcome a chance to explore even the Mediterranean, it being far wider than the bounds of Edinburgh. "Now?"

Agnes nodded.

She had been to tea once before, and it hadn't gone beautifully. Ilsa was sure, in hindsight, that she'd shocked Mrs. St. James, and not in a good way. She wasn't sure which had been the worst sin: leaving off mourning for Malcolm after six months, or missing church to go golfing. She had never been invited back, and frankly had thought she never would be.

But that restless feeling hadn't gone away, and even Robert had deserted her on their morning ramble today. She closed her book and rose. "That sounds lovely. How kind of your mother to think of me."

Agnes grinned. "Let's go!"

Not until they were almost to the St. James house did Agnes reveal why she was so keen for Ilsa to come along. "My brother will be there. He told Winnie and Bella he brought gifts, and they pestered him to bring them today."

Ilsa glanced at Agnes. So that was it; she was to be a buffer. From what Agnes had said after dinner the other night, Saint Andrew had been stern and depressing. "How likely is this brother of yours to have chosen good gifts?" she asked lightly. "One does so hate to get excited for a length of beautiful silk or a romantic new novel, only to be presented with a butter churn."

Agnes snickered. "Oh, he's probably done well. I just don't look forward to what they mean."

Her brow went up. "What they mean? Surely he doesn't expect something in return for a gift. That would make it no gift at all."

Her companion was quiet. "He does expect something," she said at last, very quietly. "And he means well, but . . . I am not eager to do it."

There was no time to ask what Agnes meant. It was only a few minutes' walk, and they had arrived already. Agnes hurried up the steps to open the door.

The St. James home was smaller than Ilsa's, narrow but neat. A babble of conversation was clearly audible from the sitting room upstairs. Agnes hung up their hats and led the way.

Ilsa followed slowly, uncertain of her reception. She had a growing suspicion Mrs. St. James had no idea she was coming and wanted a chance to judge the room before she was judged in turn.

Winifred and Isabella St. James she knew; sometimes, one or both of them would join her and Agnes for a walk on the hill. Once they had all played a spirited game of golf, with much hilarity on everyone's part. Winnie was the beauty of the family, with her mother's red-gold hair and blue eyes. Bella was dark like Agnes, with a sly wit and keen eye for the ridiculous. All of them were irreverent and amusing, and excellent company.

Mrs. St. James sat smiling on the sofa, her fair hair pinned up under a proper lace cap of the sort Aunt Jean kept urging on Ilsa. She was a handsome woman in her fifties, but more reserved and dignified than any of her daughters. Ilsa was a bit cowed by her.

It was the man in the room, though, who caught her eye. Even down on his knees in front of a trunk, he was tall. Wavy dark hair fell over his brow before he flicked it back impatiently with one large hand. He was dressed as any Scot would be, a brown philibeg with a white shirt and gray coat—much as he had been the night they'd danced in the oyster cellar.

But not, she realized as he looked right at her with brilliant hazel eyes, the way he'd been dressed in Mr. MacGill's office. Only now that she had a chance to look directly at him did she realize why she'd thought that fellow was vaguely familiar. He was the man for whom MacGill had dismissed her.

Alas. Saint Andrew was both more interesting and more disappointing than expected.

She assumed a gracious smile as Agnes tugged her into the room. "I've invited Mrs. Ramsay to tea with us today," said the other girl brightly. "Winnie, make room."

"Ilsa!" cried Bella, coming to squeeze her hand. "How splendid to see you again. How is darling Robert?"

She laughed. "Very well. He misses you, and the way you spoil him." Before she could be distracted, she curtsied to Mrs. St. James. "Good day, ma'am. Thank you for inviting me."

There was nothing in the woman's manner to

indicate surprise or displeasure. "Come in. May I present my son, Captain St. James, to you? Andrew, here is Agnes's friend, Mrs. Ramsay."

He got to his feet, looming over her as he'd done in the cellar, when he shielded her from the crowd surging up the stairs. "A pleasure, Mrs. Ramsay," he said politely.

She curtsied and smiled. Did he recognize her? She couldn't tell.

Deliberately she took the seat furthest from him and sat back to watch as he emptied the trunk.

As Agnes had predicted, he had brought excellent gifts. For his mother, he produced a length of midnight blue brocade. For Bella it was cream silk with pink flowers, for Winnie a rich green and white stripe, for Agnes deep rose. Then he gave them swathes of lace wrapped in silver paper, as fine as anything Ilsa had ever seen, along with a rainbow of embroidery floss. He brought out several new novels—making Bella gasp aloud in delight—India tea, and a small but handsome porcelain clock.

He even had things for the family's servant, the redoubtable Annag. For her there was a box of spices, a new apron and cap of fine linen, and a warm shawl of deep blue wool. Annag's lined face turned pink as she accepted them; her stammering grew incomprehensible until he teased that if she didn't like them, perhaps Bella might. Bella tossed a cushion at him, Annag smacked him affectionately on the shoulder, and then bent down and kissed his offered cheek.

Not quite the stuffy saint Ilsa had pictured.

"And the last," he said, handing out small boxes.

Sitting beside Ilsa, Agnes opened hers to reveal a silver locket on a fine chain.

"Lovely," she whispered, earning a rueful glance from Agnes.

"Oh, Drew!" cried Bella in rapture, clasping on her new bracelets of coral beads. "How did you ever afford all this?"

He leaned back against the empty trunk and stretched out his long legs. Ilsa inched her own feet to the side to avoid his boots; he seemed to take up the entire room, sitting there so easily. "These last are not from me, as it happens. They are from the duke and duchess, chosen by Miss Kirkpatrick, her companion, sent with Her Grace's cordial best wishes."

The room went silent. Agnes put down the locket she'd been about to clasp about her neck. Mrs. St. James flushed. Winnie, busy adjusting her new silver hair combs, muttered impatiently until Bella poked her.

"How very generous of Her Grace," said their mother quietly, studying the elegant brooch in her box.

The captain's gaze fixed on Agnes. "She is well aware of how disruptive this will be to all of you. She is not insensitive to your feelings, and hopes you will be able to find pleasure in the news."

"What did she give you, Drew?" piped up Bella. "Since she took the trouble to send us such lovely things. You, after all, are the important one."

He made a face. "Some stiff new suits and a great lot of work, that's what she gave me."

Agnes cleared her throat. "And a house," she said. "In England."

"England! We're moving to England?" gasped Winnie, her hair combs forgotten.

The captain ran one hand over his head. Ilsa had the thought that he'd not wanted to discuss that. "I must, to learn how to run such an estate."

"But what of us?" Winnie demanded. "Are we going, too?"

Her brother turned to look at their mother. "It means you won't have to work in the shop," he said softly. "No more fretting over unpaid bills and mortgages."

Mrs. St. James was pale. "We shall discuss that later," was her reply, her gaze flickering toward Ilsa for a moment. "Annag, please bring in the tea! So much excitement requires refreshment."

As everyone bundled away their gifts and Annag fetched the tray of tea and cakes, Ilsa leaned toward Agnes. "That's what he wishes you to do, isn't it? Go to England."

Agnes rolled her eyes. "Yes. Mama will probably go, and Winnie and Bella, too."

"But you won't," murmured Ilsa.

"What is there for me in England?" Agnes shrugged, studying the silver locket in its box.

"Certainly not a particular gentleman . . ."

"Shh," hissed her friend with sudden vehemence. She snapped the box closed. "Don't mention that!"

Ilsa subsided but caught the captain looking at her. His brow quirked as if to ask, *Is aught wrong?* She merely gave a polite smile in return and turned her attention to the repast being served.

It wasn't until after tea was done that he spoke to her directly. Agnes said she wanted to fetch something from her room and went upstairs. Ilsa waited near the door, talking to Bella and Winnie before they, too, took their gifts upstairs.

She had known the captain was waiting for a chance to approach her. She could feel his presence even without looking up to see his tall figure at her side.

"It is a pleasure to make your acquaintance, Mrs. Ramsay," he said. She tried not to react to his voice, deep and gruff and rolling his vowels like a true Scot. "I'm glad you came to tea."

"Thank you, Captain." It was hard not to look at him, and yet his piercing gaze made her feel hot and flustered. "It was a great pleasure to be invited."

He smiled wryly, as if he knew very well that Agnes had done it without telling anyone else. "Perhaps next time we meet it will be a more festive occasion."

Without your mother glaring at me? wondered Ilsa. "I suspect we've met before, Captain," she said instead.

Gold sparks kindled in his hazel eyes. "Indeed, Mrs. Ramsay," he said, his voice gone soft and intimate. "I believe we have."

She kept her pleasant smile. She knew perfectly well where it had been, and what she'd done. He was as attractive now as he'd been in that oyster cellar with his coat off and his hair rumpled from dancing, his face fierce with joy and alive with wonder as he stared at her. It had been the act of a moment's impulse when she kissed him.

Oh, if only she'd known.

"It was at Mr. MacGill's offices," she said, instead of any of that. "When he turned me out in order to see you."

His face froze in chagrin. "Ah. I was rather hoping you didn't recognize me from *that* unfortunate encounter. I never expected him to do it. I told MacGill he was wrong and he should never do it again."

"Hmm," she said thoughtfully.

"I am sorry for it," the captain added.

That was more than David MacGill had ever said to her. She gave him a gracious smile. "That is very kind of you, Captain. Of course I do not blame you for the actions of another."

The corner of his mouth rose. "Thank you."

All right. She smoothed her skirts. It was no trouble to turn the full force of her disdain and indignation upon the attorney.

She was much more inclined to like the captain anyway.

Agnes clattered back down the stairs, ready to go. She bade her brother farewell, and Ilsa followed her to the street without another glance at the intriguing captain.

"Who is the duchess?" she asked as they walked.

Agnes looked around, almost furtively. "The Duchess of Carlyle. The duke is our distant cousin—so distant he's never spoken to any of us. Our grandfather was a duke's younger brother, not that it stopped the family from banishing him like a leper and ignoring us all our lives. But Drew is, somehow, shockingly, the next heir to the dukedom, it seems."

Ilsa stopped dead and stared at her, dumbfounded. A duke! An English duke. But of course—that made sense of his visit to Mr. MacGill's office, looking as expensively trussed up as one of King George's many sons. And she'd caught the name Carlyle, too, when Mr. Leish rushed in to evict her.

But it did *not* fit with the exuberant Scot who'd whirled her around an oyster cellar and kissed her so hungrily. She wondered which was the true man, and then told herself it didn't matter. He planned to remove to England; a duke was far too grand for the likes of her anyway. Andrew St. James was fated to be nothing more than a passing acquaintance.

She forced her feet onward again and tried not to feel as though a tiny flame had just been snuffed out inside her breast. There was no reason at all to have dreamt of anything beyond that one thrilling dance—and kiss. It had nothing to do with the Scottish captain turning out to be a future English duke.

"Don't tell anyone," Agnes was saying in the same hushed voice. "It doesn't seem real to me, it doesn't! And I don't want to move to England, and *no*, it's not because of anyone in Edinburgh."

For once Ilsa didn't tease her friend about the handsome solicitor who always seemed to be in their favorite coffeehouse, ever ready to fetch them a plate of warm currant buns.

"I would miss you terribly," she told Agnes, linking their arms. "You're very welcome to stay with me. Perhaps that's the answer! Surely your brother would be far too busy in his new duties to notice either your presence or your absence."

"Precisely. I'm sure I don't need to go with him, and what's more, I won't."

Ilsa squeezed her hand fondly, but in her heart she knew Agnes might not remain so sure. If her mother and sisters went with her brother, it would be very hard for Agnes to stay behind, even if Ilsa threw open her door and invited her to stay permanently in the yellow bedroom across the landing from her own.

She sighed at the thought. In just the last few days she had become very happily accustomed to Agnes's company at home. She had someone to talk to besides Aunt Jean—someone who shared her interests and humor. Agnes came with her to lectures and the bookseller's and the coffeehouse; if Mrs. St. James didn't disapprove, she would even come along to the oyster cellars.

Ilsa was making other friends, but none were like Agnes. If she left for England, it would make Edinburgh a quieter, lonelier place.

And suddenly her opinion of the captain felt a bit colder, that he would take away her dearest friend.

Chapter Six

That night he danced with Ilsa Ramsay again.

She wore red, her bodice cut low over her perfectly plump breasts. Her coal-dark hair streamed around her shoulders as he lifted and spun her around in his arms, letting her down slowly, so she slid along his body. Her eyes shone with promise, as potent as the sheen on her rosy lips, parted invitingly.

There was no one else in the room. It was only the two of them, moving about each other more and more slowly and deliberately, every touch lingering, every glance heated. Then there was no music, just the thud of his heart and the husky invitation of her whispers as she tugged at his clothing, pressing against him as he undid the laces on that scarlet gown and tasted her skin . . .

Until a pistol went off behind him.

Drew startled awake, rearing straight up into the low ceiling and cracking his head. Cursing, he erupted out of bed and had his sword in hand before he realized the gunfire was actually Felix Duncan banging on the door.

"St. James," came his low, urgent voice. "Get up, man! You have a caller."

Pulse racing, head aching, it took a moment for the words to sink in. "What?" he croaked, wincing as he pressed one palm to the lump already forming on his skull.

"Your mother is here," said Duncan, his lips right at the keyhole from the sounds of things. "Come out and face the enemy."

He let out a shaky breath. Quietly he resheathed his sword. "Aye, aye," he called to his friend. So much for the intensely erotic dream he'd been having of a dark-eyed siren about to take him by the hand and lead him to . . .

"Idiot," he said under his breath. He was a sinner just for thinking of her that way. In penance, he dunked his whole head into the basin of cold water.

He didn't know what to make of Ilsa Ramsay; that was the only explanation for his fascination. In his mother's drawing room she was as reserved and polite as Miss Kirkpatrick, the duchess's very proper companion. She pretended not to remember the searing kiss they'd shared under the oyster cellar stairs and made a point of mentioning her abrupt dismissal from MacGill's office in his favor.

Did she despise him? Blame him? Think about that kiss every hour, like he did?

He ought not to think of her at all. Not only was she bewitching and inscrutable, he needed to focus his thoughts on his future duties to Carlyle—and a future duchess. Getting twisted up by a Scottish temptress would not help him with either.

Hastily dressed, he went out to the tiny sitting room. True to Duncan's word, there sat Louisa St. James, straight and proper on the battered sofa.

At his entrance Duncan gave a hasty bow and practically ran from the room.

Drew didn't blame him. He also did not feel up to facing his mother at the moment.

"Good morning," he said with forced cheer. "What brings you here at this hour?" A second thought struck him. "And what about the shop?"

"I've told Mr. Battie to open it in one hour," she said, naming her bookkeeper. "I needed to speak to you."

Since he'd been at her house just last night, with ample opportunity to speak, he knew it wouldn't be anything pleasant she had to say. She'd waited to catch him alone and off guard.

"This house in England," she said directly.

He ran his hands over his head. "Aye. I never meant to force you or the girls to go, but I cannot avoid it." She frowned, and he hurried on. "Carlyle is a huge estate, Mother. Thousands of acres across counties. There is a vast deal I must learn, and no time to lose." He hesitated. "The duke is in poor health. The solicitor warned me he might not last the year. He advised me not to delay my education, and there's no way I can do that from Edinburgh."

"But your sisters," she said gently. "They have lives here."

"Aye, as I had a life at Fort George. Lives change."

"You've resigned your commission?" she gasped.

He peered at her, puzzled. "I will—of course I will. Why would I remain a lowly captain when I'll have a dukedom to manage?"

"Of course." She pressed one hand to her forehead. "I didn't think that far ahead." She sighed. "When your letter arrived, I hoped it meant a legacy—more fool me! A thousand pounds, Andrew. That was all I hoped for—two thousand, in my wildest dreams. That, I thought, would be very welcome. We could take a better house in the New Town, perhaps expand the shop. With two hundred pounds each, the girls might make good marriages."

He said nothing. According to Edwards, the Duke of Carlyle had an income in excess of fifty thousand pounds per annum, and that with some effort and modernization it could reach seventy. Carlyle's expenses were considerable as well, but Drew would wager the duchess spent a thousand pounds on her wardrobe alone every year.

"I did not expect this," went on his mother in growing distress. "This—this *upheaval*! I never imagined it would overturn everything in our lives, pull us out of Scotland, make us English."

English was the worst part of the inheritance, Drew knew. One of Louisa's cousins had died at Culloden, and in the bloody aftermath her father had been imprisoned and barely survived. George, Drew's father, had used to say that it was a miracle she had married a man with a single drop of English blood.

"Mother, you won't become English," he tried to say, but she gave him such a look, he stopped.

"*You* will." She laid her hand on his cheek. "You cannot become an English duke and not change."

"Do you want me to refuse it?" Not that he could, if it were granted to him. Edwards had been very clear on that point.

She sighed. "No. I know you cannot. And in truth, I suspect we will all come to like it far more than we think now. 'Tis just so sudden." She looked at him questioningly. "But I've not asked what *you* think of it."

He stirred uncomfortably. "Never mind that . . ."

"Are you pleased, then?"

He set his jaw. "Thanks to Carlyle, I can take care of you and the girls as you deserve. And I'm not sorry at all to resign my commission in the miserable army. So yes, I would say I am more pleased than not."

Instantly she clasped his hand in hers. "Of course. We've not forgotten how you sacrificed for us all these years. And I am happy for you, truly I am . . ." She smiled, more determined than joyful. "Give me a few days to acclimate my mind to it and I will begin to see the advantages, as well."

"The duchess hoped you might."

"Did she?" Some of his mother's pride returned. "What did she think of you, as the heir?"

He made a face. "Not much at all. She bestowed an income on me with a stern admonition to make myself worthy."

Louisa frowned. "My son, not worthy! Of course you are. And a fair sight more capable than she had any right to expect, given their coldness to your father and grandfather."

He laughed. "That's it—amuse yourself thinking of a sober, parsimonious Scot inheriting the magnificence of Carlyle Castle."

At that his mother laughed. "You, sober and parsimonious! You've not been away *that* long, laddie. I know you better than that."

Still grinning, he squeezed her hand. "And that's why you shouldn't worry, Mother. You know me."

ILSA WAS JOINED by all three St. James girls on her morning ramble.

Bella and Winnie rushed to Robert with cries of delight, and he shamelessly wallowed in their fawning attention. Ilsa rolled her eyes at Agnes, who laughed.

"Has something befallen the shop?"

"Mama wanted to speak to Drew," said Agnes. "Alone."

"Rip into him, you mean," called Bella, still stroking Robert's neck.

Ilsa raised her brows in question, and Agnes grinned. "She'll be giving him what-for about that house in England."

"And then?" Ilsa knew enough nobility to know that a title—any title, but particularly a dukedom—had a mighty pull. She would wager it took Mrs. St. James no more than a few weeks to warm to the idea.

"And then we'll go live in it," exclaimed Winnie. "Drew said he would take us to London for a Season—can you imagine, Ilsa?"

"I cannot," she said, smiling even as her heart suffered a pang.

"Winnie just fancies a new wardrobe."

Winnie made a face at her older sister. "Aye, and the entertainments in London, and the society, and most of all a chance to meet people I've not known all my life!"

Ilsa laughed. "You're braver than I, my dear. I would fear making a terrible fool of myself there."

"You're not a fool, Ilsa," declared Winnie. "Never!"

"I have my moments," she murmured.

"You know a Season would require a proper chaperone and sponsor," Agnes told her sister. "And you think Mama scolds you for being too boisterous. Imagine a proper lady in charge of you!"

Bella looked up. "Aye, we would need a sponsor, but Winnie and I have a plan for that." She left Robert's side and hurried over, drawing a slim book from her pocket. "Look what we found." Agnes and Ilsa put their heads together and opened it.

The Widower and Bachelor's Directory, read the front page. *An exact listing of Duchesses, Peeresses, Dowagers, Widows, and Spinsters in Great Britain, with their places of Abode and reputed Fortunes.*

"Where on earth did you get this?" demanded Agnes.

"From Drew's coat pocket the other day." Bella grinned.

"What?"

"Don't you see? He intends to find a bride, and *she* would be our sponsor in London." Winnie's eyes grew dreamy at the thought. "We shall see Vauxhall, and the Theatre Royal, and Bond Street, and ever so many balls and parties . . ."

Agnes scoffed. "As if an English lady would be eager to sponsor three wild Scottish girls in London."

"Perhaps she won't be English," said Ilsa quietly. She had paged through the book, just to see, and found her own name listed. *Madam Ramsay of Edinburgh, with twenty-four thousand pounds and two thousand in stocks.* There were several other names she recognized.

Agnes read over her shoulder and bit her lip. She began scolding her sisters about stealing from their brother's pocket while Ilsa riffled the pages again. Who wrote this? *A Younger Son*, was the only author given.

She handed it back to Bella. "Invaluable intelligence," she said lightly. "I commend your pocket-picking talent. How shall you use it?"

Winnie ignored Agnes's disapproving frown. "Most of the ladies listed are English, aye? But not all. I propose we undertake to put as many Scottish ladies in front of him as possible before he goes back to Carlyle."

"As you said, Agnes, Drew's choice of wife will affect us as well, so why shouldn't we try to help him to a lady we like, too?" chimed in Bella. "Who will like *us* in return."

"If *he's* looking up ladies in this book, why shouldn't *we*?" Winnie gave them a dimpled smile. "Drew has no experience of Edinburgh society, let alone London. He would be hopelessly lost if he tried to decide by himself. He probably thinks one chooses a wife the way one chooses a horse. Really I think he must need our advice *desperately*."

"And did he ask for your help, Winifred?"

Bella hooted. "He's too stubborn to do that, but he certainly ought to."

"Why should he depend upon some silly book to help him, when he has three devoted sisters who know him?" Winnie smiled coyly.

"Some silly book," repeated Agnes wryly, "which is also central to your own plot."

"You know he'd be happier with a Scotswoman," put in Bella. "Just as we would."

"Not to mention Mama. Really, it is our duty to our *entire family* to do this, Agnes . . ."

Ilsa strolled after Robert, who had wandered off. It was nothing to her. Let him marry a Scotswoman or an Englishwoman or an American or anyone else. She told herself the pit in her stomach was due to the prospect of her dear friends leaving Edinburgh forever. Not that she didn't long to leave Edinburgh herself at times, but they would be going together, while she had no one with whom to explore the world. She laid her hand on Robert's back and he nuzzled her affectionately. At least she had him, even if he could be won away from her side by a handful of carrots.

The others caught up to her, and they took their walk. Bella and Winnie kept up a patter about which ladies they should introduce to their brother, with Agnes periodically pointing out flaws in their plan. Ilsa smiled at their fantasies but said nothing—not because she didn't like to think of Eileen Murray or Lady Milton with the captain, no indeed not, but because she would really miss the captain's sisters.

A distant shout made them stop and turn. "Drew," gasped Bella. She flung up her arm and waved as Winnie hid the troublesome little book in her pocket.

The captain was not alone. To Ilsa's surprise a tall man with ginger hair was at his side. She glanced at Agnes, whose face was pink but serene.

"What are you doing here, Drew?" demanded Winnie as the men reached them.

He winked at her. "Mother sent me. She wondered where you'd all gone this morning. I've been searching dress shops and milliners all over town." His gaze settled on Ilsa. "Good morning, Mrs. Ramsay."

"Captain." She curtsied. "Mr. Duncan."

The redheaded fellow removed his cap and bowed. "Ma'am."

The captain cleared his throat. "Duncan, I hope you remember my sisters. Miss Agnes St. James, Miss Isabella, and Miss Winifred. Sisters, this is my friend Mr. Felix Duncan, and mind you don't frighten him off with your usual pestering."

Mr. Duncan bowed to them all in turn. Bella and Winnie responded brightly, eyeing him with interest, but Agnes barely bobbed a curtsy.

"We were on our way home," said Ilsa. "You must forgive me, Captain, if I've kept them too long and inconvenienced Mrs. St. James."

Bella laughed. "Drew wishes we'd all gone with Mama this morning, I wager!"

"Did she scold you something fierce?" Winnie wanted to know.

Mr. Duncan stood with his hands clasped behind his back, watching the captain. Agnes's face was now pale and stony, her gaze fixed into the distance.

The captain gave Winnie an exasperated look. "No, she did not."

"Then we're going to England? When?" demanded his sister.

"Nothing is decided yet."

"Oh? How long *do* you plan to stay in Edinburgh, Drew?" asked Bella. "Surely you must want a holiday, after spending a month or more at Carlyle."

His sharp hazel eyes narrowed on his sister. Like Ilsa, he was not fooled by her innocent expression. "I have some things to see to here in Scotland, aye. A month or so, was my intention."

Wide smiles bloomed in perfect unison on her

face and Winnie's. "Excellent! Shall we go to the Assembly Rooms, then? Do say you'll come with us! It's been so long since we've been, and you did say you wanted to get out."

Ilsa was shaking with suppressed laughter. They really meant to parade a string of wealthy Edinburgh ladies in front of him. Over Bella's head, the captain shot her a quizzical look. She gave him a gleeful smile in reply, imagining his consternation.

"Mama wants us," said Agnes abruptly. "Ilsa, I will see you later. Drew . . ." She hesitated, then gave him a nod. She did not glance once at Mr. Duncan, although his eyes tracked her departure.

Bella blew out a sigh, and Winnie nudged her elbow. They bade everyone farewell and followed Agnes.

Mr. Duncan cleared his throat. "It appears you've got this well under control, St. James. You didn't need my help at all, aye?" He clapped one hand to his chest and swept a gallant bow. "Au revoir, Madam Ramsay."

Amused, she let him kiss her hand. "Au revoir, Monsieur Duncan."

He strode off, whistling, his kilt flapping around his knees. Fine knees, now that she'd got a good look at them. She wondered why Agnes could no longer bear to look at the man.

That left her alone with Captain St. James. Suddenly the empty, windy field felt small and—when she met his gaze—even intimate.

Without asking, rather as if it felt as natural to him as it did to her, Captain St. James fell in step beside her as she headed back toward town. He did not offer his arm, for which she was glad. He was so big and mesmerizing, she didn't trust herself to touch him.

"I didn't realize you were acquainted," said the captain. "With Felix Duncan."

"We have met a handful of times in the coffee-house, nothing more."

His broad shoulders eased. "I apologize for running off all your companions."

"But you have not." He blinked at her, and she gave him a teasing smile as Robert trotted up to nudge her hip. She laid her hand on his head. "Not only do I have my dear Robert, sir, you are still here."

"That's Robert?" His lips twitched.

Ilsa stroked Robert's ear. "Yes. Isn't he a handsome fellow?" She glanced up to catch a flicker of relief in his face. "Who did you think Robert was?"

The captain laughed, a little shamefaced. "I thought he might be your son, when Bella mentioned him the other day."

Ilsa sighed, bittersweetly. "I love him as much as any child, but he is only a pony." Robert nibbled the end of her shawl in retaliation, and she had to snatch it away from him. "A *naughty* pony."

"There's nothing wrong with naughty," murmured the captain, his gaze on her.

"No?" She arched a brow, intrigued.

"At the proper time and place, of course."

Ilsa clicked her tongue. "But if it's proper, how can it be naughty?"

"Being naughty at the wrong place or time might be misconstrued as . . . wicked. Certainly scandalous. But at the *right* time and place . . ."

"So a scandalous or wicked act is merely naughty if no one knows you did it?"

He considered a moment. "Yes, that's about the sum of it."

Ilsa choked on a laugh.

He flashed a roguish smile. "Some acts require a willing partner, of course, who would obviously need to know what you did. You must be certain they can keep a secret."

"Goodness, Captain," she said with an admiring glance. "You surprise me."

He just looked at her, a little smile playing around his mouth. He had a gorgeous mouth, the sort that could tease a woman to no end, pleasure her and torment her and break her. The sort of mouth she could almost feel, pressed up against her ear, crooning wicked promises as his hands did scandalous things to her very willing body . . .

Stop. She had to stop thinking things like that about him. Remember the English lady he would wed, or even the wealthy Scottish one, if his sisters had their way. Remember that he would be an English duke and was leaving Edinburgh in a matter of weeks.

"I understand congratulations are in order," she told him. "I'd no idea your family had such illustrious connections."

His eyes darkened before he dropped his gaze. "Thank you." His tone expressed the opposite.

Yes, that was better. She was much safer without his glinting regard on her. "Is it a tender subject?" she teased. "Surely not—one of the most elevated titles in the land! It is my deepest honor to walk humbly by your side, Your Grace."

He stopped. Ilsa turned to walk backward, her

fingers in Robert's mane to keep her moving away from him. "Don't," he said.

"Why?" She widened her eyes. "Is it not the sort of good fortune all men dream of?"

"Not if it spoils the conversation we were having."

Her steps slowed. "Does it?" she said evenly. "How odd. Why would mention of your grand and glorious expectations spoil a friendly conversation?"

"It does if you use it to declare ever so subtly that we are different." He opened his arms. "Regardless of what I may be in years to come, today I am just an ordinary fellow, a lowly soldier."

She laughed in surprise. "And that means we are . . . what?"

He came closer. "Friends. I hope." Despite the words, his glance was heated. "We ought to be, at any rate, since my sisters think you are one of them."

"Ah," she said. "So you think of me like a sister."

His eyes flashed. "I never said that." And he offered his arm.

She thought about it, told herself not to do it, and then slid her hand around his elbow. Goodness, he was strong. His forearm flexed under her palm and a shudder of appreciation went through her. Malcolm had been tall but lean, a rangy fellow always humming with nervous energy. The captain was as steady and solid as a rock.

She knew she ought not to have touched him.

Robert wandered off, cropping the grass as he went, and the captain stepped closer, shielding her from the breeze and making her suddenly very warm and restless.

Friends friends friends, she reminded herself. Friends did not want to kiss each other.

"I suppose," she said as they began walking again, "that your visit to Mr. MacGill's office was related to your inheritance." It made sense, after Agnes's revelation.

A hesitation. "Yes."

"Agnes has heard me mention Mr. MacGill several times, and she never mentioned he was your family's solicitor."

The captain cleared his throat. "He certainly is not. He's the duke's solicitor."

She nodded. "Then, as your friend, may I ask you something about him?"

It had been festering in her mind, the way MacGill treated her. Aunt Jean had told her that *she* was the problem; she ought not to have gone to see him alone, or questioned his judgement, or tried to make decisions about her money at all. It put people off, Jean scolded. Papa waved his hands and said he would deal with MacGill, suggesting that she was unable to do so herself, and that she was probably being a hysterical female about it anyway. And Papa would most likely tell the solicitor simply to be gentler with her, not to treat her as any sort of intelligent, capable being.

"Of course," said the captain.

Ilsa kept her gaze on the spires of town. "My question is this: What would you expect Mr. MacGill to do if you asked him to do something of which he did not approve?"

He frowned. "Something unethical? Or illegal?"

"No!"

"Then I'd expect him to nod his head and do it."

"And if he protested?" she asked. "If he told you to wait six months and refused to do it sooner?"

He blew out a breath and thought. "If he made sound arguments against the action, I would consider them, of course. One never wants to charge headlong after a stupid idea."

"But if he did not offer any," she persisted. "If he said it was a silly whim, and refused to act until you came to your senses and changed your mind."

Now he was frowning at her. "Is that how he treats you?"

"What would you do?" she asked again, feeling her face grow hot.

"I'd sack him on the spot. I wouldn't put up with that from another officer, let alone a man in my own employ."

Ilsa nodded, squinting at the sunlight glaring off the windows of the town as they drew nearer. "I thought so."

"I was told you had concluded your appointment that day," said Captain St. James cautiously. "But I fear . . ."

She gave a short laugh. "Oh, I suppose my appointment was over before it began. I've no doubt Mr. MacGill viewed your arrival as a gift from heaven above, offering him an excellent excuse for bundling me out the door as soon as he could."

"So he tossed you out." Now the captain looked and sounded quite grim.

Ilsa wiggled her shoulders to release their tension and took a deep breath. "Never mind about him. Thank you for answering my question, Captain."

He glanced at her, still frowning in that appealingly stern way he had. "Sack him, Mrs. Ramsay. I intend to."

She blinked. "Do you, now?"

"As soon as I can do so, at any rate." He sighed, then forced a smile. "Which might not be for many years."

He could do nothing until he was the duke. Ilsa still smiled. His outrage for her was more comforting than it ought to have been.

"Your sisters are very curious about your future position," she said on impulse. "If I may offer a suggestion, as a friend, you could win their hearts with a little effort."

"Ah," he said, his mouth easing. "Agnes has spoken about it."

Agnes had railed furiously against any move to England and declared her brother could go alone for all she cared. But no matter what she said, Ilsa knew her friend would be despondent if the rest of her family went.

"All of them have," she told him. "Just this morning, in fact."

He heaved a sigh so weary, so afflicted, she laughed in spite of herself. "It is the greatest trial I could inflict upon my family, apparently."

He wouldn't think that if he'd heard Winnie waxing eloquent about the parties and ball gowns she looked forward to in London. "Less than you might think. Once they realize the benefits and advantages it will confer, that is . . . Naturally, each will find something different appealing."

"What do you mean?"

Ilsa didn't even know why she was saying this. It

was much more in her interest to keep her friends in Edinburgh. And yet. It was rare to have a happy family of siblings. The St. Jameses had not had it easy in all the time she'd known them. Ilsa loved the girls like sisters, and she wanted to see them happy. She hoped they would write to her from distant, elegant London.

"Edinburgh hasn't nearly the elegant sophistication of London," she said, pushing aside her own wishes. "They are intrigued by it, but also wary of the unknown. Perhaps a glimpse of how things will be would help set their minds at ease and even make them eager."

A thoughtful frown knit his brow. "So . . . if I were planning to visit a ducal estate not far from here, to make certain it's in good order?"

"If it's a fine, elegant house, likely to impress and please, you might make a party of it," she suggested.

He gave her a look so warm with admiration and gratitude, it nearly bowled her over; her knees felt weak. "A splendid thought. I'm in your debt, Mrs. Ramsay."

Heart thudding, she waved one hand. "A trifle!" And then, before she could stop herself, she added, "Invite Mr. Duncan, too."

He stopped short. "Why?"

Ilsa cursed herself for a meddling busybody who ought to stay out of Agnes's personal affairs. "You have the look of a harried stag when your sisters swarm you. Another man might deflect some of their teasing. I thought only of your comfort, sir, in suggesting it."

Now his gaze was searing. "Did you, now?"

"What else?" She blinked at him artlessly.

The slow smile that crept over his face sent a ripple of heat through her. "I'm grateful for every moment you're thinking of me."

"The only gratitude I want is for your sisters to be pleased with their future." She was gazing back at him like a coquette; she knew it and somehow still couldn't stop herself. *Friends friends friends . . .*

He laughed. "Then we want the same thing."

"How fortunate," she murmured, knowing what he meant.

Each other. They wanted each other. Saints above, how they wanted each other.

Good Lord. What had come over her? She closed her eyes for a moment, giving herself a brief mental scold. "Here is where we must part, Captain. Good day to you."

He accepted the dismissal; with a lingering warm look, he bowed and turned away. Ilsa slowly let out her breath, covertly admiring his legs even more than Mr. Duncan's.

After a few steps, the captain turned around. "I've been wondering about one thing for some time . . . What you said to me that night in the oyster cellar."

Another flush of arousal went through her. That still felt like a moment in time too vivid to stare directly at, as if doing so would cause it to dim or fade, and she was just barely keeping to the safe side of the line she mustn't cross with him as it was. *Friends*, she sternly told herself. "What any woman would say, in the midst of such a crush," she replied lightly. "A polite thanks for your assistance."

He came a little closer. "Then I seriously misheard. I thought you said . . ." His gaze dropped to her mouth.

For a moment she felt again his arms around her, his fingers in her hair, strong and commanding. She tasted his mouth on hers, hot and seductive. She felt again the wild spike of longing that it could mean something . . .

"What?" she said, hating that her voice had gone breathy. "What did you think I said?"

He was an arm's length away; her feet were rooted to the ground. "Whaur hae ye been aw ma life?" he whispered in a deep Scots purr.

Her lips parted. Her knees almost buckled. Saints help her, she wanted to kiss him again. She wanted him to swing her into his arms and hold her close and laugh with her before he kissed her senseless.

"But if I heard wrong," he went on, his voice even lower and rougher, "'tis right sorry I am."

He gave a very proper bow and strode away, his drapes swinging with every long-legged stride. And Ilsa could only cling to Robert for balance, speechless and breathless with wanting.

Chapter Seven

He was on Duncan's doorstep before his heart stopped pounding.

God above, he liked that woman. And she might just drive him mad, with her sly glances and subtle comments that sent his mind tumbling down wickedly erotic paths. That sparkle in her eyes when he said there was nothing wrong with naughty . . . the way her gaze turned hot and lustful when he said they wanted the same thing . . .

Each other. God above, she wanted him as much as he wanted her, and he *hadn't* been wrong about her whispered words in the oyster cellar. His skin seemed to burn with wanting.

There was, however, a possible fly in the ointment, and he attacked it head-on, having no patience to wait.

Duncan was sprawled on the sofa reading. It must be a legal document, because he wore his spectacles, and Felix was too vain to wear them any other time.

"You didn't tell me you knew her."

Duncan flushed dull red. "Why should I? It's not a crime to know someone."

His defensive attitude took Drew aback. "You might have mentioned it."

"There was nothing to tell," muttered Duncan, his jaw set and his eyes fixed on the papers in his hand.

"Hmph. She specifically named you, idiot, and said I should invite you to visit Stormont Palace with us."

"She did?" His friend's face came alive with wild, sharp pleasure—before going carefully blank.

His hands clenched. "Good God, Duncan, if you had an amour with her, you ought to have told me when I asked about her the other day! Acting like you hardly knew her name and teasing me about catching her interest."

Duncan's expression froze. "Ilsa Ramsay!" he exclaimed. "Of course. Ha ha, St. James, have you been tormenting yourself imagining me making love to her?" He laughed, once more the careless scoundrel Drew knew.

"Who did you think I meant?"

Duncan pretended not to hear. "We're going to Stormont Palace? Excellent. What, and where, *is* Stormont Palace?"

He raked one hand through his hair. "The ducal property near Perth I'm to inspect. Mrs. Ramsay suggested I make a party of it, invite my family and even you. Why would she do that?"

"Did she?" Duncan brightened. "I knew I liked her. Such intelligence and wit, not to mention a splendid figure."

Drew glared at him. "Why would she want to invite you?"

"Perhaps *she* fancies an amour with *me*." Felix draped his arms over the back of the sofa and looked smug. "I trust you're going to invite her to this impromptu house party, too. I'd be very grateful."

"Not so you can flirt with her."

"Planning to flirt with her yourself?" His friend gave him an evil grin. "I told you that little book would be helpful." He wagged one finger playfully. "She's one of the finest catches in all Edinburgh. I'll expect your profuse thanks at a later time."

This time Drew managed to ignore the images Duncan's words conjured up. "If not her, then who?" he demanded as Duncan threw aside his reading and sprang to his feet.

"Who what?"

"Whom did you think I meant, when you looked so elated to think you were invited to Stormont?" persisted Drew.

"Hmm? No one," said the fellow airily.

"No." He stopped, nonplussed. "Not Winifred?" He'd been startled by how beautiful his younger sister had grown. Duncan must have noticed, too.

His friend paused in the doorway. "No," he said over his shoulder, "not Winifred. Until later, St. James." And he was gone, banging the door behind him.

Which left Drew annoyed, puzzled, and somewhat startled to realize that he had, in fact, planned to invite Ilsa Ramsay to Stormont Palace.

After the exhilarating walk with Captain St. James, when her mind had filled with wild, irrational fantasies of what might happen between the two of them, it took only a few words from Aunt Jean to send her thoughts crashing back to earth.

"Oh my dear, there you are! Heaven above, I've been so worried." Jean was waiting just inside the door, ready to close it behind her. "The streets are not safe these days."

"What has happened? I walk every morning and you don't complain."

Jean clicked her tongue in reproof. "Haven't you heard? There was a robbery at the goldsmith's shop near Parliament Square!"

"This morning?" exclaimed Ilsa. Her walk home had brought her very near Parliament Square.

"No, lass, last night! Mrs. Crawley and Mrs. Douglas were here with the news!"

"Oh." Ilsa tried not to sigh impatiently. Mrs. Crawley and Mrs. Douglas were two of Jean's humorless gossipy friends. Wearing one's hat at the wrong angle set the two of them off in a frenzy of censure. "Then the thieves were long gone by the time I ventured near."

Jean gave her a sharp look and shot the bolt on the door. "Don't make light of it! Thieves, within feet of our front door!"

Almost a quarter mile, thought Ilsa. "Robert was with me," she told her aunt. The pony had already ambled back into his room and could be heard nosing about his bucket of oats.

"Robert!" huffed the older woman. "That pony is no protection!"

"And the Misses St. James were as well, before their brother fetched them," added Ilsa, partly truthful. "I was not alone until I reached High Street, which was filled with people."

"Thank goodness." Jean exhaled in genuine relief. "But you mustn't risk it again. First these brigands breaking into shops. Next it will be houses, where someone is sure to be home, and before you know it murder will be done." Aunt Jean dogged her heels all the way to the drawing room.

Ilsa put on her smock. She'd bought more green paint on her way home and thought she would finish her painting of Calton Hill. "Thieving is one thing, murder another—far more effort and trouble. I'm sure the thieves wouldn't want to bother."

"Ilsa!" Jean inhaled so hard, Ilsa feared she might faint. "You are too careless. It's only a matter of time before the thieves turn to violence. We must ask your father to put a guard at our door. We must bar every window and make certain Mr. MacLeod loads his flintlock. And you—! Promise me you will not go out *at all* until the villains are caught."

Ilsa had been only half listening to her aunt's tirade, but at this she put up her hand. "No, Aunt. Pockets are picked every day in the streets, and still we go to the shops. I shall be careful, but I am not staying in every night."

Jean stiffened. "You must," she charged. "For your own safety."

"I shall not be careless of that," Ilsa promised, "but how can we let fear of these thieves keep us trapped at home indefinitely?"

"'Tis not fear if 'tis sensible! What would your father say, if something happened to you on my watch?"

"Aunt Jean." Ilsa leveled a firm but loving look at her. "I am no longer a child under your watch."

"Yes, you are! If anything were to happen to you, your father—"

Ilsa felt a growl rising in her throat; it must have been loud enough for Jean to hear, for her aunt fell silent, although her eyes flashed and her mouth was a flat line.

"Ye've become such a headstrong lass since Malcolm died," she said with withering reproach before she marched out.

Alone in the silent room, Ilsa regarded her pot of paint. Under Jean's watch. She should have guessed as much, when her father persuaded her to have her aunt to stay after Malcolm's death. *You can keep each other company,* he'd said. Ilsa had reluctantly agreed. Aunt Jean was the closest thing she'd known to a mother, and though Jean had been strict and protective, she'd also been loving.

Ilsa had thought Papa meant well, putting together the widow and the spinster, two women without children to occupy them. She'd thought Papa wanted a bachelor's residence again. But no; Papa had meant the child and the guardian, keeping a close eye on her again now that she had no husband to do it.

She set down her paint and noticed for the first time the drapes, hung again in front of the drawing room window. The view was once more narrow, the room once more shadowed.

Stay in, bar the doors, curtain the windows, post a guard. It was too much like Malcolm's edicts. Now that she'd had a few months of freedom, it felt like being buried alive.

That night she put on her favorite gown, a glorious emerald silk with silver spangles and miles of lace. It fluttered when she walked and made her feel like a butterfly, capable of soaring wherever her fancy took her. Malcolm would have hated it, for the brilliant color and low-cut bodice. She would not be held captive by her aunt's rigid rules, nor by her father's manipulations. She ignored Jean's furious protests and stepped into the sedan chair Mr. MacLeod had summoned for her.

The Assembly Rooms were full when she walked in. Obviously no one else in Edinburgh was huddling behind their doors in fear of thieves. In fact, her father met her almost immediately. "Ilsa! What are you doing here?"

She kissed his cheek. "The same thing you are, I expect."

He flushed even as he scowled. Papa came to flirt and dance and show off. He fancied himself a favorite of the ladies, and tonight he was dressed like a macaroni, in a striped yellow waistcoat and burgundy coat with diamond buckles on his shoes. "'Tain't the same! You ought not to be out."

"Don't tell me you're as fussy and fretful as Jean."

"Certainly not," he scoffed in outrage. "But you can't go about alone—"

"I came in a sedan chair," she told him. "And if it's not safe to walk the streets, how did you get here?" He scowled anew, and she smiled as she patted his arm. "I never thought you'd turn into a worried old woman, Papa."

His mouth firmed—to stop the smile twitching at his lips. "Saucy wench. I do not approve, but I'll see you safely home. And now that you *are* here, you must meet someone. By happy chance, Mr. Grant is in attendance, and he'll be pleased to solicit your hand for the quadrille." Without waiting for her reply, he towed her through the crowd and introduced her to the genial wine merchant.

From the polite surprise on Mr. Grant's face, Ilsa was sure her guess had been correct. All interest in a union between them was Papa's, and Papa's alone. Still, she smiled at Mr. Grant and even agreed to dance with him later, when Papa shamelessly maneuvered the poor man into asking.

Ilsa did love to dance, and she had nothing against Mr. Grant. But she had higher hopes tonight.

The St. James girls were at the far end of the room. Ilsa's eyes skimmed over the crowd, and finally spotted the captain. She had missed him, despite his height, because he was stooped over listening to dainty Miss Flora Clapperton, eldest daughter of a wealthy gentleman and rumored to have ten thousand pounds in dowry. Flora was flighty but sweet, and she could talk for an hour without drawing breath—especially if encouraged, as Winifred St. James appeared to be doing, standing beaming at her side and frequently drawing her brother's attention with a hand on his arm.

Ilsa settled herself on a chair with a good view of the proceedings. There was no harm in that, she told herself, nor in taking some enjoyment from the baffled expression on the captain's face as his sisters nudged him into marriage. She had no right to expect any other pleasures concerning him.

"You look pleased with yourself tonight," said a familiar but unwelcome voice behind her.

And just like that, her good mood curdled. Ilsa resisted the urge to get up and walk away. "I was," she said evenly, "until you appeared."

Impervious, Liam Hewitt plopped into the chair next to her, folding his arms across his chest. He worked in her father's shop, Papa's most trusted wright, but Ilsa found him deeply annoying.

There were many reasons why. He was smug. He was arrogant. He had a braying laugh. He was handsome and clever, but not nearly as handsome or clever as he thought himself. And for some bizarre and horrible yet unknown reason, he regularly inflicted himself upon Ilsa like a bad rash.

"I beg your pardon, sir, that seat is spoken for," she said.

Liam smirked. "No, it isn't. You just sat down—alone, as usual." He bumped her shoulder with his, causing Ilsa to frown at him and turn away. "Old Fletcher is trying to get you wed again, ain't he?" He shook his head with a *tsk*. "That's a fool's errand. Who's the victim?"

She opened her fan and kept her expression serene. Liam would only get worse if she gave any sign of distress or anger. "I will be sure to tell Papa you think him foolish."

He barked with laughter. "Will you! I'll tell him to his face. You're bitter medicine to force upon any man. He ought to spare himself the trouble."

"By all means." She gestured with her fan. "Go now. He is over there."

Liam squinted across the room, toward where her father was flirting with Mrs. Lowrie, a handsome widow half his age. "Not while he's at pleasure. I could hardly deny the man some sport, could I?"

"No, by all means insult his daughter instead," she said coolly. "He will be so grateful to you."

He scowled. "You're as tart as a lemon, ain't you?"

"More like hemlock." She smiled slyly at him. "Best keep your distance, Liam."

With a muttered oath he flung himself off the chair and into the crowd. Ilsa smoothed her skirts and tried not to give Liam the pleasure of ruining her evening. She was sure he disliked her as much as she disliked him, and her life would be vastly improved if he would have the courtesy to leave her be.

"How you put up with that man I shall never know," whispered Agnes St. James, sliding into the seat as soon as Liam had disappeared. "What an oily little toad!"

Ilsa hummed in agreement. "He thinks himself more important than he is, which is never good for a man to think."

Agnes glanced at her. "How can your father be so fond of him, when he's so spiteful toward you?"

Ilsa shrugged. It was true, and she had no idea why. Papa called Liam his right-hand man, one of the most talented cabinet-makers in Scotland. Every time Ilsa said a word against Liam, Papa brushed it off and defended Liam. She had little choice but to put up with the annoying man.

She flicked away a bit of dirt from her glove, tired of discussing him. "Tell me something more intriguing. How goes Winnie and Bella's plan to find your brother a rich bride?"

Finally a grin split her friend's face. "Oh, splendidly. They've made him dance with Catriona Hill and Lady Erskine already, and now they've thrown him into Flora Clapperton's clutches." Agnes peered down the room, where Flora was still chattering away at the captain. "Drew will ask her to dance simply for peace and quiet."

Ilsa laughed. "He's very good-natured, then."

"About Flora? Yes." Agnes hesitated. "I think he might have liked Catriona, though."

Ilsa kept smiling even as her stomach tightened. Catriona Hill was statuesque, witty, and intelligent. She and the captain would make a handsome pair. "If your sisters cannot have their Seasons in London, they could open a matchmaking service."

Agnes laughed as Bella dashed up. There was a handsome young man on her heels, his cheeks flushed with drink or from dancing. Bella paused long enough to lean close to the two of them and whisper, "The hook is baited! Let's see how long it takes him to bite!" before she whirled away in the arms of her partner.

Sure enough, the captain led out Miss Clapperton. She was still speaking, and as Ilsa watched—half amused, half unreasonably annoyed—Captain St. James looked up, right over Miss Clapperton's head and into her eyes.

His beleaguered expression faded. For a moment their gazes caught on each other, his so fierce with pleasure that Ilsa felt it in her soul. Then the scoundrel *winked* at her before turning back to the girl at his side and sweeping her into the dance.

Her heart was jolting in her chest. Little shocks of anticipation tingled along her nerves. She plied her fan so hard her earrings trembled. How could he *do* that to her from thirty feet away?

"Good evening, Mrs. Ramsay. Miss St. James."

Barely a breath separated the names, but by the time Ilsa recognized the man in front of them, Agnes had shot to her feet.

"Good evening, sir," she said coolly, and stalked away.

Felix Duncan watched her go, his eyes shuttered.

Ilsa also rose. "Miss St. James was just saying how thirsty she is," she said lightly. "She must be on her way to find some punch."

Mr. Duncan accepted the lie with a knowing quirk of his brow. "I wouldn't dream of interfering with Miss St. James's desires. I hoped I might beg the honor of a dance, ma'am."

"Of course."

Ilsa took his arm and they joined the long line of the Scotch reel. She loved a rollicking dance and soon was skipping down the set with her usual abandon. Mr. Duncan caught her and swung her around with cheerful vigor, and Ilsa grew breathless from exertion and laughter. When it ended, he offered his arm and they began a slow, meandering turn around the crowded room.

"I understand St. James has proposed an outing to Perth." Mr. Duncan glanced at her. "He said you suggested I be invited."

She gave a low laugh. "Goodness, he wastes no time. Are you displeased by the prospect?"

He grinned back. "Very much the contrary. I am in your debt."

"Then I admit I did suggest it. I thought the captain might want support troops if he were to be confined in one house with his sisters."

Mr. Duncan laughed. "Aye, he might! Not that he wouldn't deserve whatever torment they inflicted."

"Do they torment people?" She smiled artlessly at his guilty flinch. "You must know all three are my dear friends."

He hesitated. "I did know that."

"There aren't better young ladies in all of Scotland," she added. Her vow had been to not interfere in Agnes's affairs—but included nothing about stirring the pot a little.

"I agree," he murmured.

Ilsa heaved a sigh. "I shall miss them so, when they have all moved house to England with the captain."

Her companion stopped short. "England! The devil you say!"

Ilsa studied him closely. He hadn't known. "Didn't the captain tell you? He's considering removing there, to be near his future . . . responsibilities. Winifred and Isabella are enthralled by the prospect of a Season in London, as well."

All humor had leached from his face. "When?"

Ilsa looked at him in sympathy. "I don't know. Perhaps you should ask him, as *his* dear friend."

His brooding gaze skipped across the room. Near the windows, Agnes was in merry conversation with Sorcha White and two red-coated soldiers from the castle garrison. "Perhaps it doesn't much matter," he muttered.

"I wouldn't be so sure," she replied, watching her friend. Unless she missed her guess, Agnes was stealing peeks at them.

He must have suspected as much, too, for he inhaled deeply before turning a warm smile on her. "Only time will tell, aye? And as long as *you* don't say you're leaving Edinburgh, I shan't mourn. St. James was gone for years and I never once missed a minute of sleep over it."

Ilsa went along with it, arching her brows playfully. Let Agnes see someone else basking in his attention for a moment. "Is that right? Then perhaps you'll ask me to dance again, Mr. Duncan."

He swept a lavish bow. "I desire nothing else in life, madam."

"Life is full of disappointments," said a familiar voice beside her. "Go on, Duncan, inflict yourself on someone else."

"I apologize for this rude scoundrel," said Mr. Duncan, turning his back to Captain St. James. "Pay him no mind."

"Let the lady decide." The captain stepped around his friend and made a bow. "Good evening, Mrs. Ramsay."

He was dazzling tonight, in a vivid blue coat and green plaid. His dark hair fell across his brow in a thick wave, and when he stepped closer, she almost moaned as the heat and size of him sent a hot thrill of excitement pulsing through her. His eyes glittered, as if he knew exactly what effect he had on her.

Friends, she reminded herself unsteadily. Friends who would soon be hundreds of miles apart, forever. "Good evening, Captain. How are you enjoying our assembly?"

"Very well." He ducked his head and put out his hand. "I'll enjoy it far more if you'll dance with me."

She had to say no. Ilsa knew that even though she wanted to put her hand in his and let him whirl her around as he'd done in the oyster cellar. And if he chanced to whirl her right out the door and pull her close, she would like to kiss him again . . . and again . . .

No, no, no. She had come tonight to show Jean she would not be cowed; to show her father she would not be minded like a child; to show herself how easily the captain would divert his attention to another wealthy widow or young lady, once he met them. That's what she'd told herself when she put on her favorite gown that made her feel beautiful and confident. That's what she'd told herself when she accepted Mr. Duncan's invitation to dance and flirted with him.

All that time, she had been lying to herself. She had come because she wanted to see *him*. She wanted him to look at her with admiration and hunger in his eyes—as he was doing now. She wanted him to ask her to dance with him—as he'd just done. She wanted that thrilling, reckless kiss.

"I say, St. James, I asked first," put in Mr. Duncan.

"And the lady will decide whom she wishes to accept," replied the captain, his gaze never wavering from hers.

You. The word trembled on her lips despite everything.

Curse it all. She was in trouble.

Blessedly, she was saved by the approach of Mr. Grant, who had not forgotten their promised dance even if she had. With a smile, half relief and half regret, she bade the captain and Mr. Duncan farewell and let Mr. Grant lead her out.

It had been a close call. Nothing good could come of encouraging the captain; she did not want to spoil her friendships over a brief affair, and he was leaving for England in a matter of weeks. If only she weren't so terribly, wickedly tempted . . .

Mind what you wish for, admonished a faint echo of Jean's voice. *It's never exactly what you expect.*

Chapter Eight

The suggestion of a house party visit to Stormont Palace was received with joyous excitement.

"Oh, Drew, is it really a palace?"

"How long shall we stay?"

"What shall we do while we're there?"

He listened with a mixture of pleasure and alarm. Pleasure because they sounded so excited. Alarm because . . . He hadn't thought of how he would entertain his family; he was not *going* to entertain his family. He would have work to do, touring the estate and seeing how things were run. He'd been seduced by Ilsa Ramsay's impish smile and glowing eyes into signing his own prison sentence.

"Let's find out more!" Bella ran to the bookshelves and came back with a ragged copy of Pennant's *A Tour in Scotland*. "Stormont Palace," she murmured, flipping pages. "Here it is! 'The house is built around a large court, with extremely pleasing gardens and a cunning maze. The dining room is large and handsome, with an ancient but magnificent chimneypiece carved with the King's arms.'" She lowered the book, eyes wide. "Drew, was it a *royal* palace?"

Winnie rolled her eyes. "Of course it wasn't! All

those fine houses were built by toadies to the King, they splashed his arms everywhere." She seized the book from Bella and read on. "'In the drawing room is some good old tapestry, with an excellent figure of Mercury. In a small bed chamber is a scripture-piece in needlework, with a border of animals, pretty well-done. The gallery is about a hundred and fifty-five feet long, with most excellent paintings . . . '" She flipped the pages. "Many, many paintings, apparently." She sounded disappointed. "Perhaps it's haunted."

"Haunted!" Bella's face lit up. "Might it be, Drew?"

"By all the poor souls put to death by the English duke," put in Agnes slyly.

"With dungeons and torture racks and thumbscrews!" Winnie looked eager now, too.

"Captured chieftains left to starve in a dungeon cell! Heiresses kidnapped and wed for their fortunes and drowned in the moat," added Bella. She draped a handkerchief over her head and advanced on Agnes, hands clutching at the air. "Save me, my dear! Let me steal your spirit so I can seek my revenge!"

"Never," declared Agnes dramatically. "You are cursed to wander the earth forever, unavenged and restless, for the sin of consorting with the English!" She snatched the handkerchief from her sister's head, causing a shriek from Bella and laughter from Winnie.

"It's not haunted." Drew ran his fingers through his hair, torn between laughing at their antics and wishing he had thought this through a little better. "It's just an old house, closed up these many years, with some property that needs tending."

All three sisters stared at him in disappointed silence.

"Well, that sound enticing," murmured Winnie. "We'll have to explore the town, I suppose."

"I thought we might invite some friends to help make the party merrier," Drew said desperately. God above, he ought to have kept to his plan to go alone.

Winnie perked up, her blue eyes big and bright. "Who?"

Drew glanced at Agnes. "I thought Agnes might like to have her friend Mrs. Ramsay." She gave him a puzzled look. "And I mentioned it to Mr. Duncan, as well."

His sister's face grew pink. Drew wasn't an idiot; it had taken him a few minutes, but he'd put together that Duncan hadn't been speaking of Ilsa Ramsay or Winifred the other day. No, Duncan's face had come alive at the thought of Agnes.

He wasn't sure how he felt about that, but he was very interested in his sister's feelings. Duncan could be an ass, but he was also a reliable friend and solid mate.

"Who else?" Bella and Winnie were oblivious to the tension in Agnes's figure. "That's only one gentleman and four ladies."

"Am I not a gentleman?" he parried.

Bella scoffed. "Brothers don't count," said Winnie, "unless they serve as a conduit to other, more interesting gentlemen."

Drew clapped one hand to his heart as if she'd struck him. "No blade is sharper than a sister's tongue!"

Bella laughed. "Invite more gentlemen! Witty, single ones."

"Handsome, rich ones wouldn't go astray, either," added Winnie.

"Whom do you think I know, who is single, handsome, rich, and witty, yet still willing to spend a week with the three of you?"

They cried out in disgust and indignation, until he laughed and promised to ransack his acquaintance for anyone who promised to amuse them. Bella said she would begin packing, and Winnie wandered off with the *Tour* open in her hand, leaving him alone with Agnes.

"Agnes?" prodded Drew. "What say you to this plan?"

She stabbed her needle into the petticoat she had been mending. "Invite whomever you please. I'm going back to Ilsa's."

"What of Felix Duncan?"

Her mouth set and she leapt to her feet.

He followed her as she went downstairs and put on her hat. "Has Duncan done you a harm?"

Her face was stony. "No. You don't need to walk with me."

He did so anyway. "Do you know him?"

"Not really," she bit out, striding along the street. "No. Not at all."

Drew nodded. "If he did anything, I'd have to—"

"No." She whirled on him, eyes flashing. "It's not your problem, Drew!"

"If a friend of mine trifled with my sister, it would be."

Her chest heaved. "He didn't—didn't *trifle* with me. He just . . ." She sighed. "He's a scoundrel."

"He can be," agreed Drew. "But he's not generally cruel."

They had reached the Ramsay house. Agnes paused on the steps, biting her lip. "I don't think he meant to be. It was . . . it was my mistake."

"Agnes." He touched her shoulder. "Can you tell me? I wish I knew more of your lives here—I hope to remedy that—but know always that I care for you and will protect you to the best of my ability. I've imagined a host of horrible things and all the ways I could beat him to a cinder if he did them."

She flushed. "It's not your problem, so there's no need for you to do anything, let alone beat him."

"I won't invite him to Stormont," he began, but she shook her head, a hint of stubborn St. James pride in her face.

"Don't do that on my account. By all means, invite your friend." She glanced archly at him. "Since you were kind enough to invite *my* friend. Has she accepted?"

Drew gave up badgering her about Duncan. He would interrogate his friend about it later. Odd, how any mention of Ilsa Ramsay always seemed to divert him from whatever he was doing. "Er . . ." He grinned ruefully. "I've not actually invited her yet."

"Come on, then." She opened the door and led him up the stairs to the drawing room. Drew almost held his breath, hoping this wouldn't be a monstrous mistake.

It was instead a great surprise. Agnes opened the drawing room door to reveal Ilsa Ramsay on a ladder, wearing an ugly smock with a paintbrush in her hand. The ceiling of the room had been painted a pale sky blue at the edges, fading to white directly overhead. A plump older woman stood beside her, arms full of what looked like draperies, her face taut with frustration.

"But you cannot *do* such a thing, dear," she was protesting in a shrill tone that instinctively made Drew's spine stiffen. "It's not done!"

"It is if I do it," was her response, spoken lightly but still ringing with finality.

"Oh my," said Agnes innocently, gazing upward. "It looks like the sky."

Ilsa Ramsay turned around, a blinding smile on her face. "Exactly my intent! Thank you!" She caught sight of Drew and the smile vanished like a snuffed candle, but he still reeled from it. Alive with pleasure, bright with excitement, her face was . . . mesmerizing.

That must be it. He was entranced—bewitched.

He shouldn't like it so much.

"Captain." She put her brush back into the pot of paint balanced atop the ladder and climbed down. "I did not expect visitors."

That was obvious. There were cloths flung over the furnishings and of course the ladder in the center of the room.

"I do beg your pardon, Mrs. Ramsay."

"I brought him in," said Agnes, removing her hat. "You must blame me if you get paint on your coat," she told him before turning back to her friend. "He can stay only a moment."

"Of course," murmured Ilsa, as if that warning had been meant for her and not for him. "Aunt Jean, this is Captain St. James, who is Agnes's brother as you must have guessed. Captain, may I present my aunt, Miss Fletcher."

The draperies hit the floor with a *flump*. Eyes

still flashing at Ilsa, Jean Fletcher bobbed a perfect curtsy. "I'm delighted to make your acquaintance, Captain."

"The pleasure is mine, Miss Fletcher," he said with a courtly bow.

"Are we painting the walls, as well?" Agnes was gazing upward again. The walls were a plain, ordinary green.

The older woman stiffened. "No, indeed not."

"Yes," said Ilsa. "Here will be the horizon." She went to the closest wall, took a pencil from her smock pocket, and struck a line on the wall at chest height. The older woman gasped as if it had been a dagger to her chest. "And it will continue up to meet the sky above."

"Ilsa!" The older woman was an angry shade of crimson. "People do not paint their drawing rooms to look like the outdoors!"

Drew grinned. For a moment Ilsa's gaze connected with his, and he could swear she nearly smiled back. "*I* do," she replied.

"Let us go sit in the—the dining room." Miss Fletcher appeared to make a great effort not to look at the ceiling, the mark on the wall, the discarded draperies, or her niece. "At least it is tidy and proper in there."

"I beg you not to trouble yourself, ma'am," said Drew. "I've no wish to intrude. Agnes, perhaps another time—"

"Drew came to ask if you would care to accompany us to Stormont Palace, Ilsa," said Agnes. "We're to spend a week there, exploring the maze and hunting for ghosts."

"Ghosts!" Ilsa's brows went up in delight. Miss Fletcher made another pained noise.

"I make no promises about ghosts," Drew said, but couldn't resist adding, "on either side of the question."

"As long as you can't swear there are none, we have hope." Ilsa removed her smock but seemed to have forgotten about the cloth around her head. It showed off her neck and shoulders, and a glorious expanse of bosom; she wasn't wearing one of those kerchiefs women usually shrouded their shoulders and bosoms with. It took an effort to keep his eyes on her face.

"Then you'll join us?" he asked. "My plan is to depart in three days' time."

"Perfect." She bestowed that dazzling smile upon him and Drew nearly wobbled on his feet. "I should be finished painting by then."

This was too much for Miss Fletcher. She excused herself and stalked from the room, pausing at the door to call back sternly, "Do not throw out the draperies!"

Agnes grinned as the door closed. "You're going to throw them out?" She walked over to the pile of drapery fabric and picked up one.

Ilsa shrugged. "She keeps hanging them back up. The only way to stop her is to dispose of them."

Drew glanced around. With the windows uncovered, the room was filled with light. He tried to picture it with hills and grass painted to the line she'd marked, with a bright blue sky rising above it.

"Calton Hill," he murmured.

Her head came up in surprise. "Yes, that's right."

Drew gestured at the wall behind her. "Will you paint the Edinburgh view there?"

She came to stand beside him and studied the wall. Right now it held a large painting in an ornate frame. "An excellent thought. I hope my artistic skills are sufficient."

"Paint it as it is on a winter day with fog, and no one will be able to tell. Great gray clouds with a steeple here and there."

She laughed. "Not precisely the view I wish to capture."

"Hmm. Something more like this, then?" He nodded at the painting. It depicted five somber ladies all in black, except for the white caps on their heads and the wide, old-fashioned collars around their necks. "Family?" Drew asked doubtfully.

"No." Ilsa grimaced. "My father bought it. My aunt thinks it adds solemnity and dignity to the room."

He couldn't help it; a snort of laughter escaped him. She did the same, and in a moment both were shaking with it.

"The solemnity of a gallows," he said, lips trembling.

"Ladies that severe must send their victims to be drawn and quartered," she returned.

"Hanging is too tame for them?"

"Can't you just see them with the scythe and dagger?" Ilsa lowered her voice dramatically. "Pronouncing sentence and carrying it out on the spot?"

"And finishing in time for tea. Ah—I spy a decanter of sherry there, as well. Thirsty work, drawing and quartering."

Ilsa laughed again, sending his heart leaping.

Buoyed, he turned and swept out one hand at the opposite wall. "Paint Arthur's Seat there, beside the hearth. Our father used to take us there—" He broke off at the sight of Agnes. Lord, for a moment he'd entirely forgotten his sister was in the room, listening and watching with sharp interest.

Ilsa turned. "A splendid idea." She glanced at him, followed his gaze, and cleared her throat. "Shall we take those to the charity school, Agnes? Perhaps they can use the fabric."

"You really mean to get rid of the drapes?" Agnes came closer, her eyes skipping between the two of them. "Altogether?"

Ilsa flushed but gave a firm nod. "I do. Perhaps I'll replace them with something lighter."

"All right. And you'll come to Stormont Palace?"

Drew looked away, studying a sconce on the wall with fierce interest. Agnes had noticed something, damn it.

Ilsa wet her lips. "I don't want to intrude on your family. Perhaps I should not . . ."

"Oh, he plans to invite other people." Agnes shot a challenging look at Drew. "Isn't that right? Mr. Duncan, you said, and some handsome, witty gentlemen, as well."

"Right," he said, glaring at that sconce. "Monteith, perhaps. And Kincaid. It would only be a week's sojourn."

"Please think of me, Ilsa," said Agnes. "Don't leave me alone with them for a whole week."

Ilsa smiled reluctantly. "I shall consider it."

"Good." Agnes went and pulled the bell. "Shall we have tea? I'm famished."

"Yes, of course," murmured Ilsa.

"It was your idea," Drew told her under his breath. "Do say you'll come."

She glanced at him, her eyes wary.

His mouth quirked. "But you must promise not to give me away if I pretend to be a ghost, to give my sisters something to occupy their time."

At this her smile slowly returned, impish and conspiratorial. "That is something I would not miss seeing!"

"Excellent," he whispered, with a wink. He bowed, and as he did so, added in a bare breath, "Thank you. It looked to be a tedious journey until your suggestion."

"I hope you still think so, whilst wandering the corridors clanking an old chain," she whispered back.

He grinned and took his leave. His sister gave him a searching look, but he simply grinned at her and left, too full of . . . *something* to let it worry him.

AGNES CLOSED THE door behind the captain and folded her arms. "The trip was your idea?"

"Hmm?" Ilsa realized she was still smiling at the door the captain had disappeared through, and turned her back to it. The cloth she'd wound around her hair brushed her shoulder, and with dismay she jerked it off. That whole time she'd been standing there with an old piece of linen on her head, looking a fright. Why did she constantly find new ways to embarrass herself around him?

"Drew didn't mention it until this morning," said Agnes. "When did you suggest it to him?"

Ilsa looked at her. "When he met us out walking."

Then she retaliated for the nosy questions. "When you stormed off in disgust because Mr. Duncan was with him."

Agnes flushed scarlet. "I did not! That was not—! I—my mother needed me, and my sisters!"

"Not that you cared about that before Mr. Duncan arrived." Ilsa tilted her head. "And you were very abrupt with him at the Assembly Rooms the other evening . . ."

Her friend's chin set mulishly. "So you continued walking with Drew and Mr. Duncan for some time, for him to tell you about this house and you to make suggestions about visiting it."

"Oh no," said Ilsa. "Mr. Duncan left almost as soon as you did. Fair ran away, now that I think about it. He makes such a fine figure in his kilt. A man with good legs—"

"Ilsa!" Agnes's eyes flashed. "Are you flirting with my brother?"

She paused. She was certainly trying not to. "No."

"Why did he invite you?"

Now it was her turn to go pink. "I've no idea. You must ask him. He's your brother."

Agnes bit her lip. "You haven't forgotten that he's going to live in England and become a duke, have you?"

Not for one bloody minute. "I have not." She forced a smile. "Three days' time! What shall I pack?"

Agnes came to take her hands. "I know you've been determined to go your own way and find your own pleasures these last few months. And you deserve it, you really do. I just—I just worry—"

"What?" Ilsa drew a determined breath and met

her friend's gaze. "You worry I will callously trifle with your brother? I shan't. Even though you were right, I do like him. You never told me he was so delightfully irreverent, nor so considerate of you and your sisters."

Agnes raised one brow skeptically. As if she knew how tissue-thin that excuse was.

Ilsa threw up one hand. "The captain told me he was going to visit a house, and I suggested a house party for your sake because of your distress over his future inheritance. My dear," she said gently as Agnes jerked free and retreated a step. "That is not his fault, or his choice. You know these things—titles—are very strictly decided, not bestowed at anyone's whim. Your brother is to be commended for recognizing what it will allow him to do for his family, not just for himself, and stepping manfully into the responsibilities of the position."

Agnes sighed. "If only it weren't a dukedom! Something simpler, a baronetcy or something would be perfectly fine. Or better yet, just a fortune, unencumbered."

"Fortunes are always encumbered," said Ilsa wryly.

At this reference to her late husband, Agnes went pale. "I didn't mean—"

Ilsa shook her head. "I know. Just as my suggestion meant nothing beyond what it was."

"So," said the other woman on a sigh. "Shall you go with us? You *must*, you know, as it was all your idea and now Winnie and Bella are eager to hunt ghosts."

An image of the captain draped in ragged sheets and rattling a chain to amuse his sisters crossed her mind, and she bit back a smile. "If you wish me to come, I shall."

For Agnes, she told herself, *and her sisters.* And she would do her very best not to flirt with their impossibly appealing brother.

Chapter Nine

Drew racked his brain for which gentlemen of his acquaintance he could expose to his sisters and finally realized he only knew three.

Duncan, of course; that die had been cast, although Drew planned to keep a close eye on any interaction between him and Agnes. He was still plotting how to ask about it without Duncan giving him some mocking nonsense, as was his friend's habit in most serious conversations.

For the others, he decided on Adam Monteith, who was a capital fellow and could hold his tongue—and his liquor—far better than Will Ross; and Alexander Kincaid, who had known his family for years.

There might, Drew acknowledged privately, be another benefit to their company. They were the three best golfers he knew, and Edwards had said there was a course bordering the grounds of Stormont Palace. If the company became a bit trying, they could make an escape to the links.

When he broached the idea, none of them laughed. "Perth?" repeated Monteith in surprise. "How have you got a house in Perth, St. James?"

Drew mounded the sand to form a tee for his ball. They were playing with Duncan's equipment, as he and his father were fiendishly fond of the game. It was the wrong season for golf, with the summer grass grown tall, but that only made it more sporting. There were a number of wagers riding on the match today. "It's not my house," he said, squinting against the sun. The hole was over the rise, out of sight. He set his club against the ball, drew back, and swung hard.

"Not yet," drawled Duncan. "And if you've sent that ball into the marsh, you owe me a shilling."

Drew bared his teeth. The shilling was for a wager made earlier in the game, not for the cost of the lost ball. "'Tis not in the marsh."

"Whose house is it you intend to visit?" asked Kincaid, setting up his own ball. Drew watched critically. Kincaid was shorter than he, but stronger. His arms bulged as he drew back and swung his club. Monteith whistled in appreciation as the ball soared out of sight.

"Whose house?" repeated Kincaid.

Duncan was grinning like a cat in cream, curse him. Drew took a breath. "The Duke of Carlyle's."

Monteith laughed. "A duke's house! And why are you free to invade with a large party?"

"Because he's my cousin." Drew lowered his voice even though they were alone. "And I'm his heir."

Kincaid's brows went up. Monteith's mouth fell open. "You?" he said incredulously. "You?"

"Impossible to believe, isn't it?" put in Duncan with a devilish smile.

Kincaid threw up one hand. "His heir? Explain that—you, an ordinary captain, who must needs borrow funds for beer now and then."

Drew waved one hand, preferring to walk as he told the tale. It still gave him a vague sense of discomfort, detailing his *grand and glorious expectations,* as Ilsa Ramsay termed them—as if it couldn't really be true. The feeling grew stronger, not milder, the more people he told.

By the time they had all located their golf balls—none in the marsh—his friends were shaking their heads in amazement.

"If I'd known you were cousin to a duke," said Monteith, lining up his next shot, "I'd have asked interest on that five pounds you borrowed last year."

"If I'd known last year I was heir to a duke," returned Drew, "I would have asked someone of finer manners than you for it."

"What's your mission regarding this house?"

Drew threw Kincaid a grateful glance for the serious question. "It's not been visited in many years. The duke's solicitor wishes me to see for myself what state it's in, and make it ready."

"So he can come himself?"

Drew hesitated. "The duke is growing old. I doubt he'll come."

There was a beat of silence as the three of them exchanged glances. "Then ready for what?" asked Duncan, for once not laughing.

Drew thwacked some tall grass with his club. "The solicitor expects to sell it."

All three looked at him. Everyone knew about the slow but accelerating dispossession of the small farmers in favor of tenants and migratory workers across Scotland. If the Duke of Carlyle put his estate up for sale, the same would likely happen to the people working his lands.

"You're going to sell it?"

"St. James can't," said Duncan, the lawyer among them. "Only the duke can."

"Aye, only the duke can order it sold," muttered Drew. "From what I heard, he cares naught for his Scottish property, and the solicitor views it as a burden."

"But soon it'll be yours, aye?" Kincaid prodded.

The wind picked up, rustling the links grass. "Aye."

"Are you of a mind to sell off the Scottish lands?"

"No," said Drew. "If the choice becomes mine, I would not."

"So your visit . . ."

"Is to see," said Drew with a sharp look at Duncan. "And assess how they shall be maintained as valued assets, not sold to people eager to carve up more of Scotland."

"Well," said Kincaid after a moment. "Sounds noble enough. And you said your lovely sisters will be there?" He winked.

Drew folded his arms even as his shoulders eased. "Aye, and I'll be there, too, keeping an eye on the lot of you."

"Will you?" murmured Felix Duncan, lining up his next shot. He swung, sending his ball arcing into the glare of sunlight.

"Especially on you." Drew stamped the grass as he located his ball and chose his angle. Kincaid took out his flask and Monteith made a rude comment about the way Drew was positioning his club.

As Drew took his swing, Duncan said, casually and far too loudly, "If your eyes are on us, you won't be able to stare at Ilsa Ramsay, you know."

The ball shot sideways off his club, toward the marsh. Drew swore and advanced on Duncan as Monteith and Kincaid roared with laughter.

"Ilsa Ramsay!" said Monteith in dawning delight. "She'll be there?"

"Aye," said Duncan, sidestepping Drew and jogging after his ball. "But you'd better act quickly, lads, now that St. James is going to be a duke and needs a bride!"

Drew stopped, glaring after his friend. "Don't listen to him," he told the others. "Mrs. Ramsay is dear friends with my sister Agnes."

Monteith grinned. "Maybe so, but your eyes were fair falling from your head that night we saw her in the oyster cellar. Well done, laddie."

"Ignore Duncan," said Kincaid lazily. "He's still smarting from losing the lady he fancied."

"Oh?" Drew's ears pricked up. "How?"

Kincaid shrugged, collecting his clubs. "He can say the most idiotic things for such a clever lad, aye? Brought it on his own head, and that always makes the sting worse." He glanced toward the marsh. "St. James, you might want to drop another ball and leave that one."

Grim-faced, Drew gripped his club. "I will not." That would cost him a stroke, and the cost of the ball, all because Duncan had to shoot off his mouth about Ilsa Ramsay—doubly galling because he had a feeling Agnes was the lady Kincaid spoke of.

He tramped into the rustling grass, determined to play where he'd landed. As always.

THE CABINETRY SHOP in Dunbar's Close was large, loud, and smelled strongly of wood shavings and varnish. Ilsa made her way through it to the office where her father spent his days.

He was there, as usual, holding court before some apprentices and journeymen, with no doubt a few upholsterers and gilders in the lot. Papa liked performing for a crowd. At the sight of her, he slapped his hands on his knees and cried, "To work, lads! Why are ye all sitting about chattering like a flock of birds?"

Liam Hewitt, sitting at her father's side, looked up at her and smirked. The other men filed away, some murmuring greetings, a few giving her quick smiles. Ilsa knew them all, having grown up in and around the workshop. She waited until they were gone; Liam, as usual, remained in his chair, flaunting his special status as her father's favorite.

Liam *was* talented, Ilsa admitted. When she married, Papa had given her a gift of some of Liam's finely carved furnishings, taken from patterns by Mr. Chippendale but augmented by Liam's own designs. They were very handsome, those tables and chairs, and Ilsa tried diligently to credit his skill when she sat and ate upon them.

It never quite worked. The next time she saw him, Liam would undo all that positive feeling with one snide remark or patronizing glance. Ilsa had finally concluded that he did not like her and did not want her to like him, and so she had quit trying.

"What a surprise," cried Papa, coming forward to kiss her on the cheek. "How fare you, lass?"

"Well, Papa." She smiled and embraced him. "I see you allow a lengthy dinner hour for your workmen."

"Just relating some praise for our work from Mr. Aitcheson," he returned. "We fitted his shop with new counters, shelves, and a sturdy front door."

"Of course," she teased back. "Mr. Aitcheson wants only the best in his jewelry shop."

"That, and he's mindful of all the robbery going on lately." Papa tapped the side of his nose. "Mr. Johnstone in Queen Street, whose shop we refitted just last year, lost almost a whole shipment of tea—tea! What would any thief want with three hundredweights of tea? But Aitcheson worried for his shop, and a new lock and key will set his fears at rest."

"That, and the new safe bolted under his counter," drawled Liam.

Papa laughed. "Aye, that as well! Can't be too careful, can you, now?"

"Aunt Jean nearly had a spell the other day, worrying about thieves and robberies in town," Ilsa told him. "If you can set *her* mind at rest, I would deeply appreciate it."

He patted her hand. "Jean worries with every breath she takes. No one could stop her. She'll get over it."

Ilsa simply smiled. After Captain St. James left, Jean had come back to the drawing room, first scolding her for receiving guests in such a ramshackle fashion and then about how the discarded draperies would expose them to the greedy sights of all manner of thieves and housebreakers. She was sure the thieves terrorizing Edinburgh were shinning up the lampposts outside of houses to peer inside in search of items to steal.

Ilsa could roll her eyes at that. Anyone who stole that painting of the five grim ladies in black was welcome to it, in her opinion. But now the thieves were taking tea, of all things, and Jean would be even more short-tempered. She wouldn't get over it until someone was caught and hanged for the robberies.

"I wanted a word with you, Papa."

"Of course, of course!"

"Privately," she added quietly, as Liam kept to his seat, watching her with glittering eyes.

"Oh! Aye." He waved one hand at Liam. "Off with you, my boy. Mr. Hopetoun inquired after that pair of sofas the other day, wondering when they'll be ready to upholster."

"The end of next week, as I told him." Liam rose and swept a mocking bow. "A good day to you, Mrs. Ramsay." He sauntered past her with a smug air. Ilsa ignored him, but Papa watched with raised brows.

"Is there aught between you and Liam?"

"Nothing, Papa," she said evenly. "Why do you ask?"

He huffed. "As if I can't see! The fellow always acts as though you've twitted him in some way."

"I have not," she returned, not adding that Liam was always either spiteful, rude, or belittling to her, and sometimes all three at the same time. She had learned that Papa sympathized more with Liam's side of any story, and so she'd stopped arguing. "I like him just as much as he likes me."

Papa's eyes narrowed, but he said nothing more. He closed the door of his office and waited until she took a seat before returning to his own. "What is it that you must come to the shop? Has MacGill ruffled your feathers again?"

"No," she said. "I sacked Mr. MacGill, so he shall never vex me again." She'd felt very pleased with herself after writing the letter. She must remember to thank the captain for encouraging her to do so.

"Sacked him!" Papa reared up out of his chair. "Why, Ilsa?"

"I told you why the other day." She changed the subject before he could work up a head of steam. "I came to tell you I am going away."

"Away!" Papa looked thunderstruck at this. "Over MacGill?"

She laughed. "No! Not at all, far more pleasant than that. My friend Agnes's family is going to Perth for a holiday, and they have invited me to go with them."

"Perth!" Her father's brows lowered. "What the bluidy blazes is in Perth?"

"Stormont Palace. Captain St. James has been sent to examine the fitness of the house."

Ilsa deliberately made it sound as if the captain had been sent under orders from a commanding officer. She was not going to relate his expectations to her father, knowing that was the surest possible way to ensure all Edinburgh knew. Not only had Agnes asked her not to tell anyone, she suspected the captain didn't wish it to be widely known.

"And he's taking his family with him?" Papa was still suspicious.

"He told his sister he thought it would be a very

tedious job, and having a party of family and friends might make the task pass more enjoyably. The Misses St. James are eager to inspect the shops in Perth and explore the area."

His mouth twisted; he was still displeased, though Ilsa couldn't see why.

"Papa, you know how strained their family has been in the past," she said softly. "I believe their brother thinks to offer them a spot of pleasure and take them out of Edinburgh for a bit."

He harrumphed. "He's the tall one, aye? At the Assembly Rooms the other night? Looks a bit of a devil to me."

As he did to her. Ilsa laughed to hide how her heart skipped a beat at the memory of the captain's conspiratorial smile. "A dutiful and responsible officer, Papa. Every man must have his moments of mischief, though." She gave him a sly look. "How is Mrs. Lowrie, by the by?"

Papa's cheeks colored. "That's neither here nor there. Well, well! When are you to go? How long shall I be deprived of your company?"

"We leave the day after next and shall only be gone a week. You'll barely notice I've left."

"I will," he argued. "Jean will send all her complaints to me."

Ilsa rose. "And you will deserve them. When you persuaded me to invite her to live with me, you intended her to keep an eye on me, didn't you?"

His face froze in guilty astonishment. "What? Nay, never!"

She saw through that bluster. "I don't like it, Papa," she told him firmly. "I don't need a keeper, and if you don't mind your own business, I'll upset her so dramatically she'll come storming back to your house. You've still got no housekeeper and plenty of spare rooms . . ."

Papa jumped up, eyes flashing and brows drawn. "I had perfectly good reasons for putting you and Jean together. You don't know everything, my girl, and you can't run about on your own, like a man. You're still my daughter, and I—"

"I am my own person," she said with a warning glance. "I married Malcolm, as you wished, and I allowed Jean to come live with me because I am fond of her. But I am a woman grown, and I won't be manipulated."

"Manipulated?" He affected a wounded expression. "I'm your papa! Your welfare matters more to me than anything else in this world, lass. Ye spear me through the heart when ye speak so."

Ilsa sighed. He did think he was acting in a paternal, protective way. "Stop trying to control me."

"Control? Nay, 'tis concern for your well-being," he said indignantly. "And my duty until death."

She blinked in surprise. "My future husband might object to that."

Her father jerked. "Future husband? Who? Who is he? Have you accepted someone when you've not even admitted to me you're considering marriage?"

"No," she said, taken aback by his vehemence. "But if I did, he'd not welcome your interference in our life, either." She'd only mentioned a husband because he teased her about it every time they spoke. Now, though, he seemed quite startled and unprepared by the idea.

"Ah." Papa visibly relaxed. "If you *are* ready to marry again, why, Mr. Grant spoke so highly of you. Or that dashing Sir Philip Hamilton, over in St. Andrew's Square, would be lucky to have you, and he just bought a very fine new set of drawing room furniture, which sets my mind at ease that he could provide for you . . ."

"Good-bye, Papa." She kissed his cheek. "I will see you in a few days."

He walked her out. "All right, then, have your little adventure with the Misses St. James. But mind you come home safe and sound to me, or I'll have to order the apprentices to take up their chisels and awls, and lead my own army to rescue you."

She laughed with him and left. Yes, she did want to have a little adventure. But she wasn't so sure about coming home to her father.

Chapter Ten

The party set out on a fine sunny morning. It was almost fifty miles to Stormont Palace, and on his own Drew would have done it in a day. Instead, he bowed to his mother's wishes and they stopped for the night at an inn near Kinross.

Drew purposely kept his distance from Ilsa. Not only did he wish to prove Duncan wrong about staring at her, but she was always with his sisters, particularly Agnes. Since Agnes was still throwing around sharp looks whenever Felix Duncan opened his mouth, this wasn't as difficult as expected. Thankfully Monteith and Kincaid were jolly companions, and Winnie and Bella were on better behavior than usual.

He kept his attention resolutely elsewhere and remembered that he had brought all this on himself. He could have ridden to Perth alone and made his inspection in peace and solitude. No one would have teased him, as Bella did, or given him a hard time about the journey, as Monteith did, or scolded him for drinking too much, as his mother tried . . . or given him a small, intimate smile, as Ilsa did when they passed each other on the stairs.

So overall, it was worth it.

They turned into the gates of Stormont Palace in the late afternoon, as the slanting sun gilded the sandstone to deep bronze. Ivy spread like a spiderweb up the walls of the house, though the front was clear of it as they came along the winding drive.

Drew had been riding beside the first carriage with his mother and Bella and Winnie. Aside from one shocked exclamation and a long look at him, his mother made no response after sighting the house. Bella and Winnie, on the other hand, kept up a furious pelter of questions directed at Drew, ignoring Mother's admonishments not to shout or to hang out the windows of the carriage.

As they drew nearer, he slowed his horse to fall back to the second carriage, where Agnes and Ilsa rode with Ilsa's maid. He touched his hat as Ilsa smiled at him through the open window. "Welcome to Stormont, ladies."

"It's very grand." Agnes leaned out her window.

"But lovely," added Ilsa.

Drew nodded. If he hadn't spent several weeks at Carlyle Castle, he would have been stopped dead in his tracks by the house. It was an impressive sight, and only more so the closer they got. A pair of towers rose on either side of the front, crenelated and square. Wide steps led up to the entrance. The windows were tall arches reminiscent of the Norman Carlyle Castle, but more plentiful and graceful; it should be bright inside. He knew there was a courtyard, and a river ran near the house, but from the front it had the look of a quaint little citadel, proud and secure in its domain.

"When you said palace," said Kincaid, pulling up beside him, "I thought you meant like Hamilton

Palace, just a fine big house. This was once a royal residence, aye?"

"An abbot's," admitted Drew.

Kincaid gave him a sideways look. "And now yours."

Drew shook his head. "Not mine—not yet."

Still, he pulled up and dismounted a little bit away from the others. His mother and sisters spilled from the carriages, exclaiming and pointing. His friends clustered around the horses, one of whom seemed to have a loose shoe.

He studied the house. Palace. Castle. Either of those words fit. *Mine.* There was a word that ought not to fit, yet somehow did. A handful of servants were lining up on the steps, headed by a slim fellow with spectacles gleaming in the sun. That would be Mr. Watkins, the estate steward. They were waiting to greet him—as the nearest thing to the owner.

At Carlyle Castle he had been unquestionably a guest. Upon the death of the duke he might take possession, but while the duchess lived, it would always feel like her home. Even if Her Grace removed at once, it would take years and years to remake it in any other style and taste, and cost a considerable fortune. Not that Carlyle Castle gave any feel of home to someone who had lived in far more modest accommodations his entire life; he had come to think of it as his future quarters, significantly more lavish than those at Fort George but similar in purpose.

This house, though . . . He liked everything he could see. He liked that it was in Scotland. It wasn't his yet, but already he felt more attached to this house than to Carlyle Castle.

"This visit is off to a promising start," said a voice beside him.

With a start Drew looked down at Ilsa Ramsay, who had left the others and stood watching him. "Is it?"

She grinned. "Not only are your sisters amazed and excited, your mother has declared herself impressed."

"That is promising," he agreed.

"And you . . ." She stepped nearer, studying him. "You're also pleased."

"Am I?" Lord, he couldn't resist leaning closer. "How can you tell?"

"The way you stand. The ease of your shoulders." Her voice dropped and her eyes glowed. "The look on your face, fiercely interested and intrigued."

His heart was banging against his ribs. "Seen that look before, have you?" he murmured.

She arched her brows. "Perhaps. Have I misunderstood what it means?"

"I doubt it." If he had looked at the house anything like the way he looked at her, no wonder she thought him pleased. "It means I am taken aback by how very appealing it is. It means I find myself suddenly anticipating this inheritance with immense pleasure, unqualified by any sense of responsibility or obligation." His horse tossed his head, restless, and Drew calmed him without taking his eyes off Ilsa. "It means I like the look of it from top to bottom."

A fine flush had come over her face and her lips had parted invitingly. "A good omen," she said in a husky murmur.

"I hope so." Damn him for a sinner but all he could

think of was that the two of them would be under the same roof for several days . . . dining together . . . sleeping in bedchambers mere feet apart . . .

Let the house be full of private nooks and crannies, he thought. Let there be a vast wine cellar where two people could disappear for an hour. Let her room be next to his—

"Shall we go inside?" demanded Bella, making Drew start.

"Of course." Ilsa turned toward her with a laugh. "We were discussing that very thing, weren't we, Captain?"

"Then come along!" Bella hurried back toward her mother, who was watching them with a curious tilt to her head.

Drew handed off his horse to the groom who'd appeared. "Were we talking about the house?"

Ilsa smiled. "Of course. One hopes the interior will also please and delight."

"Or be a hollowed-out ruin, besieged with ghosts." He cleared his throat, trying to shake the urge to flirt with her even more provocatively. "I've no doubt which one my sisters would prefer."

She laughed with him, and they walked side by side toward the house, so close their elbows bumped. And that also felt so *right* Drew didn't even want to think about it.

George Watkins came forward and introduced himself. "A great pleasure to welcome you and your guests to Stormont Palace, Captain. I'm sure you'll find everything in order for your party."

Drew nodded, intensely interested in seeing the house. "I've no doubt. Will you show us around?"

Mr. Watkins was eager to do so. He led them

from room to room, bubbling over with little bits of history and lore about the house, the men who built it, the families who had lived in it, and even the furnishings and objects within it.

When Bella reached out to touch an engraved silver cup on a table in the gallery, Mr. Watkins piped up that it had been used by Their Majesties King James IV and Queen Margaret over two hundred and fifty years earlier while on a visit to the house. Bella snatched her hand away, and her mother pulled her back from the table entirely.

The furnishings in the dining room were French, elaborately carved walnut and inlaid with ebony from the time of King Louis XIV. It was rare to find examples outside of France, said Mr. Watkins proudly. Everyone studied the room in reverent silence, and Drew wondered how they would ever sit down to eat.

The large landscape over the mantel in the drawing room was revealed to be by Alexander Keirincx. "It was painted by commission of King Charles I, in honor of his first visit to Scotland," Mr. Watkins proudly informed them. "A magnificent view of Stormont Palace."

And left to hang unseen in this lonely house, thought Drew. He wondered if the duke even knew what treasures he owned in these far-flung, forgotten properties.

The bedrooms had been prepared, and the housekeeper, who turned out to be Mrs. Watkins, showed everyone to their quarters with friendly efficiency. Drew lingered with Mr. Watkins in the staircase hall.

"Mr. MacGill said you wish to make a thorough

examination of the place," said Watkins with a trace of anxiety. "I've done my best to assemble the records, which I've always tried to keep in good order, sir, but it was very short notice—"

"I'm sure we'll manage." The house appeared clean and well-kept, comfortably old-fashioned and handsomely appointed. Drew inhaled deeply. Yes, he did like this house.

It felt like home.

After a day of travel, dinner was a light repast, in the beautiful dining room with sky blue damask on the walls and a glittering gold chandelier above the long table. They retired to the drawing room, but when Mrs. St. James sat down at the harpsichord, it twanged painfully, putting a quick death to Winnie's hope that they could dance.

Ilsa wandered over to the windows facing south, across a broad sweep of lawn. Mr. Watkins had mentioned a maze on the property, and she thought she could see a corner of it. That would please Bella.

Agnes joined her. "When Drew called it a palace, I thought it an exaggeration," she murmured. "'Tis very grand."

"And very beautiful." Ilsa's eyes roved appreciatively over the room. They hadn't seen but half the house, and it was remarkable.

"Yes," Agnes admitted. "It is."

"One true benefit of your brother's expectations?"

Agnes smiled reluctantly. "A very small one."

"Some might think it crass to consider the creature comforts when deciding whether or not one favors something, but they most certainly affect one's opinion," Ilsa went on. "At times they're the deciding factors."

Agnes appeared put out by that. "Everything counts, I suppose. Not that this would be my house. It'll be Drew's."

"But you would be welcome here," Ilsa pointed out. "And if this is the forgotten and neglected house in Scotland, not visited in twenty years, what do you think the other, more preferred houses are like?"

Her friend gave her a perplexed look. "Those won't be my houses, either."

"No," Ilsa murmured, "but think of the gentlemen you'll meet, living in those houses. I daresay they'll own similar houses, and you might well end up mistress of one of them."

That made the color rise in Agnes's face, and she made an excuse to go talk to her sister.

The gentlemen joined them soon, but everyone was tired from the travel, perhaps a bit overwhelmed by the house, and when the clock chimed the hour the party broke up and everyone retired.

Ilsa had been given a room at the end of the hall, elegantly furnished like the rest of the house. It was fit for a duke, she thought, even a royal prince.

And Drew liked it.

In her mind she saw him again, standing at the foot of Calton Hill, arms spread wide as he disclaimed any pretensions despite his noble inheritance. *Just a soldier,* he'd said. Someone who could be a friend to her. Today he had walked through this exquisite house like a man planning his possession of it. It might as well have drawn a bright line between the two of them.

Ilsa smiled wryly. There had always been a line between them. She had seen it, even if she—and he—was tempted to ignore it. But it was real, and she must remember that.

She took a shawl from the wardrobe and let herself out of the room, lamp in hand. On the tour, Mr. Watkins had pointed out one door and said it led to the roof walk. Bella and Winnie had wanted to go up, but their mother overruled them, and then it had been forgotten by everyone . . . except Ilsa.

It took several minutes to locate it, but soon she was climbing the steep, narrow stair. It was a fair but clear night, and when she stepped out onto the broad castellated roof, the wind whipped at her hair, causing her to turn her face to the rising moon in bliss.

She explored the confines of the walk, which only ran along the front of the house from tower to tower. To the east was the vast ebony expanse of night sky, to the west the last indigo rays of twilight. It was too dark to see the long approach to the house, but lamps glowed in enough windows to give a sense of the courtyard below her. The air smelled of fir and heather, and she realized the faint rushing sound was the river they'd crossed on the way here. Was there a more elemental Scottish place than this? she wondered.

"Here I thought I'd have to confess to my sisters that I was wrong about ghosts," said a voice behind her.

Ilsa laughed. "Why?"

The captain came up beside her, resting his elbows on the stone and looking over. "Mrs. Watkins assured me the house was in pristine order, yet somehow a large book had wandered from the library to wedge itself in the door to the roof. The wind howling down the stair made a frightful sound, too, like a banshee promising vengeance on the intruders."

"If I'd let the door latch behind me, I'd have ended up a ghost in truth." She went up on her tiptoes to peer over the wide stone rampart again. "'Tis a long way down."

"You don't look frightened," he said with amusement.

She inhaled deeply. "Not at all. I love to be up high." A bird swooped silently overhead, a hawk or an owl hunting by the light of the moon. "How glorious it would be to glide on the wind like a bird. Can you imagine it? Standing on this ledge and just stepping off"—she extended her arms as if she would take flight—"to soar into the night."

"Would you?" He sounded intrigued. "Like Mr. Lunardi and his balloon?"

Ilsa's good humor faltered. Mr. Lunardi the aeronaut had thrilled Britain and Scotland with his hydrogen balloon ascents a few years ago. "Yes," she murmured.

"Did you see him? I understand his voyage from Edinburgh was a great success."

Ilsa said nothing. She had longed to go, had pleaded with Malcolm to allow her, but he refused. She only found out later that her husband had gone with some other men and wagered heavily on Lunardi's voyage, while she'd been forced to strain for a glimpse of the balloon from the uppermost windows of the house.

"My mother and sisters were amazed," the captain continued, not noticing her sudden silence. "I received no fewer than three letters about it—how magnificent the balloon was, how high he rose, how far he flew."

"I heard it was a marvelous sight. Would you go up in a balloon?" she asked, to divert the conversation.

"I'm not sure," he said with a soft huff of laughter. "It seems a risky business, that. I'd want to know it wouldn't crash, or catch fire and *then* crash like that French fellow trying to cross the Channel." He shook his head. "No flight is thrilling enough to warrant a fiery plunge to earth."

"No," Ilsa agreed. "Although that plunge . . . Before the impact it *would* be thrilling."

"When I have savored every other pleasure in life and want nothing more than that thrill, with no regard for the abrupt ending, I will attempt it," he replied dryly, making her laugh.

"What adventures did you dream of?" she asked on impulse. "Now that you have discovered my wild, lunatic wishes."

He was silent for a moment. "I used to yearn for the sea. I would imagine spending a life on the waves, traveling around the world with only the stars as guide and reference. Sometimes we would go out on Moray Firth and see a pod of dolphins leaping and spinning as merrily as a pack of wolfhound puppies and I would envy their freedom."

"How splendid that must have been," she said fervently.

"They were remarkable. And I used to wonder what sights they had seen, able to navigate the oceans with only the boundless heavens above them." His mouth quirked. "Beaches. Beaches are what they saw. Hurricanes and ships and beaches. They were bound to the water and could never see the amazing things on land."

"You are a realist," she said, and this time he laughed.

"And thus a cruel disappointment to you, I can tell."

Ilsa smiled bittersweetly. He most certainly was not, not to her. "My father never cared for ships," she said aloud. "He preferred to travel by coach, the finer the better. I've never been to sea."

"Well, neither have I. Marched from one end of Scotland to the arse end of England and back, but never sent aboard ship." He sounded wistful about that.

Ilsa turned toward him, resting her back against the stone. "You won't have to march anywhere anymore."

"And very thankful I am for it." He winked, his mouth still soft and amused.

"You'll have this house," she added. "An even finer benefit."

"After the army, any house with a sturdy roof, a sound chimney, and a warm bed is unspeakable luxury. Any ordinary farmhouse would suffice."

And instead he would have this exquisite gem of a house, finely furnished and beautifully situated, as well as a castle in England. He would never have to settle for anything ordinary again once he became duke, and she told him so.

For a long moment he didn't answer. "I still find it hard to believe," he finally said, very quietly. "'Tis good fortune that most people only dream of—you said that to me, aye? But *I* never dreamt of it. My dreams were far more ordinary and humble. A safe and comfortable home for my mother. Happy marriages for my sisters. Not to lose any limbs to some colonel's idiocy in the army. And someday, perhaps, a wife and family of my own to cherish."

Her heart was throbbing at his reply. "That last is not so ordinary," she whispered. "Certainly rarer than you might think."

He shifted, his shoulder brushing hers. "Well, I did admit it was only a dream."

"But now quite within your reach. Having realized the maddest dream of many—to be discovered as the long-lost heir to a great title and fortune—I assure you a wife will be far easier to come by." Ladies would line up to apply for the position, even before they saw that roguish twinkle in his eye and heard the low rumble of his voice humming with laughter.

He exhaled slowly. "So they tell me. But I feel . . . for myself . . . that I would wish a wife who didn't accept me because of that great title and fortune."

Oh, her *heart*. "You must favor contrary women, then."

"Aye," he breathed. His thumb brushed a loose wisp of hair back from her face. "I do."

Ilsa made herself laugh. "Just as I fancy leaping from this tower! Madness."

He stepped up behind her, his hands steadying at her waist as she leaned over the rampart again. "For dreaming of soaring above the earth—nay, who would think that mad? Like you, I feel certain someday someone will work out how to do it, and then who will look mad?"

Her laughter faded. Jean or Papa or Malcolm would have scolded her for being fanciful. Drew recognized the grain of real longing in her words and told her she wasn't mad.

This man was dangerous. Because if leaping from the tower wasn't madness, then surely other things weren't, either . . .

Not tonight, she bargained with herself; tomorrow, and the next day, she would be sensible. This moment was too beautiful, too rare, to spoil it with any claim of propriety.

Slowly she relaxed into him. Slowly his hands slid around her waist until she was in his arms. She should put a stop to this, but she liked the feel of it too much. She laced her fingers through his and rested against him. When he put his cheek against her temple, she turned into it, letting his lips whisper over her brow. He clasped her to his chest, his arms warm and strong around her. Ilsa soaked up the heat of his body. His heart beat beneath her cheek; it was as fast as her own, which raced recklessly whenever he was near. And when he touched her . . .

Oh, this could get out of hand so easily. He would marry someone else, but that was in the future. Tonight he was here holding her, as unattached as she was . . .

Ilsa let him tilt up her chin. She let him brush his lips against hers. She had told herself not to encourage him, that he was not for her, that she didn't need a man—but she stayed where she was, shamelessly letting him hold her and touch her until she wanted to cling to him and whisper in his ear, *Yes, kiss me . . .*

"Ilsa," he breathed, his hands moving over her back, stroking her hip, cupping her shoulder, winding into her hair. "Ilsa, what does this—?"

She put a finger on his lips. "I don't know. Don't ask me." *Not tonight.*

"You can't ignore the question forever," he murmured. "Not when we're both so drawn to each other. I can't help but think about it—about you."

Words like that made her want so much. He pressed his lips to the side of her throat, and she barely kept back a moan of desire. *Friends,* her conscience repeated feebly. *Not lovers.* "What do you think about me?"

His mouth quirked. "A great many things."

Her hands had fisted in the cloth of his shirt. With an effort she spread her hands flat, which only let her feel the rapid thump of his heart. "Mad, eccentric, impulsive . . ."

He laughed deep in his throat. "Aye, among your finer qualities." She poked his chest in mock affront, and he caught her hand and kissed that finger. "Not mad. High-spirited."

"Wild," she said in a low voice. "Everyone in Edinburgh says so."

His arms closed around her, pressing her full length against him. "Aye," he answered in a guttural whisper. "You drive me wild . . ."

Her last thread of restraint began to fray. Who could resist him when he said such things in that dark, seductive voice? Who would be hurt by one kiss? His mouth was already hovering over hers, awaiting the slightest encouragement . . . and Ilsa succumbed. She raised her chin, and finally, *finally* he kissed her properly, the way she'd dreamt of for weeks.

The kiss in the oyster cellar had been impetuous and brief. This one was not. His mouth claimed hers, hot and tender and demanding all at once. Ilsa rose up onto her toes, clinging to him as his arms went around her and he gave a deep growl of satisfaction.

"St. James? Oh—good Lord."

Ilsa flinched at Mr. Duncan's voice, snatching her hands from the captain's shoulders. His arms tightened around her but he didn't turn around, only glanced over his shoulder. "Aye?"

"I beg your pardon, I saw the open door," came Mr. Duncan's reply. He must have stepped back, for his voice was more distant. Cowardly Ilsa huddled against the captain, grateful that she didn't have to face the other man.

"Don't take the book out of the jamb," was all the captain said. After a moment he lowered his head to hers. "Caught red-handed," he whispered.

Ilsa sighed. She ought to thank Mr. Duncan for saving her from her own wicked impulses. It was full night out now, too dark to see Captain St. James's face, but his voice was still warm with invitation. They could pick up where they'd left off, on the brink of something that would forever change them from friends to . . . something more dangerous.

She eased out of his arms. Her heart still hammered, but she could think better when she wasn't touching him. "I wasn't the only one feeling restless, I see."

"Duncan is always restless. Never still, that one."

He paused as she slid a step away. "He hurt Agnes somehow."

Right. Excellent. Change the topic. She cleared her throat. "I've no idea what you mean."

He made an impatient noise. "I wasn't asking. I can see it for myself. But neither he nor she will say anything about it. They glare daggers at each other's back and get all sour-faced when you mention the other's name in their presence. It's bloody awkward to be around them. Why did you tell me to invite him?"

Ilsa choked back a shaky laugh. She wouldn't give away Agnes's secrets—in fact, she didn't even know this one—but he wasn't wrong. "They'll work it out. Or perhaps not, and it will be a feud for the ages." Reluctantly she took another step away from him, away from temptation, and shivered as the night breeze struck her anew. "'Tis late to be out, dreaming of mad things like wings to fly or swimming with dolphins. Thank you for not being repelled by my flights of fancy."

He brushed back a strand of her hair fluttering on the wind. "Hardly repelled, lass," he said in that gruff Scots tone that made her shiver again, but not from cold. "Never that."

She pulled her shawl tighter around her shoulders. "It's very kind of you to say so. And on that graceful ending, I shall go to bed."

"Aye," he said, after a fraught pause.

Come with me . . .

"Good night, Captain," she said briskly, gripping her shawl for strength, and stepped past him to go down the stairs, in great dignity and propriety, but filled with mad, wild unsatisfied longings.

Chapter Eleven

I believe," said Bella at breakfast the next morning, "there is a maze beyond the garden." She paused, looking at Drew. "Isn't there?" At his nod, she shot up straighter in her chair, eyes sparkling in anticipation. "Let's explore it!"

Drew said nothing as the table erupted in excited conversation. He was watching Ilsa, who sat sipping her tea in silence.

Regret? Unease? He wished he could tell. Her expression was serene but distant. God, he hoped it wasn't regret. Had he offended her?

He'd kissed her again last night. He'd held her in his arms for more than a startled moment, and it had shot through his nerves like lightning, searing the feel of her into his flesh. Just the sight of her, her face turned up to the night sky with an expression of rapture, her long hair rippling behind her in the breeze, had rocked him back on his heels. No one else had ever enthralled him the way she had—even before she'd declared a desire to soar into the night, unrestrained by anything like duty or inheritance or gravity.

He'd spent a long time thinking of that embrace, and their conversation, and what he ought to do about his growing fascination with her. At Carlyle Castle a suitable wife had been one of Her Grace's favorite topics. She had spoken at some length on the necessity of choosing a well-born woman who would know what was expected of her and uphold her position with grace and dignity. Drew had nodded along because who was he to argue with the woman who had been the Duchess of Carlyle for over fifty years?

And now here he sat, fascinated by a woman who was neither well-born nor English, who danced in oyster cellars and dreamt of flight. The duchess, Drew thought, would not be pleased.

That brought him up short. Was he considering *marrying* Ilsa? Or was he just losing his mind over her?

"So that's settled." Bella bounded out of her seat, jarring him from his thoughts. "We'll meet in the garden in an hour."

Drew finished his coffee and pushed back his chair. "Not I. I'm riding out with Mr. Watkins this morning." Ilsa's gaze flicked his way. "No one make a map of the maze," he added. "Don't spoil the mystery for me."

"It would take more than a map," said Alex Kincaid. "Worst sense of direction I've ever seen in a soldier."

His sisters hooted with laughter. Drew gave Kincaid an aggravated glance—his friends had seized the opportunity to make sport of him at every turn—and left to put on his boots.

When he came back down to the hall on his way to the stables, Ilsa was pacing between the tall French windows and the hearth. She wore a scarlet riding habit and held a broad-brimmed black hat. At his entrance she spun around as if she'd been waiting for him.

He squashed that hopeful thought. "You're even more eager than Bella to explore the maze," he said with a smile.

She gave a startled laugh. "I'm not sure that's humanly possible. She's talked of little else since yesterday."

"Ghosts," he reminded her.

"'Tis Winnie who yearns for a ghost." Her smile grew stronger.

Drew made a face. "Ah, yes. How could I forget?"

Still smiling, she looked down at her hands, gripping the hat, then back up at him. She opened her mouth, hesitated, then plunged on as if she'd reached some momentous decision. "I was wondering, if it wouldn't be too much trouble or inconvenience, if I might ride out, as well."

He went still. "With me?"

She blushed. "Yes. Or not, if that would disturb—"

"Of course," he said, mesmerized anew. *Anytime.*

A glow came into her face. "Thank you!"

"I don't know if there's a fit horse for you," he said, remembering with a frown. "Allow me to ask Watkins—"

"Oh no." She put out her hand, then snatched it back. "That is—I asked Mr. Duncan if he would lend me his horse, and he agreed."

Drew wondered again if he should believe his friend's disavowal of any interest in her but put that aside for now. If she rode Duncan's horse, Duncan couldn't come with them.

"The saddle," he said slowly.

The familiar wild, impish smile curved her lips. She twitched up the hem of her habit to show him that she wore boots and breeches under her skirt. "I came prepared for any chance."

His heart thudded and soared. "Then let's be off."

Watkins was waiting at the stables. Drew saddled his horse while a groom brought out Duncan's mount and Ilsa watched with barely contained eagerness. She did indeed ride astride, mounting herself before he could help her. Drew told Watkins they wanted to have a bit of a gallop first, and they set out.

She rode like a centauride. Her breeches and boots were dark, and when she looped up her skirts it looked for all the world like she rode sidesaddle, but she controlled her horse with the ease of a cavalry officer. Duncan's horse was a bit frisky but performed under her hand like a lamb.

Drew was entranced.

"Oh, that was brilliant!" she cried when they had let the horses race across a rolling meadow, clearing a low stone wall, and now had settled back into a cooling walk toward the path where Watkins was to meet Drew. "I've not ridden like that in years!"

He pulled up beside her, laughing. "Why not?" There were plenty of places for a good gallop near Edinburgh.

Her face froze. "My husband didn't approve."

"What?" he exclaimed in astonishment. "Why not?"

"He—" She brushed a wisp of hair from her face with one gloved hand. "He didn't think it decorous behavior. Proper ladies ride in carriages." She leaned down to pat the horse's neck, hiding her expression.

"But that was worth the wait! I feared I'd forgotten how."

Drew was intensely curious about her husband. Duncan had said Ramsay was a hotheaded fool who got himself killed. He wanted to ask, but checked himself. "Where did you learn to ride astride?" he asked instead.

"My father." She smiled again, the moment of tension and anxiety gone. "He decided any child of his must be a bruising rider, and I was the only one, so I received excellent lessons."

He grinned in memory. "My father also taught me. Put me on a pony when I wasn't quite three, to my mother's alarm."

"Oh, Papa didn't teach me himself. He was much too busy. I had a riding instructor from the time I was five."

Ah yes; Drew remembered that her father was a successful merchant. "He's Deacon of the Wrights, aye?"

"And a town councilor," she said somberly, before wrinkling her nose and laughing. "Yes. He wasn't at the time, though. My grandfather, his father, was the deacon then. Papa was learning his tradecraft, working long hours. And when my mother died . . ." She sighed. "I suppose he thought I would miss Mama less if I were kept busy all day with lessons."

Drew heard the thread of sadness in her voice, but her expression was calm. "I hear Deacon Fletcher is the finest cabinet-maker in Edinburgh."

"As his daughter, I must tell you he is the best cabinet-maker in all of Scotland, and therefore the world, thank you kindly," she returned pertly. "And if you'll be wanting a set of furnishings for your new domain, you'd better place your order now, for he won't jump for any man, not even a duke."

He laughed. "I'm not a duke, and it may be decades before I can afford so much as a footstool from the finest cabinet-maker in Scotland."

She tilted her head thoughtfully. "How strange that must be, knowing immense wealth and power await one, yet possessed of none of it now and completely in the dark as to when one might be."

He cleared his throat. "I've been given an income from the estate. Nothing to the duke's, of course, but generous for a humble captain." He paused. "The duchess his mother has run the estate for years, and I believe she was utterly appalled by the quality of the prospective heirs, once she located us."

"There's more than one?"

"My cousin. I've given up trying to remember what degree, but I never met the fellow before Her Grace summoned us both to the castle and said we must make ourselves worthy of her son's title."

"Or else . . . what?" She gave him that mischievous little smile.

"Or else we'd be flayed alive by her tongue, I suppose," said Drew with a curt laugh. "In all honesty, it never crossed my mind to defy her. I'd sooner tell my colonel to kiss his own arse, and that would earn me a flogging." He shuddered. "The duchess would be worse."

She laughed. "I know that type of woman well." They had come to a fence and turned to walk along it. "But only one of you can inherit. What will happen to the other?"

"Well, neither my cousin nor I have married or

had a son yet. Until then, he's my heir." A frown touched Drew's brow at the memory of Maximilian St. James, with his polished, cynical smile and calculating eyes.

"You don't look pleased by the prospect," she remarked.

"I don't think my cousin took it seriously. He's a rogue and a gambler, and Her Grace is resigned to him frittering away her money and help." The duchess had never said Maximilian's name after he departed the castle, but every day some passing comment or other would make clear her despair over him. "She strongly encouraged me to marry and secure the succession—" Drew broke off in chagrin. He'd felt so comfortable talking to Ilsa, he'd let his tongue run wild. "Forgive me."

"No, I'd already heard that."

Drew started. Here he thought he'd spilled his secrets, and she already knew? "Did you?"

"Oh yes." She gave him a sympathetic look. "I heard far more than I should have, no doubt."

Drew closed his eyes for a moment. "Bella or Winnie?"

"Both."

He pressed his knuckles to his brow. He could only imagine what his sisters would have said. "Dare I hope you might forget every word of it?"

"Captain," she said with a small laugh, "you need have no worry about *my* remembering any of it. You should be far more interested in who else they're telling."

They had come to a gate. Drew leaned down to open it, thinking hard. It didn't take long. The dance at the Edinburgh Assembly Rooms, when he'd been forcibly introduced to at least five or six ladies and maneuvered into dancing with all of them. He'd thought his sisters were just being excessively sociable. Merciful saints above.

He motioned Ilsa to ride through the gate. Mr. Watkins awaited them ahead, his placid horse grazing on the tall grass by the end of the path. "They'll be the death of me," he muttered as he rode past Ilsa, the gate securely closed again.

"On the contrary, sir," she said. "They mean to help you."

He glanced back sharply, but she gave him a jaunty wave and put her heels to her horse, cantering off down the path. This time Drew only admired her form for a moment before urging his own horse toward Watkins.

Today he wanted to see the scope of the estate, not dig deeply into the details, so Watkins led him around the property without stopping to inspect anything. He pointed out the small village, the road to the farms, the mineral springs, and the stream that fed the mill. He showed Drew the distillery and the dairy, where Stormont produced whisky and cheese famed throughout Perthshire.

"Proud we are to have Stormont sustain itself, and not be a drag on His Grace's purse," Watkins assured him. "Mr. MacGill was quite clear that we were not to request funds, and we haven't, not since the spring floods six years ago. And that was just a small amount, mind, to repair the mill," he added quickly. "'Twas soon repaid."

Drew nodded, a thin frown on his face. He had no experience of managing an estate, but surely it was odd to tell an estate steward he shouldn't ask for funds from the owner if they were needed. "So you've had no communication with Mr. Edwards, the duke's solicitor?"

"Nay, sir. Only with Mr. MacGill."

"And why is the house kept in readiness at all times?" That, Drew knew, was a considerable expense.

"Mr. MacGill's orders, sir. He does come here for a month every summer, to see that all is well."

And have a holiday at the duke's expense, thought Drew in irritation. "It was suggested that I should consider selling the property when I inherit," he said. "What do you think of that?"

Watkins hesitated. "It is a very fine estate, Captain. I'm sure it would bring a handsome sum."

Drew nodded. He knew the dukedom came with a Scottish title: Earl of Crieff. Surely a Scottish earl should hold property in Scotland. He wondered again why Edwards was so keen to sell the estate. He thanked Mr. Watkins, told him he'd seen enough for one day, and headed after Ilsa.

She had ranged off on her own, but he found her on a hill overlooking the river that wound past the palace and into the village through the mill. She had dismounted and was walking Duncan's gelding, who looked well exercised. He swung off his own horse and joined her.

She shaded her eyes as he came up beside her. "Is this all your property?"

Over ten thousand acres belonged to Stormont Palace; the answer was almost surely yes. "It's not mine, but I believe this is all Stormont. It's a question for Watkins." She glanced past him, and Drew made a vague gesture. "I saw what I needed to see today. He's gone back to . . . whatever he does all day."

Her lips twitched. "Running your estate?"

"It's not mine," he said again. "And he's doing a far better job than I would, so it's for the best." She grinned, and he shook his head. "I do intend to tell Mr. Edwards he ought to find a new solicitor, though. It appears Mr. MacGill tells Watkins to keep the estate ready for guests at all times, at great expense, yet the only guest who comes is MacGill himself." He smiled tightly. "To see that all is in order, conveniently enough for a month in the summer."

"I sacked Mr. MacGill," Ilsa said with obvious pleasure.

"I am consumed with envy." They shared a gleaming glance of amusement. God, he loved talking to her. "I apologize for not riding with you."

"Oh no, you mustn't," she cried. "I fully expected to go on my own. If anything I should apologize to you, for imposing on you when you meant to see to business."

"Imposing?" he echoed, startled. As a guest, at a strange estate, on a borrowed horse? Any host would have offered to accompany her, even if that host hadn't also been eager to seize any chance of her company.

She seemed to misunderstand, hastening to assure him. "Oh yes. I hope I didn't keep you too long. I'm quite used to doing on my own, since I was a child." The glance she gave him from under her eyelashes was oddly shy. "But it was lovely to have company."

He looked at her. A child without a mother, and

a father too busy at work to be with her. A steady stream of tutors and instructors. An invitation to Agnes to stay with her, even before there was any crowding at his mother's house. And the vision of her alone on the roof last night, gazing wistfully into the night sky and dreaming of flying like a hawk.

"I hope my company wasn't dull."

Her eyes opened wide. "Not at all!"

Drew grimaced. "My sisters tell me I am. Dreadfully Dreary Drew, Bella used to call me."

She choked on a laugh. "That's decidedly untrue."

He knotted the reins and let his horse wander. "It must be said that I've had more . . . excitement with you than with my sisters."

"Have you?" she murmured, one dark brow arching.

"*Far* more," he averred in a low voice. "And I hope to continue."

She turned and strolled away, her gloved hand brushing the tall grass beside the path. "Plans are the antithesis of excitement. None of us knows what the future holds anyway."

Drew went still. Was he being brushed off? He took a step after her. "If anything I did last night caused offense—"

"No." She put up her hand. "Nothing you did was wrong. It was my fault." Her fingers curled into a fist. "All my fault. I don't wish to cause complications for you, and yet I keep forgetting myself . . ."

He snorted. "It was not all your fault. If it had been anyone else on the rooftop, I would have gone back down without a word, aye?" He walked after her. "And who said you're causing complications? My sisters?"

"The duchess, I imagine." She raised her chin. "She encouraged you to marry. I daresay she didn't expect you to run wild with some mad Scotswoman."

He stood beside her. She was right, of course, about the duchess. But when he'd invited Her Grace's help in finding a bride, he'd never once imagined that a woman like Ilsa would whirl into his life in an Edinburgh oyster cellar and capture his attention so completely.

"The duchess also suggested I stuff my head with English politics," he said aloud, "leave off wearing a kilt, and purge the Scots from my speech. I'll admit she had some reasonable points, like learning how to manage an estate ten times the size of Stormont, but she's no' my mither nor my keeper, lass." He let his burr swell at the end. He was still a Scot, dukedom be hanged. "And I told you last night, you're not mad."

"Kissing you was madness."

He scratched his chin. "I thought it was brilliant, myself. Do it again so I can study the matter more closely."

Her cheeks were turning pink. She put one hand on his arm. "Captain—"

"Drew." He caught her hand. "You canna kiss a man and refuse to call him by name. Andrew, if you dislike Drew, but 'tis mainly my mother who calls me Andrew now."

Her lips pursed, as if she was trying not to smile. "Drew, then. But there's no good reason—"

"Good reason?" He leaned toward her. "The *very*

good reason I have is that I find you fascinating. And if you want me to stop, you'll have to say so aloud, because the way you kiss me back is all kinds of encouragement."

"But your plans," she began again.

He dropped her hand and stepped back, spreading his arms wide. "Plans? I have no plans—nor any promises made. Let's not worry about that. Let's just . . . see how things go." She narrowed her eyes at him. He grinned engagingly. "You've promised me nothing, either, and I won't hold you to anything that might happen. 'Twill all be at your desire, or not at all."

"You're a devil," she told him, now very obviously biting her cheek to keep from laughing.

He winked. "Aye, but not a blackhearted, world-destroying one. Merely one of the minor, mischievous devils, more wicked fun than evil."

She stepped right up to him, a flash of exhilaration in her eyes. Oh, this woman set his blood on fire with just that look. "I know," she said with a sigh. "And that's what makes you dangerous."

Chapter Twelve

To Bella's delight, the maze was an excellent one, tricky and confounding. No one had made it to the center. The next sunny morning, she stood up from the breakfast table and raised her hands portentously.

"I propose a game," she said as everyone looked at her. "With prizes."

"Hear, hear!" Monteith tapped his spoon on his cup.

"A race to the center of the maze," blurted out Winnie, her eyes shining.

"Winifred!" Bella glared at her. "A race, with teams and prizes, and eternal glory for the winner."

"Eternal glory?"

"If I win, I shall never let any of you forget it," put in Winnie, making everyone laugh.

"If there are no objections, we'll meet in the garden at eleven." Bella grinned. "Wear sturdy shoes if you want to have a chance."

Drew had meant to review ledgers, but this was more appealing, especially when he caught the gleeful look Ilsa shot him.

God save him. After twelve long years in the army, commanded by others, assigned to lonely barracks and constantly scrimping to send money to his family, the luxury he relished the most was freedom—to postpone a duty, to laugh, to follow a beautiful woman with her beguiling smile into a maze for who-knew-what frivolity. He spoke to Watkins, putting off him and the ledgers, and was one of the first to the garden.

"We'll draw partners so there's no unfair advantage." Bella climbed up on the low stone wall that edged the terrace. She turned her hat upside down, dropping in a handful of twisted slips of paper. "Each gentleman will draw a lady's name."

"Unfair," cried Winnie. "I won't be handicapped by one of them! I want to win!"

Monteith staggered backward, clapping a hand to his chest. "God above, now I'm frightened to be left alone with one of your sisters, St. James."

Bella chastised him loudly and shook her hat. "The prize is a bottle of aged whisky from this very estate, and a new hat from that charming little shop we saw in Perth."

Monteith nudged Kincaid. "Swords at dawn for the hat."

"And I'll take the whisky, thank you kindly," put in Agnes, making them both shout with laughter while her mother threw up her hands in dismay.

"What if I don't fancy sharing the prize?" drawled Duncan. "I like a good whisky, and I've not had a new hat in an age . . ."

"Be sure to order one that conceals your entire head, for our sakes!"

Bella flapped her hand at them. "Enough, enough. I thought pairing a gentleman with a lady would make it fair. Two ladies together, of course, would triumph before any gentleman made the first turn. Mama agrees with me, no one will argue his way out of it. So draw a name, Mr. Monteith, and if it's mine, not only had we best win, I shall indeed meet you at dawn with a sword to claim that bonnet."

With more laughing and teasing, the four men each drew a slip of paper from the upturned hat.

Drew stole a peek at Duncan's paper. The man wasn't holding it very closely. He nudged his friend's shoulder. "Trade with me," he whispered.

Duncan whipped around, closing his hand around the slip. "Why?"

"I don't like my draw."

Duncan wasn't fooled. The scoundrel smirked and folded his arms. "You saw who I have."

"No," said Drew, but Duncan scoffed.

"You're that desperate to explore with Miss Isabella?"

"Anyone other than who I drew," he retorted with a shrug, refusing to admit that he *had* seen and that he *did* only want to trade because of whom Duncan had drawn—who was not Bella. Casually he opened his hand, letting Duncan catch a glimpse of the name on his slip. "But if you won't trade, perhaps Kincaid will."

His friend's eyes narrowed. Drew turned to walk away. With a muttered oath, Duncan swiped the slip from his hand and replaced it with his own. "You owe me," he said with a stern look. "And don't be forgetting it, St. James." He strolled off to where Bella had climbed down from the wall and was handing out her pages of instructions.

Drew read the name on his new slip with pleasure and went to stand beside Ilsa. At her raised brow, he showed her the paper that bore her name.

"What a coincidence," she whispered.

"Luck of the draw," he murmured happily.

Bella finished reading her rules and beamed at them all. "Has anyone got a question?"

"Aye," called Monteith. "Is wagering permitted?"

"Yes," said Bella at the same moment her mother cried, "Certainly not, Adam Monteith!"

Everyone laughed, and Agnes said, very primly, "Not within my mother's hearing, Mr. Monteith."

"And we shall have a large, fine tea here on the terrace after our exertions," Bella added as the gentlemen began whispering among themselves and Louisa St. James threw up her hands again.

"What are we to do?" Drew watched Ilsa skim over the rules Bella had written out.

"Were you not attending? We're to find our way to the center of the maze, where Mr. Watkins—who is, I believe, the only person who knows the way through—has deposited a blue ribbon, on Bella's instructions. Then we must find our way out and absolutely lord it over everyone that we've beaten them."

Drew laughed. "And what are these rules we must obey?"

She gave him an amused glance. "Are you and your friends known cheats? The rules are primarily things we may not do. May not climb the hedges. May not crash through a hedge. May not lift one's partner onto one's shoulders to get a view of the maze from above. May not speak to anyone other than your own partner. May not lie to anyone."

"That's redundant. If I can't speak to anyone, I can't lie to them, either."

"You could point."

He scoffed. "As if I'd trust any one of them, or they me!" He shook his head. "I know for whom those rules are meant, and it's not my friends. My sisters are fiendishly competitive. If we meet Agnes in the maze, I beg you will protect me from her tripping me or knocking me unconscious with a branch."

She was still laughing as they reached their spot. The maze was shaped like a five-pointed star, with entrances on the points. Bella had drawn a line in the dirt at each one and allowed the pairs to choose their place of attack. Winnie and Adam Monteith took off at a quick jog for the far left, while Bella and Alex Kincaid darted to the closest one. Agnes and Felix Duncan appeared to be arguing over whether to go left or right, and Drew steered Ilsa around to the back, choosing a point next to the one unoccupied. It was as alone as they could get.

The hedges grew tall around them, a little higher than Drew could reach, and rustled gently in the summer breeze. It might as well have been a secluded bower.

"Ready?" called his mother from the terrace. Distant shouts confirmed everyone was.

"Do you also like to win?" Ilsa asked.

Drew winked. "You mean, do I savor outmaneuvering my sisters and showing up my friends? What do you think?"

She raised her brows, grinning. "And what are you prepared to do for it?"

He clasped her hands in his and rested his forehead against hers. "Anything," he whispered. Including losing this damn race through the maze, if it meant he could stay here and kiss her. That was worth more than winning a silly race. This was rare, this connection and attraction, and he was loath to let go of it even for a moment.

Ilsa's eyes gleamed, and she squeezed his hands. "Anything?"

"Aye." He dipped his head, his lips a breath away from hers.

From the terrace, Mr. Watkins blew a blast on the hunting horn.

"Then we'd better run," she whispered. For a brief, searing moment, she rose up on her toes and pressed her mouth to his. "I also like to win."

The world reeled around him. He'd already won, it seemed—but he let her pull him by the hand into the maze.

Ilsa was having the time of her life. Accepting this invitation had been the most brilliant thing she'd ever done.

She had ridden out three times now with him, and relished every moment. Not only was it a joy to be in the saddle again, but the estate was large and beautifully kept. They could ride for an hour or two along the paths and roads or following the river where otters frolicked in the water and beavers tended their kits. And then they'd dismount and walk the horses back, sometimes talking, sometimes in companionable silence, even in a light morning mist. He was the first man she'd met who didn't need to hear himself talk or require her to support his opinion on everything. After her father and Malcolm, it was a shock and a relief and marvelously appealing.

Today they were running like children, sprinting up and down the twists and turns of the maze. The hedges muffled sound, but occasionally a far-off shriek or laugh was audible. Ilsa couldn't help wondering how Agnes and Mr. Duncan were getting on. They'd been arguing bitterly before the start, but Ilsa had a strong suspicion that Mr. Duncan had traded names to be paired with Agnes.

Or . . . She stole a glance at the captain. Had he traded to be with her?

"Which way?" he asked as they confronted another junction.

"Left," she guessed, starting down it, only to catch a glimpse of blue through the leaves. "No, no, no," she gasped, turning and pushing him back the way they'd come. "Right! Go right!"

"Who was it?" he asked as they jogged along another curving path.

"Agnes and Mr. Duncan, I believe."

He gave her a glance. "I heard no arguing or cursing. Are you certain?"

Ilsa paused. She was quite sure that bright blue could only have been Agnes's dress, but the figure had been silent—and motionless, not darting along as they were. "Perhaps they found something better to do."

Drew stopped so suddenly she cannoned into him. He caught her in his arms and lowered his head. "Something like this?" he whispered, his hands sliding down her back to pull her tightly against him. The swing in momentum almost upended her, and Ilsa gripped his coat to keep her balance—and then kept holding on because she didn't want to let go of him.

"Perhaps," she gasped.

"God, lass," he rumbled in her ear, his lips on her neck. "I can't think straight around you . . ."

Neither could she, and it was becoming a problem. "If we keep this up," she said over the hammering of her heart, "we'll come last."

"It would be worth it. That was better than any whisky or new hat." But he took her hand again and they started off once more, darting up and down paths.

After several minutes, he stopped. "Have a look from above." He put his hands on her waist.

"That's cheating!"

"Aye, so don't be caught." He gave a roguish wink. "Just peek over and see how far from the center we are."

Choking on laughter, she nodded, and he boosted her to his shoulder with impressive ease. She clutched at his head, her fingers digging into his dark hair. He turned his face into her stomach and a shiver went through her. She could swear he kissed her there . . .

"How close?" he murmured, his lips moving against her belly.

Ilsa started—this *must* be madness; she'd completely forgotten about the maze, the race, the other people—and cautiously peered over the tops of the hedges . . .

Only to meet Bella's startled gaze, from the far side of the maze. Obviously they weren't the only ones ignoring the rules. With a wild burst of laughter she twisted, sliding down Drew's body until her feet hit the ground. "This way," she told him, clinging to his arm and barely able to get the words out.

"What happened?" His brows shot up. "Were you seen?"

"Aye," she said with a wicked grin, "by your sister, obviously cheating herself. Come!"

This time they ran around a long curving bend, into and out of a dead end, dodging left, then right, and then right again. Drew squinted at the sky and tried to judge their direction, while Ilsa closed her eyes and concentrated on the view of the maze from the dining room windows before pulling him off to the right again, around several switchback turns, and finally—

And finally they burst into the clearing at the center of the maze, where the blue ribbon still hung from the raised hand of the stone statue of Vesta. Ilsa gave a whoop of delight; Drew snatched the ribbon in one hand, and then snatched her in his other arm.

"We make a good team," he whispered, and then he was kissing her, hot and deep and utterly unabashed. Ilsa threw caution to the wind and kissed him back. Something vital deep inside her came alive when he held her. She speared her fingers into his hair and held his face to hers, kissing him as if she could devour him and somehow keep the glowing warmth he inspired burning in her chest.

She had no idea how long they stood wrapped around each other, but someone coughed loudly and ruined it. Ilsa's head was spinning and her balance was off—she would have staggered and fallen if not for Drew's arm around her waist—but she was still able to recognize the people who had discovered them: Mr. Monteith, looking smug, and Winnie, her eyes wide and her jaw slack.

Flustered, she stepped back, smoothing her hair. Drew seemed to have no such self-consciousness. He fluttered the ribbon in the air, and called, "I'm going to enjoy that new hat. Although I suspect it's to be bought on my own account, aye?"

"Mrs. Ramsay, I do hope you'll share the whisky," drawled Monteith. "Since I wouldn't be seen in the same room with any bonnet St. James might select."

They all laughed, though Ilsa could feel her face burning. Bella and Mr. Kincaid darted into the clearing, and Bella set about scolding her brother for nefarious cheating. Drew asked what proof she had, which made her turn red, and then he laughed and tied the ribbon around Ilsa's wrist with a large bow, giving her a smacking kiss on the hand. There was much laughing and teasing and indignant protest before they turned and began making their way out of the maze as a group.

The gentlemen led the way, heaping abuse on each other for their senses of direction, or lack thereof. Winnie and Bella fell behind, whispering furiously to each other. Ilsa felt awkward, walking alone in the middle. She tried not to wonder what they were saying. Winnie had seen her kissing Drew—Winnie, who was determined to find her brother a wealthy Scottish wife who would sponsor the St. James girls in London.

Ilsa acknowledged she might fit the first two requirements, but she knew nothing of London and had no desire to go there, and that was what

Winnie yearned for: a stunning new wardrobe, a dazzling debut, the chance to dance and laugh and sparkle at any number of eligible gentlemen.

Well. She sighed, plucking the ribbon on her wrist. Hopefully the girls would believe it was an impulse, the momentary thrill of victory—and not tell their mother, who already regarded Ilsa with disapproval.

As they emerged from the maze and started toward the house, someone called her name. Ilsa turned to see Agnes hurrying after them, flushed and missing her hat.

"There she is," cried Bella. "You came dead last, Agnes."

Agnes waved one hand. "I expected nothing less, when Mr. Duncan drew my name."

Everyone but Drew laughed. "Where is he?"

"I shoved him into the river for making us lose," she retorted. "Bella, didn't you promise us tea after the maze? I'm half-starved."

"Yes!" Bella bounded away, calling out to her mother, who was helping Mrs. Watkins with a large tray on the terrace.

"Did you drown him?" Drew asked Agnes in a lower voice.

She sighed. "Of course not. He's fine—sulking, most likely. I neither know nor care." She saw the ribbon on Ilsa's wrist. "Did you win, then? Despite Drew's poor sense of direction? Let's not be last to tea, men have fiendish appetites and won't leave us a crumb." And she pulled Ilsa toward the terrace, without a single glance backward for her partner.

Ilsa only wished she could be as resolute.

Chapter Thirteen

Drew had screwed his courage to the sticking point and was poring over the estate ledgers when his mother tapped at the library door.

"There you are, Andrew. May I come in?"

He looked up from a list of sheep shearing expenses. "Did you not want to go into Perth?"

After two days of rain, everyone else had been eager to get out of the house. They'd left for town some time ago—so that Ilsa could obtain her new bonnet as prize for winning the maze, Bella had declared. Drew suspected his sisters were also determined to come home with new bonnets of their own. He would have liked to go with them, but he could put off inspecting the ledgers no longer.

His mother smiled. "No. A bit of quiet is welcome. My ears are still ringing from yesterday."

Drew laughed. Winnie had organized a scavenger hunt about the house, with much running and screams of laughter and slamming of doors.

"Do you mind if I take my tea in here? I've brought biscuits and sandwiches."

"Of course I don't mind," he said with a wink, "since you brought a bribe."

"Bringing food has never served me ill, with you or with your father."

His mother settled herself in the chair by the window next to a tea tray carried in by Mrs. Watkins, and picked up her embroidery. The room was silent, save only the occasional clink of china.

Drew had never been especially fond of mathematics, and even less fond of bookkeeping. He made himself check the sums on a few pages, but everything looked in good order. Stormont Palace was as Mr. Edwards had hoped: a handsome property, well-kept and prosperous. If the duke wanted to sell it, he would have no trouble.

If it were still a ducal property when Drew inherited, on the other hand . . . It was becoming harder and harder not to plan as if it would be his. He'd grown attached to the place already.

When he finished with the ledger, he stretched his arms and rolled his head from side to side to ease the muscles in his back. He was not accustomed to sitting at a desk all day; that never happened in the army, where he was more likely to be sent out to repair roads or restore order to a restive village. At Carlyle Castle he'd been kept busy touring the estate, absorbing the duchess's lectures on the dukedom, and learning the scope of the duke's investments and obligations from Edwards. In Edinburgh, he'd been on holiday, with no ledgers in sight.

He would have to get used to more intellectual exercise. Edwards had hammered it into him that the dukedom was enormous, and even with estate agents and bailiffs and secretaries, the ultimate responsibility would fall on his shoulders. He remembered Ilsa's words—*good fortune that most men only dream of*—and ruefully thought that most men wouldn't dream of such fortune if they knew how much arithmetic was required.

"You look relieved," said his mother in amusement.

Drew opened his eyes and grinned at her. "Aye. I outlasted the ledgers."

She laughed. "Well done."

He jumped up and came around the desk, rubbing his hands in anticipation. Without a word she passed him a plate of biscuits.

"How does the estate look?" Louisa asked.

He polished off his first macaroon with a happy sigh. "Excellent, as far as I can tell."

"It's remarkably lovely. I cannot imagine why the duke never visits."

Drew had told his family the duke was not well, but not much more. "I doubt he can travel. I understand he was kicked by a horse some thirty years ago." He tapped his temple, right where the Carlyle groom had reported the hooves had struck the duke. "Here, in the head. They said he did not wake for almost a week, and was despaired of ever waking again, but when he did, his mind was not whole."

No one at Carlyle would speak freely about it. Miss Kirkpatrick, the duchess's companion, said His Grace was kind and gentle, but tired very easily. The duchess said he was unwell and not to be disturbed. Edwards had been the most forthcoming, admitting that all estate decisions had to be made by the duchess because the duke was unable.

If any ill were to befall the duchess, the estate

would be rudderless. Edwards had used that as a cudgel to persuade Drew to accelerate his separation from the army and his move to England, even though it might be years before he inherited.

"I don't think the duke has done much of anything since then," he went on, picking over the biscuits. The Stormont cook made the most delicious macaroons. "In all the weeks I spent at the castle I never even saw him."

"Goodness." Louisa paused in her sewing. "No wonder the duchess . . ."

"The duchess?" Drew repeated when his mother fell silent. "That woman could confront a full regiment charging at her and send them all fleeing for the hills."

"No doubt." She smiled wryly. "What I thought was, no wonder the duchess wishes to have you close at hand. She's lost all of her children, in truth if not in deed, and now has no one to whom to pass the estate."

That was true. Sobered, Drew nodded. The duchess was more fearsome than any general, but she had suffered terrible loss.

"The poor woman," added his mother softly. "I know you are more than worthy of the title, but I hope you will always remember the debt you owe Her Grace."

Drew looked up from the macaroons in surprise. "Debt?"

Louisa resumed stitching. "She could have done nothing, and simply waited until the duke dies. No one but God knows when that might be, and you are no near relation of hers. Instead she troubled herself to send for you, offering you an income and assistance preparing you for the inheritance. I gather she is not the sweetest of ladies, but in her position . . ." She clucked in sympathy. "I regret my earlier feelings against her."

Drew cleared his throat. "I have no hard feelings against the duchess. I'm deeply grateful to her. But I cannot overlook how very intimidating she is."

His mother gave him a stern look but ruined it by smiling a moment later. "Nor should you! It keeps a man on his toes, that!"

He laughed and took a sandwich, having finished the macaroons.

"I heard something very intriguing," remarked his mother, drawing her needle and silk through the cloth. "About you."

"Good or bad?" he asked lightly.

She smiled. "I don't know yet. I heard that you kissed Mrs. Ramsay in the maze."

He froze.

"And that she kissed you back, with evident pleasure." She snipped her thread and looked at him. "Was I told truly?"

He tried not to squirm in his chair, feeling like a boy again. "Yes."

"Do you like this woman, Andrew?"

Beyond reason. "She's charming," he muttered, not facing her.

His mother nodded. "I have no doubt the subject of a bride was discussed at Carlyle Castle."

Here Drew went quiet and still. Of course it had been—more than once. It was an important matter.

When he tried to imagine the wife Her Grace would prefer for him, his brain conjured a pale, dignified lady with a cool smile, who would send baskets to the poor and help set the fashions in London and sleep in her own bedchamber, the door between them respectably closed.

Perhaps that's who he needed as his wife—a woman who would set a good example and restrain his wilder impulses. It would be his duty to be respectable and responsible, sober and serious. Every glimpse he'd got of the ducal life showed little of fun or freedom to do as he pleased, and much like bookkeeping, he'd supposed he would get used to it.

Then Ilsa Ramsay had blazed into his life, like a comet through a midnight sky, fascinating and attracting him like no other woman ever had—perhaps ever would. But every time he hinted at anything beyond flirtation, she skittered backward. Her kiss was full of passion and joy, but her eyes held shadows he couldn't penetrate.

He'd told himself to let it happen, or not, naturally. He'd promised not to press her. And yet, every time he saw her, something inside him reacted helplessly—like an iron nail to a magnet. He didn't know what to do, half-afraid of spoiling whatever might be growing between them and half-afraid that it would wither away if he did nothing.

"Your sisters like Mrs. Ramsay very much," remarked his mother when he took another sandwich instead of replying.

"But you don't," he murmured.

Her hands stilled. "It's not that," she said carefully. "She is lovely and polite, and has been kind and generous to the girls. But . . ." She shook her head. "She's had an odd life."

He shouldn't pry; it wasn't his business; if there was anything he ought to know, Ilsa should be the one to tell him. "What do you mean?" he still heard himself ask.

"Her father is gregarious and charming, known to all Edinburgh, but she never made her debut. I suspect her aunt, Miss Fletcher, kept the young lady under tight supervision, which is unremarkable. But then she married, quite privately, and still was reclusive. I hardly ever heard her name until Agnes met her in a bookshop and they became friendly. But in the last few months . . ." A little frown wrinkled Louisa's brow. "I'm afraid I don't know what to think."

Mad, eccentric, wild . . . everyone in Edinburgh says so, whispered Ilsa's voice in his memory. She'd tried to make light of it but he'd heard the thread of pique. "What do you think changed her?"

"That disgraceful business with Malcolm Ramsay." His mother's face set in disapproving lines. "A duel! The Englishman who shot him was loud and uncouth, and the trial—" She stabbed the needle forcefully into her cloth. "I do sympathize with Mrs. Ramsay for enduring that nightmare. I only wonder if it didn't . . . unsettle her."

Drew had been gleaning scraps of information about Ilsa, and the picture they formed made his heart ache. A lonely childhood, raised by a strict aunt while her father worked. More tutors and instructors than friends. A husband who wouldn't allow her to ride, even though she relished it.

He studied the sandwich he'd been holding for several minutes now. Nothing about Ilsa suggested she was deranged or unstable—that's what his mother meant by *unsettled*. "What was her husband like?" he asked abruptly.

"An arrogant fool," declared his mother. "A gambler and a scoundrel. Nothing reclusive or retiring about him! He flirted once with Agnes and I sent him off with a flea in his ear. I'd not have let him near any of your sisters." Drew glanced at her, startled. "Others saw him more favorably, I suppose," added Louisa self-consciously. "He was handsome and he was rich."

But not a kind husband. Ramsay didn't allow Ilsa to go see the balloonist.

"How do you think she's . . . unsettled?"

This time his mother took her time replying. "It's the marked swing from quiet and retiring to bold and independent that startles me. Who is her true self? I wonder if *she* knows. Some people never can decide and settle down to be happy. They are always seeking something, never satisfied, even if they don't know what *would* satisfy them."

Drew thought of a woman who kissed a stranger in an oyster cellar, kept a pet pony in her house, and painted her drawing room to look like Calton Hill. He remembered her open joy when they went riding, and her longing to glide on the wind like a hawk. She didn't seem unsettled to him, but rather . . . adventurous. Open in her enthusiasms and decidedly not reclusive. It was hard to believe a solitary, secluded life had been entirely her choice.

"She's not unstable," he said, very softly. "And I do like her."

His mother sewed in silence for several minutes. "Does she know how much?"

He didn't reply.

"I only advise you to be clear about your intentions with a lady—any lady," she added.

That would be easier if he knew what his intentions were. Drew ate the last of the sandwiches.

"And be cautious," Louisa added gently. "It is easy to get your heart broken. Yes, even those of grown men who have been soldiers can be broken." Her eyes twinkled at his instinctive frown. "Not only should you be certain of your own feelings, you should know how she might receive them. You have a different future before you now, and you must choose a suitable wife carefully and deliberately."

"I only meant to evaluate Stormont Palace, not choose a bride." He jumped to his feet, ready to escape the conversation. "Are there more macaroons in the kitchen? I seem to have eaten all of these and left none for you."

She gave him a look of reproof. "Yes. But think on what I said."

He smiled at her on his way out the door. "Always, Mother." And fled the room, wishing he could so easily escape the nagging question, inside his own head, about his intentions and his heart.

Perth was a picturesque town set in a stunningly beautiful landscape on the River Tay. They had driven through it on their way to Stormont and the younger ladies were eager to return.

Ilsa knew that was because they'd spied a neat little millinery shop, with stylish bonnets in the window, but she was easily persuaded to go along. Winnie had read in Pennant's *Tour* that there were some handsome walks and a beautiful park. Ilsa had missed her long walks on Calton Hill with Robert, and fancied a ramble after the St. James ladies shopped.

She did have to choose a hat, though. Bella refused to allow her to decline, and the shop owner didn't help by producing a hat that was unquestionably beautiful, a broad-brimmed straw hat with a crimson ribbon and a darling spray of miniature white roses. Then Mr. Duncan led the party to a cozy inn, where they had tea and cakes.

Mr. Kincaid and Mr. Monteith declared an interest in seeing Gowrie House, site of the infamous conspiracy, while everyone else walked in the park. Agnes took the lead, with—after a long moment of hesitation—Mr. Duncan. Ilsa was left to stroll with Bella and Winnie, who were in raptures over Ilsa's new hat, Perth, and the shawl and gloves Bella had purchased as well as Winnie's new bonnet. The sunshine and exercise did wonders for Ilsa's humor, and by the time they returned to Stormont Palace she was in a buoyant mood.

She had barely stowed the hatbox in her room when Bella tapped at her door. "Come with me," she whispered.

"Why?"

"Winnie and I have been dying to talk to you."

"We just spent all day together," she pointed out.

Bella rolled her eyes. "We wanted to talk *privately*."

Oh dear. She'd been waiting for the axe to fall on that kiss Winnie had seen. "Oh? Why?"

"Nothing naughty! Just . . . private."

Ilsa hesitated. "I'm not going down to the cellars in search of a ghost."

"No, no. Nothing like that." She motioned with her hand. "Please. We would like your advice."

Being invited into a secret sister conference was too much to resist. She followed Bella down the hall to the room she and Winnie shared.

At their entrance, Winnie looked up from her position, seated on the floor. "Come see, Ilsa!" she whispered eagerly.

She realized why when she came into the room, and Winnie tugged aside a fold of her skirt to reveal a black kitten with bright green eyes, small enough to hold in one hand. Bella shut the door and hurried to drop down beside her sister.

"Who is this?" Ilsa asked in delight as the little animal pounced on a loose thread from her hem. She sank onto a cushion Bella provided.

"We call him Cyrus," said Winnie, dangling a bit of yarn in front of the kitten, causing him to leap about in a frenzy. "He's from the barn but his mama died, and Mrs. Watkins is feeding him in the kitchen."

"We plan to smuggle him home," said Bella, scratching the kitten's head. "Isn't he darling?"

"He is." Ilsa smiled as Cyrus tried to lope off with Winnie's string in his teeth, only to tumble over Bella's foot and be scooped back into the center. "Is this the advice you need? I recommend a hatbox and a bribe to your maid, and a very solemn expression as you assure your mother you're not up to mischief."

Winnie shook her head, grinning. "Why do you think we had to go into Perth? Now we have the hatbox. If that doesn't work, Alex has offered to smuggle him home for us in his baggage."

"Has he?"

"He's a great one," replied Winnie. "I'm so glad Drew invited him." She made a face at Ilsa's surprised look. "We've known Alex Kincaid for years. The Kincaids used to live near us, and he and Drew were at school together. They still play golf."

"And won't let us play with them!" Bella sounded outraged.

Ilsa laughed. A moth had flown in the window and the kitten spotted it; he began leaping about, trying to catch it. Bella wiggled the bit of yarn again, and he instantly abandoned the moth to pounce.

"We wanted to ask your advice on a"—Winnie glanced at her sister—"a delicate subject."

Bella plunked the kitten into her lap, where he rolled into a ball and let her stroke under his chin. "Very delicate. It concerns . . . a family member of ours."

Ilsa tensed very slightly. "Does it? I'm not sure—"

"But it's about marriage, and you've been married, and we've not," said Winnie in a rush. "And we can't ask Mama, obviously, because she would tell us not to interfere—"

"That's good advice," murmured Ilsa.

Bella made a face. "Listen before you advise! Please, Ilsa?" She offered the kitten, smiling brightly.

Ilsa took the ball of black fur in both hands. Cyrus was purring loudly, and when she settled him in her lap he began flexing his tiny paws against her stomach. His eyes closed and a little pink tongue poked out of his mouth. She couldn't help smiling. "All right. What is the problem?"

"Our—our family member has formed an attachment. The trouble is, it's not going well," said Bella, shooting little glances at her sister every few words. "We are not sure why, as our family member has not seen fit to confide in either of us, even though we both devoutly want nothing but their happiness."

I wonder why not, thought Ilsa. These two were interfering busybodies.

"Everyone can see that the attraction is strong on both sides," Winnie put in. "They can hardly keep their eyes off each other, especially this week."

Ilsa's hand paused mid-stroke, self-conscious. "This week?"

Winnie nodded, watching her too closely for comfort. "Everyone can clearly see how much these two ought to be together—"

"Only they are both being so dense about it!" burst in Bella.

Oh Lord, what should she say? "That's often how it goes. Attachments"—she almost choked on the word, praying desperately they were speaking of Agnes and Mr. Duncan and not her and the captain—"attachments are delicate matters. One party may not be sure their affection is returned, making them reserved, which renders the other party shy, as well."

Winnie inched forward on her cushion. "What could we do to nudge one of them—"

"Or both of them," said Bella.

"—to admit the depth of their feelings and proceed to the proposal and wedding?"

Ilsa blinked, and Bella choked on a giggle.

"Are you certain they care that deeply for each other?"

"Yes." Winnie nodded confidently.

"How did you know Mr. Ramsay was the one, when you married before?" Bella asked.

Ilsa's hand slowed and stopped, resting lightly on Cyrus's back. *When Papa told me he was.* "I suspect it's different every time," she said, keeping her tone even. "And while it may be obvious to *you*, dear matchmakers, it may not be to either of *them*. The course of true love never does run smooth."

She told herself they must be speaking of Agnes and Mr. Duncan. The looks those two exchanged fairly singed the air—sometimes with dislike, sometimes with longing. It was only her guilty conscience that made her even suspect Winnie and Bella might have their brother in mind. How could they have gone from witnessing one reckless kiss to maneuvering to arrange a marriage between her and Drew? Of course they had not. They wanted him to marry a sophisticated woman who would take them to London for a glorious Season. They had a book listing the most eligible women in Britain to choose from.

She ought to feel very relieved, and yet did not.

And now she'd let herself be maneuvered into offering advice on Agnes's love life, which she had sworn to avoid. "Your best choice is to be a kind and loyal sister to this family member, and trust that they will know what's best for their own life."

Both of them looked let down. "But what if hardheadedness or—or hurt feelings cause the other party to walk away?" Bella exclaimed. "Most people don't wish to pine away of love forever, you know."

Ilsa laughed. "Of course not. I only meant that it's not your choice to make. You would not wish them to make it for you, would you? You cannot presume to make it for either of them."

"But our family member is being a fool!"

Ilsa raised her brows. "I've not met a St. James yet who was a fool."

Bella rolled her eyes. "You have, we just see it more clearly after years of exposure to them."

"But what can we do?" asked Winnie earnestly. "To make them see reason and—and woo the other party."

"Woo?" Ilsa tried not to laugh.

"One of them has to say something," said Bella wrathfully. "And we've already stated that our family member is being an idiot!"

Ilsa stroked Cyrus's soft black fur. The purring had stopped; he was sound asleep in her lap, curled into a trusting little ball. She wondered if Robert would like him, and then told herself Cyrus was not her cat. He would go to England with the St. Jameses.

"When it comes to love, you cannot force it to flower," she said, eyes on the kitten. "It is a wild plant. It will grow, or not, where it wills, often despite your best intentions. Perhaps the best you can do is beware of its thorns and do your best to prune it."

Well did she know that. She had wanted to love her husband; for a while, she'd thought she did. Her father had arranged the marriage, but Malcolm had been handsome and eligible and Ilsa had agreed happily, eager to escape her father's house and Jean's strict rules and see something of the world.

It had not happened that way. Malcolm had been, like her father, a man about town, known in every tavern and public room. He had not wanted to change his bachelor ways and take her to the theater or the art galleries, as she longed to do. His friends, he claimed, were not a lady's society, and he would neither give them up nor take her out in their company. He expected her to sit at home, quietly reading or sewing, when Ilsa had yearned to dance and host dinner parties and go see balloon ascents. Her feelings of love had not lasted long. Malcolm, of course, had never felt any to begin with.

And as for Drew . . . She was not going to allow herself to think of love.

Bella and Winnie were gazing at her with identical disgusted expressions. "Prune it?" echoed Winnie, as if the words were blasphemous.

"Thorns?" Bella wrinkled her nose. "Does true love *have* thorns?"

Ilsa couldn't even smile at their disappointment. Not only did love have thorns, some of them were tipped with poison. "I don't know much about love, at least in marriage. Perhaps your mother will have better suggestions."

They exchanged glances of dismay.

Feeling awkward now, she handed the kitten back to Bella and climbed to her feet. "I do wish your family member great happiness, you know. I just believe she will work out on her own how to find it."

Bella gave a muffled snort.

"Hopefully before we've left Edinburgh and it's too late," muttered Winnie.

"Well." She flattened her hands on her skirt. The warm spot where Cyrus had curled felt cold now. "I will see you at dinner."

"Thank you for your advice. And—and you won't say anything to anyone about our questions, will you?"

Agnes would combust with fury and mortification if she knew. Ilsa shook her head and tapped her nose. "I swear not," she said gravely. "On my very soul."

That elicited a wan smile from Bella, and Ilsa was able to depart with a smile on her own face.

It was only in her own room that she gave in to the yawning emptiness inside her when she thought of the St. Jameses' departure for England. She leaned against the door, shuddering, and put her face in her hands. No more of Agnes's company. No more teasing and plotting with her sisters.

No more Drew, with his impertinent winks, saucy good humor, and incendiary kisses. In the moment when she'd thought Winnie and Bella meant Drew, and were trying to match him with her . . . Before the awkwardness had gripped her, there had been a searing burst of hope in her heart for one moment. That his sisters had sensed that he was in love with her. That he wanted to marry her. And even more, that they would all look on the match happily.

That little explosion of happiness inside her had caught her off guard. She had promised Agnes no hearts would be broken. It was just flirting. They were merely friends.

All lies.

She swiped at her burning cheeks. *Stop it,* she told herself. *You're being a fool.*

That sort of love is a myth.

Chapter Fourteen

The visit to Stormont Palace seemed to pass in the blink of an eye, to Drew's surprise, even though it had stretched from a week to almost a fortnight.

There was no doubt that it had been a smashing success. He'd got around to all the tenants and farms, seeing for himself that they were well-run. He saw the mill and the little village around it, the distillery, the extensive dairy operation. He had copious notes for his report to Mr. Edwards, to make his argument for keeping the estate.

Bringing his family had been a stroke of brilliance. His mother was impressed by the property and the calm efficiency of the Watkinses. Agnes had a sparkle in her eye and color in her face, even when she spoke to Felix Duncan. Drew still wasn't sure it had been a good idea to invite the man, but both seemed to thrive on their acerbic exchanges. He had always trusted that Bella and Winnie would be won over fairly easily, but they took to the grand old house with ebullient delight, from the maze race to telling stories in the vast, echoing cellars.

And the very best part of the trip: Ilsa Ramsay was there. She'd ridden out with him several mornings, making him laugh every time. To his regret, the first night was the only time they'd stood out on the roof together, but he'd kissed her in the maze, and twice on the ridge behind the mill during a morning ride. He felt like a boy, impatient to see her again whenever they were apart, euphoric every time he kissed her and she kissed him back, beset by vivid erotic dreams of her at night.

He had heard his mother's caution and tried to keep it in mind, but what pulled him toward Ilsa was stronger. He didn't know his intentions or her true feelings for him; he only knew that he liked her—very much.

With a surge of anticipation, he tapped softly at her door the night before they were to return to Edinburgh. It was late, the household having all gone to bed. He had waited until no light shone under any door, but that included Ilsa's, and there was a chance she would be asleep—

The door opened a crack. Her eyes widened at the sight of him. "What are you doing?" she whispered.

For answer he held up a length of chain, the iron links clanking faintly.

Her eyes grew wide. "No . . ."

Drew grinned. At dinner Winnie had lamented not hearing so much as a ghostly wail. He leaned closer and whispered, "Come be naughty with me, and give my sisters the fright they so desperately crave."

She inhaled. He felt the rush of breath across his cheek, almost like a kiss. Her hair fell over her shoulders in inky black waves, she wore a sleeveless nightdress that made him wish he'd brought a bigger lamp, and behind her, in the shadows of her room, was a bed . . .

"Where?"

"In the attics," he murmured, still absorbed in the smell of her hair and the warmth of her skin. The chain clanked against his knee as he forgot about ghostly pranks and thought only about her—kissing her—being wild and wicked with her—

"Let me get my slippers," she whispered, and then she turned her head and pressed her lips to his for a heart-stopping moment.

Something happened to him every time she kissed him. The closest thing like it he'd ever experienced was when lightning struck a tree near the fort as they were returning from patrol. Every man in the regiment had been knocked off his feet by the earsplitting crack, and all scrambled back up with pulses thumping, hair standing on end, feeling like they'd just won a sudden and terrific battle.

He sagged against the door as she slipped back into her room, and tried to calm his rioting senses. *Do you like this woman?* his mother had asked. *Mam, I'm utterly fascinated with her,* he silently replied.

Ilsa returned a moment later, tying the sash on her dressing gown. Drew heaved a silent sigh of mourning for her bare shoulders. "What do you intend to do?" she whispered as they crept down the corridor toward the heavy door that led to the attics.

It was so like his mother's query that Drew gave a start, nearly dropping his lamp. He glanced at her, and almost fumbled the lamp again at the exhilaration in her face. If not for that dratted chain hitting his knee, he could easily believe this was a rendezvous, two lovers meeting in the dark of night because they couldn't keep away from each other a moment longer.

Unsettled, he put one finger to his lips, and only when they had gained the staircase, with the door gently closed behind them—on hinges that were blessedly oiled into silence, thanks to Mrs. Watkins—did he speak.

"They want to hear a ghost," he said quietly. "I thought I would . . . just . . ." He rattled the chain.

She folded her arms and tapped one finger to her chin. Standing two steps above him, her bosom was right at eye level, and Drew was mesmerized by the sight. Her dressing gown was fine lawn, like her nightdress, and he could swear he spied a dusky nipple—

"You'll have to make more noise than that," she said thoughtfully. "These old houses have thick walls and floors. Some stomping, I think, and dragging the chain on the floor." She turned and darted up the stairs, into the stygian darkness, without so much as a backward look. Drew started out of his daze of arousal and hurried after her, holding the lamp higher.

"Oh my," she breathed. He could barely make her out, even in her white garments. "It's empty." She turned to him, a wicked smile on her face. "We can make *so* much noise up here."

As it turned out, the attics were not empty. No doubt thanks to Mrs. Watkins's efficiency, trunks and crates were stacked neatly at the far end of the room. Ghostly figures turned out to be furniture draped in dust coverings. But that left a long run of open space where they could, indeed, make an unholy racket. Ilsa located a heavy padlock on a shorter length of chain, which made a satisfying thump against the wooden planks. Drew mentally mapped out the floor beneath, and paced off where he thought his sisters' rooms were.

"Some wailing would be enormously helpful," she whispered.

"Wailing?" He was still thinking about the way her dressing gown shifted over her breasts as she moved.

"Remember? The stairs to the roof," she whispered. "You said it made a howl like a banshee when the door was left open."

The roof, where he'd kissed her and she'd kissed him and things might have reached a truly spectacular level if Felix Duncan hadn't been wandering about sticking his nose where it didn't belong. "Right," said Drew, his brain too fixated on that night and what might have been to make any other sensible reply.

"There's a window here," she went on. "Open it, and I'll open the door when you're ready to give Winnie her ghost, and then—"

"The wind will howl down the stairs," he finished. It was a wild, raw night outside. The windows had been rattling since dinnertime. He set the lamp aside and managed to pry open the rusted latch and shove open the small window.

The breeze that rushed in was cold and damp and raised the hair on his arms. Ilsa leaned near it and breathed deeply. "It smells of the sea," she whispered.

It smells of home, he thought. The briny tang of the North Sea was in the air, along with heather and peat. And there was a note of something else, something softer and warmer . . .

She leaned farther toward the window and inhaled. The soft warm scent tugged at him, and Drew realized that was *her,* her perfume, her skin, her hair. Unconsciously he leaned toward her, breathing deeply—

He stopped. Perhaps this had been a mistake. He'd thought it the perfect way to end the visit, this caper to make Winnie laugh and steal a few more minutes with Ilsa at the same time, and instead he'd fallen into a bottomless pool of desire. He wanted to kick the chains into the shadows and make love to Ilsa on the bare attic floor, never mind ghostly pranks.

"I'll open the door at the bottom of the stairs," he said to distract himself from that, but was unable to resist sneaking one more look at her as he turned away.

She stood in front of the window, her arms braced on the sides, face lifted in ecstasy to the night sky. Her hair and dressing gown billowed in the stiff breeze. *She* was the spirit haunting him and tormenting him, and Drew cursed at himself as he nearly fell headfirst down the dark stairs in his distraction.

"All in readiness," he said when he rejoined her, having propped open the door with a stray bit of wood and got himself under better control.

Her face was pale and eager in the lamplight. "For Winnie's sake, be terrifying."

He led the way, clanking the chain and dragging his footsteps along the floor. Ilsa followed, dragging the padlock and periodically banging it on the floor. "We should moan," she whispered at one point, and Drew had to stop and collect himself for a moment, until she let out a wail that sounded not like the passionate utterance his fevered brain had conjured, but more like a banshee foretelling death and suffering.

"That was you, aye?" he whispered over his shoulder.

"Of course! Who else?"

"I took a moment's fright that we'd unleashed the spirits of the house in truth."

She choked on a giggle, which made him smile, and then the two of them could barely carry out their spectral prank for laughing so hard.

Drew paused when he heard a door slam. It was impossible to hear voices over the keening breeze, but he tossed aside the chains and caught Ilsa's hand, tugging her toward the stairs. At the last moment he blew out the lamp, and they huddled behind an armoire under Holland covers.

"Surely 'tis naught but a stray animal," came Felix Duncan's voice, along with the glow of a lamp. A moment later his head and shoulders appeared at the top of the stairs, and he took a sweeping look around. "I see nothing," he reported over his shoulder.

"Go up, man, be bold," cried another voice—Adam Monteith, who pushed past Duncan to jog up the stairs and pose there, fists on hips, feet spread. "Show yourself, foul spirits," he boomed.

Beside him Ilsa was shaking with silent laughter. Unthinking, Drew put an arm around her, grinning, and then stilled as she pressed closer to his side.

Mam, I think I'm falling in love with her, he thought.

"Let me see!" Winnie hurried up, Bella close on her heels. They clutched each other but peered around eagerly. "Was anyone murdered up here? Is that why the ghost is in the attics?"

"No, you goose, spirits obviously need space to do their haunting," was Bella's retort.

To Drew's surprise, his mother and Agnes appeared next. His sister looked skeptical, and his mother wore an expression that made him think she knew exactly what had gone on and found it amusing against her will. Looking distinctly grumpy and still half-asleep, Alex Kincaid brought up the rear, holding another lamp aloft.

"I see nothing," said Duncan again. He yawned behind one hand. "No headless Highland chieftain, no lady who threw herself from the battlements in heartbreak. Not even the spirit of a badger who got trapped in the—Argh!"

As he spoke, Drew had silently tugged one of the Holland covers down over himself. Eyes shining with glee, Ilsa had pressed back into the shadows while Drew stepped forward, hunched over with his arms upraised. Everyone else was facing the opposite way, so when he lurched toward them and let out a long, low moan, it caused a moment of pandemonium.

Winnie and Bella gave earsplitting screams and scurried behind Monteith, who had quite lost his cocky expression. Kincaid cursed at full volume, now wide-awake. And Duncan jumped backward, almost dropping his lamp but still managing to throw out an arm to shield Agnes as she shot behind him and pressed against his back.

Only Louisa didn't move, just stared him down with her arms folded and a knowing quirk to her brow. "Very amusing, Andrew."

With a grimace, he cast off the sheet. "It was meant to be terrifying, Mother."

His sisters erupted with outraged squawks. Bella flew at him and pummeled his arm. "What on earth, Drew?"

Laughing, he fended her off. "Ow! Stop, lass. You wished to see a ghost—"

"A *real* one," cried Winnie with a stamp of her foot. "Not you!"

"We could make him a real one," suggested Kincaid dryly. "For rousing us all from warm beds to shiver in the attics."

"Tip him right out this window. He'll make a ghostly wail as he plummets to the ground, for certain." Monteith peered out the window before closing it.

"And you helped him, Ilsa?" asked Agnes. Interestingly, she had jerked away from Duncan and now stood on the opposite end of the group, her face pink even in the dim light of the lamps.

Her eyes downcast but biting her lip guiltily, Ilsa stepped forward and nodded.

"Oh," cried Bella, interest warring with indignation in her voice. "Was it terribly thrilling?"

She gave another tiny nod. "We wanted you to have something to remember," she said to Winnie.

His sister affected a pout, but Drew could see she was enjoying herself. "I suppose if there were any ghosts here, they've fled by now, having seen the lunatic who stands to inherit the place."

"No doubt. With any luck they'll follow him

home and wreak vengeance on him for disturbing their peaceful home." Monteith headed for the stairs. "My heart canna stand the excitement. I'm to bed—and plan to stay there until morning, unless you set the house afire next, St. James."

"Aye." Kincaid shot Drew a dark look. Drew merely smirked in reply.

"Well." Louisa clapped her hands. "Now that we're not needed to bring ease to a restless spirit, off to bed with the lot of you. We have a long journey tomorrow."

Still protesting and laughing, Bella and Winnie went with her. Agnes waited for Ilsa, then walked down the stairs with her. Drew overheard her ask just whose mad idea it had been, but lost Ilsa's reply.

It had been *their* idea, really, he thought. His was only the initial thought. Ilsa had embraced it, added to it, and brought relish and verve to the whole venture.

And left him more fascinated than ever.

"Showing Winnie a ghost, eh?" muttered Duncan, clattering down the stairs after him. Like the other men, he had clearly leapt from his bed and raced to the scene; his long linen shirt was on backward and his loose plaid was thrown haphazardly around him.

"What else?" Drew made sure the door was secured. After the cold breeze through the attics, it felt cozy and warm here.

Duncan raised one ginger brow. "You didn't ask me, your bosom friend, to help."

"Would you have?" Drew affected shock. "You've been out of temper since we arrived, sulking and sour-faced. I thought you couldn't wait to return to

Edinburgh. No, I never thought of you, ye feckless fool."

His friend scoffed. Ahead of them Ilsa and Agnes were arm in arm, heads together as they walked back to their rooms. "You didn't think of me because you were thinking of someone else."

"Winnie," said Drew stubbornly.

His friend laughed as he went back to his own chamber. "Keep telling yourself that, but don't expect anyone else to believe it."

A door closed, then another and another. He was left standing alone in the corridor, suddenly chilled. He cast a lingering glance toward Ilsa's door. She hadn't even said good-night.

He heaved a sigh as he let himself into his room and contemplated his lonely bed. He'd had her for half an hour, and would have to be content with that.

Chapter Fifteen

Ilsa stood by her door, her heart pounding and her skin tingling. What a magnificent lark! Even if Mrs. St. James had seen through them at once, the expressions on Winnie's and Bella's faces had been priceless, when Drew lurched at them with that dusty sheet draped over him, moaning like a wounded stag.

Just the thought made her convulse with a silent laugh again. Dear God, what fun they had together . . .

She never wanted that to end.

This was their last night at Stormont Palace. Tomorrow they would travel back to Edinburgh, where she would go back to her house and he would go back to Felix Duncan's rooms, before he packed up and left town entirely to go to England, to his English dukedom, to his future English bride.

If she wanted to seduce him, tonight was her chance.

After an interminable delay, during which she counted to five hundred, toed off her slippers, and listened at the jamb for any late-night wanderers, she cracked open the door and peeked out. The corridor was dark, illuminated only by the moonlight from the staircase hall at the far end. The house was asleep once more. She took a deep breath and slipped out, leaving behind her lamp and all her reservations about being wild and wicked.

She knew which door was his; it was, naturally, the farthest from hers, at the head of the stairs. Accordingly she sprinted, feeling her heart nearly burst from her chest, half in anticipation and half in anxiety that Mrs. St. James would open her door and step out to order her back to her own room. Surely it was a sin to seduce a man when his own mother was under the same roof.

When she reached his door, she didn't dare knock. Every squeak and creak of the house sounded loud to her overexcited brain, and she was here because she was being bold and daring anyway. Gently she turned the knob and slipped inside.

It was dark within, though the drapes at one window were open. She stayed still, clutching the door, searching the darkness as her eyes adjusted.

A rustle of cloth. "Is something wrong?" Drew asked, his tone guarded.

"No," she whispered.

"Ilsa," he said in surprise, but she could make out the shadowy room now and was on her way to the bed, where he sat up, bare-chested and rumpled.

She touched his face and put her finger to his mouth. "Do you want me to stay?" she breathed, her lips at his ear.

He shuddered. "Yes."

She smiled. "Good." And then she bit his earlobe, thrilling to the shudder that went through his broad shoulders.

Without a word he turned his head and kissed her. Ilsa opened her mouth and kissed him back, inviting, tempting, seducing.

All her life she had been told to be sensible, to do what her father, her aunt, her tutors, her husband wanted her to do. It had taken Malcolm's death for her to realize that no one ever asked if she were pleased with that state of affairs, and that other people acted to please themselves as well as the world around them. No one tried to please *her,* and Ilsa had finally realized that was up to her. For a year now she'd been trying to learn to do that, allowing herself to do things that weren't sensible or typical.

She could not think that *this* was a mistake.

Her heart had tugged her toward Andrew St. James from the moment she saw him, even before he had tempted her to be carefree and bold. She'd never had that—no siblings, few friends, no one to have fun with. She'd never felt so alive as she did with him, whether racing across the hills of Stormont on horseback or rattling an old chain in the attics. He tempted her to think she wasn't mad to crave some adventure, at the same time he proved it needn't come at the expense of responsibility and duty.

So here she was in his bedroom, his hands moving over her back, his mouth making love to her skin. This was mad, and it made her so wild she could hardly bear it.

She plowed her fingers into his hair and tugged his lips, which had wandered over her jaw, back to hers. She kissed him hard, deeply, and felt his fingers flex on her hips in surprise. With an impatient yank she pulled up the hem of her nightdress so she could climb onto the bed, straddle his thighs, and press even closer to him.

Gently he set her back on her heels. Ilsa leaned toward him impatiently until he put up one hand in silent admonishment. Much too leisurely for her taste, he untied her dressing gown and slid it from her shoulders.

She arched her back to shed it faster. His breath turned rough. Reverently his palms skimmed up her bare arms to her shoulders, then back down. Even in the dim moonlight she could see his eyes, hot with desire.

She reached up and undid the top button on her nightdress. There was a long row of them down the front. The modiste had smiled knowingly when she made this for Ilsa's trousseau years ago, and murmured about buttons piquing a man's curiosity. Malcolm had never once undone the buttons.

But Drew . . . His gaze focused on her fingers and stayed there, even as his hands continued to wander over her back.

She undid another button, and a third.

He smoothed her hair over her shoulders and ran his thumb along her collarbone, nudging aside the strap of her nightdress. Ilsa slipped loose another pair of buttons.

Drew was barely breathing now. His fingertips skated lightly over her skin, leaving scorch marks in their wake. Ilsa shifted restlessly atop him and undid more buttons, less languidly now.

The nightdress gaped open. He inhaled, a needy rasp of breath that acted like oil on the fire smoldering inside her. Good Lord how she wanted him, for his teasing winks and easy laugh and bulging arms and muscled chest. Without thinking, she dragged her fingers through the crisp hair there, shivering at the hard, hot flesh behind it and the way his abdomen flexed under her touch.

He opened his mouth and she quickly touched one finger to his lips. *No, no, don't say a word*; let her look, let her marvel at him. His eyes glittered but he lay back, sliding his hands up her thighs, beneath her nightdress.

'Twill all be at your desire or not at all . . .

She desired. She wanted him so much. She wasn't a wicked widow, just one who ached to feel and do and *be*. She yearned to be wanted for more than her fortune or social standing, to be understood and trusted and allowed to follow her own heart.

And he was the one who made her feel it all. This big, rough, handsome devil of a man, who would be a duke but played pranks like a lad.

She stripped the nightdress over her head and flung it away.

Drew let out his breath with a hiss. His hands went still on her, his fingertips digging into her flesh. His hands were large and warm on her thighs, mere inches from where she wanted him. He was waiting for her to decide things, letting her touch him while holding back himself—

"You're magnificent," she said softly. Not just physically, although she was hardly blind to that. She had never guessed a man could be so playful, so leisurely seductive in bed.

She didn't even realize she'd said it aloud until his hand cupped her cheek. "Ye make my mind go blank when ye say things like that," he whispered.

She gave a gasping little laugh. "'Tis a pity. I prefer you aware—"

With a growl he lurched upright, bracing himself on one powerful arm. "I've never been more aware of a woman in my life," he murmured, and then he was kissing her, his mouth hot and hungry on hers, and Ilsa forgot how she'd been planning to explore him and tease him. There would be time for that later—not now, when she wanted him so ferociously that she almost passed out when his hand swept up her ribs to cover her breast possessively.

And now . . . she was pressed up against his bare skin, so hot next to her own. His chest expanded on a sharp inhale; his arms closed around her, and then with a sudden twist he flipped them over, so they were face-to-face, the bed linens tangled around them, swamping her in his scent.

"I wanted to have my wicked way with you," she gasped as he raised her arms overhead, clasping her wrists in one large hand.

"You shall," he promised. "Just let me . . ." His voice trailed off as he lowered his head to her breast and touched his tongue to her nipple, hard and aching for—for just this. Ilsa sucked in desperate breaths as his fingers ran down the underside of her raised arm, his nails lightly scoring her flesh.

"You like that," he whispered against her breast. His whole hand curved around it now, reverently lifting and stroking her.

"Aye, sir."

His shoulders shook on a soundless laugh. "Good. I fair love it . . ." Now both his hand and his mouth were on her breast, and Ilsa forgot all about wanting to have her way with him, because his way was every bit as pleasurable as she could have dreamt of, and more. Now she wanted him to ravish her, fast and hard like a conquering army.

But he seemed bent on taking his time. His tongue did wicked things to her breasts, then wandered to her belly. Ilsa pulled against his hold on her wrists and he let go, allowing her to plow her fingers into his hair and urge him onward. She wrapped her legs around his chest as he tormented her.

Her skin had never seemed so sensitive and delicate. Each stroke of his fingers made her want more, harder, deeper, driving her wild. But when she tried to yank free the linen still twisted around him, he stopped her hand.

"Leave it," he rasped. "It's the only thing keeping me sane . . ."

"I don't want sane!" She pressed against him and dug her nails into his back.

"Oh?" He moved, sliding down her and taking the sheets with him. "You want madness?"

"Yes . . ."

"Desperation?" His head dipped. His tongue circled her navel.

"Yes," she gasped.

"Passion?" He licked her and she almost jolted off the bed. "You want this?"

"Yes!"

"Shh," he whispered, nipping her inner thigh. "You'll wake up everyone . . . again . . ." And then his mouth was on her, his hands spreading her legs, and Ilsa arched upward as if her body would soar right off the mattress. Pleasure coursed like lightning through her veins, throbbing in time with every purposeful stroke of his tongue.

When he slid a finger inside her, she spasmed, almost climaxing before the wave of heat receded and rose again—but then blinked out of her daze of bliss. She wanted this—so much she was shaking from want of it—but she also wanted to see him, to watch his eyes change, to hear his voice grow wild, to know she gave him as much pleasure as he was giving her.

"Drew." She pulled at his ear, then his shoulder.

He glanced up, sliding a second finger inside her. "Aye, my lady?"

She gulped for breath. All her nerves were clamoring for release. "I want—I want it together."

"As you wish," he said after a startled pause. Awkwardly he levered himself up and over, landing on his back beside her. "Be gentle with me, lass," he said through his teeth, draping one arm over his eyes.

"You want it gentle?" She scrambled up and crawled atop him, her mouth going dry at the sheer size and strength of his body spread before her.

"Well—no," he said, his voice muffled by his arm.

"Don't you trust me?"

"I do." The words were strained.

Ilsa rose above him, taking his shaft in her hand. He was thick and long, fiery hot and satiny smooth. The veins in his forearms stood out as his hands gripped the linens. "I should repay you in kind," she murmured, swirling her thumb over the head.

His stomach hollowed out, he inhaled so hard. "You could."

"I will. But I think this time . . ." She went up on her knees and guided him between her legs. "This time I will just have you like I've wanted since the night we met." She sank down, taking him inside her.

She had to pause a moment there, hands clenched on his stomach, dizzy at the way he filled her. Beneath her he lay taut, humming with tension but motionless. He had uncovered his face and watched her with eyes glowing like embers in the darkness, burning into hers.

Slowly she began to move, taking each stroke to the full length. His hips rose up to meet hers, matching her pace exactly. His hands stole up her legs to that spot he had suckled so devastatingly, and Ilsa leaned back with a moan to allow him better access. Her hands came to her breasts until Drew made a choked sound and sat up, taking her nipple into his mouth.

Now she could brace her hands on his shoulders and ride him. She could feel the tremors shaking his body, as hard and excited as the ones going through her. She could feel the moment his control broke and he came without pausing his ravishment of her breast, his hand between her legs sending liquid flame into her until it all pooled low in her belly and ignited every nerve. She broke with a gasp, clinging to him for balance as they both shuddered.

It took several minutes for her head to clear. She was still cradling his head to her breast, and pressed her lips to his temple, reveling at how slick with sweat it was. In turn he kissed her chest, right over her heart, before looking up.

"Since the night we met?" he whispered.

She smiled, combing her fingers through his damp hair. "Do you remember it?"

"Every moment." His eyes were half-closed in pleasure as she ran her thumb over his upper lip. "Why did you kiss me?"

Ilsa paused. "I wanted to." His mouth curved in delight. "It was the impulse of the moment."

"Mmm." He settled his arms more comfortably around her and turned until they lay facing each other. "Like tonight?"

She blushed. "Oh goodness, tonight was something I've thought about for days. Tonight was when my restraint gave way."

His laugh was a low growl in his throat. "Being ghostly does that to women, I hear . . ."

She tried not to, but the laugh escaped her. That laugh grew and grew, fueled by the giddy afterglow of lovemaking, until tears ran down her face and she had to swab them away with a corner of the sheet. And Drew laughed with her—perhaps a little *at* her—and gathered her close, nestling her against him so perfectly she forgot it was to be this way only for one night.

"I never knew lovemaking could be so *playful*," she gasped without thinking.

He raised his head. "No?"

She covered her eyes, mortified. "Forget I said that."

"I don't think I can," he said after a moment. "I think I shall reflect upon it with enormous pride and happiness. No man could be more flattered."

She swatted his shoulder, and his chest rumbled with laughter. Helplessly she smiled.

"I gather Mr. Ramsay took a more prosaic approach to the matter?"

She nodded. Malcolm had kept a mistress. She

supposed he enjoyed making love to that woman more. "'Twas a duty, for an heir."

That sobered him. His hands stopped on her. "Ilsa . . . if there's a child from this night—"

"Oh!" She blushed. "I doubt it. I was married six years without conceiving."

"Unlikelier things have happened," he said. "And if it did, I would do right by you and the bairn."

Ilsa went still. He was meant for someone else and she knew it. She didn't believe a child would happen, but it touched her that he would promise that. "Would you?" she murmured, thinking that most men in his position wouldn't. They would wait for the wealthy, well-born English bride.

"Of course I would." He kissed her and pulled her close. "Happily, I might add, for it would lead to more of this . . ." His fingers tickled down her ribs, making her twist and laugh again, the moment of dark thoughts fading away.

That was the moment Ilsa realized what was happening to her. His company exhilarated her. His kisses made her burn. His lovemaking made her feel like that hawk, soaring free into the night sky, and for a moment she wished with every fiber in her being that she could be in his bed every night, making love to him every night, and she suspected he wanted the same thing . . .

She was falling in love with him, and it looked to be a very hard fall. One that could leave her broken beyond repair.

"Ilsa." His voice was velvety soft and rough with concern at the same time. He had sensed the change in her even though she hadn't moved. "Don't be frightened."

She wasn't—not of him. Of what he could *do* to her, if she lost her head and gave in to the yearning burning through her veins and muscles—through her very soul. Yes, she was right to be afraid of that.

For once in her life she would be sensible and cautious for her own sake, not because someone else forced it on her. She would remember her promise to Agnes, and why she had made it.

She made herself smile. "Afraid of you! 'Tis you who ought to be frightened of me, the notorious wild widow . . ."

"Stop," he said. "You're not that."

"And here I've just seduced you like one."

He smiled, but it was thoughtful and focused now. "When we return to town—"

"No." She put her hand on his mouth. "I don't want to talk about that. I want only to savor this. Tonight we are free like the hawks and the dolphins, able to go where we choose and frolic as we please. There will be time to talk about thornier subjects later, aye?"

He was quiet for a moment. "You must know I care for you . . ."

"And I care for you!" She managed a carefree smile. "Enough to wonder if you will make love to me once more before we must face the new day, and the long trip back to town."

"Once?" His brow rose. "Twice more at least, I think. 'Tis hours until dawn."

"When will we sleep?" she protested with a small laugh as he rolled over her.

"Sleep?" He nuzzled her neck. "I'm accustomed to guard duty all night. I don't need sleep, particularly not when there's a wild, ravenous beauty in my bed."

"That would be . . . acceptable," she gasped as she felt him, once again hard between her thighs.

He laughed as she curled her legs around his hips. "I'll make you scream that someday: 'Acceptable! God almighty, that was so—bloody—acceptable!'"

She was laughing as he pushed home, but then she stopped and lost herself to him.

And when he murmured later, as she lay exhausted and replete in his arm, that he *did* mean to talk about it later, she didn't argue.

Chapter Sixteen

The next day dawned like the beginning of a glorious new world.

Despite getting very little sleep, Drew was up early, fairly bouncing on his feet as he oversaw preparations for the journey. Ilsa had stayed in his bed until the first pale glimmers of gray lightened the sky, before slipping away with one last lingering kiss.

Three times they had made love, teasing, gently, focused, and hard and fast, that last time, trying to make the most of each stolen second together. She came apart under him with an expression of such rapture, he didn't know how he would ever do without her.

"You're too bloody cheerful this morning," was Duncan's greeting as he came out, still pulling on his coat.

Drew grinned. "Why not? 'Tis a fine day for travel. We should make good time."

"Aye," said Duncan sourly. "And a long day of travel never fails to put a spring in a man's step."

"Did you not sleep well?" asked Drew in exaggerated concern. "You're right peevish this morning."

Duncan gave him a dark glance. "You might

guess why, you daft specter." He paused. "Speaking of ghostly figures, I saw another one, early this morning. Flitted right down the corridor past my door in a flowing white gown."

That made Drew pause. Duncan's room was near his. If people had seen Ilsa leaving his bedroom . . . "I told you the place was haunted," he said bracingly. "Whole regiments of ghosts drifting through, no doubt."

Now his friend was smirking. "Fortunate me to have seen one! She was very fetching, too, and blessedly silent."

The doors opened and his mother walked out, tugging at her gloves and calling over her shoulder to her daughters. Drew lowered his voice. "Aye, fortunate you. I'm sure 'twas a very gentle ghost, and not interesting to anyone else."

Duncan snickered. "For your sake, St. James, I hope she wasn't *entirely* gentle. But no, I'm sure no one else would be interested in the story." He walked off, whistling toward the horses being led out by the grooms.

After that Drew did his best to be cautious, and did not sweep Ilsa into his arms for a morning kiss the way he wanted to do when she finally appeared, looking remarkably fresh and beautiful even though she'd had as little sleep as he had. She came out with Winnie and Bella, carrying a large hatbox whose lid seemed to bounce upward every few seconds, and the three of them were absorbed in conversation. Only as they passed him did she glance up with a tiny, intimate smile that set his mood soaring again.

It was an easy trip back, and they reached Edinburgh before dark the next day. During the ride, Drew endured his friends' complaints about the ghost prank and teasing about his partner in crime with good grace; in truth he barely listened to them as they rode, preferring instead to steal peeks inside the carriage where Ilsa sat, sometimes talking to his sisters, sometimes leaning against the side with her eyes closed, sometimes sending him arch glances that almost caused him to ride into the ditch.

After the serenity of Stormont, the Edinburgh streets felt crowded, full of workmen hurrying to their dinners, carriages taking people to the theater, shops closing up, windows lighting with candles. The smells felt sharper and more noxious the closer they got, reminding everyone why the city was called Auld Reekie. After they crossed the bridge toward High Street, Monteith and Kincaid doffed their hats and called a farewell to the ladies before turning away toward their own lodgings.

Annag came out on the steps when they reached the neat little house off the High Street, fluttering her hands in happy welcome. The ladies climbed down, stretching and exclaiming at the long ride, and Louisa asked Drew to see that the luggage was carried in.

"And then I suppose you'd better escort Mrs. Ramsay home," she said with a perfectly straight face.

Behind him Duncan coughed and wore a wicked grin until Drew thumped him vigorously on the back. "Aye, Mother," he said. "Duncan, take up a trunk and be useful." Conscious of Ilsa's gaze on him, he heaved Bella's trunk onto his shoulder and jogged up the stairs.

When he came back down, his mother was talking to Ilsa. He checked his step, then slowly came near, wondering what they were saying.

"We were delighted to have you, my dear." Louisa clasped Ilsa's hand in hers. "I'm pleased we were able to become better acquainted. I know my children are very fond of you."

Drew stood like a statue, wishing he hadn't approached.

But Ilsa smiled. "Thank you, ma'am. It was entirely my pleasure."

His mother patted her hand and released her. "Perhaps you will dine with us tomorrow evening."

He caught the flicker of surprise in her face before Ilsa smiled again, wider this time, and accepted.

When his mother turned away, he told her he and Duncan would see Agnes and Ilsa back to her home. Then he lowered his voice, as he bent down to collect Agnes's trunk. "Do you remember what you asked me, that day you took tea in the study?"

His mother looked startled. "Yes, I think so . . ."

Drew glanced at Ilsa. She wore a short pink jacket over her dark blue dress, and the new hat—a straw bonnet with white flowers and a bright red ribbon. As he watched she laughed at something Agnes said, and an answering smile bloomed unconsciously on his own face. "The answer is yes," he murmured to his mother, and walked on, calling for Duncan to bring the other baggage.

"We could hail a porter," said Agnes as they walked, Duncan behind him and the ladies bringing up the rear.

"No need," Drew told her. "Unless it's too much for Duncan?"

His friend growled something rude under his breath.

"'Tis very kind of you, gentlemen," said Ilsa.

And just the sound of the warm appreciation in her voice made him feel taller, stronger, and able to carry this trunk another mile straight up the hill.

Mam, I think I'm already in love with her.

At her door the butler let them in. The pony came trotting out to receive a flurry of affection from both Ilsa and Agnes, and graciously let Drew scratch his nose. Ilsa invited them to come up to the drawing room, and Drew went without waiting for Duncan's response.

Ilsa led the way but paused in the doorway. Her shoulders fell slightly, and then she took a breath and walked in.

Drew realized why when he followed. The walls and ceiling had been repainted a muted green, no more hints of Calton Hill. New draperies hung in front of the tall windows, closed against the twilight. The stern and forbidding painting still hung opposite the hearth.

Ilsa said nothing. Agnes was not so restrained. "Oh no," she exclaimed, halting just inside the room.

"Respectable and elegant once more," said Ilsa with a forced smile.

"Indeed it is!" said Miss Fletcher from the doorway, a complacent smile on her face. "The new drapes are much lighter, as you wished."

Ilsa touched the heavy cream fabric. "Yes. Much lighter."

Her aunt went to embrace her. "I am so glad you approve. I wanted to surprise you."

"You did," Ilsa murmured. "Aunt, I hope you

remember Captain St. James. Allow me to present Mr. Felix Duncan, who accompanied us to Stormont Palace. Mr. Duncan, my aunt, Miss Fletcher."

"*Enchanté,* madam." Mr. Duncan swept a grand bow, and Miss Fletcher bobbed a curtsy, her face alive with interest.

"You are both welcome, Captain, Mr. Duncan. I trust you had a good journey?"

"Yes, ma'am." Drew bowed in turn. "Very fine weather for travel."

"And now you must all be hungry." Miss Fletcher rang the bell. "I shall send for a light supper—"

"That is most kind, Miss Fletcher," put in Drew, "but you mustn't trouble yourself. Mr. Duncan and I shall stop at a tavern." He glanced at his sister. "Perhaps you and Mrs. Ramsay would like to accompany us, Agnes. It would be unkind to put out the housekeeper, feeding so many on short notice."

Ilsa's face brightened. Agnes gave him an incredulous look. "I—I suppose, if Mrs. Ramsay wishes to . . ."

"Of course." Ilsa smiled directly at Drew, as if she knew exactly where he meant to take them. "I would be delighted."

He and Duncan made idle conversation with Miss Fletcher while the ladies went to change their clothes. Ilsa's aunt kept casting him contemplative glances, but said nothing exceptional. Still, Drew was relieved when his sister and Ilsa returned.

"Where are we going?" demanded Agnes as soon as they were outside.

"I've longed for a plate of oysters since we left town," said Drew without looking at Ilsa. "What say you, Agnes?"

His sister looked like she couldn't believe her ears. "I—I may go to an oyster cellar?"

"Is that a good idea?" blurted Duncan, which earned him a poisonous glare from Agnes.

"As your brother and guardian, I see nothing wrong with it, and I shall be there to provide any assistance necessary. Don't you wish to come?"

For a moment Drew thought his sister might embrace him in the public street. "Yes!"

They went to Hunter's tavern again, finding a place at a long table in the cellar. Drew ordered punch for the ladies, porter for him and Duncan, and oysters and other food for everyone.

Agnes, sitting beside him, gazed around with wide eyes. "Mama won't be pleased you brought me here," she told him in a low but happy tone.

"She won't say anything about it."

She looked at him in disbelief. "She won't mind *you* being here!"

"Then she can't mind you being here with me," he returned. "I'm a proper chaperone, ain't I?"

"No!"

He shrugged and gave her a wink. "Just don't cause a scandal, and all will be well. Everyone deserves a bit of fun now and then, aye?"

Reluctantly she smiled. "Yes. Thank you, Drew."

He pretended to choke on his porter. "God bless me! A kind word from Agnes St. James! Glory be . . ."

She was still laughing at him when the food arrived, deposited by fast-moving servants with large trays, swooping in to slide platters across the table and then spin away into the crowded room. Everyone ate with relish, until—as Drew had expected—

someone pushed aside a table and a man with a fiddle leapt atop it.

This time there was no mistaking it: he danced with Ilsa. Other women took his hands and he swung them around, but his eyes stayed on her.

And when the night was over, it was Ilsa to whom he offered his arm for the walk home, leaving Duncan to make the most of Agnes's good temper. He had never felt such—such *lightness,* as if everything were right in the world and he was equal to any challenge. They parted on her doorstep with a kiss on her hand and a husky "Good night" from her that made him wish he didn't have to go home with Duncan.

"You're in a pathetic state," Duncan remarked as they strolled toward Burnet's Close. "Pretending you wanted to give your sister a night out and bribing us with oysters, all for the sake of getting Ilsa Ramsay to dance with you."

Drew grinned. "Envy, is what that is. What did you do to make my sister hate you, by the by?"

Duncan cursed him the rest of the way home, and Drew enjoyed it immensely.

ILSA FAIRLY FLOATED down the stairs to breakfast the next morning. She had slept extremely well, blissfully tired from her last few days of making love to Drew and dancing with him. *If this is ruin, I shall never be respectable again,* she thought as she went into the dining room to find her aunt poring over the latest gossip sheets. "Good morning," she all but sang.

Jean looked up, her lips tight. "Did you know this?"

And thus ended the happiest fortnight of her life, with a breathless account splashed across the front page of the *Edinburgh Tattler* of Captain Andrew St. James, future Duke of Carlyle, roving through town unrecognized and unnoticed. The author of the piece mused at some length on his intentions and plans, as well as how very eligible this young, handsome, and single heir must be considered.

"Oh," she said quietly. "Yes, I did know."

Jean's face grew dark with disapproval. "My dear! Why didn't you tell me? I must speak to your father at once."

"What?" Ilsa demanded, shocked. "Papa? Why?"

Jean held up one hand and Ilsa fell silent out of long habit. "He's been very suspicious about this man who's been chasing after you, even before you went on holiday with him—"

"With his *sisters*," Ilsa protested. "Who have been my friends for many months!"

Her aunt ignored her. "When did you learn of his expectation? How could you not tell me?"

"The family asked me not to."

That made Jean turn deep purple. "And your loyalty is to them over your own family?"

Ilsa began breathing deeply. This was degenerating into one of their confrontations of old, where Jean scolded her for an hour and then sent her to her room.

She was not a child any longer, though. This was her house now, where she was undisputed mistress, and she had promised herself that she would never sit and suffer an underserved rebuke again.

"I chose my own conscience," she said, clearly

and deliberately. "I was asked to keep a confidence, and I did."

Jean did not like that. "This is the thanks I'm to have—"

Ilsa glanced up with fire in her eyes. "I do not owe you their secrets! I am not sorry, Aunt, and I will not apologize." Her aunt's mouth formed a tight line, an expression Ilsa knew too well. "When you came to stay with me, we made an agreement."

Jean gasped. "Are you accusing me of breaking it?"

"You know you are." Ilsa kept her gaze cool and steady. "I am not a child. I do not need to be managed. You do not have the right to know everything about me. You promised not to pry, not to nag, and not to undermine me."

"I never—!"

"The drawing room was painted while I was away, without my permission."

Jean shot to her feet. "Instead you would shame me before all my friends who come to call, painting the sky on the ceiling like some sort of sybarite! Your father would be cruelly disappointed in you, lass."

Ilsa was fighting back tears, half fury, half guilt. Jean had always been able to do this to her. "Perhaps our arrangement is no longer satisfactory. Perhaps you would be happier with Papa."

The color fled Jean's face. "You've grown so headstrong. I can't imagine what your mother would think but 'tis glad I am she's not here to see it." Chin high, she marched from the room.

Ilsa sat, vibrating with tension. Abruptly she jumped up from the table and rushed out of the house, barely waiting for Robert.

She was still shaking when they reached Calton Hill, Robert trotting to keep up with her. Headstrong! Sybarite! As if she were a wicked child. As if she weren't entitled to some privacy and independence. As if a painted ceiling was decadent and sinful. She was a grown woman, and her aunt had promised to respect her wishes. She paused, breathing hard, and Robert snuffled gently at the edge of her sleeve. "How could she?" she burst out to the empty field.

Robert gave her a sympathetic look before heading off to crop the tall grass.

"Have I not been clear to her?" she demanded. "Can she just not help herself?"

Robert shook his head with a jangle of his halter, and Ilsa sank down into the grass beside him. "I know," she said quietly, squinting up at the peak of the hill, the sun rising behind it. "She still sees me as a child in need of discipline. Not as a grown woman, capable of choosing her own friends, deciding where she goes, managing her own money, painting her own drawing room . . ."

And taking her own lover.

Jean would be horrified if she knew Ilsa had kissed Drew, played pranks, ridden astride, and spent the night in bed with Drew. Proper ladies, she would say, treat their reputations as if they were made of cut glass: delicate, valuable, and impossible to repair if damaged. That was certainly how Jean tried to live, never one toe out of line.

Ilsa didn't aim to thumb her nose at propriety—indeed, she didn't think she did, much. Skipping church for golf wasn't well done, perhaps, but it happened only once. Jean's notions of propriety, though, were twenty years old; she thought everything Ilsa enjoyed was a ghastly affront to decency, from walking alone on the hill to not finding another husband the moment her mourning for Malcolm was over.

"She's old-fashioned." She plucked at the grass. "And strong-willed. I knew it, and still I let her live with me. 'Tis my own fault, aye?"

Robert gave a low whinny and nibbled at her hair. She swatted him away with a reluctant smile.

And now everyone knew Drew would be a duke. Everyone would be watching him, and with whom he interacted. If they were seen in company before he left for England, people would whisper that he'd thrown her over—that he might bed a woman like her, but never marry her. Malcolm's friends had never accepted her, a tradesman's daughter, even before the nightmare of the trial. This would only stir up those whispers again.

She'd known she wasn't going to be a duchess, but she'd thought her affair with Drew might last until he left. Now she would have to give up his company entirely, for his sake and hers.

She was still sitting there, unready to return home, when something made her look up. Drew stood some fifty yards away, watching her. He looked so familiar and dear, so much *not* like a duke, that a lump sprang into her throat. For a long moment they simply gazed at each other, and Ilsa was suddenly gripped by the strangling fear that he would turn and walk away—that this was farewell, that the distance between them wasn't mere rocks and heather but something far less passable.

Then he started toward her, and her lungs worked

again. "Good morning," she murmured when he reached her.

"Good morning." He held out a hand and helped her to her feet. Robert trotted over eagerly, and Drew fed him a piece of carrot without looking away from Ilsa.

She wet her lips. "I expect you saw the papers."

"Aye." He sighed. "It wasn't meant to be a state secret, but I didn't wish for it to be the talk of the town."

"I told no one," she said quickly.

He nodded. "Thank you. My family didn't, and my mates think it'll turn out to be a lie in the end, so they didn't trouble themselves to tell."

"Mr. MacGill knew," she said quietly.

A frown touched his brow. "Would he announce it?"

She lifted one hand. "In my experience he delights in being seen in the orbit of important and powerful people."

"Ah. Well, it cannot be undone, so it hardly matters who did it." He seemed to shrug it off. "I'm glad to find you out here."

Her heart fluttered. "Oh?"

"I hoped we might have a chance to talk."

Ilsa took a deep breath. "Of course. I shall go first." He looked startled but gave a nod. "I want to assure you that I expect nothing from you," she said. "I have known for some time that you have . . . obligations that will require you to leave Edinburgh and settle in England. I know it is your duty to find a wife who can stand by your side and support you in your future role." She paused, not looking at him. "Someone who will know intimately, and be accepted by, the society you are to join, who will be able to guide your sisters in their new lives as sisters of a duke, and help them make respectable, proper marriages. Marriage is the currency of the aristocracy. It is no secret that your own marriage will be of signal importance, and while some women might have schemed to take advantage of our—our attraction, please believe I have not."

There. She was pleased with how reasonable that sounded. Only one betraying little quaver on the words *our attraction*—as if they shared nothing but a passing flirtation.

It was so much more than that to her. But she knew what had to be done, and she'd done it.

"I see," he said gravely. "Attraction."

Ilsa flushed at the way he growled the word. "Did I misspeak?"

"No," he said after a moment. "'Tis merely a mild word for it, in my opinion."

She tried to ignore the rush of pleasure that gave her. "No matter how strong, there are many factors that overrule it."

"Indeed." He folded his arms and gazed across the rocky slope toward town. "Did you enjoy yourself last night at the tavern with me?"

Ilsa blinked. "Yes."

He nodded. "Were you glad to see me this morning?"

"Yes."

"Are you sorry you spent the night in my bed at Stormont?"

"No!" She blushed at the quick glance he shot her way.

"Are you frightened of what people will say if you are seen with me?"

She stiffened. She didn't look forward to the whispers, but she wasn't *frightened*. "Of course not."

"Are you firmly resolved never to marry again?"

"I—" She bit her lip, suddenly unsure. Resolved? "No . . ."

He gave a firm nod. "So, if I have the right of it, you enjoy my company—in bed and out of it—aren't put off by salacious gossip, and haven't renounced all thought of marriage."

"You're not going to marry me!"

"Well," he said sadly, "not if you'll never have me."

Without thinking she poked his shoulder because he was threatening to make her laugh again when she *had* resolved to be very detached and assure him she was a worldly, modern widow able to have an affair without losing her head, not someone scheming to be a duchess. Quick as a blink he caught her hand.

"Ilsa." He brought her hand to his lips, then pressed her knuckles against his cheek. "Stop thinking of Carlyle. His Grace might live another thirty years, and I'll remain just as I am now—a simple Scot wanting a wife to love and cherish, and perhaps a child or two for my mother to dote upon."

"People will expect things of you," she began.

He watched her, running his thumb over the back of her hand in absentminded affection. It made her want to lean against him and let him drape that arm around her. "People," he said with mild disdain. "I've no duty to obey the wishes of a fickle mob of *people*. Surely you're not so cowed by them?"

She stood in silent indecision. Yes, she did like being with him—beyond any other person she could think of. Yes, she had seduced him because she wanted him—rather madly, and the feeling had not abated after a single night in his bed. Yes, she thought she could fall in love with him—might even already be in love with him.

And no, she hadn't set her mind against marriage. She had no interest in Mr. Grant or any of the other gentlemen Papa kept prodding her toward, but she couldn't say the same about Drew. She kept telling herself they weren't meant to be together, but every minute they spent together made her wish they were.

Her heart thumped loudly in her ears. If he wanted to court her, could she turn him away? No, she didn't think she could.

So what was stopping her? The gossips had done their worst a year ago, and she had survived. It was hard to tell herself she and Drew had no future when he was standing in front of her, because anything seemed possible when he was near her.

Perhaps there wasn't anything to lose by risking it.

"Well," she asked, her heart racing, "what precisely *are* you asking?"

His lips curled in a slow, devastating smile. "Nothing more than to spend time with you."

"Where?"

"Anywhere. The Assembly Rooms. One of Edinburgh's fine coffeehouses." His brows arched suggestively. "Perhaps an oyster cellar now and then."

She smiled. "It won't be like at Stormont Palace."

"Sadly no," he agreed, looking wicked now. "I vow it would frighten Duncan fair out of his skin if you slipped into his lodgings like a ghost." She bit back a laugh. He sobered. "My mother hopes that you will be able to keep our engagement for dinner this evening. I also hope you will come."

That made her breath catch. This was sounding very much like courtship. "Yes, of course I will . . ."

"Excellent." He glanced around, then lowered his voice. "If there weren't some people impinging on our hill, I would kiss you. In the interest of propriety . . ." He offered his arm. "May I escort you home, my dear one?"

With a warm flush of happiness welling within her, she accepted his offer and his arm.

Dinner was wonderful. Bella and Winnie had won over their mother about Cyrus the kitten, even when he tried to climb the tablecloth during the dessert course. Agnes was in excellent spirits and whispered that Drew had told their mother about their visit to the oyster cellar, and Louisa had only cast her eyes heavenward and sighed. Mrs. St. James welcomed Ilsa warmly, and made a point of conversing with her at length, something Ilsa could never have imagined a month ago.

It was so amazing, she couldn't help but mention it to Agnes after Drew had escorted them home. Her friend gave her a gleaming look. "You know why, don't you? She sees how Drew looks at you."

Ilsa's mind jumped to that last night at Stormont Palace; someone had seen something. She could only stare, mouth agape.

Agnes nodded. "Mama's no fool. She didn't *dislike* you before, but now she most certainly wants to like you."

"Oh—" Ilsa flushed with anxious happiness. "I do hope she can—"

"Would you accept him?" Agnes prodded.

"Hush! There's been no question asked to accept."

Her friend laughed. "But if he *were* to ask, would you consider it?" She clasped Ilsa's hand. "Selfishly, I hope so. You must know Winnie, Bella, and I would adore having you as our sister."

Ilsa had no memory of her mother. She had never had a sister, and Malcolm had been the only surviving child of his parents, as well. She had not thought of the fact that marriage to Drew—and it still felt dangerous even to think those words, as if they tempted Fate to spite her again—would give her a new family, with beloved sisters and a caring mother, a family who teased and laughed and annoyed and *loved* each other. Again she could only stare at Agnes, dazed.

It ran round and round inside her head as Maeve brushed her hair before bed that night. It was too good to be real, she told herself, but as she lay in her bed and closed her eyes, she dreamt of Drew tangled in the sheets beside her, looking at her with heat in his eyes and a wicked smile on his gorgeous mouth.

In the morning she came down early to breakfast, the image lingering in her mind and somehow becoming more possible with every passing hour. She drank her tea and gazed out the window, daydreaming of what might be, if it were real.

It lasted until just before the clock struck nine, when Winnie hammered on the door of her house and burst into the room, hat askew and cloak barely tied.

"Winnie," cried Agnes, leaping out of her seat. "What's wrong?"

"The shop," gasped Winnie, gulping for breath. "The shop has been robbed!"

Chapter Seventeen

Lord Adam St. James, youngest son of the third Duke of Carlyle, had been a charmer. Drew dimly remembered his grandfather as an old man, sitting by the hearth with a mug in one hand and a blue silk cap on his head, telling some amusing story of his years spent perambulating Europe, skipping out of the way of wars and blockades before settling down. Despite the terrible falling-out with his elder brother that resulted in his banishment from Carlyle Castle, Lord Adam had had a handsome income from his mother's dowry funds, enabling him to live like a gentleman all his days. Upon his death, though, the income ceased, and Drew's father, George, had used his inheritance to purchase a silk shop, confident that it would keep his family in style.

For several years it did. Not luxurious style, but affluent enough for Drew to attend school with the sons of gentlemen and wealthy merchants. Louisa taught the girls music and embroidery. The St. Jameses had not been wealthy but they had been genteel.

When George died, the summer Drew was seventeen and eager to enter university, that illusion was blown away. George, it turned out, had had a gentleman's head for business, which was to say, no head at all. He had let accounts go unpaid. He was in debt to his suppliers. The ledgers were a disaster. There was a mortgage no one had known about that must be paid.

Louisa had had to rouse herself from grief and begin to manage the shop. Drew had learned how to negotiate payments and argue with lawyers. The girls, still children, had all been put to work, sweeping threads and lint, stitching samples for the display cases. When all that had still not been enough to pay their bills, Drew had taken the king's shilling and joined the army, desperate for any income to support his family.

The shop, though, had pulled through. Thanks to Louisa's fierce efforts, it had come back to modest prosperity, providing a steady income, and thus a decent home and enough to eat.

This morning the once-neat little shop was a mess. Drew surveyed the damage in grim silence. All the drawers had been opened—a few forced, breaking the latches—and their contents scattered across the floor. The iron money box had been safe with Mr. Battie, who kept the accounts, but the stock had been pillaged. One bolt of red silk had been sliced into ribbons and strewn around the salon like a bloody sacrifice, an act of wanton destruction that made Louisa turn pale and collapse into a chair. Other bolts had been thrown on the floor and trod upon, and dozens of rolls of expensive silk were missing. It was hard to know for certain how many until the inventory could be tallied, but the cabinet where the finest bolts were usually stored under lock and key was nearly empty.

"Who could do this?" murmured Louisa into the stark silence, her hand at her lips.

A fool, thought Drew. Robberies had been plaguing Edinburgh for several months now. The other victims had been the usual sort of places robbed—a jeweler, a goldsmith, a bank. There was already a reward on offer for the capture of the thieves, and Drew, to his bitter regret, had not paid much attention to the crime wave. What could his family's small shop have to tempt a thief, when there were far more affluent shops all around?

"And what if we had been here?" Louisa went on, her voice rising. "What might those villains have done to me, or to your sisters?" She waved one hand at the slashed scarlet silk.

"All the robberies have been at night when no one is in the shops." Drew sighed, rubbing his brow. "'Tis a pity Mr. Battie didn't hear anything."

The bookkeeper lived in the rooms upstairs. He had discovered the damage when his charwoman arrived early in the morning and let out a wail. Mr. Battie had sent a boy running to tell them and then gone to the sheriff-clerk as soon as Drew and his mother arrived.

"'Tis a great relief he did not," countered his mother. "He might have come downstairs and been murdered!"

Drew doubted the man was that foolish, or the thieves that deadly. A bolt of silk could not fight back. He stepped over to the door to examine the lock. For all the tumult inside, the outside of the shop looked as it always did. The front door had been closed and the back door leading into the alley was still barred from the inside. Only a few scratches on the lock plate indicated any trespass.

"They got in easily." He looked at his mother. "Is this lock sound?"

She flushed angrily. "Sound and stout enough these past five years, Andrew! It was repaired only a few months ago!"

He held up his hands. "Aye, aye!"

A sheriff-officer arrived then with Mr. Battie, but there was little they could tell him. He assured them a report would be filed and their losses recorded, but beyond that he could only offer his sympathy. He left with a suggestion that they call upon the procurator-fiscal and offer another reward.

Louisa picked up a broom and began attacking the mess, her face set and her eyes flashing. "Sympathy! I suppose that's all he offered Mr. Wemyss the goldsmith, too!"

"What can he do, Mother? If they knew who the thieves were, they would make an arrest." Hands on hips, Drew paced through the shattered salon, searching for anything that might betray the intruders.

"Unconscionable!" Louisa muttered, whisking furiously at the piles of unraveled thread.

Drew said nothing. This invasion infuriated him, too, and part of him wanted to stalk Edinburgh every night, catch the villains and throttle them before dragging their hides to the Tolbooth jail.

The other half of him . . . He had been delicately trying to persuade his mother to sell the shop and come with him to England. Was this not the perfect motivation? *Leave all this behind,* he could urge. *Come to Carlyle, and it will be as it was at Stormont Palace . . .*

Winnie burst in, Agnes hard on her heels. "What happened?" Agnes cried.

Drew explained as their mother angrily swept, offering only a curt word now and then. Winnie, wide-eyed and quiet, hurried to help their mother while Agnes paced, her arms folded.

"This has gone too far," she announced. "This thieving!"

"Aye," replied Drew with forced patience. "Do you know who's behind it? The sheriff-clerk would be well pleased to hear a name."

She glared at him.

"Put it up for sale," said Drew abruptly. "Don't bother cleaning, walk away and be done with it all."

Louisa stopped what she was doing to stare, Winnie made a startled sound, and Agnes exhaled in obvious fury. "That's your response? Just sell Papa's shop and run off to England?"

"It's not been Papa's shop for a dozen years. It's Mother's shop."

"Don't," cried Agnes. "This is *our* shop!"

Louisa's face was red. "I cannot decide that now, Andrew!"

"Why not now?" he exclaimed. "What better time to be rid of it and all the worry it entails?"

"It's *ours,*" said Agnes with a furious wail. "Not *yours*! Nothing will ever again be *ours* if we all leave and go with you!"

He stared in amazement. "What are you going on about?"

"Everything!"

With a slam, the front door flew open and struck the wall, and Felix Duncan surged into the room, his face set in battle lines. "What the bloody blazes happened?" His gaze flew to Agnes. "Are you hurt?" he demanded.

With a cry she ran to him. Felix caught her as if he'd come explicitly to do just that, gathering her close and lifting her off her feet. And Agnes's arms were around him, her face buried in his neck.

Drew's jaw almost hit the floor. Louisa's broom clattered as it fell. Winnie broke into an astonished but beaming smile.

After a long moment Duncan set Agnes back on her feet. He tipped up her face to his and murmured something, and she nodded, keeping her back to her family. Flushed, Duncan turned to Drew. "What the hell happened here?"

"We were robbed. What just happened *here*?" Drew jerked his head toward Agnes, who whirled and glared at him.

Duncan cleared his throat. "Was anything taken?"

"If nothing was taken, I wouldn't call it a robbery, aye?"

"Stop," exclaimed Louisa sternly. "Take your arguing into the street. Agnes, run upstairs and find the master inventory book. Bella's been up there searching for an age. Winifred, find another broom and help me. This won't clear itself. Andrew." She pinned him with a fierce look. "I'll not walk away from this shop. Turn the sign in the window. We're not open today."

He and Duncan stepped into the street, still quiet at this hour, and closed the door behind them. "A simple robbery?" asked Duncan, his eyes flitting up and down the short expanse of Shakespeare Square. "Same as all the others?"

"It appears so."

"The cadies saw nothing?" Duncan pressed, referring to the City Guard who patrolled at night.

"The sheriff will be asking them, but one presumes not, or they would have raised the alarm."

"Have you any idea what the loss is?"

"At least twenty bolts ruined or missing. Mother guessed four hundred pounds, but she'll need the inventory book to know for certain."

His friend nodded. "Thank God no one was hurt."

"How many burglaries is this?" Drew had been trying to count, cursing his earlier lack of attention.

"Too many," said Duncan. "Other victims have offered rewards, with no result."

"How much?"

"Ten guineas, in one case. Some of the stolen goods have been returned or discovered in the streets or along the road to Leith. I wonder who the devil takes the trouble to rob a shop, then scatters the take around the city."

"Strange, indeed." Drew glanced at the undamaged door. "And how is it," he murmured, "that no one's seen anything or heard anything? They must not be long at their work. Look—this lock was opened as easily as if the villains had a key."

Duncan stooped to study it. "A picklock?"

"Something like that." Drew pictured the bolts of silk. "If there's more than one thief . . ."

"To carry off twenty bolts of cloth, there must be," said Duncan. "Someone would notice a cart waiting in the street."

"Precisely." He fell silent, thinking. When they'd been children and misbehaved, his father had told them confession and penitence would excuse them from serious punishment. He'd said it was more important to him that his children could admit their mistakes and try to set things right than that they take a whipping. Drew had escaped multiple thrashings by prompt confession, even though he'd been punished in other ways. The philosophy had served him fairly well ever since, too . . .

"What are you going to do?"

With a wrench Drew pulled his thoughts back to the conversation at hand. "I told Mother not to mind it too much. Seems a perfect moment for her to sell the shop and come with me to Carlyle, eh? She and the girls."

The other man's throat worked. "I didn't think you meant to make them go . . ."

"*Make* them!" Drew scoffed. "As if I could *make* them do anything! I *invited* them, to provide a better situation for my family after all these many years of being away and leaving Mother and the girls to manage on their own. But if the shop is gone, or failing, that's certainly less reason for any of them to stay."

Duncan said nothing.

"Have you got anything to say about Agnes?" prompted Drew. "Or should I assume you've apologized for whatever idiocy you committed that roused her fury?"

Color crept up his friend's broad cheekbones. "'Tis not your concern."

"No," Drew agreed. "'Tis Agnes's, and she's already told me I may not thrash you for it, more's the pity. But I would still like to know." He stepped into the street and headed toward the sheriff-clerk's offices.

"May not! *Could* not," retorted Duncan, keeping pace with him.

"I've seen you fence and box," Drew replied. "She's saving you, idiot."

Duncan tried to smother his laugh with a cough. "Aye, tell yourself all the lies you want." He motioned at the shop. "What will you do?"

Drew hesitated. "I have one idea, rather audacious. Tell me what you think of it . . ." And they put their heads together and discussed it all the way back toward Castle Hill.

IT TURNED OUT that the St. James shop was not the only one to have been robbed recently. Nearly every night while they were at Stormont Palace had seen another robbery; every morning another shopkeeper had discovered his or her premises in tumult, and every day the Highland guardsmen who walked the streets after dark could not account for it. The thieves seemed to have an uncanny sense for avoiding being seen, and in consequence a new level of fear and apprehension gripped the city.

Unfortunately, Ilsa's main source of information was a steady parade of Jean's friends, dour matrons and stern dowagers trooping through their drawing room to discuss the latest rumors about the thieves over tea and cake. Jean professed herself terrified and alarmed, but had an insatiable appetite for gossip about robberies, the more alarming the better. To escape, Ilsa spent more time than ever wandering the fields around Calton Hill with Robert, even if she felt unaccountably lonely doing so now and had to endure renewed argument from her aunt about it.

There were no more invitations to dine or take tea with the St. Jameses; they were occupied restoring their shop. She saw nothing of Drew and had only brief greetings from Bella and Winnie. Agnes spent most of her time with her family now, with Felix Duncan escorting her back and forth from the shop or her home most days.

"My mother is in a fine fury," she told Ilsa. "The thieves took the finest bolts of silk, some already promised and paid for. Now Mother is out the cost of the silk and must refund the customers' payments. It's mortifying to her, having to tell her customers that she cannot deliver their orders because we were robbed."

"But that's not her fault," Ilsa protested.

"Of course not. But one lady suggested, rather tartly, that Mother ought to have replaced the lock and door when this trouble began." Agnes rolled her eyes and threw up her hands. "It doesn't make sense, but everyone is on edge! I cannot believe no one has caught these villains. It's been months."

"Perhaps the reward offer will turn up something." Ilsa didn't have much confidence, though. The rewards hadn't accomplished anything so far.

"Drew says he spoke to the procurator-fiscal and proposed a new reward." Here Agnes grew grim again. "Of course, he also suggested Mama sell the shop and go with him to England. And perhaps now he's right, curse it, but I—I—" She stopped, biting her lip.

Ilsa didn't want to talk about that, either. A few days ago Drew had said the duke might live another thirty years and he would remain just a Scot, with no pressing need to leave Edinburgh. It was a hard jolt to hear that now he was urging his mother to sell so they could leave town immediately.

"I am certain that if you don't wish to go, you could find a way to remain here," she murmured.

Agnes pretended she didn't hear. Ilsa had been openly fishing for information for several days, since Mr. Duncan seemed to have nothing else to do but squire Agnes about town, and Agnes—for a change—seemed quite happy for him to do it, but her friend had grown more close-lipped than ever about him. Weeks ago she would have spent hours musing or ranting about the man, and now she said not a word. Ilsa felt . . . shut out.

"I think I should be at home now." Agnes flushed, not meeting Ilsa's gaze. "My mother is beset by worries and indignation over the shop, and I ought to be there to help her."

"Oh," faltered Ilsa. She had not foreseen that. "Bella—and Winnie—"

"They are no real help, and both imagine thieves around every corner. I believe Winnie would be ecstatic if our own home were broken into—the excitement! The drama! The danger! She asked Drew to leave his sword with her, which thankfully he refused to do." Agnes's eyes flashed. "Besides, I'm the eldest, and Mama relies on me more."

Ilsa did not point out that Agnes was the eldest daughter, not the eldest child. "Of course you must do as you think best," she said, making herself smile.

Agnes sighed with gratitude. "I knew you would understand! Drew said—" She stopped, coloring. "I hate to leave you alone, but of course you're not. Your aunt is here, and you have Robert and all the servants."

Only Robert provided real companionship, and he was a pony. Ilsa's smile grew wistful. "Of course. Your family needs you, and I shall be fine."

Agnes embraced her and went to pack her things. Ilsa sat in lonely silence for a moment, contemplating the new order.

She had sent a note to Mrs. St. James the day after the robbery, expressing her shock and outrage and offering any assistance she might make. The reply had been gracious and kind, thanking her for the generous offer but nothing more.

Ilsa hadn't expected much else, but since then it felt as if she had been slowly but inexorably edged out of the circle again, as before the visit to Stormont. Too late she realized she had latched on to that warmth and welcome far too quickly, seizing on their kindness and obviously making more of it than they intended.

More than *any* of them intended, perhaps. Despite what he said on the hill, she hadn't caught so much as a glimpse of Drew since the robbery. She burned to ask Agnes about him—to *know* about him, even if he were too busy to see her—but did not dare. Surely if he wished to see her, he could find time. Just a few days ago he had asked to spend time with her. It was how she had told herself things would end, but it still caused a sharp ache in her chest.

Aunt Jean came in and clucked in disapproval. "Mrs. Crawley is coming to call. You really must put on your cap, it isn't proper."

Mrs. Crawley was one of Jean's friends, though Ilsa couldn't see why. She had been widowed young and seemed to have been steeping in sanctimonious bitterness ever since. No one in Edinburgh took more pleasure in the misdeeds and misfortunes of others. Jean claimed she merely had high standards—implying that Ilsa did not—but Ilsa thought she was a raven, living off the corpses on the gallows.

She shot to her feet. "You must make my excuses, Aunt. I was just going . . ." Her mind emptied; where? "To visit Papa," she blurted. She'd not seen him since returning to town, and strangely he had neither come to call nor sent a note.

Jean frowned. "Alone? Of course not. Get Mr. MacLeod—"

"No," she said firmly. "I shall walk down High Street in broad daylight as I've always done."

Her aunt's face darkened. "My dear, you cannot—"

"I'll be home by dinner," she said, and fled.

Papa was not in the workshop. That was unusual. Mr. Henderson, the foreman, told her Papa hadn't been into the shop for days. Ilsa thanked him and left, holding her head high despite Liam Hewitt's insolent scrutiny.

But the servant at Papa's house in Forsyth Close let her in with a warm greeting, betraying no sign of worry, and directed her to the parlor. "Is aught wrong, Papa?" she asked as she went in.

"Eh?" He jerked away from the desk where he was hunched over, writing. "Ilsa! What are you doing here?"

She stopped, surprised by his belligerent tone. "I came to see you."

He closed his eyes, exhaled, and rose. His back to her, he closed the top of his desk, and when he turned around his usual, genial smile was back in place. "And glad I am of it, too! You startled me, is all."

She returned his embrace, still puzzled. "Is aught wrong?" she asked again, this time in real concern.

"Nay!" He waved one hand.

"You're at home, and not in the shop," she pointed out. "That's not like you."

He made an exaggerated grimace and thumped himself on the chest. "A touch of catarrh. The leech told me to stay home and rest."

"Oh." She blinked. Papa wasn't often laid low by illness. "You sound fine now, so it must be working."

He winked. "I'm fit as a fiddle, lass, and twice as handsome!" He led her to the sofa. "Tell me the news with you. You've just returned from Perth, aye?"

"A few days ago." Ilsa couldn't put her finger on it, but something about Papa was off. "I told you you wouldn't even notice I was away."

He scowled. "Don't say that! Of course I noticed. I've been ill, child. Have some compassion."

She laughed reluctantly. He meant a flurry of sympathy and attention. "You just said you're fit as a fiddle! I'm glad you didn't pine away for me."

Her father patted her hand. "It's not manly to pine. I missed you, aye, but I had things to tend to."

"A love affair gone sour?" she murmured with a teasing look.

"My love affairs are not your concern, and they do not go sour. I'm a gentleman, lass." He coughed, a little too dramatically. "I've had much suffering to endure, alone and unloved."

"You might have sent for Jean, if you were lonely and unwell."

Instead of laughing or rolling his eyes, he stiffened. "No reason to trouble her."

Ilsa regarded him in worry. This was not like Papa. "Something *is* bothering you. Is it the shop?" Normally his cabinetry business was quite busy.

"The shop is fine."

She bit her lip. "You've not been wagering again, have you?"

When Malcolm died, Ilsa had found gaming debts in her husband's papers. Malcolm had been a regular at the card tables; she recognized those markers, but he'd never been one for cockfighting. When Ilsa confronted her father, he admitted that he'd gone to Malcolm a few times for help covering lost wagers—only in rare moments when he was short of ready funds, he explained, and he swore he'd repaid Malcolm every farthing. After a furious argument, he'd promised to stop going to the pit behind the Fleshmarket, and every time since when she'd asked, he swore that he'd kept his word.

This time, though, Papa's mouth compressed. "Nay. Don't fret yourself."

She was not reassured. "What, then? It's—it's this spate of robberies, isn't it?"

It was a reasonable question. Not only had it consumed her and Jean, everyone in town was talking about the thieves. Papa owned a prosperous shop, full of valuable tools and with a healthy income. It was only natural he would worry about being robbed, and all the more so if he were ill and unable to watch over it.

But to her astonishment her father erupted off the sofa. "'Tis not your concern, Ilsa," he exclaimed in a temper. "Stop nattering at me!"

For a moment the words hung in the air, stinging and acrid. Ilsa went very still, as startled and cowed by his sudden fury as she had been as a child.

"All right," she whispered after a moment, when his fierce glare did not abate. "I only worried about you, Papa . . ."

He gripped his wig. "Ah, lass, you don't need to. Don't fash yourself over me, I'll come about."

"Are you in trouble?" she asked hesitantly.

He gave a bark of laughter, almost like his usual self. "Always some little intrigue or another! It keeps a man on his toes." He winked again but looked tired. "Perhaps I've been more unwell than I realized. I'm sorry, child. I'm not myself today."

"Perhaps I could help—"

He waved his hand. "Nay! You're not to trouble yourself over me." He hesitated, his face falling in heavy lines. "Well, I'll tell you. I was called to sit as juror recently on a charge of murder. It's been a weight on my mind, deciding a man's fate, and no doubt accounts for my melancholy today." Papa roused himself with a forced smile. "Enough of my troubles. You should be thinking about handsome young men, and which of them might be worthy enough to give me grandchildren. You know it's my fondest wish, to have a grandson to bounce on my knee."

A little boy with wavy dark hair and hazel eyes, and a naughty sense for trouble and fun. She closed her eyes against that useless and impossible vision. "Then you'd best take care of yourself, so you can dance a reel at my wedding. I could have five sons and you'll never get to spoil them if you don't mind your health."

He laughed and agreed before walking her out and tying on her bonnet as usual. "Ilsa, my child." He took her face between his hands and gave her a searching look. "You're the dearest piece of my heart, and a better daughter than I deserve. I don't say enough how proud I am of you, and how precious you are to me."

She clasped his hands. "I know, Papa. You're a wonderful father, and I love you dearly, too."

He smiled ruefully. "'Tis sorry I am not to be in better spirits today, but the fault is mine. Don't hold it against me, aye?"

"Of course not!" She kissed his cheek. "You must rest, though, and let Jean send you blancmanges and mustard plasters for your chest until you feel well again."

He groaned. "Anything save the mustard plasters! Would you push me into an early grave?"

She smiled. "Never, Papa. But someone must look out for you if you won't do so yourself."

He kissed her forehead. "Never you worry about me."

He bid her farewell, and she left, more unsettled than ever. Now she had her father's health to worry about in addition to everything else. Papa was not himself . . . though he was always cantankerous when he was ill. At least it had kept him from quizzing Jean about her doings and about Drew. She was quite certain Papa would rise from the brink of the grave to question her about Drew if he'd any idea how close they'd come to discussing marriage . . .

But they hadn't—not really. It had been hinted at but never directly stated. And she hadn't seen him since that lovely dinner when she'd started to feel almost like part of his family.

Ilsa pulled her jacket tighter around her despite the warm day. Once again she must have read too much into it. Not for the first time she wished she'd had more experience with gentlemen. Before she married, Jean had refused to let her go into society, claiming it would give her dangerous ideas. After she married, Malcolm hadn't allowed her to go anywhere without him, and he only took her to events and activities that he preferred. And when he'd died . . .

I'm free, was what she had thought, once the shock had worn off. She hadn't expected that, yet somehow it was true.

But then the trial happened, and she had not been free of anything. People had said horrible things about Malcolm and about her. Papa had insisted she attend the trial, garbed in black, to shame the rumormongers. By the time it was over she felt as though part of her had also been killed. Ever since, she had tried to think of herself as a phoenix reborn from the ashes of her former restricted life into a new life where she was an independent woman with a handsome fortune, and no man could tell her what to do.

It had taken her too long to realize that she had been denied so much in order to reflect well on a man—first her father, then her husband. Only Malcolm's stupid, senseless death had made it clear to her that all that privilege and advantage had been a cage instead of the means to do things she believed in and cared for.

That was why she rescued a half-starved pony

from the slaughterhouse and installed him in what had been Malcolm's private study. Why the staid draperies were now upholstering two sofas at the charity school for girls. Why she went to oyster cellars instead of to the Assembly Rooms and why she danced with soldiers and merchants instead of with gentlemen and lords, who might have wanted to force her back into the useless, idle life that had threatened to drive her mad. Why she'd dismissed Malcolm's domineering butler and hired the sensible, obliging Mr. MacLeod. Why she sacked Malcolm's pompous attorney who didn't believe she had the brains to manage her own money.

She took a deep breath. Enough pity. Neither Jean nor Papa nor even Andrew St. James would make her doubt herself again.

Tonight she should go out; Agnes had left, but Sorcha White would go to an oyster cellar with her. She would cede the drawing room to Aunt Jean and paint her Calton Hill mural in the dining room, with the golden chandelier in place of the noon sun.

And Drew . . . She blew out her breath. She would not sit around waiting for him. He knew where to find her. And if this mad attraction between them flickered out, or he decided an English bride was better for him, she would not be wrecked by it.

Things could always be worse, she told herself bracingly. *Never forget that.*

Chapter Eighteen

Drew was beginning to get a taste of what life would be like as the Duke of Carlyle.

Part of it he did not care for at all. After the *Tattler*'s sensational report, a flood of letters and supplicants looking for something from the duke appeared on Felix Duncan's doorstep. No matter how many times Drew said he was not the duke, and could not speak for the duke, none of them were deterred from begging that he put in just a word with His Grace. Duncan reported that David MacGill had indeed been the one who let the secret slip—or rather trumpeted it about—and Drew took great pleasure in writing a severe report to Mr. Edwards about the solicitor's shortcomings.

Before he left Carlyle Castle, Mr. Edwards had suggested he engage a secretary. Drew had thought that ridiculous—he was perfectly capable of managing his own correspondence—but now he was reconsidering. He *should* hire a secretary, a tall fierce one capable of standing guard, armed and intimidating, against the hordes of favor seekers.

The other side of the coin, however, was more gratifying. Being a future duke made some things immensely easier. For instance: his visit to William Scott, the procurator-fiscal. As mere Captain St. James, son of a victimized shop owner, he would have been left to cool his heels before being patronized by a deputy clerk. As the heir to Carlyle, he was escorted in and welcomed very cordially by Mr. Scott himself. When he explained that his family's business had been attacked by the thieves, Mr. Scott hastened to apologize and assure him everything possible was being done.

And when Drew said that he thought more could be done, and he had some suggestions in fact, Mr. Scott listened with attentive and respectful interest. The man agreed it was a sound idea, and suggested that Drew go argue the case to the lord advocate, who would then need approval from the Home Office in London. Mr. Scott provided a letter of introduction to smooth the way and wished him luck.

His idea, after all, was a King's Pardon, as ripe and juicy a plum as any criminal had ever been offered. It was legal absolution for all past offenses, not merely the most recent one. The skill and daring of the break-ins had suggested experienced thieves, with more than this sin on their consciences. All it would take was one thief, eager to clear his blotter with the law, to put an end to the robberies.

If he had to bear the impositions of the Carlyle title, he might as well seize the advantages.

But all that cost him several days, between riding to and from the lord advocate, and he'd not had a chance to see Ilsa since that last dinner at his mother's home, before all hell broke loose and upended his days. They'd said only a simple farewell that night because Drew had never guessed how long it would be before he saw her again.

How blissful the life of ordinary Captain St. James seemed now, when he could hardly walk out of his borrowed rooms without being intercepted and importuned by someone, let alone escort a woman up Calton Hill for a walk, a conversation, even a kiss. Now it would be noted in the newspapers if he called upon her, and Drew didn't want to do that after her speech the other day.

But he was desperate to see her.

Finally his sister gave him an excuse. Agnes had returned home after the robbery to help their mother sort out their losses, but she'd left a trunk at Ilsa's. "Would you come with me to retrieve it?" she asked guilelessly.

"Of course," he said, and saw from her smug smile that she knew he'd been dying to go.

Unfortunately Ilsa was not alone. At his entrance, her aunt and two older ladies curtsied in perfect unison before turning looks of calculating anticipation upon him. Ilsa alone gave him a smile, and he contrived to find a seat near her.

The conversation was wretched. The ladies tried to pry out of him how long he meant to stay in Edinburgh, the condition of the duke, and what his personal fortune was. They knew he had been to see the procurator-fiscal and wondered aloud about his role in the recent scandalous robberies; would he be called to the jury? They brushed aside or outright ignored Ilsa's every attempt to divert the conversation, and when Agnes returned to say her trunk was ready to be carried home, it was with mingled relief and dismay that Drew leapt to his feet and made his farewells.

Ilsa followed them to the door. "Thank you for

calling," she said as Agnes deliberately stepped away and fawned over Robert, who had emerged from his room with a brisk whinny to beg for the apple she'd brought him.

Drew gave a soft huff of laughter. "Much good it did me." He lowered his voice. "Perhaps you'll reconsider haunting Duncan's lodgings."

Some of her usual spark returned. "If only I could."

His sister was still cooing over Robert, so Drew took a chance. "Do you walk out tomorrow?"

"Yes, if the weather is fine."

"Perhaps to the Botanic Garden?"

Her face brightened further. "Yes, I could . . ."

He bowed close to her. "I fancy a walk there myself, around eleven."

With joy in her face, she whispered back, "I hope you have a very, very pleasant stroll, Captain."

ILSA DIDN'T GO often to the Botanic Garden, which was a mile distant on the northern edge of town. It was the sort of place visitors went to see, or those citizens with a passion for plants and vegetables. Jean and her circle attended lectures there presented by a professor from the university, and that had been enough to dissuade Ilsa from going.

Today, though, she pinned on her new hat and put on her favorite morning dress, and asked Maeve to accompany her and Robert. The pony tried to amble up the familiar slope of Calton Hill, but pricked up his ears to explore somewhere new.

It was early still when they reached the garden, the plants dewy and lush. Ponies were not permitted, so she sent Maeve and Robert to wander in the field outside the walls. At the gatehouse there arose a problem; she had no order to visit, and it was not open to visitors until twelve. Ilsa hesitated uncertainly until the fellow asked her name. When she told him, he bowed and apologized, and opened the gate for her.

Once inside she found herself apparently alone. The garden fluttered and trilled with birds, but no other people, not even gardeners. It was peaceful and somehow invigorating. She took a deep breath and felt her shoulders ease.

Strolling leisurely, marveling at the plants, she had made it to the statue of Mr. Linnaeus, patron saint of botanists, when Drew found her.

"A sight that does feed my poor soul."

She turned in pleasure. "Mr. Linnaeus?"

Drew came closer. "No. All I see is you." His gaze seemed to devour her. "'Tis *good* to see you."

That low growl did something inside her, quietly peeling back the veneer of decorum and propriety that muted her passionate urges. She smiled. "And you, Captain."

He offered his arm, his expression focused and intent. Ilsa slid her hand along his forearm, letting her breast graze the side of his arm to see his hand contract into a fist.

"I'm puzzled by one thing," she said as they walked around the pond. "The garden isn't open for viewing until twelve, yet the man at the gate admitted me after asking my name."

Drew had a satisfied air. "I discovered that the promise of a donation to Dr. Hope worked wonders upon his willingness to bend that rule."

She caught her breath. "You bribed him so we could walk in the garden?"

He turned up the path that led to the greenhouse, the slate roof tinged blue in the rising sun. "No," he said, opening the door for her. "I bribed him so I could have a private conversation with you and not be rushed or interrupted."

"My." She raised her brows at him. "One wonders why you desire so much privacy . . ."

His eyes smoky, Drew brushed his thumb across her lips. Ilsa's heart lurched into her throat. "You'll see."

Mercy, whispered her helpless heart. "Show me . . ."

His fingers curled around the nape of her neck. His lips skimmed across her brow. "Patience, love." He pressed a light kiss to her temple, right by her ear.

Her skin felt cold and hot at once when he released her and stepped back. The stoves that warmed the plants in winter were snuffed out, but she would have sworn there was a blazing furnace behind her. A sheen of perspiration made her shift stick to her bosom and she took a deep breath to quell it. "I hope everything is being done for your mother and the shop," she said, seizing on the most ordinary topic she could find.

"Yes." He led her through the soaring ferns and palms. "Which is to say, not much. They've no idea who the thieves are, but I've made a suggestion for running them to earth."

"Oh?"

He nodded once. "Aye. That's why I've been so occupied of late." He gave her a look. "Why I've not been to call sooner."

Her skin prickled. She was surely the most sinful creature in the world, imagining how he might have come to call, kissed her, made love to her on the drawing room sofa and made good use of the privacy offered by Jean's impenetrable new drapes. "Hmm," she said, hoping it sounded politely interested and not lustful.

His wicked mouth curved, as if he knew what she was trying not to think about. "But that's not why I hoped to speak to you."

"Oh no!" she protested, flushing from head to toe. "I—I want to know. What have you suggested? Shall you haunt every attic in Edinburgh, hoping to act upon the guilty consciences and send the thieves screaming into the streets?"

His knowing smile only grew wider. Ilsa waved one hand in front of her heated face, recalling how they'd concluded that night of haunting.

"No, a more craven appeal to the guilty conscience. A King's Pardon," he said.

Ilsa blinked. "A pardon?"

"For one man, who gives information on the rest of them." He lifted his shoulder. "To stop the robberies. Those robbed deserve to know and seek justice, and everyone else, including my family, deserves to sleep in peace. The thieves have been devious. It's almost as if they had keys, or someone opening the doors for them. They've never had to break in violently, which is surely how they've gone so long undetected."

That had not been in the newspapers. "And the procurator agreed?"

"And the lord advocate. They've sent a man to London for the Crown's approval."

Ilsa said nothing. The English Crown would be

more likely to approve such a proposal made by the Duke of Carlyle's heir.

Again Drew divined her thoughts. "My inheritance has become terribly cumbersome of late, and this is one counterbalancing advantage."

She didn't really want to talk about that, the inheritance that would take him from Scotland and probably from her. "If you didn't wish to discuss that, what did you want to tell me that was worth bribing a professor of botany for the use of this garden?"

"First, to apologize." They had come to a bench nestled in a stand of spiky palms. Drew shed his coat and spread it on the seat for her. He sat beside her, one elbow on his knee so he could face her. "I asked to spend time with you, and then vanished for days."

She waved one hand. "It's nothing."

"Not to me." He caught her hand and brushed his lips over the pulse in her wrist. "I did miss you."

"Some of that is inevitable," she told him. "Even courtship is conducted at more leisure."

She wished she could snatch back that word as soon as she said it.

"Indeed," he said in that lower, rougher voice. "And here I've come to tell you I must leave again."

Ilsa looked up in dismay.

"I've got to return to Inverness and resign my commission. It was fully half the reason I returned north, and my colonel's not the sort to countenance a mere letter."

"And are you subject to his disapproval any longer?"

He grimaced. "'Tis a deep-grained habit. But,

more to the point, I wish to be done with it." He still held her hand and now spread it open, palm up, on his knee. Idly his fingers swirled over hers. "There are other matters demanding my attention now."

"Yes." She watched his fingers as if in a daze. "Your family—"

"No."

"The demands of your inheritance—"

"No." Somehow he was closer to her, the heat of his body making her hot and flushed again.

"What?"

"You," he whispered after a moment. "Nothing but you, Ilsa." He raised her hand to his lips, sucking lightly at her palm. Ilsa gripped the bench to keep from sliding into a puddle on the ground.

"How long will you be gone?"

His eyes, glowing gold and green, flashed toward hers. "A fortnight." He lowered his head and sucked the tip of her ring finger between his lips. "Dare I hope you might miss me?"

She hooked her finger and pulled his wicked mouth to hers. "Desperately," she whispered, and claimed his lips in a kiss that felt like it had been eons in the making. He slid off the bench to his knees and crowded closer as he pulled her to him. Boldly Ilsa opened her legs and took him there, full against her.

His hand speared into her hair, dislodging the hat. His tongue teased hers. She cupped his face and kissed him back, deeply and absolutely, until his free hand settled on her collarbone, his fingers loose around her throat.

"Did you invite me here to seduce me?"

He drew his fingertips down her throat, pausing on the edge of the gauzy kerchief tucked into her bodice. "Not . . . specifically." Slowly the kerchief came loose until it fell from her shoulder. "But if the opportunity arises . . . should I refuse it?"

"Never."

The corner of his mouth crooked. "Shall I continue?"

"Yes." She let her head fall back as he pressed his mouth to her throat. "Will someone come in?"

"No," he breathed, his hand spanning the small of her waist and urging her forward on the bench. "For fifty pounds Dr. Hope would keep out the King himself."

That was enough for her; when his hand skimmed up her calf, she put her arms behind her and arched her back, a wanton pagan sacrifice to his desire.

"I want you," he murmured against her skin.

"Yes," she gasped as his fingers stroked between her thighs. A spasm rippled through her as he touched her again with intent.

And there in the midst of exotic plants from around the globe, she let him seduce her, his hand under her petticoat and his mouth on her breast. When she felt climax licking at her nerves, she reached for him, dragging up the front of his kilt until he rose up on his knees and fitted himself against her aching center, thrusting home with a harsh moan that pushed her over the edge. Tears gathered in her eyes as they moved and strained against each other, absorbed in each heavy stroke of his flesh joining hers, each hungry gasp, each urgent touch and stroke and hold until he broke and shuddered in her arms. Still shaking from her own climax, Ilsa clutched his shoulders, pressing her mouth to his neck, damp from exertion.

I love him, she thought with a start of amazement. *I love him.*

After several minutes he lifted his head and gazed at her. She smiled back—good heavens, she might never stop smiling from the euphoria thrumming through her veins. His own lazy but happy expression sent her heart soaring.

"A fortnight," he whispered. "With only this to warm my heart and blood."

She moved, undulating against him, and he caught his breath. "Perhaps it will encourage you to return sooner."

He grinned. "God willing."

He helped her restore her clothing, and then sat on the bench holding her hand while she leaned against his shoulder, telling her about his trip to see the lord advocate. Rarely had Ilsa felt this blissful sort of joy; his hand, so large and strong around hers, his body so solid and wonderful beside her. Was this what love matches were like?

"I'll come to call when I return," he told her when they finally walked out. It was nearly noon, when the gardens would open to other visitors. He tried to argue that he would see her home, but she told him her maid and Robert would be enough. It would be hard enough to conceal the happiness bubbling inside her without him; she was afraid that if he walked back into Edinburgh beside her, it would be in all the newspapers tomorrow that Wild Widow Ramsay had thrown herself at the next Duke of Carlyle. "You'll be here?"

She laughed, reaching up on her toes to kiss him one last time. "Where would I go? You're the one who keeps leaving again and again."

He cupped her jaw and kissed her on the forehead. "I may go mad from missing you these next several days."

And I you. She tugged the cloth at his throat back into place, having dislodged it during their frantic coupling. "You shan't," she said firmly. "How shall you find your way home if you run mad?"

He laughed and let her go, reluctantly. "Then I shall ride like the wind, throw diplomacy to the dogs, and race back as if the banshees were after me."

And at that moment, it felt as if Fate was smiling upon her, deciding to repay her for her lonely childhood and indifferent first marriage by showering pure happiness upon her.

She should have known better.

Chapter Nineteen

Drew left the next morning for Ardersier in strangely high spirits.

He had expected to have done this already. When he left Carlyle Castle, he'd planned to spend a week with his family in Edinburgh arranging their move to England, assess Stormont Palace in a few days, return to Fort George to resign his military obligations, and then relocate to Carlyle to assume his role as heir. He would be back within two months, he'd assured the duchess and Mr. Edwards.

That deadline had already passed. The brief trip to Stormont Palace had turned into a visit of two weeks' duration. He had lost another several days to the Edinburgh thieves and what to do about them. And, of course, he'd spent time with Ilsa, which he had not foreseen at all.

Not that he regretted it in the slightest. In fact, as he traveled northward, he spent considerable thought working out a new plan. Fort George was the first step—he had savored for too long the prospect of resigning his commission in front of Fusty Colonel Fitzwilliam—but everything else would be different.

In this plan, he wasn't going back to Carlyle.

What he'd told Ilsa was true: the duke could very well live decades longer. As convenient as it might be for Edwards to instruct him in person, Drew thought he was perfectly able to learn via letter. If Stormont Palace could be run efficiently and smoothly without the duke setting foot on its grounds in twenty years, Carlyle Castle could get along very well with him in Edinburgh, particularly since he had no actual authority as long as the duke lived.

And the duchess had said only that he should endeavor to become respectable and sober. She'd wanted him to find a suitable wife. At the time Drew hadn't known a single suitable woman, but now that he had met the most suitable woman imaginable, there was no need for Her Grace to introduce him to any others. Ilsa might not be the bride the duchess had had in mind for him, but she was genteel, wealthy, and beautiful, which the duchess could hardly fault.

And Ilsa possessed one advantage which obliterated any and all objections anyway: he was absolutely in love with her. He was going to stay in Edinburgh and court her properly. If he could persuade her to marry him despite the Carlyle inheritance, he'd willingly risk the duchess's disappointment.

He reached the fort after several long days in the saddle, arriving in a cold mist that made him doubly glad to be quitting this spot. He found his old quarters shut up and dark, and his man MacKinnon sharing whisky with the men.

"Captain!" He leapt to his feet. "I'd no warning of your return."

Drew almost laughed. "Because I sent none. I want a word, MacKinnon."

The sergeant was amazed by his news. "A duke!" he repeated. "A bloody duke of England!"

"'Twas a shock to me, as well. But as it's true, I'm done with the army."

MacKinnon nodded in awed agreement. "Aye! A man would be a bloody fool to stay in!"

Drew clapped his shoulder. "You've been a good man for me, MacKinnon. If you also wish to be done with this . . ."

The man hesitated only a moment. "Nay, Captain. I've family in Inverness." A crooked grin crossed his face. "And ye couldna pay me enough to live in England—not you, nor a duke."

"Aye," said Drew, straight-faced. "If you're ever desperate enough to change your mind, though, I'll have a place for you."

His interview with the colonel was entirely gratifying. "Duke of Carlyle?" repeated Fitzwilliam, thunderstruck. "His heir?"

"Aye," replied Drew placidly.

"You claimed you had naught to do with the family!"

"I never did," he agreed. "Until they discovered I stand next in line for the title."

The colonel continued to glare at him. "I thought you'd deserted."

"There's no reason why you should have," was his cool reply. "But now I've come to resign my commission, so it matters little to me what you thought."

That seemed to remind the colonel that the lowly captain he'd regularly assigned to oversee road repair had suddenly become someone with influence and status, and he grew a great deal more accommodating and cordial, to Drew's amusement.

He had allotted three days at the fort to pack his belongings, settle a few debts, and make his farewells. News of his good fortune spread through the fort like wildfire, though, and he was entreated to stay for several dinners, each including many rounds of toasts and huzzahs. He would not miss the army, but he would miss his men and his friends among the officers, and the thought that this was farewell forever weakened his resolve. His three days stretched to six, then eight, after which he swore off any more celebrations. The last one, thrown by the men of his own regiment, left him severely off-color and intensely glad he didn't have to form ranks that morning.

"No more, aye?" he said groggily when MacKinnon brought in water and set out his razor.

"Aye, Captain. Not if you're to leave tomorrow."

Drew groaned at the thought of a day in the saddle, even one that led him back to Ilsa, and draped one arm over his face. "Don't speak of that now. I may not be able to stand before then." Rain pattered on the windows, making travel unthinkable. It was a good day to stay abed and let his head recover.

MacKinnon was still chuckling when a knock sounded on the door. The sergeant returned a moment later with a letter in his hand. "By express messenger, sir."

"Express?"

MacKinnon nodded. "From Edinburgh. He says he's to wait for an answer if there is one."

Drew lurched upright, ignoring the ferocious

pounding in his head unleashed by the action. The handwriting was Felix Duncan's—who knew he meant to return soon, who wouldn't bother sending a messenger for anything but a crisis, let alone an express messenger who rode through a storm and waited for a reply. He tore it open, scanning quickly.

His curse made MacKinnon look up. "I need to leave now," said Drew, staggering out of bed. "Send someone to saddle my horse and arrange for my baggage to be shipped south. And tell the messenger I'm going with him back to Edinburgh. Find him a fresh horse."

"Now, sir?"

"Within the hour," said Drew grimly, and he reached for his boots.

Chapter Twenty

Scandal broke like a dam bursting: a leak here, a trickle there, until the whole edifice gave way in a flood.

The sheriff's office had been swamped with leads after Drew left town. Mr. Duncan heard it from the procurator-fiscal's office and told Agnes, who confided in Ilsa during a morning walk with Robert.

"That is excellent news," she exclaimed, thinking Drew would be pleased that his plan was working.

Agnes nodded. "It's been a great comfort to my mother. She was terribly unsettled by that shredded red silk. It looked like blood, she says, and she has nightmares the villains will come back for us." She shivered.

"I thought Mr. Duncan and Mr. Kincaid were coming by to keep an eye on things," said Ilsa in concern.

"Oh! They were. They do." Pink-faced, Agnes cleared her throat. "We'll be relieved when Drew returns, though."

Ilsa could only agree.

Rumors sprouted and multiplied like weeds, each more shocking than the last. A thief had been identified, in possession of some of the stolen property, but had escaped the officers. Unspecified evidence had been located. There were several more members of the thieving ring still at large. There had been an attempted escape from the Tolbooth prison, aided by a corrupt officer, and was only foiled by a passing maid's cry of alarm. A fortune in stolen gold had been recovered, buried in a field. The stolen goods had been shipped to Amsterdam, and the mastermind of the thieves had taken flight on board the ship after a fierce battle with the sheriff's officers on the docks of Leith.

Ilsa followed the rumors with interest, wondering if any were true but as absorbed as every resident of Edinburgh. Her aunt was similarly transfixed. Every day Jean scoured the newspapers, which she then dissected in breathless indignation with her gossiping friends. Ilsa had little patience for these discussions and generally went for a walk when one of her aunt's visitors was announced.

The worst of the lot was Mrs. Crawley, as usual. She became a daily fixture in her widow's weeds and fluttering shawl. Ilsa took to leaving the house early and staying away, to avoid any chance of meeting her, but one morning she erred, returning from her walk as Mrs. Crawley mounted the front steps.

Her instinct was to hurry back to the fields. She had approximately six seconds to consider it; to curl her fingers into Robert's mane to slow him down; to duck her head and start to turn away.

"Mrs. Ramsay! There you are!"

She clenched her jaw to keep from cringing. She was not fond of Widow Crawley and would have kept walking away if it wouldn't make her aunt livid. She turned back, a polite smile on her face. "Mrs. Crawley. How delightful to see you."

Mrs. Crawley advanced on her with hands clasped in front of her like a bishop castigating a sinner. "And how surprising! You are always gallivanting about, it seems."

"Alas," said Ilsa. "I hope my aunt has conveyed to you my highest regards every time I missed your call."

"She has, of course. Miss Fletcher knows what is proper." Unspoken but not misunderstood was that Ilsa most definitely did not. "I trust you will join us today."

Ilsa made a noncommittal noise in her throat as she headed toward the door. "Indeed. Let us go in." *And get it over with,* she added silently, wishing she'd been fleeter on her feet and had fled at the first sight of Mrs. Crawley.

The widow eyed Robert with disgust as he clopped up the steps. "Really, Mrs. Ramsay, you cannot bring a pony inside the house!"

I'd rather bring in him than you, she thought, opening the door. "He's a very small pony, hardly anyone notices him. And he is so dear to me—aren't you, Robert?"

He gave a soft snuffle in reply as she ruffled his mane.

Mrs. Crawley seemed to grow several inches with outrage. "I am shocked that Miss Fletcher allows this." She raised a scolding finger. "Your butler ought to be awaiting your return to admit you. And that pony ought to be in a stable. One must make some allowances for a young widow whose mind is disordered with grief, but this is beyond the bounds of reason! If you would allow me to guide you, like your own mother might desire—which surely you must welcome, having been without her for so long—"

"Oh dear, Robert, no," said Ilsa, removing her hat. Robert had begun nibbling at the fringe of Mrs. Crawley's shawl as she stood reprimanding Ilsa, and now was slowly unraveling the whole thing as he pulled on the yarn.

The widow gave a cry, snatching her shawl free. Robert tossed his head and tapped his front foot on the marble floor, then trotted off toward his room.

"Show Mrs. Crawley in to see Miss Fletcher," Ilsa told Mr. MacLeod, who had appeared at the closing of the door.

"You will be joining us, of course?" demanded the widow.

"I shall be in as soon as I refresh myself," replied Ilsa, that same determined, polite smile carved on her face. With a suspicious sniff the woman followed the butler up the stairs.

Slowly Ilsa went to her room. A walk to Leith and back would refresh her greatly and outlast even Mrs. Crawley's visit. But Jean would scold her fiercely, so she smoothed her hair and brushed the grass from her skirt, and went to the drawing room with all the eagerness of a condemned soul facing the gallows.

The two women were ensconced on the sofa when she arrived, a large refreshment tray nearby. Jean's guests tended to stay awhile. Ilsa quietly seated herself, resigned.

They were discussing the recent burglaries—again. Or was it still? Ilsa let her mind wander. It had been a full week since the pardon had been offered. She thought again of Drew and wondered if the news would reach him all the way beyond Inverness. She sighed silently, wishing he would return. A fortnight, he'd said, and it was only two days shy of that.

"But you must know, Mrs. Ramsay!" exclaimed Mrs. Crawley.

She blinked, startled. "Must I?"

"Why yes." The woman gave her a sly smile. "You're acquainted with Captain St. James, who will be a duke."

Her throat closed for a moment. "I am."

The widow's eyes gleamed, and she pounced. "Then you must know something. The fiscal is eating out of the captain's hand, he is. I warrant the captain knows all!"

"I've no idea," she said cautiously, her heart thudding.

"No?" Mrs. Crawley leaned forward, her small blue eyes hungry. "And him here all the time?"

"He is not here all the time."

Mrs. Crawley's smile was spiteful as she moved in for the kill. "Perhaps he told you when you met him out on the hill."

Ilsa froze. Jean stiffened. "What is this?"

"Didn't you know?" Mrs. Crawley, the evil witch, stirred her tea and looked to Jean. "I hear they meet frequently out there."

Her aunt turned to her with an expression of such censure that Ilsa's stomach cramped. "I had no idea," said Jean icily.

"I'm sure not," murmured Mrs. Crawley with patently false sympathy.

"We met by chance," said Ilsa, her heart stuttering in alarm. "Often when he is looking for his sister—"

Mrs. Crawley made a derisive noise. "Indeed!"

And suddenly anger boiled over within her. This was how the gossips had hounded her last year, with innuendo and suggestion that Malcolm's fatal duel must have been over her, that she must have had an affair with that horrid Englishman, who had done everything he could to encourage the story—not a word of which was true. Jean had made her endure it in silence, saying it wasn't dignified to defend herself publicly. Never again.

She jumped to her feet. "Are you accusing me of indecency, Mrs. Crawley?"

Mrs. Crawley started at the counterattack. "Well—" She glanced sideways at Jean. "One hates to think that—"

"Does one?" Ilsa raised her brows. "Does one also hate to suggest it without evidence?"

"Ilsa!" hissed Jean.

The widow's face turned scarlet. "I never!"

"Good," said Ilsa. "I accept your apology." She turned toward the door without a word of farewell, only to be brought up short by the butler.

"Mrs. Arbuthnot, ma'am," he said to Jean.

Ilsa's jaw tightened. Another scandalmonger. She wasn't going to stay and face three of them.

But Mrs. Arbuthnot burst in, lappets and dress fluttering. "My dears, have you heard?" she cried before Ilsa could escape. "There has been a breakthrough!"

Jean and Mrs. Crawley gasped in unison, and urged Mrs. Arbuthnot to come sit and tell all. The woman was only too happy to oblige; she was breathless from hurrying to tell them. Ilsa lingered at the door, curiosity momentarily overwhelming her outrage.

"'Tis very momentous news," Mrs. Arbuthnot gushed. "As you know, my brother-in-law Mr. Hay is in the sheriff-clerk's office, and he tells me they have apprehended one of the villains!" She flapped her hand at Mrs. Crawley's indrawn breath. "For certain this time, Lavinia!"

She paused for breath and accepted the cup of tea Jean urged upon her. "He's a very low, criminal sort—English, of course. He wants that pardon! Clearly he should go to the hangman, too, but we must be consoled by the thought that he is revealing all the secrets of Edinburgh's criminal elements."

"But has he told them who was involved?"

Mrs. Arbuthnot nodded. "Apparently he informed the sheriff of at least one accomplice, and hinted that there is yet another, the mastermind of the whole plot."

"Good heavens!" Jean clapped one hand to her bosom, riveted. "Who is the mastermind?"

"Now, he hasn't said yet," replied the woman with a trace of disappointment. "Mr. Hay thinks he wishes to extort something else—as if a King's Pardon isn't enough! But he did give some clues, which have tantalized the sheriff to no end! Oh, thank you, dear." She took a sip of tea and accepted a plate of cake.

"What are the clues, Cora?" demanded Mrs. Crawley, her weak chin quivering. Ilsa thought she was annoyed not to have been the first to hear—and share—this news.

Mrs. Arbuthnot shook her head. "He didn't name the man, Lavinia. He said only that it's a prominent man of the town, and that it'll cause a great stir when he's revealed."

"What else?" Jean wanted to know.

Mrs. Arbuthnot knew plenty. "He—the thief who turned, that is—is a nasty bit of goods called Browne. Mr. Hay heard that he led the sheriff to a set of false keys, which so far have opened the doors of Mr. Wemyss's shop, Mr. Johnstone's shop, and there are several other keys they've not identified yet. Imagine it! The thieves had keys to the burgled shops!"

Ilsa barely heard the ensuing excited conversation. Drew had mentioned keys . . . and so had Papa.

Papa was not only a cabinet-maker; he was also a locksmith. And she thought he might have done work for one of the victims—a grocer who'd lost a great deal of tea.

No. It was madness to think Papa would be involved in the robberies. He was one of the most respected men in town, a deacon and town councilman. What's more, he was a wealthy man, with a successful shop. Why would he risk all that for petty thieving?

There was no more prominent locksmith in Edinburgh, though. And it would cause a mighty stir if someone accused him of thieving.

She closed her eyes and bit down on her lip, furious at herself. Papa! It couldn't be.

But he did have a weakness for gambling, and he had been tense and twitchy the other day when she mentioned the robberies. He'd told her to mind her business. He was ill, she argued to herself, even as her feet started moving toward the door. It meant nothing; there were dozens of locksmiths in Edinburgh, to say nothing of criminals skilled in picking locks. This villain, Browne, was surely casting about for someone else to throw to the wolves, to secure the pardon and save his own neck. He probably made the keys himself.

A new thought struck her even as she slipped out the door and hurried downstairs. Papa should know in case Browne did mean to accuse him. She seized her hat, flung a shawl around herself, and bolted.

She was running by the time she reached her father's house, where he was putting on his hat to go out. "Papa, have you heard?" she demanded.

He frowned at her. "Why are you screeching at me, child? I've not got time to talk now." He took up his walking stick and motioned her back out the door, held open by the servant. "If you wish to walk with me, come."

She followed him into the street. "Mrs. Arbuthnot came to call today and what do you think she told us?"

"Some gossip of illicit love affairs?"

Ilsa shook her head. "It was about the thieves."

He snorted. "What can she know? I've never met a sillier woman."

Ilsa smiled fleetingly. "Her brother-in-law is in the sheriff-clerk's office, and she heard from him that they have a thief in custody."

"Oh. Aye. I knew that."

"The man wants the pardon, of course, but he says he'll inform on the other thieves. Papa, Mrs.

Arbuthnot said he gave the sheriff a bunch of false keys, which fit the locks of shops that were robbed."

"And?"

"Papa!" Ilsa tugged at his arm, but he only raised a brow at her, his pace unchanged. "He said he would accuse a prominent man of the town, and you're a locksmith. You told me you refitted the lock of one of the victimized shops." Now that she was saying it aloud, it sounded even more ridiculous.

"Half the shops in Edinburgh have had their locks refitted. Every wright and locksmith has been busy from morning till night," he said, with a certainty that made her wilt in relief.

"Of course," said Ilsa, calming down. "But what if one of the thieves worked in your shop—?"

Of a sudden he stopped, gripping her arm. "What?"

"Well—it's possible, isn't it? Your apprentices learn how to fit locks . . ."

His eyes narrowed, and she had the sense he was furiously angry. "Cora Arbuthnot ought to keep her mouth closed, and the same for the blabbering fool who put that word in her ear. Surely you don't think my lads would do such a thing?"

"No!" She lowered her voice until it was barely audible. "But perhaps it is something to prepare for. If she's telling the matrons of Edinburgh . . . well, people may start to suspect *you*. Mrs. Crawley was there, and she'll tell everyone in town."

"'Tis arrant nonsense, and I'll not dignify it with a response." He relented at her expression. "Forgive me, Ilsa. I swear to you on your mother's grave, I had nothing to do with this thieving."

She exhaled in unspeakable relief. "I knew you couldn't have. But why—?"

"People will say anything when they feel the hangman's rope tightening about their necks." He patted her hand. "You heard the story that there was a pitched battle on the docks at Leith, no? Complete with a cavalry charge and cannon. Twaddle." He made a face of disdain.

"But if people believe it . . ." She faltered. "Don't let them drag you to the hangman, Papa, just because people have lost their heads."

"Aye, you're right. Edinburgh wants to hang someone. Too many robberies, too many losses over too many months."

"But you've been worried," she began.

Her father's mouth eased. "Not for myself, and not on this matter. A man who used to work for me has been locked in the Tolbooth. I'm going to see him now. John Lyon is a good lad. His mother begged me to look in on him, fearful he's fallen in with scoundrels. If I can save him from the gibbet, I must make an effort, aye?" He looked away from her. "He's not even your age, child. A young man with a wife and a babe on the way."

She took a calmer breath. "Of course. You must try to help him." She didn't remember John Lyon but she could picture his type: a young wright trying to support his family, falling prey to a scoundrel in the numerous taverns and gaming pits around town. It didn't take much to trip up a man.

Her father bade her go home and not to worry about him. Feeling much better, Ilsa did. She avoided her aunt, who was pestering Mr. MacLeod to physically bar every door and window now that the thieves might have keys. To avoid an argument about safety she stayed in that evening. After the alarm she'd given herself today, a quiet night had some appeal.

But in the morning, a grim-faced officer from the sheriff-clerk knocked on her door. Papa was gone from Edinburgh.

Chapter Twenty-One

That day was the beginning of a nightmare from which she couldn't wake. Jean sent the sheriff's officers away with a flea in their ear, but when she closed the door on them, she looked at Ilsa with worry in her eyes.

"My dear, did you know William was leaving?"

"No," Ilsa exclaimed. "As I told the officers."

Jean nibbled her lip, a shocking sign of distress for her. "They will discover the ladies were here yesterday. They will think we warned him of something."

Ilsa swallowed. "I told him what they said—and he denied everything, Aunt. Categorically."

The older woman stiffened. "Naturally he did! William would never engage in such behavior!"

Ilsa nodded and didn't say what she was thinking: *But he secretly fled town within hours.*

The newspapers exploded with wild and lurid charges against Papa, not only of the robberies but of every sordid thing a man could do: lewd behavior at the raucous Cape Club, rumors of multiple mistresses, tales of ruinous gambling at the cockpits, and more than one charge of cheating.

It was as if the entire town had been simply bursting for this chance to destroy William Fletcher. His name entirely eclipsed those of the two common thieves actually under lock and key.

Agnes and her sisters visited, and loyally proclaimed they didn't believe a word of it.

"If I were unjustly accused, I would go into hiding until I could clear my name," was Winnie's confident assertion.

Agnes nodded. "He's surely gathering proof of his innocence, to silence every chattering biddy in this town. Have faith, Ilsa."

She managed to smile. "I do."

"If only Drew would return," burst out Bella, ignoring the furious motion Agnes made at her. "He would put a quick end to this nonsense." She noticed her sister's agitation. "What? You know he would, Agnes. Now that everyone knows he's to be a duke, they all listen to what he says. He could shield Ilsa from this evil gossip. How rude of him not to be home already!"

Ilsa flinched as if a blow had landed against her heart. She wished Drew were here, too, even as she shuddered at what he might think. Drew's own family had been robbed, and he had gone to great lengths to get the pardon offered, driving the authorities to finally make a bold move to catch the thieves. No matter what she believed, Papa's disappearance made him look very guilty. Would Drew believe in him if all the authorities in Edinburgh didn't?

"Drew *will* be back soon," Agnes was saying, "and this will all be sorted. Any man would defend himself, and Mr. Fletcher will want to clear his name. Winnie is right."

Her sister beamed. "Of course I am! You mustn't worry, Ilsa."

Their support buoyed her, but when they left the walls seemed to close in. She yearned for a walk, but people would stare at her, even more than they had for her companion pony.

The next days were worse. The sheriff's officers came again, armed with orders to search her house. Jean took to her bed and Ilsa huddled with Robert in his room, pressing her face into his neck to muffle the sounds of officers tramping through her home, prying into her life and belongings, looking under the beds and in the wardrobes, rifling her neat little library and writing desk for any betraying evidence against Papa—or her.

They suspected her of warning Papa. Mrs. Arbuthnot, no doubt, had told her brother-in-law of her visit, and Papa's servants remembered her coming to see him. Ilsa told them she knew nothing to warn her father of, but she feared they didn't believe her.

Agnes brought Mr. Duncan to offer his assistance. "Out of my own concern for your safety as well as in St. James's stead," he said.

"Felix is a solicitor," Agnes put in. She knew Ilsa had sacked Mr. MacGill. "If you need any advice."

Ilsa managed a smile. "I do recall. And I thank you, sir, but I don't know what there is to be done."

Jean's friends deserted her. Where once someone had called almost every day, now no one came. Jean's defiant confidence had gone silent; she sat in the empty drawing room and stared at nothing, the very proper drapes closed protectively. When

Ilsa ventured in one day, her aunt asked in a low voice, "What will become of us, without William?"

"He'll be back," she said firmly. "I know he will."

"Back?" Jean reared up in sudden wrath. "How can he come back, Ilsa? He is ruined!"

"He'll come back to clear his name."

Her aunt stared at her before subsiding onto the sofa. "No, child. I've tried and tried to tell you, and now you see the brutal truth of it. A good name once ruined is lost forever."

Ilsa's temper sprang up as quickly as her aunt's. "How dare you say that! Papa is innocent."

Jean slashed one hand. "He will forever be doubted! Lavinia Crawley always says—"

"A pox on Mrs. Crawley," said Ilsa loudly. "And Mrs. Arbuthnot, too, if they have turned you against your own brother."

Her aunt's face turned red. "Yes, you will always blame me when I have done nothing but try to keep you and your father on an honest, respectable path. And now William has ruined himself beyond all hope—and the gossip will ruin *us*, too—" She stopped, covering her face with both hands.

Ilsa bit back a dozen replies—that Jean had delighted in salacious gossip about others, that Papa was innocent, and what good was a sterling reputation if it couldn't withstand mere rumors?

She had to get out; she was going mad without exercise and fresh air. She put on a drab brown cloak, pulled up the hood, and slipped out, leaving Robert behind—Mr. MacLeod had to take him out for his wandering now, to her bitter regret.

She made it a few streets, clutching the cloak at her throat, before a man fell in step beside her.

"Running off to retrieve the stolen goods?" he asked in a booming voice. "Where did your dearest papa hide the bounty from the goldsmith's? Or the bolts of silk? I wonder, did he steal those for you?"

With a start Ilsa recognized Liam Hewitt, her father's head wright. "Leave me alone," she bit out.

He smirked. "'Tis a public street, and we happen to be going the same way." Even though she sped up, he kept pace with her. "What a dark day this must be for you, Madam Proud and Haughty." He laughed. "Although, just wait until he's caught and hanged!"

Never had she hated someone as much as she hated Liam in that moment. He was deliberately baiting her and drawing attention to her; people were turning to watch. Tomorrow the gossip rags would be full of *this*, she thought in despair. "Don't say such a thing," she whispered harshly. "That will never happen!"

"No? Why not? Mrs. Ramsay," he said with sly, affected surprise, "did you help Deacon Fletcher escape?"

It felt like the entire street full of people, shopkeepers, chairmen, running boys on errands, ladies with servants at their heels, gentlemen on their way to the counting house and coffeehouses, had stopped to watch and listen—and judge. Her face burned and her skin crawled. "Stop," she pleaded again, low and furious. "Please."

"Am I making you uncomfortable?" His eyes gleamed mockingly. "Not so proud and disdainful anymore, are you? All these years you've thumbed your nose at me and now you're begging for my help." He clicked his tongue. "Not that it'll save him from the hangman."

She whirled on him, shaking with fury. "How dare you?" she demanded. "I don't care if you hate me—I certainly despise *you*—but how could you walk the Canongate exclaiming that Papa will be hanged, at the top of your lungs? After all he did for you? He's treated you like his own son!"

Liam smiled bitterly. "Hardly. But I suppose it might look like that to a spoiled daughter. I daresay he took to me because you were such a disappointment."

Her throat was raw and her hands were in fists. "Stay away from me," she said, quietly but clearly, "or I will summon the law."

"Oho!" He laughed as she turned and walked away, slipping on a cobble in her haste. "Summon the law as much as you like! I daresay they'll be coming for you soon in any event."

She reached home and slammed the door behind her, leaning against it until her shaking subsided. She hid her face in her hands and squeezed her eyes shut to hold back tears of humiliation. It was no secret Liam disliked her, but Papa had been his mentor, his patron. He had taken Liam into the shop when he was a young man, training him and grooming him to manage the business himself someday. How could Liam betray Papa like that?

"Ma'am." Mr. MacLeod approached with sympathy in his eyes. "Are you well?"

"Yes." She swiped at her face and untied her cloak.

"This was left on the step earlier. I took the liberty of peeking inside very briefly, to make certain it wasn't . . ." He paused. "Dangerous."

She gave a joyless huff and took the slim wrapped packet, the string loose. "Thank you, Mr. MacLeod."

Inside was a familiar book. *The Widower and Bachelor's Directory.* Puzzled, Ilsa checked the wrapping, but there was no note. Only when she held the book in her hands did it fall open, to a heavily marked page.

Madam Ramsay, Edinburgh, had a thick black line drawn through it. As to her fortune, the amount had been circled and labeled *embezzled,* and the stocks had been marked *stolen.* Across the page was one phrase, writ large: *mad, immoral, and spurned by all decent men.*

She stared at that for a long moment.

For twenty-five years she had followed every rule, every stricture. She had obeyed her aunt as a child, married the man her father chose, done her best to honor and obey her husband. All those years of following the rules had left her with a pristine reputation, but no friends. Her marriage had been distant and cold. She'd been desperately lonely and unhappy. All she had asked, in the months since her mourning ended, was to have a few friends, wear what she liked, and have some fun. Mad? She'd got a pet pony and learned golf, which everyone played. Immoral? She'd gone to oyster cellars and taken walks on the hill, like so many other ladies did. Spurned by any decent man? She'd fallen in love with Drew, the most honorable and decent man she knew, and she'd thought he might be falling in love with her . . .

She ran to the drawing room and burned the horrid little book and its spiteful words. If only she could wipe out the tide of rumor and gossip so easily. *William has ruined himself beyond all hope—and the gossip will ruin us, too,* lamented Jean's voice in her memory.

She pulled the fireboard into place to block the ashes of the book from sight. As long as Papa was missing, no one would believe he was innocent, or that she and Jean had known nothing. Jean would be little help, paralyzed by despair over her lost respectability. Papa *had* to come back—and if he did not come back soon, Ilsa would have to find him. It was the only way to save them all.

The point was driven home two days later by David MacGill. The solicitor came to call on her this time, with no pretense of affability, bearing a letter from her father, which he thrust at her as if it scorched his hand.

"This was delivered to me today and I want no part of it," he said acidly.

Ilsa gripped the letter with rigid fingers, desperate to read it but unwilling to open it in front of him. "Did you read it?"

He flushed. "Of course I did not. You see there, it is still sealed."

"It would be easy enough to seal again."

The solicitor's expression could have soured milk. "Nevertheless, I did not," he snapped. "I have no wish to become entangled in Deacon Fletcher's troubles. If he were here, I would inform him that I am no longer able to represent him. My other clients find it unseemly."

Other clients like the Duke of Carlyle. Ilsa suspected MacGill knew Drew wanted to dismiss him, and was trying to avoid giving any reason for the current duke to do it.

"Well," she told him, unable to resist a parting shot, "we both know how you abhor supporting anything *unseemly*."

He understood what she meant—their old argument about shares of the William Cunninghame company, with its trade in slavery-dependent tobacco and sugarcane. His face thunderous, he barely managed a curt farewell. He hadn't even sat down.

The moment MacGill was gone she broke the seal and tore open the letter, praying it would offer solace, comfort, hope—an explanation.

It did none of those things.

She was still reading it, over and over, when Jean opened the door. "Did you have a caller?"

Ilsa looked up with stricken eyes. "Did—did Papa say anything to you?" she faltered. "Before he . . . left. Anything at all about his business, or anything troubling him, or *anything*?"

Slowly, warily, Jean came into the room. "No. Of course he did not—he never did." She hesitated. "Why?"

"Mr. MacGill has brought a letter from Papa."

With a muffled sound her aunt rushed to the sofa, snatching the letter. Her breath sped up as she read. "No," she whispered, her restrained facade beginning to crack. "No!"

The letter was, to all appearances, a farewell note; Papa spoke of his love for both of them, and how dear family was to him. He swore he could never harm his own blood, and he was determined to spare them any shame or upset. He begged their forgiveness for any hurt he had caused either of them and closed with a humble wish that they might forgive him for taking his leave this way.

Not one word professed innocence. The prosecutor would see it as a confession.

"Oh, Ilsa—he will be hanged—" Jean's voice broke.

With a curse that made her aunt jump, Ilsa leapt to her feet. "There must be an explanation—some reason he would write that letter. It's not like him."

"No." Jean sounded dazed. "It's *decidedly* not like him . . ."

Ilsa seized her aunt's hands. "If anyone will save him," she said fiercely, "it must be us. No one else believes he is innocent. Will you help me?"

Jean's lips trembled. "I don't know how I can."

"To whom would Papa go in a time of need?"

Her aunt shook her head. "No one. *He* is the head of the family—everyone looks to him." Her chin wobbled again. "He is such a good man, Ilsa, so generous and kind, no wonder everyone loves him so—" She broke off with a sob, obviously having remembered that no one seemed to love William Fletcher now but the two of them.

But Ilsa inhaled. "Of course!" She embraced her startled aunt. "I know where to look."

She sent Mr. MacLeod out to make arrangements as discreetly and rapidly as possible. The need to leave Edinburgh raged like a fever consuming her.

She meant to tell no one, but Agnes came to call. Ilsa didn't want to lie to her few friends and had told Mr. MacLeod not to admit anyone. Agnes, though, was not deterred and argued her way past the butler.

"What are you planning?" she demanded breathlessly upon bursting into the drawing room.

Ilsa squeezed her hands into fists. "What do you mean?"

Her friend closed the door with a bang. "I saw it in the papers, that your father contacted you. Was it really a confession?"

"Of course not! He's innocent!"

Agnes nodded. "I know. But I also know you, Ilsa. What are you going to do?"

She hesitated. Would Agnes tell anyone—specifically her brother? Unwillingly she thought of Drew; he had been gone three weeks now. He must have been delayed at the fort.

Not that she could ask him to help her, not with this. Ilsa was keenly aware that she was probably breaking some law. Drew had his family to think of, his future position, the duchess whose displeasure he feared. "I don't know what you mean. What could I do?"

Agnes's eyes darkened in anguish. "The rumors—"

Her spine went rigid. "They're wrong." She turned away. "I don't listen to them."

There was a rustle, and Agnes appeared in front of her, taking her hands. "You don't have to be alone. Let me help you."

She struggled. Agnes was intelligent and thoughtful, and Ilsa was about to explode from the anxiety building inside her. But telling Agnes would make her friend an accomplice. What if she argued against it? Ilsa couldn't spare any of the hope and bravado she'd scraped together. "What would you do?" she asked, unable to resist. "If it were your father."

Her friend didn't hesitate. "Go after him. Demand an explanation. I would want to know the truth, and why he fled and left me to face the storm alone. I—I would need to see him again because I would not be able to believe it without that."

Her lips parted in gratitude, and she gripped Agnes's hands. "Yes," she said in a low voice. "Exactly."

Agnes gave a nod. "Let me go with you."

"Absolutely not." Ilsa released her and stepped back. "You know nothing about anything." Sheriff Cockburn had already come to see her again, stern-faced and curt. Mr. MacGill had told him about the letter, though not the horrible, guilty things it said. Ilsa had had to show the sheriff the letter. Brazenly she told him she did not think it was Papa's handwriting, and that she thought it was an attempt to cast false aspersions on her father. The sheriff hadn't been convinced, but he'd gone away.

Frowning in frustration, Agnes paced away. "When are you leaving?"

Ilsa said nothing. After a moment Agnes sighed and came to embrace her. "Promise you'll be careful," she whispered tearfully.

That, at least, she could do. Ilsa nodded. "Would you look in on Robert?" she asked on impulse. "It would be a great comfort to me."

"Of course! We shall walk him out every day and spoil him with apples and carrots."

Ilsa managed to smile.

"I would do more," said Agnes urgently. "We all would. Drew—"

Ilsa held up a hand to stop her. Even if Drew were here, she couldn't ask him for help. And Drew *wasn't* here, so it didn't matter anyway. "No, Agnes. There's nothing you can do."

Only she could do this, and the fewer people who knew about it, the better.

Chapter Twenty-Two

Drew rode into Edinburgh late, later than he should have been on the road, but heavy rain had made the journey agonizingly long.

Felix Duncan leapt up at his entrance. "There you are!"

"Had to go by way of Aberdeen. A bridge near Croy was washed out." He peeled off his dirt-caked coat. "What's happened?"

It had been six days since Duncan's letter reached him in Ardersier. It had taken the messenger three days to get there from Edinburgh. Nine days without information had nearly driven him mad.

Duncan followed him into the other room. "I wrote to you as soon as I heard a whisper of Fletcher's name. The sheriff was reluctant to act on rumor—the deacon sits on the bloody town council—but things have got worse. Fletcher tried to see Browne, who's claiming the pardon, in prison—"

"What?"

"Aye. He was allegedly there to see a lad in for nicking some bread from a grocer, and asked to see the famous thief, recently caught. The keeper refused and he wasn't pleased by it. The next day he left Edinburgh on an early coach, with no word to anyone. Told his servants and foreman he would be gone a few days and gave them leave."

"That looks guilty as sin."

Duncan made a grimace of agreement.

"And what of Ilsa?" Drew splashed water on his head. His back strained and ached at the motion, and he thought longingly of lying on the comfortable bed under the eaves. Instead he lowered himself into the chair and pried off his boots for the first time in two days.

His friend hesitated. "It's not gone well for her, in town. The sheriff thinks she must know something. He sent his men to search her house, which led the whole town to believe she's an accomplice. The rumors are licking like bonfire flames at her feet."

Quietly he swore. "Agnes?"

"Has been to see her," confirmed Duncan. "Including just today. She had to argue her way into the house and declares she practically shoved the butler aside to gain entrance. She thinks Mrs. Ramsay is about to flee town herself, to find her father and bring him home to prove his innocence." He cleared his throat. "And, coincidentally, escape the gossip, I imagine."

Drew rubbed his face with both hands. "Damn." He glanced up. "Agnes is sending you word, eh?"

Duncan flushed. "She turned to me for advice in your absence, and she's the only one Mrs. Ramsay will speak to. I offered Mrs. Ramsay my support and assistance directly, which she politely declined. But I'll tell you this—she's frightened, and with good reason."

Drew nodded. "Thank you." He levered himself

up and went to the desk. "Take one more note to Agnes for me, and I'll be in your debt."

THE CARRIAGE WAS waiting early the next morning. Mr. MacLeod took out her trunk and helped the driver stow it. Ilsa, who had not slept, pulled up the hood of her cloak, hugged her white-faced aunt good-bye, and stepped outside, eyes down. It was the first time she'd left the house since that horrible day Liam intercepted her, and she felt exposed and vulnerable just descending the steps.

"Ilsa! Ilsa, wait!"

She flinched. There went her hope to leave quietly and unnoticed. Why oh why hadn't Agnes respected her wishes?

"Have you come for Robert? Thank you," she said as Bella St. James, the fastest of them, flung herself in front of the carriage.

"Wait, please," the girl begged as her sisters dashed up, out of breath and, in Winnie's case, hatless. "You can't go off like this, you can't!"

"I must," she said in a low voice. "Please keep your voice down."

Winnie squeezed her hands together, looking anguished. "You can't think anyone blames you!"

Oh, but they did. Ilsa had Mr. MacLeod send out a boy to buy all the papers, and there was rampant speculation that Ilsa and perhaps Jean, too, had urged Deacon Fletcher to flee. The St. James girls must know it. She looked at Agnes in reproach, feeling betrayed.

"It's not right—it's not fair!" cried Bella.

"Life seldom is." Her voice sounded brittle to her own ears. "Go home, *please*."

"Drew is back," whispered Bella urgently. "If you'll only wait—"

God help her. "I have to go," she tried again.

"We worry for you." Agnes, the turncoat, stood an arm's length away, pale but composed. "We don't want you to race off into danger."

She lowered her voice even more. "We discussed this yesterday, and nothing has changed for me. Can you not do me the courtesy of trusting me to know what I must do and not do? Have you no faith in me?"

Agnes was blinking hard. "We *have* faith in you," she said, her voice quiet but trembling with emotion. "We are your friends, and we don't want you to get . . . hurt."

Ilsa swallowed. *Arrested,* was what Agnes had almost said. Their concern made her eyes sting, but they didn't understand. How could they? They probably didn't notice the faces peering from neighboring windows, but she did; she was used to them now, because she'd seen people stop outside her house to gawk and whisper. She'd seen the sheriff's officers stroll up and down the street several times a day, casting watchful eyes upon her door. She knew Mr. MacLeod had disposed of numerous items left on the steps, though he never would tell her what they were.

She was glad her friends didn't know about all that, but it reminded her that she couldn't let them dissuade her from the only course of action open to her. "Thank you for taking care of Robert. He would be so lonely with only my aunt."

Agnes bit her lip and glanced at her sisters. Tears slipped down Bella's cheeks. Winnie's gaze flitted from Agnes to Ilsa and back, as if begging one of them to relent. Ilsa's heart ached. She didn't want to part on bad terms with such dear friends.

She bowed her head and murmured, "Tell your mother I am terribly, terribly sorry for the damage to her shop. Tell your brother . . ." She paused. "Tell him I said good-bye." The word made her throat thicken, so she shook her head and said quickly, "No, don't. Don't tell him anything. I must go."

"Ilsa, please wait—talk to him—" whispered Bella.

Mr. MacLeod held the carriage door open and she climbed in, feeling both protected and imprisoned in the box of the carriage. The St. James girls drew back, whispering furiously among themselves. A small throng of people had collected across the street, avidly watching. Ilsa settled herself in the carriage, determined to ignore them even if their scrutiny made her skin crawl. *The thief's daughter,* she imagined them whispering. *Fleeing with the stolen funds, no doubt. Perhaps they ought to lock her in the Tolbooth to bring her vile father out of hiding.* This town which had been her home all her life had changed into something different in the course of a few days.

A thump on the back of the carriage made her jump. She knocked on the side panel. "Go!" The carriage started forward, then stopped, and the door opened again, giving her a jolt of alarm that she would be dragged from the vehicle by an angry crowd.

To her amazement Andrew St. James swung inside, closing the door behind him with a snap.

For a moment a wave of relief, longing, hope, even joy rose up inside her. It seemed an eternity since she'd laid eyes on him and now here he was—somehow he'd made it back to town and raced to her side.

When it was too late.

"What are you doing here?" was all she could gasp. She knocked on the side of the carriage again. "Go!"

"Don't do this." He reached for her hands. "Don't go. Tell the driver to stop the carriage."

Ilsa recoiled. "What?"

"Ilsa," he said urgently. "Listen to me. You can't help by running after your father."

She stared at him. How she had wished Drew was here, and now what he was saying . . . "That's not your decision to make."

He exhaled impatiently and dragged one hand through his hair. It was getting long, and there was stubble on his face and dark circles under his eyes. "I'm trying to persuade you, not command you."

"With what argument? You leap into my carriage and tell me to stop without so much as asking *why* I might have made this choice—"

"Why did you?" His head came up, his eyes intent on hers.

Ilsa flushed, thinking of the cruel stares and the horrid little book and Liam's mortifying display. She had no wish to describe that humiliation. "I have good reason."

"And I have good reason for asking you not to go. Will you listen to me?"

Jaw tight, she turned her head to stare blindly out the window. She couldn't refuse him and yet this was not what she had so desperately wanted from him.

"Leaving, particularly this way, at this time, looks very bad," he began carefully. "It suggests you know where he went." A pause. "Do you?"

She glared at him in outrage.

Drew sighed. "It also makes people think you're part of his plot."

"He didn't do it," she said through her teeth.

"Right." Drew nodded. "Supposing that's true—"

"Get out!" She lunged for the door. "If that's what you have to say, get out of my carriage!"

He stopped her, his hand covering hers. "Not until you hear me out. Ilsa, I want to help you—I am here as a friend."

"By persuading me to sit back and let my father go to the gallows? That is not a friend," she said before she could stop herself.

He went still, something flickering in his eyes. "I never said that."

"Supposing that's true," she said mockingly, throwing his words back at him.

His eyes closed in defeat. Ilsa gave another rattle at the door, and his hand convulsed on hers. "Let me go with you, then."

She swallowed the word *yes*. It came so readily to her lips with him. "Why?"

"Please." His free hand opened in appeal, then closed into a fist. "Please don't charge off alone, into God knows what, because you're frightened and hurt. I won't stop you but, please . . . let me come with you."

Frightened and hurt. How small those words felt to describe the days of anguish she'd suffered. She knew it wasn't his fault and she didn't want to argue with him—she still longed to throw herself into his arms and hear him tell her it would all come out well, somehow—but her heart and nerves had been shredded raw, she hadn't slept in days, and it was too much.

"Why?" she demanded bitterly. "You have no idea what's been said about me and my family this week, how our supposed friends and neighbors have turned on us, called me and my aunt accomplices, liars and thieves as bad as Papa—"

DREW HELD UP his hands as her voice rose. Agnes had warned him that Ilsa had been through hell in the last two weeks, that she looked haunted and tense and was not herself. He still wasn't prepared for the changes in her. Three weeks ago she'd been bright and carefree, smiling dreamily in his arms, the picture of poised elegance and beauty—except when she whispered in his ear to ride her harder and bit the side of his neck as they combusted together.

Today her eyes were red-rimmed, sunken, and shadowed. She'd lost weight and she looked as exhausted as he felt. She wore a plain gray dress, as opposite her former garb as possible, and he felt how her hand shook beneath his as she wrestled for the door handle.

"I won't," he promised, trying to gentle his tone. Saints, he was tired, and in consequence he was doing this very badly. "I won't stop you."

Her throat worked. "Why would you even want to come with me?"

"Because I care for you!" He plowed his hands into his hair, striving for calm and logic when his brain seemed to be tripping over itself. "Because

I've been mad with worry since Felix Duncan sent a man pelting up to Fort George to warn me there were dangerous rumors about your father. I got on my horse and raced back. I don't know what you've endured, beyond what Duncan and my sisters poured out on me last night—and I'm not sure I even understood half of what they said, since they spoke all at once."

She inhaled sharply. "Did you send them this morning? To stop me?"

He looked up in dismay. His sisters had roused him and Duncan from their beds early this morning, clamoring to know what he'd learned during the night. Winnie and Bella had been loud opponents of everything he proposed to do, certain that he was mucking up his one chance to help Ilsa. Agnes had listened to him, and to Duncan, but when her sisters ran out, saying they would stop Ilsa if he would not, she went with them. He'd told them not to go, not to cause a scene for Ilsa's sake, and still they'd bolted from the room before he was fully dressed. "I tried to hold them back. They would have had me break down your door in the middle of the night to keep you from going."

Ilsa turned her face to the window, where the scenery had shifted to the farms and meadows that lined the road south. They were almost free of Edinburgh. If she tossed him out now, he would have a miserably long walk.

Her next words cut deep. "You said you would return within a fortnight," she said, her voice wobbling.

"I'm sorry," he said quietly, cursing himself for giving in to all the entreaties to stay for one more farewell dinner. He hadn't thought there was reason to hurry. "It took longer than I expected."

She nodded stiffly.

"If I had known—or suspected—I would have rushed back," he added.

"No," she said. "Of course you shouldn't have. It is not your problem, nor your fault. I know you could not have changed anything had you been here."

But he heard the pain. Perhaps he couldn't have changed anything, but she wouldn't have had to endure it alone. He was in love with this woman, and when she needed him, he'd been drinking with his mates a hundred and seventy miles away, in perfect ignorance of the ordeal she was facing.

"What happened?" He'd heard from Agnes and his sisters, from Felix Duncan, from the sheriff-clerk and the procurator's deputy. None of them could tell him what he most needed to know.

A single tear slid down her cheek. Hastily she swiped it away. "A nightmare."

With a harsh sound he caught her hand and pulled her across the carriage into his lap. Ilsa resisted for a moment, but he wrapped his arms around her and she melted against him, her hands creeping around his neck.

"There," he breathed, holding her close and stroking her hair. "I've got you, love. We'll sort it together."

It felt so good to hold her again, even like this. For a long while she simply let him; Drew murmured mindlessly, assuring her that he wouldn't leave her again, that they would survive this, that she didn't have to carry the burden alone.

"What did you mean?" she whispered eventually. Her fingers had curled into his neckcloth, like a child, and his jacket beneath her cheek was damp. "You said I should not go alone into God knows what. What do you fear?"

He shifted her in his arms. "Never mind that."

"Tell me," she said, in the same numb voice. "If you want to go with me, be honest with me."

He shifted her weight and tried to choose his words with more care than before. "I only meant that you don't know whom or what you'll encounter, and what they might do to you."

"I only want to find Papa." She sounded drowsy.

He rubbed her back, wishing she would sleep so he could, too. He'd snatched no more than an hour of sleep before his sisters beat down Duncan's door. Now that he was with her, holding her, exhaustion was pulling hard at him. "Are you entirely certain he'll want to be found?"

Ilsa jerked upright, her head cracking against his chin. "What? Of course! He is my father—!"

"And he left without telling you where he was going." Drew froze, suddenly wary. Christ, why had he said that? "He didn't, did he?"

She stiffened. "That's twice you have suggested I know where he went and even helped him flee. What do you mean by that?"

"Where did you tell the driver to go?" he countered, his mouth once more running ahead of his tired brain.

She set her jaw. "Do you think my father is guilty?"

He didn't give a damn about William Fletcher. "It doesn't matter."

"It matters to me!" she cried.

"I'm not interested in him, guilty or innocent," Drew growled stubbornly. "Only in you."

"You said you wanted to catch the thieves." She put her hands against his chest and pushed. "You proposed the King's Pardon. The sheriff listens to you, the procurator-fiscal, the lord advocate . . ." Her gaze jumped to his, her eyes widening. "Did you follow me today to help them find Papa? Is that why you are here? You were determined to find the thieves . . ."

His muscles turned to stone, and he set her back on the opposite seat. "No." The word was hard and bitter on his tongue.

Ilsa pressed a hand to her mouth as though she would be sick. She blinked rapidly and he tensed to fling open the door and help her out. His own eyelids felt gritty from lack of sleep, and the carriage was warm, rocking back and forth over the well-worn road. When Ilsa leaned back, pale but more composed, he exhaled a sigh of relief.

"I can't make you trust me." He opened the window next to him for some air. "But I'm not lying. I'm not here at the behest of the procurator or the sheriff." He let down the shade on the other side to block the morning sun. "Agnes said the sheriff's officers came to your house."

"They searched it." She leaned her head against the wall of the carriage, the energy visibly draining from her. The smudges under her eyes looked even darker when her eyelashes fluttered closed.

Drew sighed. "Try to rest," he said gruffly. They could talk later. He had leapt into her carriage on faith and instinct, and that would have to be enough for now. Gently he spread the folded lap rug over her.

She blinked at him with unfocused eyes. "This is a nightmare," she mumbled again.

He cupped her cheek and brushed away the track of her tear with his thumb. "It is," he whispered. And there was nothing he could do to stop it.

Chapter Twenty-Three

They stopped in Dunbar, near the coast. He could smell the brine in the air even before they climbed down from the travel chaise. Drew had deliberately not asked again where they were headed, and Ilsa had not volunteered the information. She slept for some time and woke quiet and subdued. From the glances she stole at him, he could tell she didn't trust him.

The worst of it was, she was right not to. Once she fell asleep, he was paradoxically unable to close his eyes. He'd watched her for hours while dissecting and scrutinizing everything he knew. Drew had no intention of helping the Edinburgh sheriff apprehend William Fletcher, but neither would he exert himself to save the man unless it was necessary to help Ilsa. Because no matter how he tried to slant and explain the apparent facts, they looked very bad for Fletcher.

Duncan's letter to him at Fort George said only that Thomas Browne, a common criminal familiar to the sheriff-officers, had come forward to claim the pardon. Under questioning, he readily gave up one accomplice, Edward Stephens, a fellow known for gambling and long suspected of thieving, who was apprehended on the verge of boarding a coach for Berwick in possession of stolen goods.

But Browne had also declared that the leader of the ring, the mastermind of every operation, was still at large, with the tantalizing hint that it was a highly respected citizen of Edinburgh. Rumors sprouted at once. Stephens had done odd jobs for Fletcher, and Browne told the officers the thieves had used false keys to open the locks of the robbed shops. Within hours Deacon Fletcher's name had come up, and Duncan had sent his letter express at dawn the next morning.

Drew hadn't slept the previous night because he'd roused the deputy procurator from his bed and demanded to know all. It was a shameless abuse of his newly elevated status, and he did not care. Unfortunately what he learned was that things had only got worse for the deacon.

Browne's accusations were credible, detailed, and complete, in the sheriff's eyes. He had led the officers to a bunch of keys hidden near Fletcher's cabinetry workshop in Dunbar's Close, which opened a number of victims' doors. Stephens had become far more cooperative when it emerged that his wife had helped sell some of the stolen goods; in exchange for her freedom, he told the officers where to find more items waiting to be smuggled to Berwick. The goldsmith had identified several pieces as his.

Browne refused to name the mastermind; he wanted a reward for that, not just a pardon. Suspicion had already fallen on Fletcher because of the keys and where they were found, and the fact that William Fletcher was known to have been hired to repair or replace locks at some of the burgled shops. Officers had uncovered Fletcher's history of wagering—and losing—at the cockpits. It was circumstantial, but highly suggestive.

Once the man fled Edinburgh, though, both Browne and Stephens swore that William Fletcher was indeed the planner and instigator of their robberies, that they shared their spoils evenly between them, and that he'd told them often that if any of them got caught, he would leave them all to twist on the rope. No one, he'd allegedly boasted, would believe *he* was a thief.

Everything fit. The sheriff believed Browne and Stephens. Drew couldn't see a reason not to.

He knew it would be harder for Ilsa. Drew's own father had certainly fooled him, charming and genial, never hinting that he'd mortgaged the silk shop and gone into debt. It wasn't as bad as robbing half of Edinburgh, but it had taken Drew years to repair the damage and cost him his chance at attending university, as he'd dreamt of doing. Ilsa had been raised as a beloved only child, adoring and adored by her father, and she would defend him to the last. Drew didn't even plan to try convincing her.

He drew a deep breath of bracing salty air as she stepped stiffly down. "I'll secure rooms," was all he said.

She didn't look at him. "Thank you."

He took two rooms and asked for dinner. Fortunately the inn was almost empty, and the innkeeper was able to offer them a private parlor. They ate in silence.

"Will we travel again tomorrow?" he asked after a while.

Her glance was dark with suspicion. God, how he hated that.

"I'll speak to the driver if we are," he added. "Tell him to make preparations."

She reached for her wine. Most of her dinner was still on her plate. "No, I don't think so."

He nodded. So Dunbar was their destination, not merely a waypoint. Coaches left for England every day, and the harbor offered flight abroad. Did Ilsa suspect—or know—her father was here? Fletcher had left Edinburgh several days ago; it would be foolish for him to linger so near for so long, but then again, no one had found him yet.

"Shall I go with you tomorrow?"

"No!" She flushed and rubbed her temple. "Please don't ask me questions," she said softly. "You say you don't care whether Papa is innocent or not, but I do care, very much. I accept that I'm the only one who believes in him, but I don't want to argue and defend myself to you. Isn't it enough that you're here?"

"Aye," he said after a moment. "Go on to bed. You look about to drop where you are."

She gave him a sad, searching look and got to her feet. "Good night, Captain."

He sat for a long time at the table, that final word racketing around in his brain. *Captain*. Not Andrew, or Drew, let alone anything more affectionate. She kept her distance and didn't trust him enough to tell him what she meant to do. The easy warmth and powerful attraction between them might never have been.

Drew gripped the back of his neck. His feelings had not changed. Hell, even though William

Fletcher appeared as guilty as sin to him, he would have extended that King's Pardon to Fletcher, if he could have, damning any protests from the lord advocate and no matter that his own mother's shop had been victimized, just to save Ilsa from further heartache.

There was no chance of that, obviously. Not only had Fletcher been named the mastermind and chief conspirator, he had fled like a guilty man.

So think, he told himself. *How* can *you help her?*

Ilsa was not surprised to see Drew when she came down early the next morning. Yesterday he'd worn his red coat and Stuart tartan, looking every inch the King's man—the King, whose pardon had been dangled in front of a thief to coax him into blaming another man for the robberies. Even though it was Drew, whom she'd yearned to see and hold again, the red coat had jarred her.

Today he wore a more familiar dark green jacket and plain kilt. He still wore a sword at his hip and a dagger in his belt, but she felt more at ease. A full night's sleep no doubt also helped. Being out of Edinburgh made her feel like she could breathe again—and, she knew deep in her heart, so did Drew's presence, even if she didn't quite trust his assurance that the sheriff-clerk knew nothing about it.

"Do you go into town?" he asked over breakfast.

"It's not far," she said vaguely. "I fancy a walk after the long drive yesterday." She hated not feeling able to confide in him.

He looked down. His hair had grown, and dark curls fell over his forehead now. She gripped her teacup to avoid stroking them back. She knew how his hair felt tangled in her fingers, when she held him close and kissed him. "When shall you return?"

She wiggled her shoulders. "A few hours."

"Excellent." He drained his mug and stood. "I've a few things to do, as well."

Ilsa was taken aback, but if she wouldn't tell him where she went, she couldn't ask where he went. "Very good. I will be ready to leave when I have my hat."

They walked together into the town with minimal conversation. Ilsa was covertly studying the stone houses and trying to remember Jean's directions, and Drew seemed absorbed in his own thoughts. When Dunbar Castle rose in front of them he bade her farewell. "Are you certain you wish to go alone?" he asked again, his gaze probing.

She fisted her hands, digging her fingers into her gloved palms. "Yes." She wished she was as confident as she sounded. "I shall see you back at the inn."

Drew only made a polite bow and turned, going toward the harbor. She watched him for a moment, wondering where he went and why, then resolutely turned away, heading east. It was near the beach, Jean had said, whitewashed with blue shutters.

Ilsa found it after a half hour's walk. With great trepidation, she knocked on the door. Pleasantly but determinedly, she asked to see the mistress of the house. She was shown into a neat parlor, and a woman about Jean's age came in.

"Mrs. Murray?" said Ilsa. "Miss Mary Fletcher, as was?"

"Aye," said the woman curiously. "And I've not the pleasure of your acquaintance."

"You do, but it's been many years. I'm Ilsa," she said. "William Fletcher's daughter. And I need your help to save him from the hangman."

DREW FINISHED HIS errands in good time. Dunbar had a small but active harbor. It might offer a departure point, but there weren't enough ships for a man to slip away unnoticed, as there were in London or Glasgow.

No, he was certain that if Fletcher had been here, it had been only briefly. More likely Ilsa had come to see someone who knew something, perhaps unwittingly. That only made him more on edge, prowling the streets, trying to plan for a number of possibilities.

Finally he turned back toward the inn, riding his new brown gelding and leading another on a rope. He missed his own horse, but he'd pushed that animal to the limit riding back to Edinburgh from Fort George, covering two hundred miles of bad road in six days. At the same time, the close confines of the carriage yesterday had made his skin crawl. He couldn't see anything or anyone from inside a carriage.

He left the horses at the inn. Ilsa hadn't returned, and restlessly he walked out again. Her plan was mad, whatever it was. Either Fletcher was hiding here, stupidly lingering within a day's ride of Edinburgh while the rewards for his capture were spread all over Scotland, or he'd left already, and Ilsa would have only made the sheriff more suspicious of her.

He was terribly afraid for her. If she knew how to find her father, then she'd lied to the sheriff. Under

Drew's midnight badgering, the procurator's deputy admitted that they thought she already had. They knew Ilsa had gone straight to her father after a gossipy friend of her aunt revealed that someone had come forward for the pardon, and that Deacon Fletcher had fled town the next morning. David MacGill told Sheriff Cockburn that Fletcher had sent him a letter for his daughter, which he had delivered to her. Cockburn had gone to see Ilsa at once, and thought the letter was very nearly a confession. Ilsa had claimed it wasn't her father's handwriting, suggesting Mr. MacGill had written it himself, but Cockburn didn't believe that. They were sure she knew something and was hiding it.

Drew cursed as he paced the road toward town. He'd argued to the deputy for two hours that night that Ilsa couldn't have anything to do with the robberies. She'd been with him in Perth during the worst run of them, where he and Felix Duncan could attest that she'd neither sent nor received communication from Edinburgh. What's more, she had no reason to steal, having a handsome fortune and—unlike her father—no known penchant for gambling or unsavory companions. Her only possible crime, Drew had insisted, was loyal devotion to her parent, which was not illegal no matter the state of that parent's soul. Did they really mean to arrest a woman without evidence of any kind?

The deputy had said of course not, but that if she had any information, Drew should strongly encourage her to bring it to him. For her own sake.

Instead Drew had gone with her when he couldn't persuade her to stay. He'd known he would all along. Whatever the truth of her actions, he couldn't stop thinking of Ilsa saying that she was used to going alone, being alone, doing things alone. He didn't want her to do *this* alone. Especially not when he suspected the sheriff would have men following her, to see if she led them to Fletcher.

Which was why he hadn't told the sheriff.

Or his family.

Or the Duchess of Carlyle.

He was already far beyond when he'd promised to return to Carlyle. As the weeks slipped by, he had put off his letter to Mr. Edwards again and again. It still lay in the desk in Duncan's spare room, barely begun, containing nothing of import except David MacGill's unsuitability. And now there was no way to finish it—he had no idea where he was going or when he would return, or if he was inadvertently helping a wanted man escape the King's justice, all because he had lost his heart to a bewitching, exuberant Scotswoman with a loyal, loving spirit who wanted nothing to do with his English title.

And that woman had been gone a long time. He hesitated, not wanting to risk her trust again but unable to shake off the feeling of unease. *Damn it,* he thought, and lengthened his stride toward Dunbar.

ILSA MEANT TO stay only a little while, but once Mary started talking, it was hard to leave. After the horror of the last fortnight, it was such a relief and a pleasure to speak fondly of Papa with another person who believed him innocent.

Her head was full as she walked briskly back toward the inn. It was a splendidly beautiful day and she filled her lungs, heartened not only by her visit with Cousin Mary but by the exercise and fresh air. She hadn't dared go out after the scene with Liam, and her soul seemed to unfold and heal a little in the warm sunshine.

She was thinking of what she would tell Drew—she couldn't send him away, nor did she want to anymore, but she was determined to keep him in the dark as much as possible, for his sake—when someone said her name behind her. Like an idiot, she stopped and turned, only to realize with alarm that the two men approaching her were not friends.

One of them doffed his hat, which did nothing to soften his implacable expression. "Mrs. Ramsay, a moment of your time, if you please."

She clutched the hem of her jacket and kept her spine rigid. "Who, pray, are you, sir?"

"George Williamson, ma'am. King's Messenger for North Britain." He motioned at his companion. "And Mr. Hay, sheriff-officer of Edinburgh."

Mr. Hay was Mrs. Arbuthnot's loose-lipped brother-in-law. Her heart stuck in her throat. She managed a nod and resumed walking. "Regrettably, I am in a hurry. Good day, sirs."

They fell in on either side of her. Sweat beaded the back of her neck. She ought to have let Drew accompany her. "We can talk as we go, ma'am."

"I'm sure I have nothing interesting to tell you." She kept her eyes straight ahead and walked as briskly as her feet would go.

"Perhaps not," agreed Mr. Williamson affably. "But perhaps you'd be so kind as to oblige us by answering a few questions."

"Where is your father now?" asked Mr. Hay. He was a big fellow with hard, squinty eyes and a suspicious expression.

"I don't know," she said evenly.

"Have you any idea where he might have gone?"

"He has frequently expressed a desire to see Paris," she replied. "I suggest you seek him there."

Mr. Hay growled. Mr. Williamson smiled, but she sensed his patience was waning. "Anywhere else? Where does he have family?"

"My grandparents came from Perth, but they have both passed away," she told them truthfully. "His only sibling, his sister, resides in Edinburgh with me. You already know that." Mr. Williamson didn't blink. "And his cousin Mrs. Murray lives here. I've been to visit her, in fact. I assure you she also knows nothing of his whereabouts, but by all means inquire with her directly."

"And you've just come on a whim to see her," said the officer cynically.

"I wished to leave Edinburgh," she said, her voice growing tight. They showed no signs of leaving and the inn still seemed a league away. "Perhaps you can guess why, after your fellow officers searched my home and gave everyone to believe I conspired with the criminals."

"Not all the criminals," Mr. Hay said with a sharp look. "Only the one. Your father."

She swallowed. Her heart beat a sharp tattoo against her breastbone. Would they seize her? Would they arrest her? Would they tell Drew, or arrest him, too? Had he led them to her, or had she led him into disaster?

Then the man himself appeared over the rise of

the road, and she couldn't stop a gasp of relief. Both officers looked up.

"What luck meeting you here, Captain," said Mr. Hay sardonically as Drew approached. "Mr. Cockburn thought we might. He sends his regards."

"Very kind of him. Convey mine to him, sir." Drew barely bowed his head at the officers. "Mrs. Ramsay, I apologize for not meeting you sooner."

"I enjoyed the walk," she said with a smile, trying to hide how fast her heart was racing. "I had a delightful visit with my cousin. You were too kind to indulge me."

"I am delighted to hear it." He looked at the men flanking her with unmistakable hauteur and command. "Is that all?"

Mr. Williamson cleared his throat. "Nay, Captain. We've a few more questions for Mrs. Ramsay."

"Oh?" Drew's brow arched impatiently. "What are they?"

"Where did William Fletcher go?" demanded Mr. Hay.

"I don't know—"

"Ah, ma'am, we can't truly believe that," said Williamson almost regretfully.

"The lady answered your question." Drew's tone was icy.

Williamson stepped forward, hands raised to placate. He spoke to Drew, his voice low and calm. Mr. Hay leaned closer to Ilsa. "What did that letter mean? The one your solicitor brought?"

"I showed it to Mr. Cockburn." Her throat was tight. "Though I doubt my father even wrote it . . ."

"Convenient story, that." He took hold of her arm. "Obviously there was something hidden in it, wasn't there? Some clue that made you hurry all the way to Dunbar to see a distant cousin for a few hours."

"Let go of me," she said, her voice trembling. "I can visit family if I wish."

Instead he took a pair of manacles from his pocket. "You'll have to come back to Edinburgh, Mrs. Ramsay."

The sight of the manacles sparked a panic inside her. He meant to chain her up and drag her back to town—lock her in the Tolbooth—bully her and threaten her and, most horribly of all, keep her from finding Papa and clearing his name. She pulled against his grip, and he gave her a sharp shake, so hard her teeth clacked together.

"None of that, now," he growled. "You've got a fair bit to answer for." He squeezed her wrist into the manacle, so tightly she cried out. She twisted, trying to pull away from him, and he yanked her back against him.

Then he gave a shout and shoved her away, so hard she sprawled on her face in the dirt. For a moment she couldn't breathe; her head had hit the ground, knocking off her hat, and the dirt and rocks of the road scoured her cheek. Ilsa struggled to sit up. Mr. Hay glared at her, one hand clapped to his chin, where a long thin scratch oozed blood. Her hatpin, she realized.

Then Hay jerked backward, his small eyes going wide in surprise.

From Ilsa's position sprawled on the ground, Drew towered like an avenging angel as he threw Mr. Hay to the ground and stalked after him. He snarled something and put his boot on the man's chest as Hay attempted to scramble to his feet, sending him flying again. Once more the officer tried to get up, and this time Drew let him, only to fell him with a punch that made his head snap around. Mr. Hay didn't move when he hit the ground for a third time.

Flexing his hand, perhaps still breathing fire, Drew turned to her. "Are you injured?"

Wide-eyed, she shook her head.

For a moment they stared at each other, until something shattered inside her breast. With a strangled sob she scrambled up from the ground and flung herself at him. He caught her with both arms, hauling her off her feet and covering her face with kisses. Crying, still shaking, she kissed him wholeheartedly, clasping his face between her hands.

"You hit him," she sobbed between kisses.

"He hurt you," Drew replied. His wounded hand stroked over her hair; her hat was somewhere in the dirt. He touched her scraped cheek, his mouth flat with anger. "You looked so terrified—you're sure you're not badly hurt?"

She nodded, her lips trembling.

"Good." He kissed her hard once more, then set her back down and stooped over Mr. Hay. He came back with a ring of keys and unlocked the manacle from her wrist, flinging it and the keys into the tall grass of the field. With a grunt he heaved the officer up off the road, hauling him several feet away into the grass.

"Where is the other?" she asked fearfully.

Drew glanced over his shoulder. "Over there. He tried to stop me from coming to you."

The country here was lonely, rising and falling in gentle hills. Drew jogged back to where Mr. Williamson sprawled, a thin trickle of blood on his mouth. He carried Mr. Williamson to where he'd left Mr. Hay, and settled them both with some care.

"Are they dead?" she whispered. She'd only managed to retrieve her hat and stood watching in awe.

"Nay. They'll wake soon. I only want to buy time." He took her hand and set off at a brisk pace in the direction he'd come from.

Ilsa hurried along behind him. "Time for what?"

"For us to leave," he said evenly. "When they come around, they'll go to the local sheriff and then we'll be in the fire." He gave her a fraught look. "We have to go now. I hope you learned what you needed."

The local sheriff would arrest them both. Drew had assaulted law officers, one of whom would probably say she had stabbed him when he tried to subdue her. Terrified, Ilsa nodded.

They reached the inn and she ran up the stairs to her room. Drew followed close behind, whispering to her to gather only a change of clothes and any papers, and to pack the rest in her small trunk. A few minutes later he tapped on her door and handed her a wrapped package, which turned out to be a pair of breeches. "Dress to ride," he told her.

A quarter of an hour later they rode out on two strange horses, which apparently belonged to Drew now. Without a word Ilsa took the lead, choosing the road leading southwest.

They rode for an hour before speaking. "What of our things?" she finally asked.

"I left a note and some coin for the chaise driver, asking that he return your trunk to your aunt in Edinburgh. I explained we would go the rest of the way by horseback." He lifted one shoulder. "One less person who can tell anyone where you're bound."

She nodded, feeling as if she were in a play on the stage, wholly unreal and fantastical. They were wanted criminals on the run now. Merciful heavens, how her life had changed in a few short weeks. Had it really been little more than a month since she'd run through the maze at Stormont Palace with him and spent the night in his bed, her greatest worry being how to sneak back to her own room unseen?

"I take it you know where we're heading," he said, breaking the silence.

"Yes." She hadn't meant to tell him, but there was no longer any doubt that they were in this together, for better and for worse. "Glasgow."

Chapter Twenty-Four

They kept well clear of Edinburgh, running south as far as Melrose before turning west. The Lowlands were far easier traveling than the rocky crags of the Highland Cairngorms he had so recently raced through. Vastly relieved to be on a more maneuverable horse than boxed in a carriage, Drew kept a keen eye out for any more followers.

There would be hell to pay for what he'd done in Dunbar. Neither Williamson nor Hay would suffer any lasting harm, but Drew had burnt his authority and respectability to ash by assaulting them and fleeing with the woman they sought.

Williamson had told him in no uncertain terms that Ilsa must return to Edinburgh. Drew had been trying to convince him otherwise when Hay shoved her to the ground, having already locked one manacle around her wrist.

Well. There was no going back now. Ilsa rode ahead of him, her back straight, as at home astride the hastily acquired horse as she had been on Duncan's long-legged gelding. They didn't talk much, but there was no need. She no longer avoided his eyes, and that alone eased the tension in his heart.

Of where they were headed and what they would

do there, he thought very little. It didn't matter. He had bound himself to her, like a liege knight to his queen, and where she led he would follow.

The first night they stopped on the edge of a quiet little wood, where the grass was thick and soft and a stream ran nearby. Ilsa nibbled her lip at the prospect of sleeping in the open, her eyes flitting up and down the road behind them.

"Don't worry," he assured her, unsaddling the horses and setting them to graze. "I'll keep watch."

"Wouldn't it be better to find an inn? We'll be defenseless out here . . ."

He put his hand on his sword. "Cold words, lass. I've been an army officer for a decade, and ye fear for yer life in my hands?" He shook his head, and she smiled reluctantly, as intended.

Later, when they had a small fire going and the horses were snuffling quietly nearby, Ilsa crept close to him. "Thank you," she said, drawing up her knees under her chin.

"For what?" He watched her, his arms folded across his chest as he leaned against a sapling.

The fire flickered on her unbound hair, blue-black in the dark. "For following me. I was cruel to you in the carriage."

"You were wary."

She looked at him, her eyes midnight pools. "I was wrong. I'm sorry for the things I said."

"We're all wrong at times. No sin in making certain of someone."

She touched the knuckles of his right hand. They would be sore tomorrow; the officer was a big fellow, and Drew had hit him hard. "You struck the sheriff-clerk's officer. Two of them." Her fingers ran over his. "If you hadn't been there, they would have arrested me and made me go back to Edinburgh."

He flipped his hand and grasped hers. "It didn't happen. Don't dwell on it."

"No," she whispered, staring at their clasped hands. There was an ugly bruise circling her wrist from the manacle. "Because you didn't let it." She raised her eyes. "I know where Papa's gone."

Drew's stomach clenched.

"I did not know before I spoke to Cousin Mary," she went on, staring at their little fire. She made no effort to pull her hand from his. "Mary is his only cousin. The Fletchers are a clan of small families. When my mother died, Mary came to stay with us for a few months. I believe she hoped Papa would marry her." A faint half smile lit her face. "Papa was so handsome and charming and clever, everyone was in love with him . . . He did not marry her, though, and she went away and married someone else, but they remained deeply fond of each other. Talking about him with her was wonderful."

Drew wondered if Ilsa counted too much on Fletcher's charm. "Then those men will find her and demand she tell them what she told you."

Finally some animation returned to her face. "She'll tell them these charges are lies! Mary would take any secret of Papa's to her grave, but she doesn't even know what to tell them. If I'd been thinking clearly, I would have figured it out without going to Dunbar, but I'm still glad I went. Mary had heard rumors and was worried. Talking to her reminded me. Papa will go to the Lord of Princes."

He stole a quick, alarmed glance at her. Did

Fletcher mean to take his own life? "What does that mean?"

"It's a solicitor in Glasgow. Archibald Lorde in Prince's Street. Papa says he looks like an archbishop and calls him the Lord of Princes, as a great joke."

Drew couldn't keep back a bark of laughter. Perhaps Fletcher was more cunning than he'd thought. "It would take Cockburn's men a long time to riddle that one."

"It rather sounds like a suicide, doesn't it?" Incredibly, she laughed, too. "I'd entirely forgotten him. Papa knows I don't approve of his investments in tobacco, so he never speaks of them to me. Mr. Lorde was engaged because he's in Glasgow, where most of the trading companies are based. If Papa is in need of funds, he could turn to Mr. Lorde, particularly once he'd cut his ties with Mr. MacGill.

"Mary mentioned fondly the annuity Papa settled on her at her marriage." Ilsa sighed. "Jean has one, as well. Papa has a generous heart. But Mr. Lorde pays those. It's much too humble for the great David MacGill, I suppose," she finished dourly.

"Will this Lorde cooperate if he knows your father is wanted in Edinburgh?"

She gave him a look. "Papa's not guilty, which Mr. Lorde will understand."

MacGill hadn't. Drew let it pass. "If he has papers from Lorde in his home, the sheriff will find them and visit Glasgow."

"They haven't found them yet—or at least, they didn't mention it to me," she said slowly. "Papa might have taken those with him . . ."

Which sounded like the act of a guilty man. Again Drew didn't say it.

Ilsa freed her hand and twisted to face him. He leaned back and watched her, his hands flat on the ground beside his hips. Tentatively she leaned forward and pressed a light kiss to his cheek. "Thank you," she whispered.

"For what?" He turned his head slightly, inhaling the scent of her skin, and let his lips skim her cheek.

"For coming back. For being concerned for me. For staying with me even after I told you to go away, when you could have gone back to your happy life in Edinburgh and left me to muddle along as I entirely deserved."

"I care for you." He caught her chin and feathered his mouth over hers. "A great deal. I couldn't bear it if something terrible happened to you."

"Thanks to you, it didn't."

"Nor will it," he growled, and then he kissed her as he'd wanted to do for weeks, deeply, hungrily, completely. Her mouth opened under his and she pressed up against him, her hands at his shoulders, in his hair, tugging at his neckcloth.

Her dress came loose under his hands. Impatiently he lifted her, setting her astride him and pulling down her bodice, baring her to his starving gaze. Her skin was pearly pale in the moonlight and his hand shook as he trailed his fingers down her throat, slowing as he reached the swell of her breast above the confines of her stays. She watched him, her lips parted, her hair streaming over her shoulders, as she undid the knot at his neck and opened his shirt.

Drew's head fell back in helpless surrender when she leaned forward and pressed her mouth there, to the pulse at the base of his throat. This woman had enthralled him and captivated him; if she left him forever tomorrow, he would never forget her or stop wanting her.

She kissed her way up his neck as her hands moved around his shoulders until she gripped his hair, tugging his face back to her. Rising up on her knees, she rested her forehead against his, her breath light and rapid against his lips.

"I love you," she whispered. "I'm sorry, Drew, I've tried not to—"

With a harsh exclamation he seized the nape of her neck. "Why are you sorry for that?"

"Because I'm ruined now, and dragging you down with me." She touched the corner of his mouth, shadowed by three days of beard. "I can't stop, though. I still love you. I still want you. I think I always will."

He pulled her face to his and kissed her even as he tumbled her backward onto the soft summer grass and yanked down her stays just enough to taste her plump nipple. She moaned and clutched at his hair, her knees coming up around him, and he rucked up her skirts with both hands, spreading her satiny soft legs, completely bare all the way up.

He touched her, stroked her, marveled at the way her eyes widened, reveled in the ragged gasp of want she made, and then he was inside her, where he longed to be, held tight in her arms and legs as she begged him for more, her teeth on his skin making his nerves crackle like lightning had struck him, her hips rising to meet his every thrust with the same urgency and hunger, until she broke and shuddered beneath him, so tight around him, and he let go and poured his very life into her.

But her words festered in his mind—*I'm dragging you down with me*—and he didn't know what to say. All his hopeful plans laid on the road to Fort George seemed built on sand now, with the high tide of reality rising to wash it all away. She was no longer respectable, and he could no longer count on the good graces and indulgence of the duchess. There would possibly be warrants issued for their arrest soon.

The only thing he could say was the one truth he still knew. Holding her close, he pressed his cheek to hers and whispered, "Let the world go hang. I love you, Ilsa."

And will for all time.

Chapter Twenty-Five

Glasgow was a small but handsome town, with houses built of stone and many impressive public buildings. It was a great hub of commerce, though the main harbor at Port Glasgow was several miles down the Clyde; here was where the tobacco lords built their mansions and flaunted their wealth, princes among the merchants.

Ilsa surveyed it with weary eyes. They had avoided inns for the last few days of hard riding across fields and through woods and along narrow rutted roads that were impassable except by horseback. Drew had promised her a proper room tonight, with a hot bath and fresh clothes, and she was irrationally eager for it.

They bypassed the large and well-known Saracen's Head Inn and took a room in a small establishment away from the main street. Drew kept his word; servants were hauling in the bathing tub even as they climbed the stairs. He left her with a rueful smile and a soft touch on her cheek, saying he would be back in an hour.

Ilsa knew he was as tired as she was. When they slept in the open, he'd been awake and watching every time her eyes fluttered open. He only shrugged and called it army training when she protested, but she was keenly aware how much he'd done for her.

She peeled off her dirty clothes and sank naked into the tub when the maids left, content just to soak in the hot water and not feel linen against her skin. Unfortunately, that left her free to examine the darker corners of her mind and the thoughts that had been quietly growing there.

When she left Edinburgh, it had been on a wave of righteous indignation that Papa was being framed and slandered. It was easy to embrace a bold course when it was only her own reputation and name at stake. She believed in Papa; of course she would find him and save him, and curse the gossiping tongues of Edinburgh for saying otherwise. She was a lonely warrior waging her battle for redemption, and she was fine with that.

But now she was not. In her moment of weakness, when she gave in to her own longing and let Drew accompany her, she had yoked him to her quest. She knew he didn't believe in Papa's innocence. She knew he was only here because he loved her, more than he ought to do and far more than she deserved.

And because of that—because of her—he had thrown away his good name and sterling reputation.

A gentleman had fled town with a woman suspected of helping a wanted criminal escape justice. An officer in the English army had attacked and subdued officers of the law. The heir to a dukedom was probably wanted on charges in Edinburgh right now, and his disgrace would hurt not only him but his family, his mother and sisters, whose approval and affection Ilsa had yearned for so desperately.

She wondered what the very proper English duchess at Carlyle Castle would say when she heard about Drew's actions. Then she shivered and thought no, she would prefer not to know. It was bad enough thinking what Mrs. St. James would say. Ilsa's throat tightened as she remembered how it had felt to think that she might have a mother in her life, in those few halcyon days before Papa's fall from grace shattered her world.

And that exposed the most painful thought, the one that had been festering in her mind since Dunbar. She had told herself Papa was innocent, that these charges were lies from front to back, that when she found her father, he would confidently assert his innocence and explain his disappearance in some of the same terms Winnie had used: he had left town to avoid being unjustly accused; he had gone to amass evidence proving his defense; he planned a triumphant return with the forces of truth and justice on his side.

But now . . . she was not so certain.

Drew's questions, which she had dismissed with such scorn, had privately unsettled her. Would Papa want to be found? Why hadn't he reassured her and Jean before he left? Why had he left at all? What had he meant by that horribly guilty letter?

What if he weren't entirely innocent?

What if he weren't innocent at all?

What if she had lured Drew into ruin and disgrace for a lie?

She loved him more than anything in the world—

more than Robert, more than Papa, more than her independence. And she had ruined him.

The door opened behind her, and Drew came in with a package under one arm. Ilsa clasped her arms to her chest; while he was out taking care of things, she had been lying in the cooling water staring at the ceiling. "You're back," she murmured.

"Aye." He set the package on the bed. "A dress and unmentionables. Not very fine ones," he said with a note of apology. "I've scant experience buying ladies' garments."

She felt sick but made herself smile. "I gave my clothes to the maid to wash. Anything clean will be a luxury. Thank you."

His mouth quirked. "Since I made you send everything else back to Edinburgh, 'twas the least I could do."

He had done that so they could escape the sheriff-officers sent to arrest her. Ilsa put her hands on the edge of the tub and got to her feet. "I don't mind."

His gaze seared her from head to toe. "If you need anything else," he said in a low, gravelly voice, "tell me."

There wasn't another man in the world equal to him. No one else would have done what he had done for her, even when he thought her conclusions were wrong and her quest was doomed and it would cost him dearly.

Ilsa stepped out of the tub. "There is one thing . . ." She crossed the room toward him, water trickling down her bare body. She stopped in front of him and slid her hands up his broad chest, pushing the dust-covered jacket from his shoulders. With steady hands she unbuckled his belt and pulled the plaid free, letting it fall. She undid his neckcloth and the buttons of his shirt before stripping that off him, too.

He stood rigidly, his breath uneven. "Ilsa, you must be exhausted," he tried to say, but she put her finger on his lips.

"This is what I need," she said, and pushed him with her fingertips toward the bed. Without resistance he sank onto the mattress, falling back on his elbows, his eyes burning as he watched her.

I know this cannot last, she thought as she went down on her knees. *I know he's not for me*. She dragged her fingertips down his stomach, taking a wicked thrill from his harsh inhalation. *I know these will be my last days with him. And I will let him go without a fight because he deserves someone much better than I.*

She made love to him with her mouth, as he had done for her, until he pulled her up and rolled her under him to sheath himself in her body. Ilsa dug her nails into his back, hooked her legs around his waist, and urged him to ride her harder, wanting it to last forever, desperate for the oblivion this incendiary passion offered.

And when he slept beside her that night, his arm strong and comforting around her, she clasped his hand to her lips and whispered once more, "I love you."

And that's why I'm going to let you go.

DREW WAS READY to tear Glasgow apart to find William Fletcher.

He sensed a change in Ilsa when they arrived. A sort of melancholy seemed to steal over her, casting a shadow over everything, even when she looked at him and smiled or pulled him close in bed. The nearest thing he could compare it to was soldiers strapping on their weapons in anticipation of a battle, preparing to face their doom.

They located Archibald Lorde's offices in Prince's Street. Ilsa spoke to the clerk, who told them to wait while he disappeared into the inner sanctum.

After a lengthy wait the clerk ushered them back. Lorde was a tall, pale fellow with a beatific smile. "Mrs. Ramsay, Captain St. James, pray be seated."

Ilsa waited until the door was securely closed. "Mr. Lorde, I am here to see my father, William Fletcher."

Nothing betrayed the man. "I'm sorry, madam, I have not seen him."

She nodded and bent over the desk, reaching for the pen. "Of course not," she said as she wrote on a piece of paper. The solicitor watched with one brow raised. "If you should happen to see him or hear from him, give him this." She dusted the page with sand to dry the ink and held it out. "Please, Mr. Lorde."

He sighed. "Mrs. Ramsay. I don't know what you mean."

"I understand." The paper remained steady in her outstretched hand. "Please, sir."

With a jerk of his head he indicated to leave it on the desk. "I really can offer you no hope."

"I understand. I will return tomorrow afternoon, though, just in case." She curtsied. "Good day, Mr. Lorde."

Out on the street again, Drew asked, "What did you write?"

"I wrote that Cordelia would be ashamed of him." She tugged her cloak around herself. "Cordelia was my mother. If Papa can be lured out, her name will do it."

That night he finally broached a question that had been nagging at him. "What will you say to him?"

She was silent for a long time. "When I was young, my father was an epic figure to me. Larger than life, the handsomest man alive, clever and witty and charming. Everyone admired him. I remember walking with him and ladies would drop their handkerchiefs in front of him. He always retrieved them with a gallant word and bow. I said Mary would have wed him—so would any number of ladies about town."

"Why did he never remarry?"

"I think he liked the attention too much," was her soft answer. "Why wed one woman when you could command the attentions of a dozen, flirt with them and dance with them and always have a smiling, fetching woman vying for your attention?"

To have a companion, he thought. *To have someone to comfort and support you. To share life's joy with. To give your lonely, motherless daughter a mother and siblings. To love and to cherish.*

"It was not merely ladies," she went on. "Men the breadth of town respected and deferred to him. My grandfather founded the cabinetry shop and was a deacon before him, but Papa is a brilliant carver and crafts beautiful pieces. He would have been successful if he'd started from nothing, but he has held an elevated position all his life. Losing that . . ." She sighed. "I imagine if you asked him, he would say he'd rather die than be shamed and reviled by those who used to solicit his advice and good opinion. He is a proud man."

Her hair had wound around his fingers. Drew fingered the silky lock. "You don't think he'll return to Edinburgh."

Barring incontrovertible proof of innocence, Deacon Fletcher faced a daunting prospect in town.

This time Ilsa's answer was almost too quiet to hear. "I don't see how he will. But I need to hear it from him." She looked at him in the darkness, touching his chin. "What did you do when your father died? Agnes told me it was not easy for you—"

He let out his breath. "No. We didn't learn of his failings until he was gone."

"But you endured it," she murmured.

His arm tightened around her. "There was no choice. He was gone, but my mother and sisters were still here, still in need, and I had to provide for them."

"Agnes said you were to go to university."

"Once upon a time," he said after a moment.

"What did you hope to study?"

"Astronomy. Mathematics. I fancied going to sea." It was like a distant dream to speak of those things now.

"Instead you went into the army. When Agnes told me, I thought it a very unimaginative choice." Some life sparked in her voice. "A clever fellow would have chosen piracy."

He grinned. "Daring thought! Stupidly I thought the army would pay more reliably."

Her shoulders shook with a small laugh. "And less fear of hanging."

He closed his eyes at the word. She seemed to shrink in his arm, realizing what she'd said. "Yes," he rallied. "More fear of dysentery, though."

"Yet you survived. All of you."

His arm tightened around her. "Yes. Not unscarred, but whole and able to carry on and find happiness and joy."

To that she made no reply, but she clung to his side all night.

Chapter Twenty-Six

Ilsa didn't know what to expect when they returned to Prince's Street the next day. This time they waited almost an hour, and her hope, already thin and tenuous, began to give way.

She was sure she was not wrong; Mr. Lorde had seen Papa. But he could not make Papa see *her* if her father refused. And if something had happened—if Papa had been discovered—she would be forever tormented by the thought that she might have endangered him. She began to regret coming, and almost hoped Mr. Lorde would tell her to go away.

But finally the door opened and they were shown into Lorde's private office, and another man was there, too. Tall and lean, wearing the garb of a common laborer and his natural hair, stood William Fletcher. Ilsa caught her breath with a sob and flew to him before she knew what she was doing.

"Ilsa, love," he whispered, holding her tightly. "Oh my child, what are you doing here?"

"I came to find you! I've been so worried . . ."

He squeezed her to him again, and for a few minutes they simply held each other.

Finally she pushed back to see him. His face had aged since she saw him, the lines deeper and his skin paler. Or perhaps it was the effect of seeing him without his usual fine clothing and wig styled in the height of fashion; his hair was short, faded brown heavily sprinkled with gray. She would have passed him on the street and never recognized him. "Why, Papa?" was all she could ask, heartsick.

He sighed and eased out of her grip. "Because I couldn't bear to hurt you or Jean. I've made mistakes in my life, but always did my best to shield you from my failings. I never wanted you to be tainted by association."

It felt like an iron hand gripped her chest. "Papa—are you saying—you can't be admitting—?"

"Come." He motioned toward chairs at the table behind them. "Sit. I want Lorde to explain things to you." He gave Drew a long look, but said nothing.

She resisted. "Papa! Did you—did you do it?" Her voice at the end was that of a frightened child.

"Come sit," he said again. "I can't stay long. Lorde, bring the documents." Obediently the solicitor moved to the table, a sheaf of paper in his hand.

"Tell me," she pleaded. "Did you?" Drew was watching with a concerned frown, and a wave of mortification washed over her, that she had dragged him into this and been so spectacularly wrong. *I believe in Papa,* she'd insisted again and again. She'd thought the nightmare would end when she found her father, and instead it was growing worse by the second.

"I've told Lorde to convey everything absolutely," Papa went on, stubbornly ignoring her questions. "There are deeds and stock certificates, although he will sell those."

Helplessly she looked to Drew. He stepped up

beside her and urged her into the chair before turning to Papa. "Deacon Fletcher, you have to tell her if you know. Who really committed the robberies?"

Papa's hands went still on the papers, his face expressionless. Ilsa reeled, clutching Drew's hand. His fingers closed around hers, providing an anchor as her world pitched off its axis.

"You do know, don't you," Drew added quietly.

Her father sat motionless. Mr. Lorde looked vigilantly from him to Ilsa and back, saying nothing. "I do," Papa said at long last, very quietly. "But I will not give him up, not even if it costs my own life," he added as Ilsa jerked in her chair.

"What? But *no*—Papa, you can clear your name! Of course we will try to help this person—explain to the sheriff—you cannot let this charge go unanswered—"

"No!" He recoiled from her outstretched hands. "No, Ilsa. I will not. Do not argue," he added sharply. "I said no, child, and that is my final word."

Tears sprang to her eyes. Drew was watching Papa, a pensive look on his face. At her glance he put his free hand on her shoulder.

Then he spoke. "Is he your son?"

The quiet question seemed to echo in the room. Ilsa's mouth dropped open. Mr. Lorde pursed his lips. And Papa . . .

Papa's mouth closed in a hard line.

"What?" She turned to Drew again, in outrage this time. "Why would you say that? I have no brother!"

Her father glared at Drew. "You're the fellow who's caused such a stir in town, aren't you? The one everybody leapt to accommodate like lackeys. I'm not impressed by a fancy title, lad, especially one you've not even got yet. Keep to your own business."

Drew did not flinch under this. "A man would only go to such lengths to protect a few people. Someone beloved, someone dearer than life to him. It's not you, Ilsa, and I cannot believe it's your aunt. You told me you've got no uncles, no other aunts, no cousins, and your grandparents are dead. That leaves . . . a son."

The anger that had animated her father had drained away as Drew spoke. Now he put a hand over his face. "Stop." His shoulders slumped. "Yes. He's my son."

Ilsa thought she might faint—might have already fainted and was imagining the whole scene.

"I've been a terrible father to him all his life," her father went on, seeming to age before her eyes. "This is the least I can do, save his life."

"It's a terrible thing he's done," said Drew quietly.

"Who?" Ilsa asked at the same moment, unable to form any other thought or word.

Her father turned to her. His handsome face sagged in defeat. "Please understand. I—I was young. I was careless." He paused, his throat working. "I met his mother and was smitten. Things . . . got out of hand. I never meant to . . ." He sighed. "But I could not hold it against the boy. I supported him and his mother ever since and did what I could for the lad. But I could never claim him. I didn't dare, even though it had been my dream for a son to inherit—" His voice broke, and he reached for her hands. "Forgive me, child. I thought I could keep the secret, provide for the boy, and raise him almost as my own."

"Does he know?" asked Drew. Ilsa was grateful one of them could form coherent questions.

Papa eyed Drew for a moment, a muscle working in his jaw. "Yes, he does." He looked back to Ilsa. "Don't hold this against him. He's known, and envied you, his entire life. 'Tis a hard thing for a man to bear."

And hard for a daughter to learn, she thought bitterly. "Why didn't you tell *me*?"

"I always feared you would discover it. It was never my intent."

"But why?" she protested.

Papa hesitated a long time. "He's your age, Ilsa. Only two months older."

No. That meant—that meant Papa had been unfaithful to her mother, not in the later years when Mama was ill but before, when they were newly married. He'd always told her theirs had been an incomparable love match and declared he'd never married again because he would never love another woman as much.

"I realized what a fool I'd been when your mother told me she was expecting you," he said. "I ended my—my flirtation, sobered and aware of how reckless I'd been. But it was too late. Anne . . . was also carrying my child. I pledged to support her, but she wanted more. She . . . she told your mother and broke her heart." Papa hung his head. "I promised Cordelia I would never tell you about my betrayal."

It was all Ilsa could do to breathe.

"Your mother was never strong again after you

were born and the midwife said she shouldn't have more children. When she died, I resolved that the promise I made to her would guide my life, and I tried to be the best father I could be to you, child . . ."

"Who is he?" asked Drew.

Papa looked up, his mouth a firm line. He would not answer.

"Liam Hewitt," said Ilsa faintly. Papa started but didn't deny it.

She had wondered for years why Liam disliked her so much, and why Papa always tolerated Liam's rudeness and insolence. This explained why Papa had always favored him and promoted him so rapidly in the cabinetry shop. It even suggested why Mrs. St. James's shop, small and modest, had been robbed—Ilsa had gone to Perth with them for two weeks. People had seen her walking on the hill with Drew. Liam had always taken pleasure in spiting her, and hurting her friends was the nearest thing to hurting her.

And it was all because Liam had known of their connection, while she had been kept ignorant, like a child.

Suddenly furious, she flew at her father, pounding his chest with her fists. "How could you? How could you not tell me something so important? How could you put our lives in front of him like that, making him resent and despise us? How—?"

Drew pulled her back, sitting beside her and wrapping his arms around her. Papa, who had not defended himself, stared long and hard at the way Ilsa clung to Drew.

"How are you certain he's the one?" she demanded,

slightly calmer but her voice still throbbing. "Doing this."

He gazed at her with sadness and resignation. "Several of the victims were patrons of ours. They were robbed weeks after Liam supervised the installation of new locks and doors. I began to suspect . . . Well, I tried to protect him. I discovered he has a weakness for the cockfights, as I once did. I tried to dissuade him from them and paid several debts, but I heard he's been playing deep again, and losing. One of the men arrested is his known companion, a low fellow who would do nothing but debase him and poison his mind."

"Thomas Browne," murmured Drew.

Papa nodded. "When Browne claimed the King's Pardon, I feared Liam was involved. I tried to see Browne—hoping against hope he would deny Liam had scouted the shops and made duplicate keys—but they refused to let me see him. And then I heard my own name implicated, making clear what Liam meant to do. They'll leave the other fellow to hang, cast the blame onto me, and Browne and Liam will walk free. The keys were likely made in my workshop. I've no doubt more evidence will be found there. It will appear beyond question. I daresay Liam will profess himself shocked and dismayed, and completely ignorant of my crimes."

"Papa," Ilsa pleaded. "How can you allow this?"

His hand on the table closed into a fist. "I cannot send my only son to the gallows. No matter how abhorrent his actions, no matter the cost to me. I cannot, Ilsa. Do not ask it of me."

"But if you explain," she began, a little wildly.

"If you drag me back to Edinburgh, I will confess," he warned. "I am decided, Ilsa."

She collapsed in her chair, bereft. He would confess to a crime he didn't commit to save his son, who had betrayed him, regardless of what it did to his daughter, who had believed in him when no one else did. Between the two of them, Papa was choosing Liam—over her.

"What do you mean to do?" asked Drew.

Papa seemed relieved that the confession was over. He cleared his throat and nodded at Lorde, who had been apparently absorbed in his study of the grain of the oak table beneath his hands. The solicitor leapt into action, sliding a thick document to him.

"I've made over my will." Papa glanced at Ilsa. "Almost everything to you, Ilsa. A bequest to Jean, of course, a remembrance to Mary, annuities for the servants, a few charities. And . . ." He paused. "Two hundred pounds to Liam. At one time I had thought to leave him the workshop . . ." He shook his head, avoiding her numb gaze. "I pray he uses the sum to start fresh and make the most of this escape." He gave her a faltering smile. "Do some good with my money, my dear. I know you have thoughts on this matter, and I trust you to do right with it."

She couldn't think of that now. "Are you going to harm yourself, Papa?"

He flinched. "No. No! Never think that. If I meant to do that, I never would have seen you today." Mr. Lorde shifted and coughed, but Papa shot an irked look at him. "Quiet, Lorde. I'll tell her if I want to. I'm taking passage on a ship bound for America. They call it the New World, and I shall be a new man there, no longer William Fletcher but . . . someone else. Someone better, God willing."

There were no tears left in her. Ilsa gazed vacantly at the papers he put in front of her, dimly heard his assurances that Lorde had everything worked out and would help her, and only roused when Papa rose.

This was farewell, she realized. Forever. She flung herself into his arms and thought her heart would burst at the thought of never embracing him again, never hearing his welcoming cry, never seeing his irrepressible wink and nod again.

"How will you dance at my wedding?" she said against his chest. "How will you spoil my children?"

His hands were gentle on her hair. "There, love," he said tenderly. "I'll kiss you now for your wedding." He pressed his lips to her forehead, then raised his gaze to Drew. "Take care of her, lad."

Ilsa ignored that. She gripped her father's jacket and shook him. "When do you sail? Let me come say good-bye."

"No, child—"

"If you want my cooperation with this lunatic scheme, you'll grant me this," she said fiercely.

His mouth twitched, in that half-irritated, half-amused way he had. "All right," he agreed, and kissed her once more. "Tomorrow night on the tide. The *Carolina*, bound for New York from Port Glasgow."

"And you have funds?"

Finally he smiled. "Aye. Lorde has divested all my shares with Mr. Cunninghame, which you so despised. I've enough for a new start."

Lorde showed them out a back way, in case anyone had remarked their entrance. "He can't have planned this in the last few days," Ilsa said to the solicitor. "How long has he been readying this plot?"

"Several weeks, ma'am." His eyes were sympathetic. "Not to this extent, but he told me to sell the Cunninghame shares months ago and to retain the funds here in Glasgow instead of forwarding them. I believe he was even then guarding against the possibility of something like this."

She nodded and they left.

"Where do you want to go?" asked Drew in the street.

Dazed and overwhelmed, Ilsa looked up at him, squinting against the sunlight. He'd let his beard grow and his hair was definitely curling now under his bonnet. Booted feet braced apart, arms folded over the plaid that crossed his chest, he looked more Highland outlaw than English duke.

"Can we walk?" she asked wistfully. "I miss our long walks on Calton Hill—I wish Robert were here—"

She missed her old life, the one where she painted her ceiling and danced all night and flirted with a handsome soldier and kissed him and fell in love with him. How charmed and easy it looked now.

He understood; without a word Drew offered his arm and they turned north to the garden grounds.

Chapter Twenty-Seven

The next day they rode eighteen miles down the River Clyde to Port Glasgow. Drew saw Ilsa's eyes scanning the streets of the town—looking for her father, he thought. She'd been quiet since they'd parted from him yesterday, and he wanted to give her space to accept her father's actions.

They took a room in a clean little inn near the church. The town was a heaving mass of activity: wagons ferrying cargo to and from Glasgow, sailors and merchants on the docks and in the coffeehouses, children and servants darting through the narrow streets. The harbors bristled with ships' masts, the wide expanse of the Clyde sparkling behind them.

It was a simple matter to discover the *Carolina*. She was a large ship rocking at anchor near the mouth of the harbor. The shipping agent pointed out where passengers were to board the launch to the boat, leaving them nothing to do but wait.

For hours there was no sign of him. The sun was setting, and sailors had begun ferrying people out to the *Carolina*. Drew was beginning to wonder if Fletcher had lied to Ilsa about his plans, unwilling to face another emotional confrontation, when a figure strode around the corner of the customhouse with a large pack over one shoulder. Ilsa tensed but Drew held her back. "Don't call attention to him," he murmured, and she stilled, holding tight to his arm.

Fletcher came up to them and doffed his cap. His expression was calm and peaceful today, and his eyes were full of love as he looked at Ilsa. "You came."

"Of course I did." She even managed a smile. "Your daughter is not the sort to fall into a fainting fit, sir."

He smiled at that. "Well do I know it! And how proud it makes me." He let down his pack. "You're a better daughter than I deserved."

"Papa." Her eyes shone with tears as she went into his embrace. Drew turned to scan the docks one last time, giving them a moment of privacy. He'd silently kept an eye out for any more officers following them or Fletcher but had seen no one suspicious. He hoped there were none. *Let Fletcher get away with this,* he thought. For her sake.

"There now." Fletcher stepped back, taking out his handkerchief and dabbing at Ilsa's cheeks. "Don't waste your tears on me. Wish me a bon voyage and be happy." He glanced at Drew. "And I wish you great happiness."

She pressed his hand. "How can I write to you—?"

"Ah, child." Regretfully he stepped back. "You know you can't. I don't know where I shall go, in any event."

"All right," she said, remarkably poised in Drew's opinion. "Then you must write to me. Somehow. I expect you to find a way, Papa. I will look every month for a letter from my distant cousin in America."

His mouth quirked in reluctant amusement, and he winked. "God willing that he does write to you someday."

A shout from the launch made them all look around. The bell in the church began to chime the hour. Fletcher hesitated. "Good-bye, lass," he said to his daughter. "God go with you."

"And with you, Papa."

Her father's mouth twisted into a sad, trembling smile. He gripped her hand to his heart. "Saints, I'll miss you."

Her chest heaved. "I know. But this is better than me missing you because you're in a crypt in the graveyard." She bent her head and kissed his hand, then gently disentangled her fingers from his. "They're waiting for you."

"Better they than the hangman," he quipped. The moment of emotion over, Fletcher slung his pack onto his shoulder and turned toward the shore. The men waiting in the launch were untying the ropes, and he picked up his pace, trotting along the short beach and down the dock until he climbed into the craft.

Ilsa's face was calm as she watched him go. The sailors cast off the last line and shoved the launch out to sea. Fletcher gripped the gunwale as the boat rocked from side to side, but managed to lift his cap for a moment. The afternoon sunlight glinted on the sprays of water thrown up by the oars as the men bent to their task, taking William Fletcher away from Scotland and the hangman—and his only daughter.

Ilsa didn't move until the boat had grown too small to pick out of the swarm of boats in the harbor. In the distance, sailors were climbing the *Carolina*'s rigging, setting the sails. Finally her shoulders slumped in a silent sigh.

"He can never prove his innocence now," said Drew quietly. "He can never return to Edinburgh, if not Scotland entirely."

"I know," she murmured. "But he'll be safe. Perhaps one day I'll tire of it here and follow him to America."

They returned to the inn and took a light dinner. Ilsa's eyes kept straying to the window overlooking the harbor, and Drew knew she was trying to pick out the *Carolina* among the ships beginning the long journey to America.

"What will you do?" he asked when they had gone back to their room, which faced east—Edinburgh, not America.

It was no small question. Fletcher had made a detailed plan. He had left a letter with Mr. Lorde, professing his intention not to expose his family to the indignity and shame of a trial, which Mr. Lorde would convey to the Edinburgh authorities at an appropriate time. He would also bring Fletcher's will and execute it, once Fletcher's death was accepted. Ilsa would affect deep grief and astonishment, even to her aunt—for they had both agreed Jean Fletcher couldn't keep the secret as closely as it must be kept.

"I'll use some of his money as restitution for those who were robbed. I don't need it or want it. If people must think Papa the thief, they can know that his family tried to make them whole." She sighed. "I don't know what to do about Liam. If Papa had told me before, I might have found some compassion and warmth for him. But he has caused my father's ruin, and I cannot forgive him." She glanced up at Drew. "But I cannot condemn him without betraying Papa's escape. What does that make me, that I would allow such a man to go free?"

"I think it means you have a steadfast, loyal heart, full of mercy."

She nodded. "What else can I do?"

He should reassure her that her plan was noble and decent, the best choice she could make among all the bad options. He could vow to see that Liam was punished in other ways. He could simply comfort her, now that the die was cast.

Instead he went down on his knee in front of her and took her hands. "Marry me."

Her eyes widened.

"I know you think you've led me into criminal behavior and caused me to ruin my name and reputation," he plowed on. "You did not. I did everything of my own free will because I choose to be with you and fight your battles and stand by your side. I know you dread my inheritance and believe I would do best to marry an Englishwoman. But . . . *I* do not. I did allow Her Grace to believe she would advise me, but I don't need her approval—or her advice. And if you don't wish to live in England"—he took another deep breath before breaking the solemn promise he'd given the Duchess of Carlyle—"we won't. We can stay in Scotland. Perhaps the duchess would allow us to live at Stormont Palace if it suits you. If Stormont can be administered from England, then Carlyle Castle can be administered from Scotland. I'll find a chaperone to take Bella and Winnie to London for a Season." Her face was blank with surprise, no matter how he searched for a hint of reaction. "We can solve this," he said urgently. "Together. If you could trust me enough to try . . . I would never dismiss your thoughts or concerns. I love you to distraction."

Ilsa's mind, which had been a maelstrom for days, seemed to pause, settle, and calm at those words. She had told herself she must give him up, but . . . he did not wish to be given up. Nor did she want to do it. Drew had been her greatest adventure, her favorite companion, her truest friend, her most passionate lover.

Was she fool enough to throw that away in a fit of pointless sacrifice?

Was she too afraid to meet the challenges she might face as his wife?

No, Ilsa realized, she was not. She was not afraid of anything when he was beside her. And she was free, after all—free to bestow her heart where she chose, free to step out of her boundaries and make a bold decision. Free to learn from her father's mistakes and do better, as he had urged her.

She was free to decide that she *would* make their marriage work, no matter what was demanded of her as a duchess someday. She would fight for what she wanted, and for whom.

"You would really marry a wild hellion who keeps a pony in the house and paints the sky on the ceiling?" she asked. "A wild, wicked woman who will ride astride and seduce you in every greenhouse we spy and play ghost in your house?"

"Haunt me forever," he whispered.

of anxiety and tension soft- ... ved. Part of it, she realized, had ... in her dread of parting from him, on top ... sing Papa. But now she wouldn't—ever.

The first real smile in weeks, trembling but wholehearted, curved her lips. "Yes."

Chapter Twenty-Eight

They reached Edinburgh a week later, man and wife. Ilsa had thought he would want to wait and have his family there, but Drew waved that aside. "They'll only insist on a delay so they can order new gowns and plan a lavish breakfast."

She had to laugh. "Who needs all that?"

"Not I," he declared, stroking his jaw, now covered in a dark beard. "I'm beginning to relish being an outlaw, freed of all civilizing influences."

And so they were married in a Glasgow chapel, Drew in his now-ragged kilt and long hair and Ilsa in a hastily altered gown from a dressmaker in Trongate Street. Through it all they grinned at each other like children pulling off the greatest prank in the world, and when the minister pronounced them married, Drew lifted her off her feet for a kiss so passionate, the minister coughed and his wife giggled.

When they reached Edinburgh, his family descended on them with cries that changed quickly from alarm and curiosity to happiness. Even though they arrived late, Louisa St. James brought out a bottle of fine sherry to toast them, enfolding Ilsa in a warm embrace and murmuring how pleased she was to have another daughter.

Bella, Winnie, and Agnes mobbed her. "I *knew* he wanted to marry you," cried Bella joyfully. "Thank heavens you said yes!"

"Oh, Drew, well done!" Winnie flung her arms around his neck before running back to Ilsa's side. "And you, accepting him even when he looks like a hermit from the mountains!"

Drew struck a pose at that, stroking his beard. "Oh, Winnie, how you tempt me to worse . . ."

She put out her tongue at him. "As if you ever cared what I think! Only now you'll have to bow to Ilsa's wishes . . ."

"You will have your hands full, taming him," whispered Agnes with a laugh.

I won't tame him, thought Ilsa with a secret smile at her new husband. *I love him wild.*

Going home to Jean was bittersweet. The news of her marriage pleased Jean, but the rest . . . Ilsa had rehearsed her story, but when she said Papa was missing and she didn't believe he would ever be found, her aunt gave a single heart-rending wail before collapsing in silent tears that smote her heart. Only Drew's presence gave her the strength to keep her word, and not whisper to her aunt that Papa was safe. Instead she held her aunt and wept with her, hoping that someday it would be possible to tell her the truth.

Drew went to confront the furious sheriff-clerk and procurator-fiscal, once more respectably shaved and dressed like a proper Englishman. He put the fear of God into David MacGill, the "turncoat solicitor" as Ilsa called him, excoriating the man for his management of Stormont Palace and threatening to have him sacked. He offered one last chance for the man to win back his favor by defending Ilsa. Spurred into sycophancy again, MacGill provided a fiery argument that dissuaded the sheriff from action against Drew or Ilsa—indeed, he even wrung an apology from the sheriff for searching her house.

When Mr. Lorde arrived in Edinburgh three weeks later with the sorrowful news that a man fitting William Fletcher's description had been hauled, drowned, from the River Clyde, the authorities were all too ready to accept it. It was printed in the paper, along with a smaller notice that victims of the recent robberies should apply for aid to Felix Duncan, who had agreed to handle paying out the funds Ilsa set aside from Papa's estate.

Ilsa held Jean again as her aunt shed more tears, but this time grief mixed with relief.

"He would prefer this rather than be hanged by his neighbors and former friends," Jean choked. "But oh! How I will miss him, my dear."

"He is at peace this way," was all Ilsa could say.

Mr. Lorde offered, with Drew's strong endorsement, to spare her meeting Liam, but Ilsa refused. She had decided she must do this for herself—and for Papa. She sent for him, the half brother she'd never really known or liked, and they met in the drawing room of her house. Drew lurked outside, making sure Liam knew he was there.

"So," Liam drawled in bitter amusement when Drew had gone out and closed the door. "I suppose I should congratulate you on your triumph. A future duchess! How pleased your father would have been. He always was one for appearances and influence."

Ilsa regarded him steadily. "As you know, my father was discovered drowned in Glasgow."

"Tragically," said Liam with a cold twist to his lips.

"Thank you for your condolences." Ilsa picked up the letter Mr. Lorde had brought. She had seen it before, that terrible day when Papa revealed the truth, and couldn't wait to get rid of it now. "He made you a bequest in his will, which his solicitor provided to me. This was left among his papers for you."

Looking smug, Liam took the letter.

"I know you never cared for me," Ilsa went on. Drew had told her to leave it, but she had to know why Liam hated her. "But I always remarked Papa's particular preference for you. It was exceptional. I've long wondered if there was some other connection between you and Papa."

Her half brother leaned forward. "Never told you, did he? No wonder, given your behavior of late."

"You know," she said, unable to stop herself, "someone did hint to me, once, that you might be his son."

Liam drew back, startled. "Did they?"

"Is it true?"

Some of his smirk returned. "Aye. It is."

Ilsa nodded once. "I am sorry Papa never told me."

"Sorry!" His mouth bent cruelly. "Were you sorry that he was in love with another woman and not your mother? Were you sorry to hear that he did have a son, the son he yearned for but was unable to claim because he was too afraid of your reaction to the news?"

So that was it. Papa had wanted a son so desperately he had let Liam believe that only Ilsa kept him from claiming him publicly. And Liam, smoldering in envy and resentment, had finally struck back at both of them.

She gave him a grave look. "No. I'm sorry for you. He was a wonderful father, tender, kind, and caring. And what's more, I would have accepted a brother, had he come in love and friendship." She got to her feet. "Thank you for coming today. I hope your legacy brings you fond remembrances of our father."

Scowling Liam tore open the letter and scanned it, reading that he had been left two hundred pounds and nothing else. His face turned red. "How—this is an insult!" He leapt to his feet with a howl. "I am supposed to inherit the workshop in Dunbar's Close! He promised me!"

"Did he?" asked Ilsa calmly. "I didn't know that. He left that to me."

"What will you do with a cabinetry shop?" he snarled.

"Sell it, I suppose," she said with mild surprise. "I've already spoken to Mr. Henderson. Papa would want it to go to another wright."

Liam took a step forward. "How dare you," he said, low and furious.

Ilsa stood a little straighter. "How dare I?" She lowered her voice. "I am *very* conscious of what you did for him—and *to* him. If you provoke me, I would have no hesitation in suggesting the sheriff investigate whom Thomas Browne gambled with—and how much that person lost in recent months." She folded her hands. "I suggest you accept this with grace and take Papa's advice to better yourself. He forgave you, Liam, but God detests a sinner."

He breathed like a bellows. "You . . ."

"I had nothing to do with any of it. If I had, you would have received nothing." She reached for the bell. "Good day, Mr. Hewitt. And good-bye."

Chapter Twenty-Nine

Four weeks later

Carlyle Castle looked much the way he remembered it, though now tinged with the colors of winter instead of spring. Drew braced himself for a chilly reception. Not only had he missed the duchess's six-month deadline, he'd only written to the castle after everything in Edinburgh had been resolved.

Ilsa studied the cavernous entrance hall as they waited to be shown to a room. It was the most forbidding part of the castle, in Drew's opinion, and if it were ever his home, he would remove the arms bristling on the walls and the statue of Perseus holding the head of Medusa. "Intimidating," his wife murmured to him.

"Ghastly," he whispered back, making her laugh quietly.

The duchess was not pleased at their late arrival. "You were expected back weeks ago," she snapped.

Drew laid his hand over Ilsa's. "I had good reason, Your Grace."

"Hmph."

"When I left here months ago," he said, "I had no idea what lay ahead."

"You asked for my advice on that," she replied tartly.

"I did." Drew stole a look at Ilsa. "As so often happens, the best of intentions were made a mockery by Fate."

"Fate." The duchess looked at Ilsa. "This is your explanation, I suppose. An affair of the heart."

"No," said Ilsa calmly. She had shown no sign of being intimidated or cowed. "It was more than that. It was the meeting of two souls meant to be together, and all efforts to deny it were in vain."

"All true," said Drew with a small smile at his wife.

"You say all efforts to deny it." The duchess stroked her fat ginger cat. "Why must this predestined match be denied?"

Drew hesitated, but Ilsa seized the bull by the horns. "Because my father was accused of being the mastermind of a ring of thieves terrorizing Edinburgh, ma'am. Because I tried to help him, against all good advice. And yet Andrew stood loyally by my side, defying every precept that would have sent him back to Edinburgh and to you. Only the deepest affection could have caused him to do that."

"That is true." He brought her hand to his lips. "And I would do it again in a heartbeat."

The duchess looked from one to the other. "Thieves! You shock me, Captain."

"I cannot regret what I did for love," he told her.

She gave an impatient sigh. "I had such high hopes for you . . ."

"And he has not disappointed you." Ilsa sat forward. "Would you wish your son's heir to be a man led only by others, cowed by the opinions of gossips? No, I am sure that you would want a man of firm convictions and morals to step into the ducal title. How else can you be certain he will uphold the dignity and reputation of your family against any slings and arrows that may come? Whatever my failings, you must credit that the captain has acted in a manner that could not be faulted."

The duchess all but gaped at her. Drew sat in tense silence, waiting . . .

"I see it is the most severe case," said Her Grace at last. "A *besotted* love match."

Ilsa beamed. "Yes, Your Grace."

"I could not meet the demands of the title without the support of the woman I love." Drew nodded at Ilsa in solidarity. "Nor am I willing to attempt it."

After a moment the duchess sighed. "I see I have no say in the matter."

"What God has joined together, let no man put asunder." But Drew bowed his head. "We would welcome your blessing, though."

For a moment she looked between the two of them. "I have a little experience of this now, you know. Maximilian was here a month ago, also with a wife in hand, and I gave him my blessing."

Drew looked up in surprise. "Maximilian?"

"Your cousin," said the duchess with a touch of droll humor. "You remember him. The one who laughed and mocked me the entire time he was here."

"Yes," he murmured hastily. He'd not thought much of his cousin since that brief meeting. "I hope he is well."

"As well as you appear to be," said the duchess, amused by his surprise. "Happily married and respectably employed. I was pleasantly astounded."

"That is very happy news," said Drew after a startled pause.

"Well. I wish you both happy. If that is all . . ." She started to rise, but Drew took a deep breath and raised one hand.

"There is one more thing, Your Grace."

She raised her brows in surprise.

"I have a request," he began. "One which will, I believe, be to the benefit of Carlyle as well as to me. I beg the grace and favor of Stormont Palace."

"Well!" She sat back in her chair. "You astonish me, Captain. That is not what we agreed."

"The Stormont estate is well-kept and prosperous," he forged on. "It's kept in readiness only for the convenience of the solicitor, but it is a very fine home. My family spent several days there, evaluating it, and all fell under its spell. My bride and I would like to spend several months of the year there, with the remainder here."

That was the compromise he and Ilsa had reached. Nine months at Stormont in Scotland, three months at Carlyle in England. It suited them both, and he did not see how the duchess could disagree. He was sure she had no more wish to have him under her feet than he had to be here.

At least, he hoped that was so.

"But you have so much to learn," she protested.

"And I will devote myself diligently to it," he replied. "Running Stormont will be invaluable experience, on a more modest scale than Carlyle. It is a jewel, more valuable than Mr. Edwards believes. I submit that the duke should not sell it. Allow me to run it for a few years before any decision is reached.

"And if Stormont Palace can be maintained in excellent condition from Carlyle, surely I can learn what I need to know by directing the Stormont estate. Mr. Edwards will be able to instruct me on the particulars of the castle, and I will be here for three months of the year. In addition," he added, sensing an objection rising to her lips, "my sisters desire a Season in London. I will have opportunity to make connections and establish myself in town during the course of launching two sisters into society. I have no wish to neglect that aspect of the position."

"I thought you had three sisters," she snapped.

Drew hid his grin. "Only two will be in search of husbands."

"Hmph," she muttered. "I knew a Scot would be trouble."

"Your Grace." Ilsa got up and knelt beside the duchess's throne chair. "I would also like your blessing. I know I am unprepared to fill your shoes—and suspect I never could—but I am wholly committed to helping Andrew fulfill his role with grace and honor. I hope you can see that he and I are devoted to each other, and to our duty to Carlyle. It is a weighty responsibility, and one best served by a couple, standing at each other's sides and loyal to each other." She bowed her head, like a knight before the sovereign.

The duchess stared. Incredibly, after a moment she extended her hand, which Ilsa clasped reverently. "Perhaps you will do, Mrs. St. James. Humility and determination will take you far . . ."

When they walked out into the garden later,

Drew was still marveling at her performance. "As if you could never fill her shoes!"

Ilsa smiled. "I meant it! What she has done is impressive. Miss Kirkpatrick told me the duke has been invalided for nearly thirty years. In all those years, every responsibility has fallen on the duchess, with no one to support her. And in that time she has buried three children, all the while knowing the duke's health is poor and she will inevitably lose him, too." She shook her head. "I admire her to no end. I am not sure I could bear up as she has done."

"Of course you could," he said, but Ilsa shook her head.

"Don't say that," she said somberly. "Until one has been in that position, it is impossible to know—or to judge."

"Yes," he said at once. His mother's words came back to him, about how much the duchess had lost. Ilsa understood that more deeply than he did. "You're right."

She smiled up at him. "Of course I am."

He chuckled, and they walked on, laughing together when Ilsa pointed out that they obviously could not live here because Robert would trample or eat all the flowers.

When they had been there a few days, Mr. Edwards asked Drew to take a turn in the bailey yard with him. Since Drew spent hours closeted with the attorney every day, he wondered at this. Ilsa had struck up a friendship with Miss Kirkpatrick, the duchess's companion, and the two ladies were having tea in the lavish Green Salon, so he agreed.

"I am sorry to say that His Grace has taken a turn for the worse," said the attorney as they walked.

Drew started, almost gaping. All his plans rested on the duke's continued health.

"I tell you this in strictest confidence," added Mr. Edwards.

"Of course," he murmured, his mind racing.

"Your intention to spend only three months of the year at Carlyle . . ."

"Mr. Edwards." Drew stopped walking. "Do you mean to say . . . Should I expect—?" He couldn't even say it. Ilsa had been so pleased with the Stormont compromise.

"As to that, I do not know." The attorney gave him a brief smile. "Fate is unpredictable, is it not?"

"Yes," agreed Drew slowly.

"Perhaps it will not matter so much to you." Edwards paused with a troubled look. "Her Grace does not wish me to say this, but . . . you may not bear sole responsibility for Carlyle."

What? "I understood there was no nearer heir."

Edwards bobbed his head as he walked. "No known nearer heir, no."

"Mr. Edwards." He was stunned. The last seven months, he had believed Carlyle was to be his—unalterably, incontrovertibly, inevitably. "Speak plainly, if you please."

Sunlight reflected off the attorney's spectacles as he faced Drew, obscuring his eyes. "The fact is, I cannot. Her Grace wishes me not to, but I cannot, in good conscience, allow you to believe the title and estate will indisputably be yours."

"What the hell does that mean?" he exclaimed.

Edwards looked away. "It means what I said. There is no known heir nearer than yourself, but there are . . . possibilities. Remote ones, I assure you." He paused. "Most men would be angry at learning this, but when I heard of your desire to live at Stormont Palace, to stay in Scotland, I wondered."

"Wondered what?" he demanded.

"When Maximilian was here a month ago, we had no idea where you were or if you would return safely. I felt obliged to inform him of that fact, and his reaction indicated he would greatly prefer not to inherit." He paused, tilting his head. "I suspect your bride would also prefer to remain in Scotland and has only accepted the dukedom as the cost of being your wife."

Drew jerked in surprise.

Edwards nodded sagely. "I cannot blame her. The dukedom has not been an unalloyed blessing to most of the men who held it, and even less so to their duchesses. To my knowledge, it has caused more suffering than pleasure."

"Thank you for those warm and encouraging words," said Drew after a shocked moment.

The attorney waved one hand. "No, no. It is that way with all titles—did you not know? The responsibility is enormous and the privileges immense, but those who think them the keys to endless indulgence and gratification . . ." He shook his head. "I do not mean to accuse you of such thoughts, Captain."

"I hope not," muttered Drew, his mind racing. "You're telling me I may be supplanted by another heir."

The attorney hesitated. "I am telling you there is a possibility."

"Why wasn't I told this before?" He raked one hand through his hair. "Why wasn't my cousin? Was this used to intimidate us?" Drew had no love for Maximilian, but he reacted instinctively to the unfairness of the man being tormented with the prospect of an inheritance he didn't want. If there was another heir, nearer than Drew himself, both he and Maximilian deserved to know about it, after the way the duchess had intervened in their lives.

"Because there is nothing, as of now, to tell."

"I have tried to be very conscious of the magnitude of my duty," he began.

"Admirably so," agreed Edwards.

"I have persuaded the woman I love to move to England for three months of the year. I have prepared my family to discard their old lives and assume new places as members of a ducal household. I have resigned my commission and diverted the course of my entire life for this inheritance out of duty." Drew was furious. "And now you tell me there is a *possibility, perhaps,* that it will all be for naught?"

"No." The solicitor motioned to keep walking. "Under no circumstances will you emerge without advantage. I am authorized by Her Grace to grant you immediately the property of Stormont Palace—outright, Captain, not mere grace and favor."

"She's giving me the estate?" he repeated in shock.

"She is. That is—His Grace the Duke is," amended the attorney. "In recognition of your efforts and diligence thus far, and due to your persuasive arguments in Stormont's favor." He glanced at Drew.

"Think of it as a wedding gift from His Grace, with Her Grace's blessing."

"But—" Drew shook his head. It was too much to comprehend. "You're telling me I may not inherit. How likely is that?"

The attorney took a long time to reply. "A slim chance," he said at last. "Perhaps one not even worth mentioning. I regret any unease I've caused you, but in your shoes . . . I would not wish to be kept completely in the dark."

"And the duchess has known this from the beginning?"

Edwards bowed his head. "She has. It has been her strong belief that the possibility is so distant as to be unworthy of discussion."

"But you don't agree." Drew pressed one hand to his forehead, reeling.

Mr. Edwards came closer and put a hand on his shoulder. "If His Grace should die with no other heir identified, it will not matter," he said quietly. "Your claim is clear, and I would file suit for it without delay. Once a title is granted, it cannot be withdrawn, no matter how many heirs emerge later. I only spoke, confidentially, because you must know what will be asked and discussed upon His Grace's demise. The Crown will wish to be sure there is no nearer claimant before they grant Carlyle to you."

"What should I do?"

Edwards smiled. "Nothing, Captain. There is nothing you *can* do, except what you have planned. Take your bride to Stormont and be happy. As you desire, we shall be in contact by letter."

"Yes," he said, still severely disconcerted. "The management of the estate . . ."

"As to that, I have good news. A new estate steward has been engaged and is already handling business in London. By the spring, I expect he will be in residence here." Edwards pushed the spectacles up his nose. "And may I say that it will be a great relief to me, sir, to have you and Mr. Montclair both tending to the estate."

"Right." Drew managed to nod as the attorney bowed and left him.

Saints. Another heir? He wished the attorney had spoken more plainly—and sooner. But he went to tell Ilsa anyway.

Her eyes lit up. "The duke has given us Stormont Palace? For our own?"

He nodded. "But this other matter—"

She laughed and kissed him. "That also sounds like good news to me!" She put her arms around his neck. "To have Stormont Palace and a connection to the ducal family, but no weight of duty and obligation? What could be better?"

"But you might not be a duchess," he said, smiling helplessly.

She wrinkled her nose. "What a relief that would be. I married you in spite of it, you know, and if I can manage to avoid it, so much the better."

Finally he laughed. "You're a rare woman, Ilsa St. James."

She went up on her toes and pressed her lips to his. "You knew that months ago."

"Aye," he agreed, holding her to him. "That's why I fell in love with you."

Next month, don't miss these exciting new love stories only from Avon Books

Devil in Disguise by Lisa Kleypas

Lady Merritt Sterling, a young widow who's running her late husband's shipping company, knows London society is dying to catch her in a scandal. But when she meets Keir MacRae, a rough-and-rugged Scottish whisky distiller, all her sensible plans vanish like smoke. They couldn't be more different, but their attraction is raw and irresistible.

The Duke Goes Down by by Sophie Jordan

Peregrine Butler's privileged world is rocked to the core when it is revealed he was born *before* his parents' marriage and therefore is *not* the legal heir to the dukedom. Facing ruin, Perry must use his charm and good looks to win an heiress—and ignore his fascination with Imogen Bates, the alluring chit who is intent on sabotaging his efforts.

The Viscount Made Me Do It by Diana Quincy

Hanna Zaydan has fought to become London's finest bonesetter, but her darkly appealing new patient, Thomas Ellis, Viscount Griffin, threatens to destroy everything she's worked for. The daughter of Arab merchants is slowly seduced by the former soldier — even though she's smart enough to know Griff is after more than he'll reveal.